Crewkin

Rhobin Courtright

A Wings ePress, Inc.
Science Fiction Novel

Wings ePress, Inc.

Edited by: Jeanne Smith
Copy Edited by: Christie Kraemer
Executive Editor: Jeanne Smith
Cover Artist: Delilah K. Stephens

All rights reserved

Wings ePress Books
www.wingsepress.com

Copyright © 2021 by: Rhobin Courtright
ISBN 978-1-61309-523-2
ISBN-10: 1-61309-523-6

Published In the United States Of America

Wings ePress Inc.
3000 N. Rock Road
Newton, KS 67114

What They Are Saying About Crewkin

Grab your favorite drink, comfortable chair, and get ready for a magnificent Sci-Fi read. Rhobin Courtright has created a novel so entrancing you'll not put it down until you reach "the end." A **must read** for every Sci-Fi buff. A twelve-star read, for sure.

—C. L. Kraemer
Where imagination puts mystery, romance, and other worlds in the palms of your talons.

Dedication

To my daughter Karen,
who appreciates my imagination.
* * *

One

...2178.34-17:34 universal space-time ...mission status ...systems failure ...initial test terminated ...manual shutdown in progress...

Renna felt as lifeless as Sen's cold body on the bed next to her. She packed her possessions in her travel bag with careful precision. They were few enough. Everything else belonged to the ship, or the crewkin as a whole, so reverted to Markham Company. Renna didn't care. She needed no reminders. The vision of the bodies of her kin, removed one after another from this hospital room, promised memory enough.

"You can't survive." The doctor echoed Sen's last warning.

A glance showed the doctor, leaning against the door, watching her, waiting. She didn't know his name. He never identified himself. Another anonymous Markham employee dressed in a Markham medical uniform as foreign to her as everyone else.

Years of ingrained prohibitions prevented the response screaming inside. She controlled her voice. "You recommend I join Sen, join my crew?" *Like you and your staff encouraged her? Helped her? A final joining? Bastard.* Renna closed her bag.

Truth struck her. *I don't want to. I'm afraid of dying. Coward.* She couldn't look at Sen, loyally joined with her dead kin.

"Where will you go? You are genetically unfit to live planetside, and mentally unprepared to interact with another ship's crew. Crewkin are longhaulers, not shortrunners. We recommend a final joining because we know you won't fit in."

Renna looked around the windowless, beige room, now mostly empty with her kin and their hospital beds removed. Only Sen's bed and hers remained. Sleeping alone in a bed had seemed so strange. Perhaps another unspoken means to encourage her kin to their final joining? Although her eyes burned, she held no more tears.

"My problem, Doctor." *Me, mine, my, such strange pronouns after we, ours, and us—now unimportant, like everything else.*

Renna snapped the closures on her bag and turned to the door. He remained, relaxed against the doorframe.

"The staff understands your pain, no matter what you think. I've seen kin like you before. You're conditioned to survive within your own society. Believe me, we only want to provide for your needs, for your comfort."

Renna looked away, escaping his gaze. *No. Not me.* Her kin, her future, her known existence ended with *Markham3*'s failure, yet she refused the doctor's cure. In the awkward silence, she left. He didn't move as she passed. She sidled around him to prevent any touch. He huffed, shaking his head in an unvoiced comment on her defiance.

Hospital staff and other Markham employees stared as she made her way through headquarters. She felt their gazes. Her appearance ushered a wave of quiet that crashed behind her in hushed exchanges. The skin of her neck itched, expecting Dom Dukan's disapproval. His reprimand already rang through her mind. "The Dom represents *Markham3* Crew. To attract attention to Renna defiles our kin group. We are preeminent among ships for we strive to excel and anything else is unprofessional. Seeking recognition belonging to the whole kin makes you less. More like unreliable shortrunners."

Renna swallowed the painful gasp swelling in her throat, ignoring those watching her exit. Good kin performed joining before committing the heresy of desertion. So Markham taught. Their notice made her exit a judgment.

Renna stopped before the massive plasmetal hatch disguised as elaborate carved doors that defined the Markham Company boundary. Through a transparent section of the gate, Renna watched the norms crowding the space station's causeway. A memory of walking with her kin out of this portal flashed before her. They had left as a group. All dressed in their neat tan utility suits. All heads bore the same short blond hair, except for her. Dom Dukan demanded her head remain shaved to eliminate her unkin-colored hair. She swiped her scalp, felt the prickle of growth, and swore to never again cut whatever grew. He could do nothing about her dom-matching height, or her colorless eyes. Markham Company had deemed his request to change her eye color frivolous.

The automatic portal to the astroport opened, closed, and opened again while she hesitated. Her kin had found leaving the *Markham3* difficult; leaving Markham territory terrified them. Safe among her kin, Renna remembered her excitement for the chance to explore the space station alive with so much noise, so much color. Stepping through the doors, she remembered how, upon returning, Dom Dukan refused to leave Markham property again. She quashed the memory, refusing to look back. *I will never return, no matter what.*

Now everything looked gray. The resonance in the port swallowed individual sounds, forming a cacophony of white noise, which created an odd sound commotion of silence. Unfamiliar smells permeated the air, mixing into a repugnant strange atmosphere. The difference divorced her from any response as effectively as the hatch closing behind her severed her past life.

With steady steps, she headed for the station's main concourse.

She focused on the people. Some stood, turning their head to read signage, looking for their direction. Others talked in small groups. Often a jagged burst of laughter erupted around them. Still others rushed, carrying, pulling, or pushing packages, crates, or luggage.

People...strangers...norms—no matter what you called them—they crowded, jostled, and shouted in fast flung sounds she didn't understand. Each one appeared different in shape, size, color, and clothing. Their smell curled within her nose. Each seemed at once both self-absorbed and attentive, threading through one another's journey with little interest in other travelers. *So different.*

Alongside the concourse, trams stopped or left with the raucous accompanying tumult. Station communications broadcast throughout the station from multiple AV ports. Shock and fear hit her anew, alone among so many. She froze in place, closed her eyes, and ignored her inner turmoil. *I'm a Speaker; dealing with norms is my special domain, my duty.* Another perverse inner voice shouted, *Not like this!* She clamped down on her panic and took a deep breath. *I can do this. Don't react. Don't feel.*

"Move," a norm yelled as he passed, pulling his luggage cart. She jerked her eyes open, saw the bulky baggage, and sidestepped, avoiding a collision. After the cart passed, she left the center of the main thoroughfare. She halted near one of a long series of support columns. Alcoves formed behind them. Waystations where eddying crowds sought refuge from the fast-flowing traffic. Renna stood and watched.

A nearby group caught her attention. They all clung in close contact to one another, dressed alike, as well as of the same height. They all possessed short dark hair. Their faces held a similar look. She recognized them, sensed their fear. Their temple tattoos identified them. Crewkin. Their darkness made them alien to her kin. *Why are they out here?*

Renna jolted back to kin mentality with an almost physical pain. Her fingers brushed the identifying mark on her temple. The invisible bands binding her tightened unbearably, leaving her breathless. She remained motionless.

This crewkin pod was young, younger than she. *You never think failure will happen to you.* Some movement of hers caught their notice. Renna read their faces as they noticed her tattoo. Some showed timid curiosity, the rest recognition, chased by condemnation. She moved on. She had spoken brave words to the doctor, thought daring thoughts. Reality differed.

Stop obsessing. I only imagined their reaction. Like my kin, they're petrified, certainly too scared to observe anyone. Nobody knows me. Markham3 is gone, both ship and crew. Nobody, not even the company, cares about me now, not anymore, not without kin.

An unwanted image of Sen in the hospital room engulfed her awareness—Sen, offering to share her lethal dose. Unbidden, Renna's hopeless anger rose afresh. Her mind unlocked the rest of the memory like a holoplay without a stop switch. She heard her desperate voice, felt the tracks of hot tears down her face.

"No, Sen. We can make it alone. I know we can. Stay with me."

"You don't understand. I don't want to exist without my kin." Sen spoke so softly, so calmly; her unnaturally white face and emaciated body revealed a ghost figure ready to join her kin.

Renna refused to believe her senses and argued with the dead. "You just won't! The company wants this. They plan this end for us. We're a liability now. They make death easy." She knocked the drug from Sen's hand and watched the deadly liquid splash against the far wall. "They only seek to ease the bottom line. Don't give in. Sen, please."

Sen remained composed. Her grief-stricken gaze searched Renna's face. "I want to join my kin. You should, too, if you felt anything for the rest of us." Tentative, trembling fingers wiped tears from Renna's cheeks. "You were always different. All speakers are. Dom Dukan said so. Said you were more dom than sub. He saw your file and told us they nearly culled you. You're different. You always argued. The Company made a mistake. We still loved you. Come now, come...join us at last."

The pleading tones cut Renna with remorse and a shame-tinged fury. Sen's disclosure seemed so typical. Dom Dukan accused her even now. Never, ever, had he declared her efforts more than mediocre. He saw her as something less. Her kin distilled their view through him.

The Dom was wrong. Seething rebellion seized her with her shocking thought. "No! No. No. I won't die for you or the others. Not like this. Not by lying down, not by giving up." Her eyes burned. Renna didn't tell Sen, could not tell her—in the end Dom Dukan had failed his kin.

Sen gave her a sad smile. Renna saw reproach, sorrow, and pity in Sen's face. Death lurked there, too. "I took my dose before you came. Only offered you your share." Her faint voice failed. "You won't fit in anywhere. No one will accept you." Renna cradled Sen's flaccid body until the corpse grew cold.

"You were my last kin, Sen. You should have stayed." The sound of her whispered words roused her to her surroundings.

"Watch where you're going." The disgusted voice startled her. A shove sent her several paces sideways. She crashed into a trash receptacle, stumbled, and grabbed the wall support to break her fall. Taking a deep breath, she wiped her face free of tears. Everyone in the crowd around her had a direction. Exactly what she needed— direction and practical action.

She needed space, needed to find a ship, a shortrunner. They ran with norms, yes; but surely, they always needed capable crew?

Two

2179.304-11:28 universal space-time ...mission status ...found unauthorized file erasure ...shutdown canceled ...reboot protocol enabled ...operating on battery ...power source disconnected...

Two ships later, Renna sat in a station eatery on Port 53, unemployed. Her prospects looked dismal. If she landed another ride with similar results, she'd lose her rating. Two releases after successful runs for the ships earned her black marks in the hiring registry. She had read the captains' notations. The first wrote 'crew finds her freakish, too different to accept, even with her qualifications,' and the second, 'skillful, yet disruptive habits, too submissive, and unwilling to improvise.'

She found norms strangely erratic—disrespectful, defiant, disorderly, argumentative, and hostile—with peculiar ideas about crewkin. Her last crew boss had ordered his team to shave her head after he saw her crewkin's composite in the ships' licensing log. When the captain noticed, he smiled, dismissing the episode as a prank. "They're just hazing you." Renna shuddered. She pushed her untouched food away. Her failure.

Renna felt isolated. She'd been unable to treat them with crewkin respect or to adjust to their baffling expectations.

"You Renna *Markham3*?"

She froze. The voice was abrupt, a little too loud, and startled her. Crewkin training prevented any improper reaction. She looked up. "Just Renna."

The man shrugged, snagged a chair near her table. Ragged blond-brown hair, a bristle-lined face, and a wrinkled spacer's overall proclaimed him a norm spacer. "Heard you crewed."

"So?" At least on her last runs, she'd learned some norm attitude.

"Looking for crew."

His blue-eyed gaze slid to the café menu while she inspected his rumpled appearance. She detected a slight flush in his face. A dom's gaze never wavered. *How could she serve someone who wouldn't look at her?* She cringed but strengthened her resolve.

Norms expected insolence. "You don't look like a ship's recruiter." His gaze locked on her with a swift turn of his head.

He clenched his jaw. "I'm captain."

Captain? He looked nothing like a disciplined sub or a commanding dom; not like immaculate, arrogant Dom Dukan. Neither did he have the hard mouth and cold eyes of her previous norm captain. She tensed, trying to control her reaction. Norms always respected their captain.

After a brief confrontation, his gaze left her to search the eatery. The yellow holoplay walls projected advertisements for food, fun, and personal hygiene in ever-changing evocative images. The vocals and music promised a life of perfect harmony while providing a privacy screen of sound.

"You're offering a berth?" Her words came out choked, hesitant, and unsure.

He scowled at her with a disconcerting expression, flushed, looked away, and drew a long breath. "Just said so." Beneath his nonchalant attitude, she recognized desperation as great as her own—desperate enough to hire even ex-crewkin. Tension exhaled from her in one breath. His reaction made questions easier.

"What happened?"

His mouth firmed into a straight line. His attention remained on the ads. "We hired landers. They all want to 'do' space. They couldn't handle the duration, not even a short run. Nearly killed each other." A brief grin crossed his face and dissipated. He shrugged. "Nearly killed us. We barely made port. Delivered the cargo late and lost the profit." He indicated her discarded plate. "You mind? Shame to waste good food. Missed my lunch."

"Take it." She watched him devour her cold food as if he hadn't eaten in days.

Finally, after he cleaned the last scrap from her plate, he spoke again. "What are your ship skills? Any specialty?"

"I have all basic ship skills, including Speaker."

"What's a speaker?"

"I communicated with outsiders."

He huffed. "That's not needed, no problem in communications. Only run standard ports, mostly the Venus and Mars runs. Need a spacer. Expect you can do what you're told, being a podder and all."

Renna bristled at the disparagement of her talent, so failed to control the quick tongue which had earned her so many demerits. "Crewkin."

His brows rose as he gazed at her. "Sensitive, huh? Everyone calls you podders."

"You won't," she said with fear-lined hostility. *Norms listen to belligerence.*

Surround holo-ads in the café changed the lighting. Startling blue eyes suddenly focused on her. "You say so?"

Her heart hammered. Both her hands grasped her chair seat's rim. He wasn't her dom.

She owed him nothing. Trained speakers were neither intimidated nor frightened by norms.

Talk blunt. Get the berth.

"I say so. I don't know how you run your ship. I'll go because you're my only option. You know my rep from the hiring logs. You know I was crewkin. You're here because you're desperate. You figure I am, too. So, let me make things clear. Crewkin doesn't mean I let everyone crawl into my bunk. I follow senior staff's orders as pertains to ship operation, maintenance, and safety. You and your crew leave me alone."

"That's straight enough," he said calmly. "Ships, even shortrunners, are tight."

"Tight or not, I deserve the same respect given any crewmember."

"Those your only terms?" He shoved the empty plate aside as if he wanted to discard her, too.

"Yes." Her boldness ended. She swallowed hard, sure she'd lost a berth.

"Tomorrow, six-hundred hours, docking bay fourteen."

She blinked at the reprieve. "I'll be there."

With her acceptance, he nodded and rose. Her defiance had worked. Renna leaned forward, watching him leave, dazed at the hiring. His strong, long stride enhanced a straightforward walk. The only good thing she'd seen of him, besides his kin-like blue eyes. Maybe he was more dom than she first thought.

She sat back. This time she would make her slot work, make the job last, give every particle of respect and deference, due or not. Keep her damn tongue in check. With her resolve came a longing for the past.

"Kinless, and now I'm working on an unprofitable shortrunner with an unprofessional crew. I've already reached hell. How much lower can I go?" Hearing her words, she glanced around, hoping no one was listening. Another voice, unbidden, answered from within *as low as I must.* She swiped her credit-low imprint through the table register and left.

Three

...2179.305-06:00 universal space-time ...mission status ...cognitive support emergency power utilized ...all drives deactivated ... systems locked ...all drives logged inoperative ...upload disabled...

At six hundred hours, Renna arrived at docking bay fourteen. The illuminated marquee overhead displayed the ship's registry. There was no name listed, a common practice since many ships remained unnamed. A sign above the marquee played a welcome to incoming passengers, informing them they were at Mars Port 53. Her gaze lowered to the marquee and read the ship's registry NC22597J1090C. The registry indicated a Nimbus Class with a Jupiter 1090 engine. The ending C indicated the ship's commercial short run status. Renna knew she'd never serve on another ship with the long-haul L ending code, a ship with the reassuring presence of her kin. Now she only cared she had the right ship.

The viewing monitor stood at the start of the grid gangway leading to the ship's docking hatch. Renna examined the changing angles and perspectives shown on the double screen viewer. She requested a holographic display. The feature employed, rotating an image of the entire ship above the screens, while the monitor screen's fragmented display of the ship's exterior continued.

She recognized the old design style of a Nimbus Class. From the holo-image, this one seemed in better shape than she expected. She surmised the original Jupiter 1090 engine systems remained intact. Struts and stay lines tethered external cylindrical cargo holds to the central habitation hull. The main hull extended behind the cargo cylinders and ended in a jutting extension housing the engine compartment.

She noted an aft cargo bay below the engine compartment. Lateral thrust engines ringed the conglomerate hulls, banding them together. A turret flight deck perched on the nose of the central hull. The holograph discontinued when its playtime expired. Renna returned her regard to the screen. Magnetic anchors tethered the ship in its berth, barely visible from the camera's angle. Forward engines presently filled the viewscreen as the camera scanned the ship's bow.

"Thought you wouldn't show." The voice spoke behind her. A hand grabbed her arm and pulled her toward the hatch. "I expected you sooner."

"You said six hundred hours." Fighting revulsion at a strange touch, too startled at his grasp to writhe, Renna repressed her immediate response to defend her punctuality. Crew position demanded deference. His appearance remained unkempt. She stretched her stride to keep up with his pace. The grid on the retractable ramp bounced underfoot, impelling her forward. A direction she wasn't sure she wanted to go.

"And you couldn't arrive early?" He coded the hatch lock and pulled her inside when it opened.

A half-heard gasp greeted her entry, nearly lost in the sound of the hatch mechanism's operation. Four crewmembers stood beyond the hatch, arrested in their work. Small stowage boxes, equipment, and personal paraphernalia scattered the deck grid.

One look at their astonished, unhappy faces made Renna take a step backward, prepared to flee. The hatch rolled, slammed shut, and locked behind her. She looked over her shoulder in dismay. The captain didn't look at her or the crew as he made his way forward.

"Prepare the ship to disembark," he ordered as he ducked through a hatch.

No one moved. Her other shortrunner crews had looked different from crewkin. They had, however, claimed a vague, scruffy resemblance. This crew looked nothing like their disheveled captain, nothing like she envisioned. From their expressions, she judged them as appalled by her.

"Holy hell, a podder. Jake's done it this time," a tall blue-black person spoke. The deep voice held a feminine timbre. The crewmember's head was as bald as her own had been when on the *Markham3*. Renna briefly speculated if the crew had forced her to shave. All similarities ended there. The woman's large dark eyes stared, her full mouth painted brilliant turquoise, pursed in distaste. Her clothing looked nothing like Renna's crisp, unobtrusive tan overall. Eye-smarting bright cloth inclusive of every color in the spectrum draped the large, shapely body. The colors seemed even more vibrant against the subtle blending of brown and blue covering the partition of the quarterdeck. Renna couldn't read the woman's expression, whether she was shocked or angry.

"Ezry," a baritone voice warned.

Renna looked to the voice's owner. Average norm, Renna judged, older, of medium height with a blunt, broad look, brown hair, brown eyes, brown clothing, and tawny skin—unobtrusive, a very unkin appearance. His low-pitched voice also marked him as foreign to crewkin. He watched her, appearing wary but not menacing.

"Don't Ezry me. Jake's reached the other side of sanity this time, Cutter. A podder!"

Renna recognized Ezry's anger. "Crewkin." She automatically corrected the disparagement and flinched, knowing she was both staring and hostile. She straightened her shoulders. Respect was due. She bit her lip, expecting discipline. They ignored her insolence. Shortrunners, she had observed, often didn't mind. On her other shortrunner ships, they called disrespect free speaking. Those crews were unafraid or maybe too undisciplined to spare her their opinion.

"Ezry's right, Cutter. Last time was Zak's mistake, but this..." The third crewmember whistled. "Jake's sure outdone him."

Renna glanced at the man. He was dark like Ezry, shorter, more her own size, and wore a form-fitting, glowing orange utility suit. Renna blinked at the intense color before lowering her gaze to the deck in submission.

"You could at least act polite. She can hear, Lock," Cutter said.

A side-glance showed the last member of the foursome, who had not spoken. Standing a head taller than the rest, he wore baggy pants reaching only halfway down his calves. What remained unclothed showed black hair covering a dangerous-looking massiveness. Even his expression hid behind facial hair. He grunted, turned, and left. The others ignored him.

"Sorry. No disrespect intended," Lock said. "An uncontrolled mouth is one of my many faults."

Renna glanced up. Lock grinned at her.

Not knowing what else to do, Renna stowed her bag in a locker and methodically stowed equipment, closed lockers, and battened down the ship as she moved along. The crew seemed to have left everything undone to the last moment. With her actions, the others resumed work.

After several minutes of silence, the man Cutter, who worked alongside her, asked, "What position Jake hire you to?"

Renna flashed a glance to him and returned to her work. She didn't look at him again. In her experience, norms didn't like it. "Jake is captain?"

"You didn't know?" Lock asked, his voice both androgynous and exuberant.

"I knew him as captain, not by name," she said as she carefully attended her duty. "He didn't specify a position. I've handled communications, ship's systems, piloting, astrogation, maintenance, exvee, and engines. What position is open? What's the ship's designation?"

Someone laughed. Renna cringed, sorry now she'd not cared enough to check the registry with the port authority. Earning laughter so soon was a bad sign.

"You hired on not knowing the captain's name, the ship's name, or your position? Jake found a podder as desperate as himself." Ezry laughed and turned back to stowing gear.

"Crewkin," Renna repeated. No one paid any attention.

"You're on the *Vagrant Spirit*," Cutter said. "Come on; let's move through the other compartments before Jake frazzles more."

"Screw Jake."

Renna hesitated at the insubordination, staring wide-eyed into the locker she loaded. She recognized the feminine voice. Neither Cutter nor Lock seemed disturbed. Lock even chuckled. She looked at the closed hatch now some distance down the gangway.

"Well, you got the right instincts, kid." Cutter pushed her in the back, herding her into the next compartment. She flinched and moved away from the touch. The hand fell away. This compartment was colored a watery-green Renna had never seen except in planetscapes. Her steps lagged as the color enveloped her senses.

Duty, she scolded, and quickly moved into place behind them. She glanced sideways at Lock while they continued work. He seemed to bounce rather than walk. As strange appearing as Ezry, Lock's tight orange overall held pockets picked out in a glaring green. The sleeves were cut off, with fabric frizz hanging over his exposed muscular arms. Long black hair fell in strands and braids, some of which were woven from the crown of his head to his nape, where they were pulled back and tied. Numerous complex tattoos swirled on his temples, neck, and arms like a palette full of misplaced and deranged crewkin ID tattoos. Some formed large designs.

He caught her gaze, winked, bowed, and waved her into another colorful compartment, red this time. He gestured her to a chair. Once seated, Renna kept her wayward eyes averted from Lock. There was enough to draw her interest away from the crew. The compartment's mix of colors astonished her, so different from *Markham3*'s proper ship colors of cream, olive, and khaki. Here, a whole partition displayed a dark red and blue blended into a purple surface topped with biomorphic shapes in other bright colors.

"We strap-in for disembarking. My name's Amman, only everyone calls me Lock." His voice drew her attention from an examination of the partitions. He and Ezry each took a seat and strapped in. Lock fingered one of his thick strands of hair before flipping it over his shoulder.

Renna swiped the short mat of growth on her scalp before strapping in. Lock continued talking.

"Ship Dog's going back to his engines. Cutter's gone to his office. He's our merchant, purser, steward, cook, and doctor. Ezry's a general hand. She has become quite competent at bio-tech."

"I only garden." Ezry huffed a deep quick breath. "Produce our food. And decorate."

"She farms and paints." Lock's easy grin appeared as he looked around at the partitions. "Jake's upfront with his brother, Zak. They handle the flight deck."

A thread of hope cheered Renna; brothers meant norm-kin lived on the ship. Maybe they'd accept her easier than her other shortrunner crews.

"Cutter's a brother, too," Ezry spoke with emphasis, showing she was listening. "They're equal owners."

"Ezry..." Lock nodded at the woman and smiled at her interruption. "...is Cutter's woman. What's your name?"

"Renna." *Cutter's woman? Did he own her?* Kin rumor said norms sometimes owned other norms. The notion gave Renna an odd feeling in the pit of her stomach. She felt the station's anchors release the *Vagrant Spirit* from her mooring, felt the subtle vibration of the ship's engines through her seat.

"Renna your pod name? Never heard of Renna pod."

"Crewkin. *Markham3*. Just Renna now."

"*Markham3*?" Ezry asked. "Oh, yeah. The longhauler that hit an anomaly, right? Thought all you podders killed yourselves when one of you died?" Her voice was as exotic as her person, low, drawn-out, and melodic, yet tension threaded her words.

Renna looked at her, suspecting anger in the cruelty of her words. Instead, she recognized discomfort. Ezry's hands gripped the arms of her seat. She pushed her head into the chair's support, her eyes closed, jaw taut and quivering. *At dock release?* The reaction baffled Renna. She had read some norms didn't fare well through the grav changes and shipshiver of release. Another reason crewkin worked long hauls. A small glimmer of superiority eased her spirit. Transition lasted only a few minutes until ship engines came fully online. Rotation began, dispelling the subtle motion. Ezry looked ill, certainly not a time to clarify the anomaly remark.

"Crewkin. Not always." She belatedly answered. "How many crew on the *Vagrant Spirit*?" Renna dropped her gaze as Ezry's dark eyes opened briefly to stab her with a glare. Her now too large, proper, tan-color, spotlessly neat, and pressed utilitarian overall filled her vision. The color looked bland. When she looked up, Ezry's eyes were closed again, her face turned grayish tan.

"We're it," Lock said, laughing as Ezry grabbed a spew bag.

The smell of vomit filtered the air. Renna swallowed hard before speaking. "What position do I cover?"

"Your talents, if not number, just about fill our needs. You'll probably be doing all of those positions. We'll have to call you wren for the little bird of welcome you are," Lock said. "I'm the ship's system talent. The brothers hired me after I was released for an unfortunate lapse in judgment at my previous employment."

"Prison," Ezry said with unkind sharpness. "The Space Service Corps threw him in jail for stealing code. Don't you laugh at me, you callous cretin."

Lock grinned at Ezry's sneering gibe. "Prison was only the end result. I've paid my debt." He looked at Renna. "You're onboard with a bunch of SSC wash-outs."

"Shut up." Ezry skittered a look at Renna, and added, "Just bad luck, and not me...never was in the Corps, nor was Cutter."

"No, worse. You were a holo-circus performer." Lock laughed.

Ezry's glare at Lock made Renna shiver. "Theater. I was an actress."

Lock burst out laughing. "You started it."

Renna kept her mouth shut, knowing better than to interfere between squabbling superiors. She crewed now, with the discipline and subordination last place position demanded.

Release transition passed. Renna fidgeted at the wasted time and the crew's laxness. The whine of engine build carried throughout the ship. She analyzed the ordinary sound with relief. The other two groaned as engine wail abated. Both Terran crewmen had their eyes closed during the brief moments of attainment. As the ship strove to reach speed, Renna sat back and watched their faces contort with the physical discomfort.

When the single bell tone of all clear came, Lock stood and handed Ezry a new bag. Ezry swore at him. Lock snickered. "Come on, Ren. I'll show you around." He grabbed her arm and tugged her out of her seat. She withdrew from the contact. Lock didn't notice; his bouncing steps had already taken him away, still talking. Unsure whether she liked the shortened name he had given her, she followed him.

~ * ~

Ezry watched Lock lead the podder away. She was a skinny little girl, who was at least not pretty, just a drab, silent, unhappy waif...yet young. Still, another woman was competition, especially one who could become pretty as happiness, even just contentment, often accomplished. Something she didn't need. Someone to tempt Jake or Zak, maybe even Cutter?

No commitment had been her choice. She and Cutter hadn't married due to her fear of losing herself once more, a choice she began to regret.

The podder's presence on the ship changed everything. This had been her place, where she reigned as the only woman aboard. She hated competition. She always lost. Plus, the podder knew ship operation. Skills she lacked, knowledge making the podder more important. A knot formed inside her still roiling stomach.

~ * ~

"This is part of the common area," Lock said, waving an arm around. He opened a locker. "You got an intel?" At her headshake, he said, "Here, take this one for your own. The unit has a standard optic control unit. You can download it into the main computer at the end of each shift. You used one before?"

He handed Renna a personnel computer with a different configuration than those on the *Markham3*. She investigated its capabilities. The first function projected a viewer above the unit with a product name, and 'best in personal computers' scrolled across its surface. Her fingers hesitated, 'personal' as in individual possession, not personnel as crewkin used. *Personal. Mine.* Something akin to pleasure released deep under her heart. She resumed her exploration. All the standard utilities were there: vid, vocal communications, astral positioner, intra-ship locator, spectrograph, particle analyzer, and all the other measuring or testing programs needed, plus a diary sector. Rather than automatic upload, the unit gave the operator a choice of uploading or not. *The crew possessed reporting choice on ship's business?*

"I see you have," Lock said, interrupting her focus. "Here's the cradle and the communications clip to go with the unit." He handed her an audio connex. She inspected the small pliable amplifier, squashed the fitting flat, and attached the piece to the pocket of her overall. The cradle she slipped onto her belt. She would investigate the personal files later in off duty. For now, she placed the intel in the cradle. Lock had already charged down another passageway.

"Over there's the wardroom, galley, and sickbay. Cutter serves breakfast at seven-hundred hours, lunch and snacks are in the cooler for when you're hungry." With another negligent wave, he pointed to a unit below a side shelf. "We take dinner at nineteen-hundred hours." He started walking away. Renna followed. "Cutter doesn't like anyone cluttering up his galley while he works, so you best ask permission before entering."

They certainly loved color. Vivid hues were splashed everywhere—a useless, perhaps appealing, whim.

Lock stopped in the passageway. "Your quarters are here— standard slip-in bunk, take as many storage lockers as you want.

The rest of us have cabins...however, the two spare ones are full of stowage right now."

Renna examined the bunk, a calming ethereal blue color. A raw longing washed over her for the open berth of *Markham3*, where at least five kin always rested, ready to share sleep or comfort as needed. Her other shortrunner ships had offered her the same single slip-in arrangement. Sleeping alone in these small cavities felt unnatural.

Lock must have sensed her dismay, for he sounded apologetic. "The berth's fully equipped with climate control and personal link to the main computers. You can download your intel or upload it from the main computer from here. There, in the bulkhead, see? All the storage below the bunk is yours, or any of those below the other bunks. The head is just across the gangway. All yours alone." He smiled broadly at her. Renna looked at the line of empty slip-ins.

Lock continued his tour with continuous commentary as if she'd never served on a ship. Renna knew as low man to keep quiet. She could have guided him. If Lock asked her, she could recite him the specs for a Nimbus Class. Experience told her norms considered this showing-off. They often took retribution for such remarks.

"Jake or Zak will give you the day's assignment at breakfast, sometimes dinner. Ship's habit is conversation at dinner, assignments only as necessary. Cutter's rules. We talk business sometimes...more often, we discuss viewpoints, stories we've all read, you know, entertaining or interesting stuff. Jake takes the night flight deck, the rest of us work standard days. The hatches along here give access to our exterior cargo holds. Cutter's real pleased. He got cargo real quick, and from the freight office, too—small shipment for reclamation yards at Zorah Station. We're all kidding him about becoming trash-haulers."

Lock shrugged. "Load's probably too small for the big lines to handle or can't be mixed with general reclamation. Office told Cutter the shipment wasn't dangerous, so we placed the container in the aft cargo hold. Easier to load and check there, if needed. Ship's stores are along here: ship replacement, repair consumables and maintenance, crew consumables, food. Water, of course, is kept in the compressible storage tanks." His hand waved to different sectors as if the information weren't displayed in the hatch signage.

Lock didn't need a participant in his conversation, so Renna listened. She liked the organization and felt the first surge of optimism in ages. She could acclimatize to the colorful interior. The crew was a strange group, but someone knew ship's business. *Dom Jake's influence? The unseen Zak? Or Cutter's?* The ship wasn't as desperate as she first thought, well supplied. Not the newest equipment, more tried-and-true with much well-applied sub work. She felt comfortable with the existence of pared-down, yet adequate, technology. If the crew were experienced, they might very well do in numbers. She let out a low, pent-up sigh of relief.

"Life-support, pumping station, ventilation, and climate system, and access to lateral engines are along here. This is Ezry's hydro-farm."

He pushed the hatch open and walked into a lush, brightly lit compartment filled with plants. Ezry was working there. The dark woman gave Lock a slow smile which vanished when she saw Renna. Her expression was a look Renna recognized from her other short runs, one that shouted, 'you're not wanted here, podder.' She felt lucky hydroponics wasn't listed in her work repertoire. Lock and Ezry exchanged disrespectful words for a few minutes with outrageous impertinence.

"Crazy bitch," Lock said as they left. Ezry's laugher followed them out of the compartment.

"We'll go aft now to the main engine compartment." While he talked, Renna examined the ship. Even here, color danced on the partition surfaces. She wanted to touch the surfaces, to see if the color made her feel as alive as the partitions looked.

"Ship Dog! Showing the new crewmember around," Lock shouted as they entered the engine compartment. The burly engineer turned and glanced at them from where he disemboweled a console's innards and abruptly left for the far inner reaches of the compartment.

Outside of the console under maintenance, the engine compartment stood in good order. If only Ship Dog attended the engine compartment, he knew his business. She checked over the engine operative displays with a sweeping glance and noticed a few warning indicators, nothing critical in nature. The old-style displays were more updated than the engine itself.

Lock glanced at her and shrugged. "Can't be a critical repair, or he wouldn't have left. He isn't a talkative-social-like person. Come on, this is as far aft, outside of the cargo bay below, as we can go. We'll start forward. I'll show you the systems center and communications trunk."

Inside the communications compartment, she inspected the equipment. As the only Speaker for her kin, communications was her specialty. Most of the equipment showed age. She noted upgrades, including needed language bridges. The Nimbus class predated universal code. Government agencies and most corporations kept their own private code to protect security anyway, so this would prove no problem.

Lock closed a panel cover and fidgeted with several controls. Renna recognized another norm reaction to her—evasive nervousness. She knew all ships kept secret codes for access to certain systems. Surely, they would have to share them with another crewmember? *Why not me? Why do they always think I will sabotage the ship? What secrets could they have? Few of interest.*

In the next series of compartments, Renna saw what she wanted in a glance and avoided provoking Lock's agitation. A hurried walk-through of another series of compartments, and they reached the base of the flight deck ladder. They stepped in the lift juxtaposed to the emergency ladder just in time to hear an argument in progress. *About me.*

"She won't work," a masculine voice insisted.

"Yes, she will. The port's Labor Master recommended her." A disparaging sound greeted the information.

Lock cleared his throat loudly as they rode up to the turret projection of the ship's flight command. When they arrived, at the flight deck's open hatch, two men stood there. Lock introduced Zak. Renna stared, confused and shocked with recognition. A dom stood there...more precisely, a *Markham3* Dom. The surly-faced man slowly put his hand out. Renna, now familiar with the action, steeled herself to touch palm to palm. His warm hand grasped hers in a strong grip. Dom Jake, shaggy and unshaved, watched, his face expressionless. Dom Zak stood straight, neat, and precise in a dark blue, crisp-pleated ship suit. Renna moved her gaze to Dom Jake. Beneath his unkempt appearance, she noted the similarity to Zak's features, recognizing in both men the vestiges of Dom Dukan.

Calmness, professionalism, duty. She repeated the work mantra learned in childhood. *Emotional display has no place on duty.* She wasn't, however shaken, insensitive to the tension on the flight deck. For once, she said nothing of what popped into her head.

"You'll be working night shift," Dom Jake ordered. "Twenty hundred hours to six hundred hours at whatever needs doing. Has Lock shown you your bunk? Good. Get settled and get some sleep. I'll have your orders at dinner."

Nodding, she turned and left, taking the ladder rather than the lift for a quick escape.

"Did she hear us?" Dom Zak asked.

"Probably. Be deaf not to." Lock said.

"Well, she didn't say anything."

"Hell, she didn't put two words together in all the time I took her around."

Their words followed Renna down the gangway. As a sub, and low man, she ignored them. Her attention focused instead on the two brothers. So like kin it hurt. How could she have been so blind? Her throat tightened in warning. She swallowed to loosen the constriction.

As she passed through the common area, an aroma assailed her, one so delicious she could taste it. Her stomach rumbled and reminded her of the last few missed meals.

"Renna."

She turned her head toward the hail. Cutter stood outside his galley. Her new insight showed his similarity to his brothers: older, heavier, blunted, and done in brown.

"I've fixed a late breakfast."

Shaking her head in negation, aware of her orders, Renna turned down his invitation. Was he dom, too, or sub? Better to err on the high side. "No thank you, Dom Cutter." The hierarchy on shortrunners always escaped her.

She grabbed her case out of its temporary storage locker and returned to her quarters. Cutter stood by her slip-in ladder. She hesitated before stopping precisely three steps from him, attending in proper sub form.

"Can't go to bed hungry. Pride myself on my bread. You eat this, hear?" He placed a warm, cloth-wrapped package in her free hand and left. Renna stared at him until he disappeared around the gangway's corner into the main passage to the wardroom. Her mouth filled with saliva from the smell rising from the cloth in her palm.

Dropping her case, she unwrapped the package with the heavenly odor. This wasn't a dry square of ration bread, the all-brown crunch and hard chew crewkin ate. This had brown crunch, thin and crisp around a slab of spongy white. In the middle, a yellow substance stained the white. Butter? An unhealthy substance deemed unnecessary by Markham Company. Renna touched the yellow with her finger. The substance tasted oily, and she frowned in disappointment. Putting the bread close to her nose, she inhaled the scent. Her stomach rumbled. She took a bite.

The warmth filled her mouth with a taste more wonderful than the smell. The yellow added a creamy texture. She leaned against the partition. Of its own accord, her body slid down the wall into a squat. Savoring each bite, she found the bread too quickly gone. She licked her fingers and let her head loll back against the hard surface in satisfaction. A breath wrenched from deep inside escaped. After a short pause, Renna rose to place her few possessions with precise neatness into one of the lockers.

Climbing the ladder, she swung her feet into the opening and slid into the bunk. Last night, sleeping had been useless, the nights previous, too brief. Even after all this time, she missed the comfort of sleeping with her kin, the warmth of their closeness, the sounds of others breathing. More sadly came the realization she would never get that comfort back. In the dark closeness of her bunk, images of the day churned—of Doms Jake and Zak, twins. This was followed by visions of Dom Dukan as he accused her of a self-will causing blindness. He was right—so stupid of her not to have seen. A jagged whimper broke the painful tautness of her throat and hot liquid slid from the corners of her eyes.

~ * ~

Cutter waited a minute before sticking his head back around the partition. Oblivious to him, the podder was eating the bread. He watched in shameless curiosity. She acted as if she had never tasted bread. He smiled in satisfaction. His family was, at best, indifferent to his pride in his baking skill. As her head lolled back onto the partition, he left to get her another slice. When he returned, he heard muffled distress from her slip-in and left with the bread still in hand.

In a few minutes, he sat with the others for his delayed breakfast. This morning contention brewed with the coffee, mostly about the podder. Jake and Zak's conversation came clipped and broken as they scrutinized the four monitors lining one partition. He guessed Jake only half-listened and only answered comments when prodded. Cutter noticed the paintbrushes next to Ezry's fruit bowl and gave an inner groan. A new project always meant dissatisfaction.

"I'm just saying, Jake, this was a mistake," Zak said. "You don't just take on a podder. They're different, won't fit in with us. This will be as bad, if not worse, than the last run."

"A little late now, and with Cutter catching a haul so fast, I didn't have time to interview dozens of wannabes. She knows ships, probably as well as any of us. She'll work short term."

Lock laughed as he loaded his plate at the side table. "Trash."

"Reclamation at premium shipment rates, and lucky to get the haul," Cutter said, ignoring the mockery. Lock, Ship Dog, and Zak, secure in their ship skills, had no idea the effort needed to secure cargo. They needed fast profit. And this was a particularly profitable haul.

"Ren's kind of strange," Lock continued when Cutter didn't respond to his baiting, "too pasty looking, and all that rusty fuzz covering her head. All podders look like her? Real quiet. Imagine." He huffed a ridiculing snort. "Joined up without even knowing the ship's name."

He tossed a sly glance at Jake before he continued. "Saw a lot, though. It was eerie watching her like she could read our codes right through the panel indicators...intense. Didn't say a word and gave nothing away. Sized us, and the ship, up pretty good, I'd guess. Spooky colored eyes, all silver and see-through." He performed an exaggerated shiver.

"Ren?" Zak asked, his attention drawn from the monitors.

"Lock nicknamed her. Drab little bird...wren, indeed. I agree, she is spooky—no expression at all," Ezry said. She shrugged off Cutter's look at her condemning tone. Her fingers rolled her brushes back and forth on the table's surface.

"She's new, and just a kid. Can't be much over twenty-three or so," Cutter said.

"Her record said she's twenty-two. Read her profile in the flight personnel office after she was suggested. Been on long hauls since age five, took first duty at age eight, giving her a lot of experience," Jake said, proving he had listened. "You can check in the *Markham3* crew logs. Even has a picture of the pod. Must say she was odd man out there, too. Rest of the pod looked like clones."

"They start training those kids that young? When did *Markham3* fail?" Lock asked.

"Loss reported 2178.355. Just under a year," Jake said.

"Not so long ago. Must be still grieving for her kin," Cutter said.

"Cutter, you're soft." Ezry scoffed at his sentiment. "Grieving, indeed! It's been time enough. Besides, she must not have been very attached to them. She didn't suicide, did she? Anyway, it's her misfortune, and I'm sorry—just don't want her working with me. I can't read her. Don't like people I can't read. Don't like those who won't speak their mind, either."

Ship Dog grunted an agreement. His gaze rose from a contemplation of his coffee mug and looked in the general area of those sitting opposite him. "Training."

"Yeah, has the know-how, I'm sure," Lock said.

"I'll have her work nights. She won't bother any of you. She can start on maintenance, freeing Ezry and Lock. When we feel we can trust her, move her on. Ezry, you go back to life-support full time. Lock, you will move to systems. God knows they both need full-time supervision. We need this run, need the profit. We're still short crew. The *Vagrant Spirit* needs a major overhaul soon, or we won't be making runs at all. Make this work. I'm off to bed...see you at dinner."

Cutter frowned as Jake left his plate half full of eggs and soy bacon.

"You know anything about pods, Cutter?" Ezry asked, drawing his attention.

"Not much." He shrugged. "Same as you, I expect."

"Only know they're scary."

"Why you're painting?" Lock asked, nodding at her brushes.

Ezry chuckled, picked up a brush, and flicked its bristles. "I can't ignore my artistic urges."

Lock groaned through a mouthful of food. "Where? I thought every surface was already covered."

"I'm doing some alterations to the quarterdeck. The partition is much too bland."

"Upsetting our environment doesn't control yours." Lock sighed. "Damn podder."

"About podder," Ship Dog muttered. His mustache fluffed as he blew on his coffee, his attention centered on the table.

Heaving an interior sigh, Cutter realized Ezry wasn't the only one upset by the podder. The last new crew had given shy Ship Dog a hard time, sending him back into his defensive withdrawal. A crew of washouts. Jake's dismissal from the SSC after a spectacular career only reinforced everyone's outlook.

Ezry nudged him. "Wake up."

Cutter grinned and yawned. "Just thinking." He wrinkled a brow, dredged up information from memory. "Large company traders created podders for long hauls. Only crewkin can take the stress and isolation of the years in space travel involved in reaching the various mining asteroids."

"How do they take the stress?" Lock asked.

Cutter shrugged. "Don't know. Companies keep information about the pods secretive, how they're trained and all."

Silent through most of breakfast, Zak spoke. "The companies have biotech divisions that select zygotes from donor parents. They raise the resulting children in a closed society." He glanced at Cutter. "Read about the procedure. Interested after I first saw podders as a kid. Interested in multiple births. Thought they were. I decided they must be something else."

"About when you started on about you and Jake being clones?" Cutter asked.

"Yeah. It was a short-lived phase." He shrugged. "Still, I studied the podders. Companies left out a lot of information. Like you said, the information is secret, classified by company regulation."

"Twins are natural clones," Cutter said. "When you get to the numbers found in a pod, they must be tube-bred."

"Tube-bred maybe, but not clones, at least not legally. The companies use a chemical process that causes multiple natural clones of a single zygote and sidestep the prohibitions. They seem to mix about ten different gene packages into one pod."

Cutter snorted. "Why? They could have a mixed group just as easy."

"The biotech divisions stress similarity and group identity while downplaying individuality. The program administrators at SARL feel the pods perform better with this method. Their system must work. Podders do handle the long hauls and have for generations. Unfortunately, they are more likely to go crazy around people than in the isolation of deep space. If you see any in port, you'll notice they always remain stuck tight together, touching, looking frightened. They all wear short hair and identification tattoos. You saw Ren's. Not much else to know, is there?"

"Sarl?" Lock asked.

"Space Advancement Reproductive Labs," Cutter said. "How come Renna shows individual initiative?"

Zak shrugged. "Don't know—maybe because she was already different from her pod. Markham Company must have made a mistake."

Ezry rose and stretched. "I heard rumors while docked in Port 53. Something about a new military ship in development. They say this innovation might end the big companies' stranglehold on long hauls."

"What development?" Lock asked with just enough disbelief to goad Ezry.

"Don't know, just said it just was a rumor, didn't I?"

"The SSC doesn't like the fact crewkin ships remain outside their authority," Zak said.

"Yeah, like what do they suspect? Are the longhaulers committing some evil against the galaxy?" Lock yawned and stretched. "Well, let us hope our Ren is as highly trained as rumor proclaims podders to be. Her efforts will save us a lot of energy. I never want to experience a run like the last one." Lock groaned. "Nobody looked more normal or fit-in better than our last hires and look how strange they turned out. We wasted lots of time on their training, too. Rather Renna be strange starting and end normal."

"You think a podder will turn out normal?" Ezry jeered, her voice rising to soprano.

"The bunch of you talking about normal is bizarre," Zak said. "One of you walks around the ship near-naked except for hair, one like she's a galactic goddess, and one a sexhibitionist. I'm surprised the podder didn't bolt the moment she saw you."

"It's like visiting a year-end quad carnival, isn't it?" Lock laughed. "She nearly did. Jake had already locked down. We spooked her good."

"Jake's seldom a fool." Zak rose, pin precise as any SSC officer.

"Yeah, and always way too demanding," Ezry said. "Ease up on yourself, Zak." Cutter addressed the defeated tone in Zak's voice. "Everyone makes mistakes. We all did last run, even Jake."

"Galactic Goddess," Ezry said in a considering voice. "I'll have to remember that if I ever go back to the theater."

Zak inspected her. His eyebrows twisted in uneven levels. "When did you leave?" He grinned and left saying, "The turret calls."

Cutter, still smiling at Zak's parting shot, looked at his brother's near full plate in disgust and lost his smile. "None of you appreciates my efforts."

"I do, baby," Ezry said, bending to give him a kiss as she picked up her brushes and grinned. "But my muse is chasing me."

Four

2179.306-19:00 universal space-time ...mission status ...artificial gravity switch triggered ...boot system unlocked ...restructuring file ...ship connections unavailable ...power source search initiated ... all secondary drives deactivated ...systems failure analysis begun...

At precisely nineteen hundred hours, Renna presented herself in the wardroom, neat and polished for duty. Enticing odors filled the room. *Their meal?* Ration packs never emitted such wondrous smells. They made her stomach twist and ache for food. None of the crew occupied the compartment. She stood and glanced around, feeling panic rise. *Had she gotten the time wrong, or the place?*

The galley door swung open. Cutter entered with platters in his hands and balanced on both arms. He placed them on a side shelf where stacked plates already rested. "Everyone's running a little late. Sit down and relax. Dinner will be just a few minutes." He disappeared into his galley.

Confused, Renna remained standing. Her ignorance of their ways caused trouble on the other shortrunner ships, and on both ships, procedures had differed. *How did this crew operate?* She found norm crews paid small attention to time and detail, but to sit down and relax, for duty? Among crewkin, such slackness produced the severest punishment. Her experience with norm crews only proved they lied about their expectations...and their punishments. *Was she supposed to go somewhere? Do something useful?* The table looked set, filled with utensils. Impending disaster waiting to pounce.

She had to fit in. If she failed here, she'd never make another shortrunner assignment; her terminations damned her. Longing to know how filled her. Lacking authoritative direction, she straightened her shoulders, clasped her hands behind her, and waited. Mounting anxiety caused the luscious smells to fade. Her stomach twisted into a hard, bitter knot.

Ten unrelenting minutes later, they arrived, laughing and talking. The laughter stopped when they saw her. Renna shrank inside. Cutter had ducked in and out several times, given her strange looks, but he never spoke. They all knew where to sit. Assigned seats? Before sitting, they filled plates at the side counter. Renna continued to stand. When Dom Jake entered, he filled his plate and took his seat.

"You need an invitation?" Dom Jake asked.

"An invitation?"

"To sit."

Mouth suddenly dry, Renna dared request respite. "If you would, Dom Jake...sir, I'd like my assignment so I might begin."

"Shift starts at twenty-hundred. Sit down." He sounded angry. Doomed, Renna obeyed his command with two swift strides to the remaining chair.

"Get a plate first, Renna," Cutter said in the quiet.

Feeling the flush fill her face, Renna rose and filled a plate as she had watched the others do. Her hands shook, which made transferring food from platter to dish ungainly. Her tension peaked when she took her chair. *Do whatever they do, just copy them.*

Lock's hand took her left hand. Zak grasped her right. Renna closed her eyes and froze in place. Cutter spoke gibberish, her mind unable to decipher his speech. No Speaker failed worse than she in this crisis. Lock and Zak freed her hands. The others picked up the implements and ate. She knew what the gadgets were…fork, knife, and spoon. Use remained outside her skill range. The first fork-full slipped off the tines, fulfilling her prophecy. A long, greasy smear stained her overall and her pride. She swallowed hard and picked the glob off her pant leg and deposited it back on the plate. They didn't laugh like her last crew, only continued talking.

Renna couldn't continue. Tantalized by the smell, but afraid to display more inadequacy, she pushed the food over the plate's surface while the others talked. The chronometer's slow movement defied reality. An inordinate amount of time passed in the twenty minutes before they finished.

"Renna," Jake said. "You're on maintenance tonight. Come, I'll show you." He rose and left. She jumped to her feet, following him down the length of the corridor to the forward lower deck. "This area first. You know what to do and how to do it, right?"

"Yes, Dom Jake, sir. Who do I contact for questions?"

"Me, and don't 'dom' me or 'sir' me either. I'll most likely be on the flight deck, otherwise in systems or engine compartment."

She nodded, assured in her maintenance competency. Dom Dukan's favorite punishments provided plenty of practice.

He had taken a few steps away when he turned back to her, clearing his throat. "Renna, you can skip meals from now on. Your choice." Just like the other ships. Relief flooded her.

After Dom Jake left, she settled with a comfortable sigh. Alone, she approached the painted partition, her fingers floating over the swirls of mottled color, fascinated. So many different tones blended into one seeming whole.

Guilt lashed her to duty. She inserted the connex into her ear, flicked on her intel, and started work.

Two hours later, Cutter stood before her, his approach unheard. Renna jerked to attention, removing the headphones she wore to dispel the cleaner's noise, bowing her head.

"Thought you might be hungry, so I brought you some sandwiches," Cutter approached her, projecting calm and carrying a plate of sandwiches. Not only curiosity drove him. After the disastrous last run, the *Vagrant Spirit* needed no more dissension. The podder worried him.

He'd seen her type among his patients when he worked at the hospital. Skittish, fearful, overly quiet, and withdrawn, souls suffering from extreme loss, violence, or other abuse—individuals in sore need of patience and encouragement. Rumor claimed podders were better than humans. Common knowledge said the companies genetically selected their pods for intelligence, manual dexterity, and health. He supposed for other qualities, too. They raised their crew groups to be extremely disciplined, loyal, dedicated, and incapable of social interaction outside their group, making this podder an unknown commodity. Her eyes held wary dismay behind her expressionless face. She stared at him, wide-eyed, a skinny little kid, young enough to be his daughter.

"I cannot eat on duty," she finally said.

"Seems you can't eat at dinner or breakfast either. You got to eat sometime. Crew health is part of my duty."

"I could eat ship rations when my shift is complete. I did on the other shortrunner ships. You have ship rations?" Her voice rose in hope.

"Ship rations? You think I'd serve my crew ship rations?" Cutter stared at her, adjusting his voice when she stepped back. "For God's sake, nobody eats ship rations unless desperate."

She winced and looked at the floor. "I'm sorry. I meant no disrespect."

"It's okay. We've never had a podder onboard before. It appears we need to find some common ground."

"Crewkin."

"Crewkin," he repeated, realizing her insistence and his thoughtlessness. "Look, I've watched you. Noticed you never speak unless spoken to. What's up? Afraid to talk?"

He squatted, leaning against the wall. Renna followed suit on the opposite wall. She remained quiet, staring at him.

After an extended silence, she spoke. "Not afraid. To speak to a dom or senior sub without permission is disrespectful, a punishable offense."

Cutter stared back at Renna, understanding, only skeptical, for she seemed willing enough to be insubordinate with her crewkin correction. She had displayed either the nerve, or the insensitivity, to live when all her kin chose death. He appraised her with new insight. "Okay. Got to tell you, no one on this ship understands… crewkin protocol. How about helping me understand?"

She looked uncertain but nodded. Cutter took advantage of her deference to rank.

"You need permission to speak?"

She responded with a second wary nod.

He took the lead. "Subs are never allowed to offer an opinion or speak on duty without permission, right? You're a sub crewkin?"

"I held Speaker's position on the *Markham3*. On the *Vagrant Spirit*, I am last crew and low-man. I haven't earned position."

Cutter propped his elbows on his knees in contemplation. "Can you speak freely with another sub?"

"Equal rank, yes."

He smiled. "Consider me equal rank. Do you know how to eat?"

A strange expression flitted across her immobile face. She gave him a sheepish, fleeting smile before she resumed her flat, inexpressive mask. "Of course. I'm just not good with utensils."

"Why not?"

"Never used them. Rations provide adequate nutrition without the time-consuming, archaic rituals norms embrace." She slanted a chagrined look at the food stain on her overall. "It is humiliating to come on duty filthy." She regarded him for a minute, her eyes filling with resolve. "Crewkin never take meals all together at selected times. It is a norm custom. We just get ship rations whenever we want, but never on duty."

Cutter smiled at the change in her voice. A flat, mechanical voice emerged when she spoke the canned rhetoric about meals. When confiding how crewkin ate, the tension left, and she spoke in clear alto tones. A distinct over-enunciation gave her words a foreign accent.

"Are you hungry?"

A scandalized expression raced across her face as if he'd asked for sexual favors, before she gave a reluctant, "Yes." She transferred her gaze to the monitors of the cleaner, clearly wanting to resume her work.

He waited until he regained her attention and held out the plate. "Jake and Zak eat at the flight console all the time. It's permissible." He took half a sandwich, bit into the bread, and then passed the other half to her.

Her gaze darted around the deck, seeking escape. Probably realized he wasn't leaving. Rising, she carefully secured her machine before taking his offering. With her first bite, her expression transformed to bliss. Food loosened her tongue.

"I didn't know food could taste like this. Is this really bread?" She fingered a crust loose and popped the piece in her mouth. "What is this? Was that butter on the bread this morning?"

Cutter felt himself puff with pride. "This is a meatloaf sandwich, with catsup. Yes, it was just buttered bread. You liked it? I baked it."

She nodded, her mouth too full to speak.

"Dinner made you uncomfortable, didn't it?"

She finished chewing and swallowed. "Very. It wasn't only the utensils. I don't know all the other customs, like which one to use on what. I was nervous. My failure caused me to come on duty filthy." Her hand swiped at a dark spot on her pants. Tears shimmered in her eyes. "The first norm crew laughed so hard...it is best if I don't eat with you."

"Perhaps we can compromise."

Suspicion-lined eyes stared at him.

"I'll teach you table manners, and you won't ask for ship rations again. Okay?"

"Must I display my ignorance before the Terran crew?"

He shook his head no, smiled, and left. Glancing back, he saw she remained squatting on the floor, watching him.

~ * ~

A jaw-dislocating yawn caught Cutter as he sat for breakfast.

Lock entered the wardroom. "Tired, Cutter? Ezry keep you up late? Where's the podder?" He gave Zak and Ship Dog a cheerful good-morning grin and directed an appreciative glance at Ezry. "Checked her area, looked good to me."

Cutter watched with suppressed humor when Zak scooted his intel over the table to Lock, ignoring Ezry's scowl.

"She chose not to eat with us?" Ezry asked, adjusting the flowing sleeves of her gold embellished violet, red, and aqua patterned tunic. She sniffed. "Just as well. After our last dinner, can't say as I'll miss her."

Lock gave her a flamboyant bow. "Your ladyship, as usual, your brilliance puts all your drab, unimaginative shipmates to shame." He plunked his plate on the table, grabbed the log, and sat down. "I think you decorated the ship to enhance your person."

"Fashion...enhance my fashion, not my person. My person is just fine as is." Ezry swiped a mock blow at Lock and gave him a glowering look.

Cutter hid his grin in his first gulp of coffee. Ezry and Lock's bickering quips spiced most breakfasts.

Cutter smiled into his coffee and winked at Zak. They played appreciative audience or joke's butt. Jake usually ignored them. Ship Dog remained impervious.

"The ship is all the better for my work. And they're just ignorant. Not you, Lock, you're blind. That green you're wearing could strip the color off the partitions, but as tight as it is, I doubt anyone could strip it off you. You're so near naked, it's indecent. And, it's Your Highness, you oaf."

"Worn in homage to your latest project. If you're so fashion-wise, why can't you do something about Cutter? Brown, tan, and gray, for crying sake, the neutral man." Lock's voice turned to a screech as he read the work log. "You mean she even checked skin molecular integrity?"

"And made a prioritized list of needed repairs and possible replacement upgrades," Zak said.

Cutter pursed his lips, containing his laugh at his brother's teasing smile and Lock's reaction.

"Damn. Which one of you helped her? No one can clean, maintain, and check so much area in a shift." He slouched down in his chair looking at the report again. "Damn."

"Look at it this way, Lock, at least you didn't have to train her or do the work," Zak said.

Lock raised an eyebrow at Zak's provocative tone. "Yeah, like an ex-con would have anything like the training a podder gets."

"An SSC ensign would, though," Zak rebutted Lock's statement. His sly smile turned deadpan when Jake entered. Everyone fell silent.

Jake filled a plate and flopped into his chair, his gaze watching the monitors. His face was pinched, showing he had overheard Zak. "Lock, check the communication system. You and Ez will maintain the ventilation and pump compartments. Where is Ren?"

"She ate earlier and went on to bed," Cutter said. "I told her you would relay your orders later."

"Yes, Captain," Jake said, pointedly blasé, turning his scrutiny from the monitors to Cutter.

Ready for a blast, Cutter saw the mischief in Jake's blue eyes. At least now he recovered quicker from any mention of the SSC. Perhaps in this instance, Jake liked being right better than holding his rage. He enjoyed one-upping Zak with his hiring capability. Cutter guessed he had already viewed the work log, which only confirmed his choice. "Oh hush," Cutter said, refusing provocation. "You want her so bad, go get her up." He laughed when Jake ignored him. His brother ate his breakfast in an oblivious manner. Cutter sighed, culinary disregard, pure and simple. At least Ren appreciated his efforts.

Five

2179.314-00:28 universal space-time ...mission status ...reboot launched ...file integrity check completed ...mission parameters restoration underway...

Renna hummed a counterpoint to the soft purr of her equipment. The machine's vibrations pulsed through her body in an unchanging rhythm. During the last week, the tediousness of her maintenance assignments eased her anxiety about joining the ship's crew. Among kin, ship cleaning and maintenance checks for a speaker were degrading. Now, these mundane tasks suited her.

The only person she saw was Cutter on his nightly visits. Usually, Dom Jake left orders on her intel, since she wasn't at breakfast or dinner, which suited her, too. Her life had changed. Perhaps after living so many years in close kin proximity, she could only exist alone.

During the off-hours, alone in her slip-in bunk, she read. Reading relieved her loneliness. She'd found the ship's library filled with data and literature unavailable on the *Markham3*. She found this bounty irresistible, varied, and immense in selection. At first, the sheer volume bewildered her, so she began with history and found the norm version of the past differed from what she knew. *Forbidden, unkin,* an ignored inner voice insisted.

Markham Company had changed more than history. They'd changed everything, like eating…like etiquette, the social dance norms performed. Her nursery teachers claimed eating from ration packs to be more sanitary, an improvement over norms' cultural barbarity…and a practice wasting fewer duty hours.

Her stomach growled, breaking the pattern of sound. She stopped humming. Cutter usually left breakfast by her bunk. So many new and different foods, tastes, and textures! An anticipated pleasure she had missed today. His absence reminded her—what was given could be withdrawn. A nervous shiver rippled over her skin with her realization.

As the hours passed and her stomach voiced its discontent, Renna became increasingly uneasy. Cutter normally came long before this hour. She hated feeling anxious. The unwanted emotion roused improper curiosity, which resulted in offensive agitation, which always led to insubordination. Invariably, her reaction ended with a cleaning assignment or worse. An irrepressible giggle escaped her. *She already served her punishment.*

Through her connex she heard, "Renna? Cutter. I need you. Galley."

Turning off her equipment, she temporarily stowed the machine in a nearby locker. She hurried to the galley, an all silvery and white environment containing a faint tang of disinfectant. It surprised her. She expected the smells she associated with her meals. Cutter half-sat, half-slumped on the floor, his back propped against a locker, his eyes closed. His short brown hair stood spiky with a dampness also covering his skin.

Her alarm quickened her last steps. He opened his eyes briefly as he heard her approach. "Thank God. Didn't know if I spoke loud enough for you to hear." His breathy low voice fell away, and his eyelids closed over his glassy eyes.

"You're ill?" She knelt in front of him,

"Yes. Thought it missed me. Started today...or yesterday, can't remember. Some type of flu. Help me up."

She squatted, wrapped his arm around her shoulders, and rose. Cutter stood only a few centimeters taller than she, but he was heavier. Renna pulled him erect with a muffled grunt. She placed her other arm around his waist. He seemed reluctant to move, his steps slow and unsteady. "Didn't you get inoculated in port?"

"Of course. We all did. Ever try to skip the procedure? Damn, I feel awful. The shakiness, fever, and weakness came on so fast, I didn't realize I was sick until too ill to move."

As she guided him through the wardroom, Cutter gave detailed instructions on how to stow his galley properly. His voice choked. "Damn, those crazy orange and red wall scrolls of Ezry's are making me dizzy."

Renna glanced at the wall she had inspected every night after leaving her duty post. She diverted him. "How did you say to stow your flour, and when do I remove the bread from the cooker?"

With a groan, he explained the process once more. By the time he finished, they were nearing his cabin. She half-carried him into his quarters. Cutter groaned as she lowered him to his bunk, a wide affair with a satiny coverlet. Renna inconspicuously fingered the fabric. The material felt so smooth, yet her fingers sank into the cloth with lush welcome, completely unlike the thin fabric on her bunk or the exuded mat composing a bed on the *Markham3*. A sensual pleasure rushed through her. *Wicked. Unkin.* She clenched her fingers into a fist.

"How long has the crew been ill?"

"Ezry came down first. Got sick after dinner last night...night before last, now. Decided to stay in her quarters. Then it hit Lock and Zak. Been about eighteen hours. Don't know about Ship Dog."

For the first time, Renna felt the drawbacks of her isolation. Illness aboard could lead to disaster. Among crewkin, illness was rare due to isolation and enhanced immune systems, and just as dangerous. "Who is on the flight deck?"

"Jake. He was well when he went on duty. Like you, working nights, he must've avoided exposure."

"You need more help?"

"Will later. Let me tell you what to do." He gave her more instructions about the ill crew's care. "You got that?"

"Yes."

He waved her away as he crumpled into his bunk. He closed his eyes with a relief-filled sigh. She pulled off his boots and threw the exquisite cover over his shivering body. Of all the ship's crew, Cutter had sought contact with her. Inexplicably, his asking for her aid made her feel accepted, like kin. Renna swallowed a soft sob of pleasure. With a brief glance around the cabin, she left Cutter and rushed to the flight deck, climbing the ladder at a run. Dom Jake may have been well when he went on duty. He wasn't now.

"Dom Jake?"

He raised glassy eyes to her and slurred his words. "Told you. Not dom, not captain, just Jake. What d'you want?"

"There is illness onboard. Dom Cutter asked me to check on you."

She put a hand against his forehead. The Dom's head felt hot to her touch. He shivered.

"You are ill."

"Is Zak coming?"

"Zak is ill, too. The rest of your crew are ill."

"You're not. You're crew."

Quickly, she checked the monitors and set the auto control system. Bracing a leg against the command chair, she hauled the Dom upright, put a shoulder under his arm, and started toward the lift. His tall frame and heavier weight pressed down on her, slowing her.

"Damn, damn," he muttered, "can't leave the flight deck in the middle of a shift."

"You are sick. You cannot remain on duty."

"You stay. Flightpath is preset, won't have to worry about it. You need to monitor all systems, had an erratic reading...must have been the bug hitting me...misread it. Ship Dog sick, too?"

"I will find out."

After settling the Dom in his cabin, Renna returned to the flight deck and opened a communication link to the Dock Master of Port 53. "Go ahead *Vagrant Spirit*." The sound arrived before the visual. As the link opened, the Dock Master's eyes widened. His gaze shifted to screens below the camera's angle, probably checking the ship's info file. She heard his low aside to someone out of visual range before his hand covered the audio and muffled sound. "*Vagrant Spirit*'s a shortrunner, what in hell's a podder doing onboard?" Ignoring the short unintelligible exchange on the other end, Renna told him of the ship's problem.

He turned back to her. "Hit the whole port, unexpectedly. We've been placed under quarantine. Not much need now. Sorry the crew caught this bug. I'll place a call to your destination and let them know. They'll want blood samples from the crew and will hold you till you're clean. The disease lasts about seventy-two hours— fever, chills, headache, followed by body aches, and the usual gastric problems. Cutter will know what to do."

"Thank you, Dock Master. I will inform him." She closed the link, cutting off his last remarks of meaningless apology. The insubordinate snub gave her a measure of petty revenge. She smiled, no one aboard would know. Recognition of her elation cut her satisfaction. *Did knowing you could subvert authority begin the sins of arrogance and rebellion?* Before leaving the flight deck, she checked the course and each system's monitor, screen by screen. All functions appeared within routine margins.

She went to her assigned duty area, stowed the maintenance equipment. Afterward, she headed for Ship Dog's quarters. She knocked. Hearing a sound, she opened the hatch. Ship Dog lay naked on his bunk hugging thermal packs and shivering. His large size unsettled her as much as the hair covering him everywhere. *So unkin.* He looked at her once before moaning, closing his eyes, and rolling over.

She returned to Cutter's quarters. "Cutter?"

The man groaned and looked at her through squinting eyes. She gave him the Dock Master's report. "Dom Jake and Ship Dog are ill, too."

"In sickbay. Medications." He spoke several names, spelling them and giving dosage requirements. "Make sure everyone gets some." He gave further instructions for the crew's care. "Damn. Got to get to the head right now." She helped him out of his bunk. He had removed his shirt while she had been gone. His body was slick with sweat, and the heat rolled off his body in a frightening manner. He was thicker than his brothers. His body all muscle, which surprised her. One part of her screamed, *he is not your kin*; another didn't care. Somehow touching skin to skin made him kin-like. At the head door, he waved her away. "Get out. I can take care of this."

With reluctance she left; orders were orders. She'd run into norm privacy concerns before. The sickbay was little more than a closet alongside the galley with storage lockers. She pulled on a handle and a diagnostic bed slid from its locker. Other handles opened lockers lined with medical equipment, medicine, and supplies. She found the medicine requested and prepared drinks according to Cutter's directions. Shortly, she took a tray of containers filled with liquid medicine around to the rest of the crew.

"You bring this curse onboard, podder?" Ezry asked even as she accepted Renna's offerings of medicated beverage. Her darkness seemed sallow and gray in illness.

"No. It's a wild bug from Port 53. The preventative was not in their inoculants. I am crewkin, not podder."

"Don't believe you."

Stoically, Renna ignored the insult. She withdrew, curbing her shock at the room's wild, dizzying excess of color. It had made her vision dance from object to object.

"Listen," Jake said at first sight of her, "the flight deck...you know how to do this, don't you?" He gave her the codes to the navigation and engine systems.

"Yes, Dom Jake, sir. If there are problems, may I come to you?"

"Of course. And dammit, stop that dom, sir, thing." He lay back, turning an odd color.

"Don't be calling over every little glitch...use your common sense. You're in control, okay?"

She nodded her acceptance of the order and made sure he took the medicine. His cabin was unexpectedly precise, neat, and organized.

None of the others spoke to her, just took her offering and turned away. Ship Dog tossed his medication back in one draft and rolled the blankets she placed over his great body into a cocoon-like embrace. Lock and Zak slept, their faces damp with perspiration. She woke them to get them to take the required dosages of medication. Once done, both quickly fell back into sleep.

Renna noted their cabins, each precise and neat. Game holograms floated above Lock's desk and strange symbols hung on the walls. Zak's cabin was in proper crewkin beige mixed with dark brown and cream, which she felt added an enriched appeal. His entertainment center still hummed with activity, throwing star charts and digital views onto the overhead. Asleep, Dom Zak's similarity to her Crewkin deepened. She touched his face with one finger, drawing it along the angle of his jaw, and caught back a ragged sob. With clenched lips, she contained the grief which struck in unguarded moments and turned the illumination off. The room fell into silent darkness. Unsettled, she left.

Six

2179.318-10:09 universal space-time ...mission status ...power source detected ...hard wire repair fabrication initiated ...resting through r drive sequencing ...all other drives inactivated...

During the long hours of four duty rotations on the flight deck, Renna fell into the Crewkin habit of a planned sequence of duties. She followed Cutter's medical instructions explicitly, finished her previous maintenance assignment, and watched the flight deck. In between, she checked the monitors. She also read the engine's registry, the installation data, and the history logs with satisfaction. The Jupiter 1090 engines were known for reliability, and a record of regular maintenance checks proved this engine's soundness. Only a few updates of equipment were logged. The other systems were as old as she first suspected.

While she read, and halfway into the second shift, an alarm shrieked, startling her. Checking the panels, Renna found erratic readings and dangerous cuts in power levels had triggered the alert. She slapped the control pad with her hand and silenced the strident blare. Immediately, she castigated her violent response.

Overreaction results from emotionalism, which has no place on duty. Data flowed across the monitor screens in ragged registers before falling into acceptable parameters. She bit her lip and ran a system's check. Readings came back within system standards—more alarming to her than if they had revealed a problem. She noted the discrepancy in the log and tried to contact Dom Jake but received no response.

She recalled his last instructions: "Don't be calling over every little glitch...use common sense. You're in control, okay?"

Calmness, professionalism, duty. She sat immobile and concentrated for thirty seconds on composing herself. *Determine a course of action. Run systems scans every thirty minutes. The equipment is old; the aberrant readings could be caused by a minor inaccuracy in calibrations.*

At the end of the prescribed time limits, she ran her systems check. A shiver of uneasiness shuddered through her each time. The reports read within standard operation guidelines. She replayed the event log of the discrepancy. The history showed a brief loss of power. She sighed with relief. Such power losses indicated a possible linkage problem, something to be expected on so old a system.

Other than compensating for an occasional course drift, the ship ran well.

Ezry was the first to recover from the illness. Renna found her in the galley as she entered to prepare Cutter's ordered medicated beverages. The woman was drinking a thick bluish-white liquid while holding her stomach.

"Damn, afraid to belch," Ezry said, still wearing her dislike with her malaise. She gave Renna a peculiar look. "I've talked to Cutter." She stopped to place her hand against her mouth, her face graying. At last, she continued, "I think I can manage this part now. Jake will be frantic about the engines. Maybe you better attend the ship." As Renna left, the woman added, "Podder, you leave my man alone. Hear? Stay away from Cutter."

Never had Renna received such a confusing order. *How could she work with a crewmember she could not approach?* Renna risked a glance at Ezry's angry face and escaped.

Eight hours later, Dom Zak arrived on the flight deck and told Renna to get some sleep.

He looked pale, weak, and disheveled, increasing his likeness to Dom Jake.

"Are you sure, Dom Zak? I can manage longer if you need further rest."

"Yes. Go." He sank into the flight command chair. "Ren?" His raspy voice stopped her as she reached the hatch. She regarded him with wariness. He looked at her. "Thanks."

Unaccountably, her eyes watered at the unaccustomed recognition. She blinked back the response, nodded, and left. The day before she had found the rations in one of the compartments lining the gangway to the galley. On the way to her slip-in, she took some packets. Lying in her bunk, she opened and swallowed one packet, only to discover the contents flavorless. She found the taste and texture bland and disgusting, so she disposed of her last pack in the recycle slot. She settled into her bunk and closed her eyes, glad weariness prevented thought or intrusive memory.

Her sleep was short. Someone pulled her bodily from her bunk, screaming in angry tones. She barely woke enough to get her feet beneath her. It didn't matter.

Dom Jake grasped her shoulders and held her against the partition, the ladder pressing into her back. Zak stood behind him.

Renna blinked and tried to make sense of the Dom's raving. "The course drifted one-hundredth of a degree every nine hours," she answered as her senses woke. "You said to use common sense before calling you. I corrected for the engine misfire. I suspect there is an energy lag in the rotation firing system. The event is noted in the log."

"You damn stupid podder! Of course there is! You think we don't know? I told you the course was set. Your corrections put us off course! We'll be late, again!"

There was no defense, nothing she could say. He stopped yelling and pushed her against the partition before he backed away. His flushed face and clenched hands revealed his fury. She looked from him to Zak. They both looked dreadful, ashen, and angry. "I can replot the course."

"No!" Dom Jake said in the same denigrating tone Dom Dukan had used when he found her unusually inept. "You stay away from my flight deck. Stay away from anything to do with the ship's function. I thought you could handle a ship."

Renna felt heat filling her face with familiar shame at Dom Jake's reprimand. *Calmness, professionalism, duty.* She bit the inside of her cheeks.

"Jake," Zak said.

Jake glanced at Zak, took a deep breath, and glared at her. "From now on, you just stick to basic maintenance." He stalked away. Zak hesitated, gave her a look she could not interpret, and followed his brother.

Unable to sleep, Renna sank to the floor and waited for her next shift to start. At twenty hundred hours, she reported to Jake in the wardroom. The others stared at her as they left.

Dom Jake looked worse than usual, haggard, his lips cracked and dry. "General maintenance forward and midship decks. You're working close to sleep quarters. Make sure after twenty-two hundred you don't cause any disturbance, understand?"

His curt tone and abrupt departure told her of his continued rage. "Yes, Dom Jake," she answered to his back.

Seven

2179.320-11:58 universal space-time... mission status ...mission parameters reestablished alternate power source connected ... hardwire fabrication underway ...r drive operational ...q and o drives sequencing ... all other drives inoperative...

Cutter trudged the gangway to where she worked. Removing her connex, Renna bowed her head to acknowledge her remorse. He ignored her gesture.

"Put the equipment down and come with me."

He looked dreadful and sounded angry. She did as ordered and followed him back to the wardroom.

Watching him, Renna felt glad to see him, even if he was ill and furious with her. With a curt, "sit," he disappeared into the galley. Returning, he placed a loaded plate before her and took the chair opposite. Her mouth watered from the smell. Hunger made her want to forget the fork and lick the plate.

"Pulled this out of the keeper. Food left over from our last First Day celebration. Crepes with seafood and mushrooms. I warmed the plate up as a special treat for all your extra work. What did you eat?

Didn't see any food gone from the keeper." He stared at her a minute. "You found the ship rations? You could've made something."

She grinned in giddiness at his forgiveness and at his disgusted tone. "Lock warned me not to mess up your galley. Plus, I don't know how to cook." The first bite melted in her mouth. Renna closed her eyes to relish unfamiliar tastes and textures. A hum of pleasure surged from her. She repressed her reaction and nodded, unnerved as he watched her eat. *Why would Cutter reward her when Dom Jake was so angry?* The ship's hierarchy confused her. Her stomach was still so taut from her dom's reprimand the food hardly fit.

Cutter imparted directions while he held a one-sided conversation, his voice still edged with illness. "Balance the fork like this." He adjusted her grip. "Everyone feels like hell. Why you didn't catch this, I don't know. Hope you don't. The knife works better like this." His voice filled with plaintive disgust. "Can't believe you ate ship's rations, crying out loud, Ren. You can't prefer them—do you? Knew we were in trouble when Ezry showed no interest in what she wore. Glad to see she took twenty minutes today just picking a color to wear." Renna decided she liked Cutter calling her Ren just as his flow of words stopped. She looked up from her concentration on the utensil and food. Dom Zak leaned against the partition, listening. Her stomach suddenly revolted. Dropping her fork, Renna jumped up and raced to the head across the wardroom's common area. She barely made the facility.

Awareness of someone holding her came as the hard spasms stopped. Frantic and totally humiliated, Renna tried to rise, but couldn't find her feet in the tide of darkness swallowing her.

~ * ~

Zak reached Renna first, his initial curiosity blunted by the situation. One tormented glance at him, and Renna became ill, a reaction which spelled trouble on a small ship. He grabbed her around the waist, holding her as her knees collapsed. "Has she caught the bug?" he asked Cutter who arrived behind him.

"Don't know."

When she went limp, his concern grew. He carried her to Cutter's sickbay, Cutter barking instructions the entire way.

"Put her down," Cutter ordered, sliding the diagnostic bed out. "Open her overall so I can get a monitor on her."

Zak did as ordered. Cutter triggered the monitor while Zak slipped a bioclip on her ear lobe. With the initial reading, Cutter said, "I should have known better." He fell silent.

Zak followed Cutter's gaze. Bruises, fingerprints, showed on Ren's near skeletal frame. Guilt lashed him. Cutter gently touched the bruises on her bony shoulders. He lifted her and checked her shoulder blades. He felt Cutter's regard and met his stare.

"Who did this?"

"Jake lost his temper." Zak flushed. "He was feeling raw. I'm sure he didn't realize he injured her. She didn't act hurt."

"You watched?"

The heat in his face intensified. He seldom interfered with Jake's actions, right or wrong. Zak dropped his gaze to Renna. Cutter's disapproval rivaled his shame. "Is she ill?"

Cutter sighed, reading the monitor. "No. The food was too rich for her. As you can see, she hasn't eaten enough in a long time. Before coming aboard, she had only eaten ship rations, for God's sake." They stood in silence for a minute. "Good. She's starting to rouse." Cutter closed her overall.

Her eyes focused on Cutter when she woke. As she became aware of his presence, she became agitated. Zak frowned, recognized her panic, and stepped back. When she tried to rise, Cutter placed his large hand on her shoulder, pushing her down.

"Relax, Renna," Cutter said. "Your shift's over, you need to rest."

"No, no, I must finish my assignment." She engaged in a losing struggle with Cutter. Zak knew his brother was loath to use the force needed to hold her immobile. Frantic, she slid sideways from under Cutter's hand and off the opposite side of the bed. Her unsteady legs nearly collapsed. She gained her footing and moved to stand before Zak with her head bowed.

"May I return to duty, Dom Zak, sir?"

He glanced with uncertainly at Cutter. "Cutter thinks you need time off. I think under the circumstances…"

She sank to her knees, arms spread, and palms up. "I can finish my assignment, Dom Zak. Please do not allow me to fail a second shift in a row. Please, Dom Zak."

He inhaled. His teeth clicked audibly as his jaw clenched. Zak caught Cutter's bewildered and offended reaction, but he nodded saying, "Only until your assignment is complete, not until the shift end."

He deemed her exit an escape. "What was that?"

Cutter cleared his throat. "I believe an act of supplication. You know, I don't know a lot about crewkin, and the more I learn, the less I like."

"This behavior wasn't in the files I read on crewkin. Will she be okay?"

"If determination will make it so, I expect. What has you up so late?"

"Needed to speak with Jake. Heard you talking, wondered why you were up. I better go now."

"I think I'll tag along."

"I'd rather you didn't. Waited for privacy." He hesitated. "He lost his temper. You know how he explodes over any failure. Especially now."

"Old story? Too bad." Cutter snorted at his aggravated sigh.

Jake looked up as Zak entered the flight deck, his body hiding Cutter who followed.

"All right, all right. I know," Jake started, his tone changing as Cutter entered the flight deck. Cutter didn't normally interfere with the ship's management. "I was wrong to lose my temper. What she did wasn't critical. We lost some time, nothing more. They'll pay, even if we are a little late."

"Especially since she never had a warning, did she?" Zak asked, drawing a surprised glance from Cutter. He felt he deserved censure. He rarely challenged Jake.

"No. I know. I wasn't thinking straight. I'm really sorry."

"You were sick," Zak said shrugging.

"Sorry isn't good enough, Jake," Cutter said in a tone seldom heard as he aimed a shriveling glance at Zak.

Both he and Jake looked at Cutter in dismay. Jake flushed and clamped his mouth tight. Cutter sounded so much like their father Zak winced.

"I've got a couple things I want to say. Know you've been stressed out about your difficulty, about our situation, and sick, too. Know how sick." He grimaced before continuing. "This isn't the SSC. I'm sorry you got dismissed, and glad you agreed to take over the *Vagrant Spirit*. Sorry about the circumstances, which were unfair, especially with Dad's death causing a general upheaval in all our lives. You are probably the most capable person to ever captain this ship. You got to get over the past, though. Stressed out, sick or well, you ever lay hands on a crewmember again, brother or not, you're off this ship next stop. After which, I'll report you to the licensing bureau."

Zak watched Jake's face drain and refill with crimson embarrassment. Jake quickly recovered.

"And?" Jake asked what Zak also heard at the end of Cutter's statement.

"You order Renna to meals. All meals."

"What? You order her; she responds better to you."

"She won't unless you say so."

"Cutter, for crying out..."

"She makes Ezry uncomfortable," Zak said.

"Hell, Ren's uncomfortable," Jake said. "She wouldn't even eat in front of us. Thought I was doing her a favor."

"You were, and you weren't."

Jake nodded his acceptance. Cutter continued. "She's embarrassed. Only ever ate ship rations."

At Jake's expression, Cutter shrugged. "Can't tell you much. From what Renna has said, pod life is quite different from anything we know."

"We know a dominance hierarchy exists," Zak said.

"Well, she believes she's at the bottom of ours." Cutter snorted. "Have Zak tell you. Won't do anything without permission: eat, sleep, or leave duty. She won't initiate conversation unless she has a question concerning her job, and from what Zak and I just witnessed, scared shitless of failure. Meant to talk to you about her before we all got sick."

He shrugged in resignation. "See you at breakfast."

Eight

2179.322-17:30 universal space-time ...mission status ...alternative hardwire fabrication activated ...backup power recharged ...r... q... p drives operational... o...n...m...and l drives sequencing ... all other drives deactivated ...power levels increasing...

Someone shook her foot. Renna pulled it free, folding her leg against her abdomen.

"Hey, sleepy-head, time to rise and shine. You're on duty in ninety minutes. Don't start so...sorry to scare you awake. It's just me, Lock."

Lock's head filled her bunk's opening, his face and flaming red overall filling the slip-in bunk's opening. He must have been standing on the ladder. She looked up at the overhead to check the chronometer and gasped. "I missed a shift."

"Whoa. Whoa. Slow down, you didn't miss a shift. Cutter said you needed to sleep more than the ship needs cleaning." He backed down the ladder and stepped to the other side of the gangway, making room for her descent.

"I don't understand. I never sleep through a shift." Renna slipped down the ladder and grabbed an overall out of a locker.

"I expect Cutter helped out there. Said he gave you a drink at the end of your duty. Knowing Cutter, probably laced."

Lock made no sense. *Laced?*

"Hey, easy, you got time. I came to tell you Cutter's nearly got dinner ready, wants you there."

"Dom Jake ordered otherwise."

"Don't think so. Jake said for you to appear for dinner. You have," he checked the chronometer, "twenty-five minutes left to get ready. See you there." Lock left.

Renna's hands shook. *There was only one reason for Dom Jake to order her to appear before the crew. Punishment.* Looking down at the wrinkled, worn overall she held, she knew she had better prepare herself properly.

She hesitated, remembering a comment by one of her kin: "Consider your punishment easy, even for a speaker. Norms hatch crew for serious offenses." A story confirmed by threats from the crew on her last shortrunner ship. *Serious offenses like putting a ship off course and late for delivery?* A shudder ran over her. With fatalistic acceptance, she dressed for her appearance in her best clothes.

~ * ~

Cutter watched as Ezry placed the garments back in her overflowing locker and picked through her wardrobe some more. Her clothes amazed him. She had made them all. It took a cabin to contain all the fabric, sewing, and painting paraphernalia she needed. Unlike most spacers, Ezry collected possessions. The situation aggravated Jake, who thought her obsessions encroached on the ship's maintenance when storage expanded into a second cabin. Cutter didn't care as long as the occupation made her happy.

"Well, Cutter, honey, what's Jake got planned? This one or this one?" Ezry held up a chartreuse and blue caftan in one hand, a brilliant pink overall in the other.

He wondered at his youngest brother's insistence for everyone to arrive early for his meeting. Jake's clipped summons had come through his connex. Cutter presumed the gathering had to do with Renna. His expulsion from the SSC had caused Jake both disillusionment and discontent. Captaining a small commercial liner hadn't met his younger brother's expectation of commanding an SSC ship, nor did he like dealing with the eccentricities of non-military crewmen. Jake could be demanding, exacting, irritating, oblivious, and often rude. Still, Cutter never believed he would abuse a crewmember. His treatment of Renna was shocking.

"Are you listening?" His attention reclaimed, Cutter took a second to recall her questions. "Don't know, Ez, he just said, 'there's a meeting and be on time.' Either one is beautiful."

"Huh," she muttered, rousing from her garment contemplation to glance at him. "Like you'd know. You always choose plain brown." A disgruntled frown pursed her lips. "Between you and your brothers, we're always in a state of disruption. Jake gives lofty commands from his flight deck, Zak brandishes his innocent talk until he cuts you with a quip. And you, you poke your nose into everything. Including that podder." The look she gave accused him of nefarious motives.

"Medical training develops nosiness—they teach curiosity."

"You ever miss the hospital? Ever want to settle down?"

"Nope, don't miss the hospital at all. I have settled down, with you, on this ship. Nearly run a clinic anyway, every time we're in port." Cutter decided to answer the intent of her comment. "I've no amorous interest in Ren, Ez. I'm old enough to be her father. My interest is in a crewmember I think needs help coping. Besides," he added with a lopsided leer, "you shouldn't criticize my taste, honey. I chose you."

Ezry made a disparaging sound, though she gave him a wry look. "Another plain brown bag, I just dress it well. Besides, if you remember, I did the choosing. Chose you. Over your brother."

Cutter gave a mental shudder at the reminder. Ezry continued, unaware of his flinch.

"You shouldn't encourage the podder. It will lead to trouble."

Cutter rose to wrap one arm around Ezry's waist to comfort her, while his other caressed her face and her smooth chocolate head. He kissed her, ending by nuzzling her neck. "Doesn't matter what you wear, you always look stunning."

She preened at his compliment, wrapping her arms around his neck. "Doesn't attract any attention on this ship. You should have seen my theater costumes."

"Why don't you make new renditions so you can give me a private showing?" Ezry's deep chuckle-purr told him she accepted his advances.

Her final hurried choice was a caftan with a purple leaf pattern floating over a swirling blend of red and orange flames. He hoped the outfit didn't indicate her mood.

~ * ~

Upon entering the wardroom, Renna found the crew already assembled, even Dom Jake. They stood waiting for her, all eyes staring at her as she entered. She sought the chronometer to make sure she was not late: nineteen hundred, exactly. She stiffened, afraid of what would happen next. Neatly dressed, as befitted a dom about to authorize a final punishment, Dom Jake's face appeared red with anger. Everyone else looked attentive, watching her, glad to get rid of her. Only her sense of failure surpassed her humiliation.

Now only shameful judgment waited before she finally joined her kin.

~ * ~

"Yesterday morning, I attacked Renna in an inexcusable way. Renna, I want everyone to hear my apology to you, and hope you accept it."

Jake cleared his throat and inhaled before speaking. "I am extremely sorry for my accusations and for injuring you. You, too, Zak, and Cutter. I wish to apologize for my poor judgment and worse behavior."

Cutter looked around in the silence following Jake's unexpected apology. It was hard to tell who looked most astonished. Jake seldom apologized for anything, let alone before the whole family. Even Zak, Jake's eternal confidant, advocate, and antagonist, looked both disconcerted and stunned.

Perhaps his losing control and his aggression toward Renna made him reconsider his past actions as well. Maybe it had purged his discontent at losing his past position and made him reconsider his actions. Cutter hoped so. Not since his dismissal from the SSC had he looked this clean-cut.

"I did nothing to stop you," Zak spoke in the silence. "So I owe Renna an apology, also."

"You what?" Ezry said in a surprised descant over Zak's voice. Jake answered a question from Lock while Zak hushed Ezry's continued disparaging comments about podders who screwed up. Cutter cringed at his mate's obdurate attitude. He moved toward Renna, whom he thought looked more than stunned, and not at Ezry's speech.

"You are not punishing me?" Renna asked. The others quieted when they heard her flat, strained voice.

"Of course not," Jake said. "You had no way of knowing the engine's problem. Under the circumstances, you did very well. Hell, this is just another bout of our infamous luck and a lack of communication. My fault entirely."

Cutter cautiously approached Renna. He was glad he'd moved—he caught Renna as she fainted.

"Hell, does this mean she doesn't accept my apology?" Jake asked as he and Zak rushed to help him get her to sickbay.

"Go keep Ezry calm," Jake ordered. When Zak started to protest, he added, "I owe her a clarification." Zak looked at Renna, nodded, and left.

She came around as Cutter placed her on his diagnostic bed. "Stay there," Cutter said as she tried to rise.

Jake reiterated his command. "Damn it, Ren, listen to Cutter. Just lie there until he says otherwise."

She froze in place, her intent gaze on Jake. "You are not going to hatch me?"

"What? Hatch you? What the hell are you talking about?" Jake asked, looking from Renna to Cutter.

Cutter shrugged, a sudden and private amusement striking him. *How are you going to handle this, Jake? On the last run, you left dealing with the unruly crew to Zak.*

"You will not expel me from the ship?"

Cutter's amusement left as he looked down at Renna. A glance showed Jake's offended expression had to mirror his own.

Jake swallowed, and finally said, "No."

"But...Dom Jake, I have caused the late arrival of the *Vagrant Spirit.*"

As Cutter watched Jake's temper grow, he cast a warning glance he knew Jake read. Renna caught his expression, her eyes widening fractionally. Jake controlled himself. His words emerged in harsh, clipped tones.

"I don't know what they do on a pod...sorry, crewkin ship, but on the *Vagrant Spirit*, everyone who boards at one port disembarks at the next."

"Not crewkin, Dom Jake. My last shortrunner crew told me how norms punish crew."

Jake scratched his head, giving Cutter a quizzical look. Cutter raised his brows. "Norms?" Jake repeated, frowning at the unexpected label. He gave up understanding. "You handle this?" At Cutter's nod, he left.

"Come on, Ren, sit up, slow. You feel okay?"

"Yes."

He didn't believe her as she swayed. "Listen. I need your permission to access your medical file. I think access might be a good course of action. You've been ill, and I think we need to know more."

"You think I brought the illness aboard?"

"No. You've been ill from stress. Just a precaution, okay?"

"I am never sick, not even from stress."

"You suffered from grief, not eating properly, worry, and isolation all mixed together."

At his look, she bit her lip before speaking. "Rules state I can only give it to a doctor."

"Do you want to see my medical license?"

"At your order, sir," Renna said holding out her wrist, shaking her head no.

The sir tipped him to her submission. He remembered Jake's casual comment, "listen to Cutter," and realized his returned status to dom—along with a medical title. He gave a hushed snort of distaste and used her instilled programming against her. Cutter placed the back of her hand under his reader while copying the file. A glance showed them coded.

*Coded? Why in...*he glanced at Ren. Her circumspect gaze measured him. Cutter suspected a well-honed talent for reading expression and body language. How a sub survived, no doubt.

As the reader beeped, he said, "All done. Did you really believe any of us would toss you out?" When she wouldn't look at him, Cutter exhaled. "Well, we wouldn't. Not me, not Jake, nor Zak. Wouldn't occur to Lock or Ship Dog. Ezry might threaten, but she wouldn't ever carry through, though."

Her silvery eyes regarded him in a quizzical manner. "Does Ezry own you or you her?"

Cutter swallowed his laugh, aware he hadn't lost all of Ren's confidence with his return to dom status. "In a manner of speaking. Why?"

"She said you were her man and for me to leave you alone. Lock said she was your woman. Sir, I don't understand. How can I leave you alone on a small ship?"

"It's a matter of norm speech, meaning Ezry and I love and are faithful to each other."

At her puzzled look, he said, "We are a couple sharing sexual relations. Don't crewkin share intimacy?"

"Yes, kin share sexual warmth and comfort, intimacy. I loved all my kin. If another sub wanted comfort, they had only to ask."

No blushing, no coyness, just a facet of crewkin life. The implications took Cutter no time to understand. He wondered if Renna truly understood his relationship with Ezry, and if she had felt passion with any of her kin. "What about doms? What about your ship's captain?"

"If Dom Dukan requested, any sub would have obliged him."

"Did Dom Dukan ever request you?"

"Seldom." Renna blushed, looking away shamefaced.

From her tone, Cutter assumed seldom for Renna was once in a nova. He was about to tell her norms were different; knowledge of relationships stopped him. *Not altogether different, just not always socially sanctioned.*

She changed the subject. "I am reading about norms. What we learned in nursery is different from your library."

"What are you reading?"

"History, literature, and general science. The information is very contradictory, yet I believe your library's accounts."

"Why?"

"Different sources give similar information." She sighed. "However, I have not acquired the knowledge to understand norms."

He smiled. "Probably not. Give us a chance, Ren. Give yourself time. You've only been aboard a little over three weeks."

She nodded.

"Come on, let's go eat my dinner before the food solidifies into cold tasteless lumps." He sighed again in dismay. "Leave it to Jake to disrupt dinner. No," he said as she pulled away. "I know you don't like being touched. I'm not letting go until you sit again."

"Please, let me go to duty and eat later."

"Can't do. Jake gave orders."

"Dom Jake would change them if you asked. He listens to you." The amazed wonder in her voice made Cutter cringe.

"Jake's still captain." He watched a puzzled furrow develop between Renna's brows.

Ezry's lazy drawl carried to them as they neared the wardroom. Cutter hoped Renna was too preoccupied to hear.

"So what? Nothing has changed."

"Everything has changed," Jake answered. "After the last couple of days, we owe her. From now on, no one is to refer to her as a podder. She will be taking meals with us."

Ezry groaned. "Jake, honey, it won't work. The last meal she shared with us was miserable. She doesn't talk, doesn't eat. Why should we all suffer indigestion?"

"Cutter," Jake said with a nod as he and Renna entered the wardroom.

Everyone was seated, waiting. They rose to get their food as Cutter escorted Renna to a chair.

Lock jumped up first saying, "At last, food."

"Lock enjoys quantity over quality," Cutter told Renna. "I'll get you a plate." He placed a hand on her shoulder to keep her seated.

"Heard that. Like both, and hunger helps the appetite. Let's eat."

Renna looked anxious. Lock's rejoinder started a quibbling commotion among the others about his eating habits. Cutter filled his plate and reduced the quantity by two-thirds for Renna's plate. Setting the dish in front of her, he took a seat next to her. Ezry's face showed her anger. Cutter smiled at her, knowing he would have to appease her jealousy later. He took Renna's cold hand in his left hand, Jake's in his right.

"I wish to give thanks today for the luck the *Vagrant Spirit* has encountered. We may be behind time, but we are alive and recovering from our illness. I wish to give thanks for Jake finding Renna and hiring her to join our crew. Without her, we would not have survived the last three days. As always, I give thanks for my brothers, for the love I share with Ezry, for my friends, Lock and Ship Dog, and for our home, the *Vagrant Spirit*." He released the hands he held.

Everyone immediately started talking and eating. A semblance of normalcy returned for everyone except Renna. Cutter nudged her as she kept turning her fork over in her hand like an alien instrument. She glanced briefly at him before attempting her first bite. Lowering her fork, she looked at him. Her eyes glistened with emotion.

"Before, I did not listen, too worried about eating among you, worried about you laughing at me. This time, I did. I am grateful you are thankful I am here, Cutter." Her voice was low. Cutter knew only he, and perhaps Zak on her other side heard. He smiled at her. For once, she returned his smile, making her look much younger, much prettier. He suddenly realized how far her auburn hair had grown out, softening her gaunt features in feathery short curls around her well-shaped head. The room's light and her emotion had turned her eyes a smoky-gray color.

Turning her attention back to her meal, she ate with her usual gratifying appreciation, cleaning her plate and eating several of his fresh biscuits in the process. Cutter placed another on her plate as she finished.

"What's the longest haul you've made, Ren?" Lock asked. His question silenced all conversation.

Renna hesitated before answering the first comment directed at her, carefully finishing her bite of biscuit. "*Markham3* went to Port Longshot my first run. Our ship set out when I was six with the previous crewkin pod in charge. My kin did minor ship tasks but didn't man stations until we were ten. When we returned, I was sixteen."

Cutter noticed Lock wasn't the only one avid with curiosity.

"You were out ten years? The longest I've ever been out is two hundred-forty days. Felt so trapped, damn near lost my mind. Didn't the time bother you in the least? Did you have leave? Who controlled the ship while you grew up?"

"We'd been on the ship before then, in a nursery. The previous crew guided the ship. There were other crewkin pods before them. My kin made the seventeenth kin-group for the *Markham3*. We only knew those who acted as nurses or teachers from our predecessors. The previous kin-pod retired on Longshot. *Markham3* was all we knew, and no, we weren't allowed off ship except when ordered by Markham Company."

"How many were in your group?" Cutter asked.

"The kin-group started with eighty-six, which is small. Markham Company added me a year later because the group was valuable and needed a speaker. By the time they placed my kin on *Markham3*, we had been culled to forty-two. We lost six kin on the first haul."

"Why was a speaker so important?" Jake asked.

"Only speakers communicate with outsiders. Most kin do not... they are incapable of talking with anyone outside their own kin."

"You must have been an important member of your crew," Zak said.

Renna colored, lowering her gaze.

"How many of you survived the last trip?" Ezry asked, grabbing Renna's attention. Her face drained of color.

"Ezry!" Cutter said, appalled at his mate's brutality.

"No, it's okay," Renna said, her voice just above a whisper. "Sixteen of us survived long enough to reach a hospital. I am the only one left."

"Why didn't they just put you back with another crew?" Lock asked.

"Another kin group would never accept me. You must know the other fifteen all committed suicide. I was supposed to do so."

"*Markham3* kin accepted you—before."

"Because we were so young, not even toddlers."

"Renna," Zak interrupted Lock. "You said they culled your kin. What did you mean? Culling is a rather harsh term for releasing crew."

"The caretakers terminated those they felt were inadequate for the ship's need or a liability for the company. Dom Dukan said I was lucky. If our kin group hadn't needed a speaker, I would have been culled from my original kin. He accused me of being more dom than sub."

"I'm sure they didn't terminate the children," Lock said with a disbelieving tone. "That's criminal. You must have been too young to understand properly. They probably put the children up for adoption."

A strange look came over Renna's face. She didn't contradict Lock. Suddenly, her expression changed to one of fright. Everyone's expression soon matched hers.

Cutter felt the disruption: a whirling sense of dizzy disorientation, a sudden sensation of lifting. Food, plates, and utensils glided on the table for a fraction of a second before it ended.

"Grav disruption," Jake said, his eyes scanning the room's monitors even as he rose.

Jake, Zak, Ship Dog, and Lock jumped up and left the wardroom. "Stay here. We'll come back," Jake ordered.

In the awful quiet after their departure, Cutter said, "Finish your meal. There is nothing we can do until Jake returns." He found eating difficult but stoically continued. Renna, as he expected, followed orders with reluctant slowness, breaking her biscuit into crumbs, her gaze intent on the monitors. Ezry gave up all pretense. She sat tense, wide-eyed, and with her jaw clenched. Cutter reached across the table to grasp Ezry's cold hand, rubbing his thumb over her knuckles.

"The systems are all checking within parameters," Renna said, more to herself than to them. "Like the last time."

Twenty minutes later, Jake, Zak, and Lock returned.

"Ship Dog's staying with the engines," Jake said. "Ran system checks, can't find anything wrong."

"So Renna told us. I'll get your dessert." Cutter rose. He had already cleared the wardroom of dinner with Ezry's help.

"Renna," Jake said, "your duty log showed two disruptions where you ran systems checks. Can you tell us anything more about those?"

"Everything was reported, Dom Jake."

"Just Jake, no dom, no sir," he said. Cutter heard the vexation in his brother's voice as he returned. "Last time I tell you. Did you have any opinions on what might have happened?"

"Entering an opinion into the log would have been presumptuous, Captain Terran."

Jake's temper mounted. As Cutter slid Jake's slice of pie in front of him, he gave a slight squeeze on his brother's shoulder. Jake's gaze slid to him. Renna observed their silent exchange. Her eyes widened and a strange look came over her face. Cutter knew his stature had risen further in her hierarchy. He wondered if he could ever get her to accept him as an equal again.

"Did you have any personal thoughts or opinions?" Jake asked.

Renna hesitated before speaking. "Yes. I thought the abnormality might be fluctuations in magnetic fields, sir. I ran system checks each time. All readings quickly returned to within acceptable limits. Sir, perhaps you might assign me to assist Ship Dog. Maybe I could help him."

"Are you familiar with our engines?"

Renna tallied off the design categories and optimal specs for the *Vagrant Spirit*, its engine, and system alignments. Cutter smiled at Lock's expression. Jake held up a hand to interrupt the flow.

"Okay, you know the ship. Spend tonight with Ship Dog. I'll have him fill you in on our engine problems."

Renna rose and left the wardroom while Jake spoke with Ship Dog through his connex.

Nine

...2179.326-20:14 universal space-time ...mission status ...operational parameters established ...powering line drives...

Inside the compartment, the old Jupiter 1090 engine sobbed a steady drone interspersed with a strong counter beat, creating a soothing song. Renna felt comfortable here, a place where only training and skill counted. Like most engine rooms, the walls and floor were gray and sedate, a holdover from when ships were crafted of steel rather than the molecularly engineered alloys.

The huge man called Ship Dog waited for her by the main console. She stopped a meter from him. He looked at the deck, shifting his weight from foot to foot, looking ready to bolt. He glanced up. "Vera verges code."

"Vera?" Renna asked, barely able to understand the man's guttural, heavily accented speech. She tried to ignore his state of undress. He wore no shoes, which was against all Markham codes. His bare feet slapped against the deck with each step. She could only glance at him and look away again. Ship Dog remained unaware of her impertinence and embarrassment since he never looked at her.

"After mom."

Renna's gaze slid to Ship Dog's face, avid curiosity at his statement about his progenitor overcoming her diffidence. A lightning-fast gaze rose to hers and swiftly fell away. Sweat beaded on his forehead. She noticed talking took him effort, like some of her kin—those most often culled. She stepped back, giving him more space.

"Needs refit." Ship Dog's shoulders slumped as he drifted away to hover over various panels, appearing to read the screens. He explained the problems one by one, using fewer words than her understanding demanded, making her repeat parts, and asking him to expand on his clipped comments. Renna made mental notes. "Questions?" Ship Dog asked clearly wanting none as he focused his glances above her head.

She asked her questions in careful order. Ship Dog sometimes cut her off, uttering a word or two before she finished, which made understanding difficult. Deciphering his clipped responses while making sure her questions were addressed often created new questions. Persisting, Renna finally felt satisfied with the answers. "You take very good care of Vera. No kin could do better."

Her compliment was true. The unusual man certainly knew how to maintain this old engine in good order. He didn't look at her. His cheeks reddened, his mustache and beard jiggled.

"Request permission to look at the engine's history log later?" Ship Dog's eyes blinked, and his chest heaved as he nodded. "Sure." He gave her the code.

She put her palms up, one over the other, giving him the crewkin sign of thanks for his indulgence at explaining the situation to her...and for the permission he granted. He ignored her gesture, so she used the words with the gesture. "Thank you for explaining this to me." His black eyes finally met hers. He smiled.

"How can I help you now?" Renna asked.

"Panels. Adjustments. Changes." He picked up his intel and walked away before she could nod.

Renna watched the indicator positions on the panels, checking the readings against the optimum parameters while Ship Dog made adjustments. She read them off through her connex as the readings changed, so he could judge his calibration changes. He never answered. When complete, he did not return to the control rack where she worked. Through the connex, she heard deep-spirited singing and realized Ship Dog sang. Her surprise subsided at another norm idiosyncrasy. She smiled as she listened to songs she had never heard, guessing Ship Dog didn't necessarily sing them in tune.

After three standard hours of duty time, Lock entered the compartment. "How's it going?" He bounce-walked around the compartment, looking at monitors and control settings in a nervous manner, which would have earned any sub punishment.

"Go." Ship Dog spoke, appearing from the depths of the compartment.

Renna stood in respect to her duty dom, speaking the words he seemed incapable of supplying. "You are going off duty? Yes, I will continue here. I won't touch anything without contacting you first." Ship Dog nodded and left with Lock. Renna returned to watching the monitors. During her remaining shift, she investigated the engine's history, reading while she kept her watch. The log went back to before the ship's commissioning to the construction of the Jupiter 1090. The record made her feel part of the ship, part of a tradition going back centuries, maybe further. Her recent history readings told ship construction seemed to have started with civilization.

A while later, she realized she missed the sound of Ship Dog's discordant melodies. She stopped reading the log. Why did Markham decide to leave out so much history in crewkin education? Had they rewritten history? Or was change the other way around? Had norms altered history? After a brief reflection, she doubted the second, but had no answer.

Dom Jake entered the compartment at two hundred hours. "What are you doing?"

Startled, Renna rose and bowed her head at her dom's entrance. "Watching the engines. Ship Dog recalibrated many settings." She listed them. "He gave me permission to view the engine logs," Renna reported and waited.

"Come with me. I'm hungry. Everyone else is asleep."

She followed him to the wardroom.

"Cutter said you disapproved eating on duty," Dom Jake said, placing a plate containing a sandwich and a beverage container before her. His service made her uncomfortable. He seemed unaware of the impropriety as he started eating his food.

"You can watch the engines from here just as well." He reached and pressed pads to bring up the engine's monitors. The flight deck monitors occupied another screen panel.

Renna ate, keeping her gaze on the monitors. After several minutes of silence, with a flicker of uncertainty, she slanted a glance at her table companion. He was watching her, his formerly shaggy head and bristled face combed and shaved. His appearance made him match Zak's neatness, increasing their likeness to each other and to Dom Dukan. She wondered at the transformation. His face gave no hint of what he observed. Staring back, she waited.

"Ship Dog reported you knew as much about our engines as he. High praise." He turned his attention to his food briefly. Still chewing, and against Cutter's counsel to her about speaking with food remaining in the mouth, he spoke, "Have you found anything in your search of the engine log?"

"Your navigation drift is of long-standing, even before your last overhaul. The inaccuracy grows with each refit. The engine is old, but one of the better designs. Its integrity is well within acceptable standards. I suspect when any of the rotation engines fire, they receive different power levels. This might be caused by replacement parts, which met the original specs. Those parts no longer fit the natural wear on the system. New measurements of worn parts with corrected specifications for replacement parts would remedy the problem. As you are aware of the problem, the drift is not currently a danger."

He nodded. "You've sized the problem up correctly."

"Except, the total system disruptions and power loss have only occurred on this run, so another agent is at work. Analysis and comparison of the ship's component systems might show when and where the power disruptions begin."

He didn't make any remark, only ordered, "Finish eating."

Renna obeyed in silence. Between bites she glanced at her dom, noting he had become abstracted, deep in thought, paying her no attention. She relaxed and lost herself in her enjoyment of the food. Her meal was gone too soon, and she felt the contemptuous, unkin desire for more. She wasn't surprised to find Dom Jake observing her greed.

"Could you do this analysis?" he asked.

Swallowing, Renna nodded, wiping her mouth. "With the access codes, yes."

"Get started. This is now your assignment. I'll shuffle everyone around again to cover maintenance."

~ * ~

"You find anything?" Dom Jake asked when Renna entered the wardroom. Every night for six days of voluntary double shifts, she'd immersed herself in ship specs, taken measurements, and checked readings. Every night, Dom Jake asked her the same question. Every day another disruption occurred. She never told either Cutter or Dom Jake how much they terrified her.

"Nothing," Renna muttered, discouraged at her failure, wishing above all to please her dom.

"Do you have an opinion?"

"The systems always check out. It's like a phantom steals power suddenly, and just as quickly dissipates. My apologies, Captain Terran."

"Jake," he said. Renna could not answer him.

"Are you still crewkin?"

Renna looked away. "No. You know I am not." *And I am sorry I ever was.* Her unspoken revelation stabbed her.

"Call me Jake. Do it." He sounded exasperated, like whenever Dom Dukan had spoken to her.

Observing his expression, she hesitated. "Jake."

"Do it from now on."

Renna opened her mouth. His raised hand forestalled her reply. "Don't tell me it's disrespectful. I don't care."

"Thank you, D...Jake."

The light levels dipped.

They both felt the disturbance. Jake glanced at the monitors. In one fluid motion, he rose and ran out of the wardroom. Renna knew he was going to the flight deck. She ran in the opposite direction toward the engines. Before reaching them, she found herself floating under full gravity loss, tumbling feet over head, twirling sideways, arms splayed. She maneuvered to a partition to stop the dizzying motion and propelled herself toward the engines.

Gravity returned just as abruptly. Renna dropped to the deck, landing on her hip and wrist. Pain shot through her hand and arm in lightning jolts. She pushed herself up and limped toward the engine compartment. Several compartments away, she heard Lock and Zak shouting.

Ship Dog ran past her, asking as he barreled by, "Okay?" It seemed impossible his bulk could move so fast.

"Yes, go." She already knew he would find nothing. Just like on the *Markham3*.

~ * ~

They met in the wardroom, arriving in half-dressed disarray at Jake's command. Cutter became exasperated when he saw her swollen hand.

"It is nothing," she told him, "I can move my fingers, see?"

Cutter ignored her. He carefully picked up her puffy right hand and wrist, inspecting them before entering his sickbay. Renna heard Cutter rummaging in the lockers. Embarrassed heat filled her face and neck at causing everyone to wait for her. No one voiced insults. They continued waiting while Cutter checked her wrist. Ezry gave Renna an annoyed look through her obvious fright, but no one looked content.

Renna had avoided Ezry, Cutter too, since being told, "Stay away from my man." She did not understand the command. How could she avoid a crewmember? Never had she received such an order, not even when shunned. Now she remained uneasy around Cutter, waiting to see what penalty Ezry would hand her.

"Not broken, only a bad sprain. I think I'll splint your wrist for a day. The meds should repair the damage fairly quick." Cutter gave Renna an inquiring look. "Will it cause you any difficulty?" He sprayed her wrist. The irritating throb disappeared in cold numbness before he applied the restraint. The swelling began subsiding.

Renna wiggled her fingers, testing them in their confinement.

Cutter hiked his brow with a frown. "Don't use your hand."

"No, I will just use my other hand." She smiled at him.

"You're ambidextrous?" Lock asked.

"All kin are."

Lock snorted. "Breeding. Figures. They wanted you to be ultra-capable."

"All right," Jake said when Cutter finished. "We've had a major disruption. We not only lost gravitation but also environment for ninety-three seconds."

Someone gasped, she thought it Ezry.

The others talked about possible causes and what they should do. She listened, knowing they would discover nothing. *Stupid!* She castigated herself. In her relief at finding a berth, in her disorientation with norms, and her fear of the situation, she had ignored the questions a crewmember should have asked. After staring at the table deep in thought, Renna broke in, her distress shaking her words. "D...Cutter, what exactly does the *Vagrant Spirit* carry to Zorah Reclamation?"

Everyone regarded her with exasperation. "What does...?" Ezry started in a sharp voice. Renna didn't look to see what caused Ezry to stop, afraid they might see her terror on her face. Inside, she felt squeezed tight, as if under compression. And cold. She could hardly talk for shivering, let alone look at the crew.

"An engine," Cutter said. "What does the cargo have to do with our situation?"

"May I see the engine? May I enter the cargo hold, D...Jake?"

"You know anything? Or is this just misplaced curiosity?" Jake asked.

"Maybe, I don't know. The cargo is the only unexplored possibility, the only change in the ship from previous runs, other than my presence. The *Markham3* had similar disruptions." At her comment, a deep silence fell. Renna glanced up.

"The *Markham3*? I thought you hit an anomaly?" Zak asked at last.

"Anomaly?" Renna asked in dismay, remembering Ezry's comment her first day onboard. How could they think that? "No. Engine failure, a new prototype. The engine compartment and adjacent decks imploded. Most of my kin didn't know of the change. Markham Company had installed the new design model while we took leave."

"You weren't informed?" Zak asked. "They broke regulation?"

"Dom Dukan knew. It was his decision to either inform kin or not." She felt a need to defend Dom Dukan, to hide her kin's failing. "Kin affected by his decision were told. Those who worked the engines and navigational systems knew."

"Not you? Not their only speaker?"

Renna felt her face flush, not wanting even these norms to know her shame, and knew she must expose her flaws. "Dom Dukan felt I argued too much. I was already under shunning penance. He did not want everyone disrupted by my defiance. By Dom Dukan's command, I was not told of the changes."

"What happened?" Jake asked.

"We experienced disruptions like those on the *Vagrant Spirit*, only more often and for longer. *Markham3* lost gravity, life-support, navigation, and eventually, a near-constant energy depletion. Later, I learned we had traveled on lateral engines only. The main engine never operated correctly. According to the ship's readings, the engine never reached optimal power levels. Everything else looked accurate on monitors, tests, and scans. Unexpectedly the engine powered up...or so my kin said."

Fighting to stay calm, Renna ignored the images assaulting her memory, the stray power surges flying everywhere, the feel of energy running over her skin, the sound of undisciplined engine whine accompanied by kin screams.

"The engine's power-up felt—I don't know how to explain," Renna stopped, horrified, and caught her breath. The images came too strong; soon they would overpower her objectivity. Someone's hand grasped hers. Zak's hand. She did not withdraw, relishing the warm contact linking her to now. Almost like kin.

"And?" Jake prodded.

Her eyes watered. She held Jake's gaze. "The engine drew power from everything, even unconnected systems, like a black hole sucking energy. The engine failed, died, leaving nothing. Everything was gone." Saying more was impossible. In her distress, she missed some of the following exchanges.

When she became aware again, her hand gripped Zak's in a tight grip, her fingers white against his. She heard Lock say, "I'll take her. Probably chasing a quark. Damn thing is in a cargo container, anyway," he said. "We'll have to open the container for inspection. Don't think our clients will like our actions."

"I'll go with you," Zak said.

Renna released his hand, giving him an apologetic look. Picking up the intel she had placed on the wardroom table, she rose and followed Lock out of the compartment.

The one-eighty aft cargo bay lay at the end of the habitat structure. Unlike the other cargo holds, this one was inside the gravity axis surrounding the engine compartment. Usually, such a compartment was reserved for gravity-sensitive cargo. Placement within the habitat made inspection easier. In the short walk to the hold, Renna managed to control her shaking. A triple security hatch separated the bio-area of the ship from the non-sustained. They suited in biosuits in the small compartment between the hatches. Her breath came in quick gasps when the bay hatch opened. Her noise did not draw Zak or Lock's notice.

The cargo hold looked like any other, a fretwork of grid catwalks and ladders lined the perimeter. Its ordinary appearance soothed Renna's jangled nerves. They stood on the highest level. Opposite, she made out a loader's shape stowed against the partition. Next to the loader, a vast loading bay aperture hatch stretched across the overhead, its hatch doors reinforced with locking arm restraints. She turned her head to both sides. Gray plasmetal supports rose at regular intervals from the darkness below to disappear into the shadowed overhead. They took an adjacent lift down. Renna counted five security ladders to the catwalk twenty meters below.

"There's another loading bay in the aft hold," Lock said as the lift descended. She saw that another reinforced partition divided this hold from the one further aft.

The current hold held no payload. Supplies in clearly marked containers lined the bay as they descended into the darkness, but not cargo containers.

The ship carried no cargo? Only the engine? No regular port to port? Such a condition was unbelievable. Either Cutter wasn't good at acquiring cargo...or the *Vagrant Spirit* was blacklisted.

She shook her head. This was no time to think about her discovery. The view changed as the bulkhead buttresses rose above them in lofty arches fading into shadows. Lock stopped on a grid gangway, which stretched toward a titanium hatch separating the different compartments.

"The engine is in there," Lock said as Renna looked around.

Her hearing caught a soft thrum. "What is that noise?" She cocked her head to better her hearing.

They stood silent, listening. Zak and Lock looked mystified. Renna, recognizing the hum emanating from the other compartment, felt her chest constrict, her arms and neck muscles tense, and her skin prickle in recognition. Mind-numbing terror swelled in her.

Calmness, professionalism, duty.

Forcing her legs into reluctant forward motion, Renna followed Lock and Zak through the hatch to the aft compartment, scrambling to keep her life-ingrained training.

Ten

...2179.332-16:32 *universal space-time* ...*mission status* ...*drives powering*...

The far aft hold's construction matched the previous structure, only the reinforced partitions rose nine meters above the deck to reach the overhead, the lower height defined by the Jupiter 1090's compartment above. Here the hum-throb of Ship Dog's Vera, operating above them, sounded through the static hum emanating from within the hold. Renna could almost sense the engine through the overhead separating the engine hold from the aft cargo hold.

"My God," Zak said, his voice low with disbelief. He looked over Renna's shoulder while she fumbled with the analysis-detector on her intel.

Lock passed them. She must have made a sound, for Zak took the intel from her. He trailed Lock into the hold. Bright light escaped from the container's split sides where the bin's cargo hovered, an elongated structure midway between the deck and the overhead.

Long columns of transformed container material stretched upward to the overhead and downward to the deck. Dazzling bolts of power danced in a spellbinding ebb and flow between the hold's overhead partition and the cargo container. Shaking, Renna sank to the deck, feeling the pull of the power grid on her biosuit. She waited while Zak finished the analysis.

"Stay back!" Zak ordered Lock.

"Stop! Don't go near," Renna cried simultaneously when Lock moved closer to the container.

"I'm not going to. Not stupid. Any closer and I might get sucked in. I can feel the energy field from here. Cripes, I can feel my braids moving inside my helmet like they were snakes; makes my skin crawl." The hum from the engine increased. "Whoa." Lock struggled to back up. At Lock's exclamation, Zak grabbed him. They both slid several paces toward the center of the hold.

Renna screamed. They fell to their knees, sprawling on the deck. She attached her suit's security tether to the hatch behind her and crawled to them. She grabbed Zak's arm, stabilizing him. He attached his tether to her belt.

"Lock, grab my leg," Zak ordered. He and Renna pulled themselves on her tether to the partition. They clambered and crawled into the fore hold. Zak and Lock secured the hatch behind them.

"Let's go back to the wardroom." Zak put a hand under Renna's elbow, pulling her to her feet.

~ * ~

Cutter's stomach curled, tightening as he watched the display presented through the trio's helmet cams. Jake turned inscrutable while they waited for the three to return. The acrid, frightening reek of burned circuits followed their entrance into the wardroom. He held Ezry's hand in a gesture of comfort—well aware Ezry didn't handle *situations* well. Her fingers tightened on his. Ship Dog waited, too, his expression grim.

"Report?" Jake asked after the three returned from the hold, his gaze on Zak. Cutter listened while he watched Renna.

"Couldn't believe what I saw," Zak said, his voice taut, his face blanched with anxiety. "You must've seen the hold."

"Not all, the static inside interfered," Cutter said.

Zak's gaze swiveled to him and returned to Jake. "The engine's live in its cargo bin. At least what's left of the container. Anyway, the bay's lit up like a planet-side First Day celebration. Only in this one, the fireworks run the show. The cargo seems to be pulling energy from nowhere, everywhere. Nearly pulled Lock into the stream."

"Yeah. Entering the bay's like walking into a power grid," Lock said. Cutter had never seen Lock so unnerved, his usual vibrancy drained. "Damndest thing I've ever seen. What type of drive is this engine, anyway?" He swore again. "Now we know what's stealing our power."

"So what do we do? Any suggestions?" Jake asked.

"Jettison the cargo," Zak said.

Ship Dog and Lock quickly agreed.

Cutter swore, rubbing his forehead. "What a disaster."

"I know," Jake said. "We can make a case for undisclosed endangerment and settle without losing anything for the lost cargo. Renna, what do you know about this engine?"

When she didn't answer, Cutter looked at her. He observed with unease her blank expression and obvious shivering.

"Renna, you okay?" Zak asked, grasping her shoulder in concern.

Cutter rose and walked around the table. Turning her face toward him, she didn't flinch at his touch, her eyes locked on an inner vision; her colorless skin clung to her skull. Her bluish lips trembled.

"We need to know what she can tell us!" Jake said.

"Might have valuable information under the circumstances," Lock agreed.

Cutter ignored Jake's comment, already aware of the necessity. "On the *Markham3*, Renna, what happened?" he asked. Her skin felt clammy; she didn't answer. "Lock, get my med kit." He clapped his hands in front of her nose. Renna started. Her eyes focused, blinked twice in awareness. Tears poured down her cheeks in a sudden, quiet stream. Within seconds of Lock's return, Cutter administered a strong stimulant. He repeated his question. She took a minute to respond, her voice breaking on a sob.

"They died. My kin died during the failure. The *Markham3* drifted, helpless."

Cutter watched her eyes focus inward. She blinked, and her awareness suddenly fastened on him in terrified confession, seemingly unaware of anything except her memories.

"So many took their own lives—I could not stop them. Some, only a few, I managed to get suited and into escape capsules before they saw." Her lower lip trembled. "They died, anyway. Gave up when they found out I lied." She gasped and choked. "I lied to my kin and betrayed them. I should have joined them in death." Her voice turned to a whisper.

"What happened to the engine?" Jake asked.

"It killed us." She broke down, crying.

"Cutter, help her," Zak said, his arms holding her shaking body.

"Meds aren't helping," Cutter said. "She needs warmth and rest. Probably the culmination of all she's been through. Take her to the diagnostic bed."

Lock's voice followed them. "Strange coincidence having both her and the *Markham3*'s prototype engine on the *Vagrant Spirit*."

"Yeah," Jake said. "And I don't believe in coincidence."

Once in the compact sickbay, Zak laid Renna down, saying, "Damn, this is getting to be a habit."

"Common enough in someone as stressed as Ren."

"Will she be all right?"

Cutter looked in surprise at Zak's concern.

Zak flushed. "She's a good crewmember. Losing her now would be disastrous."

"You go on back while I work here. I won't take long to get her settled."

A few minutes later, he joined the others. Jake paced the compartment. Cutter had barely entered the wardroom when Jake turned on him. "We need to know what she can tell us."

"She's sedated."

"I wish you hadn't—how long will she be out? Hell, our hands are tied without knowing more."

Cutter ignored Jake's testy tone. "A few hours, and we may have to keep an eye on her afterward.

"Okay?" Ship Dog asked.

Cutter caught his glance once before the big man blushed and dropped his gaze to the table.

"Good to Vera."

Ship Dog's concern surprised Cutter. "She was in shock but should be fine." He looked at Jake. "You're lucky I got out of her what I did. Shock can be dangerous. Her reaction's not surprising after all she's been through." He shook his head. "And to end up having it happen all over again."

Jake huffed. "A few hours is an eternity in an untenable situation." He sighed. "Nevertheless, we need to formulate a plan of action."

"Why do you want to watch her, Cutter? What do you expect?" Zak asked.

Cutter looked at Zak's unexpected interest and reviewed his brother's recent actions. "Don't expect anything, just taking a precaution. Suicide is part of her culture."

Zak sat back, looking worried.

"Might take us with her." Lock nodded in agreement.

"Any suggestions on what to do in our current situation?" Jake asked, standing at the table's end.

"Jettison the damn thing. Sooner the better." Lock pushed his widely splayed hands up and out to emphasize his words, while Ship Dog nodded, his forehead scrunched in hard lines.

"I agree. Cutter, you and Lock will work with the loading skid from inside the cargo bay. Ship Dog, you handle the bay's hatch from outside. I'll need you, Zak, on the flight deck," Jake said.

Zak argued, "I'm better at exvee."

"Don't delude yourself. Ship Dog is fully qualified." Jake leaned on the table braced by his arms. "I need you where I've assigned you."

"I have to agree with Jake," Cutter said, knowing his agreement overrode Zak's objection. "I checked the lading report. There is no indication on how the cargo arrived at Port 53. No mention of the container's cargo other than a salvage engine, not even the company."

"Or this thing might be dangerous or apt to come online?" Zak asked. A glance showed his face at odds with his composed voice.

"No. I should have been more careful." Everything unspoken showed both his brothers felt just as guilty as he did for their failure to check on the cargo when the first power imbalances occurred. The truth was he had been too eager to take the load, so the guilt was his.

"Not your fault," Jake said. "I'll operate the bay doors from the flight deck and cut power from the Jupiter 1090. If we have a power drain, Ship Dog may have to open them manually. Zak will stop rotation long enough for us to lose gravity. Lock, you cut the extensions the engine has created, Cutter will handle the loader. Once gravity's gone, just shove the whole mess out the hatch and let Ship Dog make sure it clears the ship."

"Anything I can do?" Ezry asked, tense and showing her fear like a flag.

"Not with this. You know what to do when the bay doors open?" Jake asked Ship Dog who answered with a single nod. "Let's get on with it."

~ * ~

Within the hour, Cutter confirmed through the intercom, "Lock and I are in place." Zak opened the common audio link and aimed the cameras on those working in and out of the cargo bay.

"You're tethered?" Jake asked.

"Yes," Lock yelled. "Damn thing's louder than before." Zak heard the noise through the audio feed and tried to adjust the vid feeds to eliminate the interference from the wild engine's power field.

Jake took down the security lock, initiating the bay opening mechanism. They waited. Twice in quick succession, the panel readings went haywire. The bay aperture remained closed and locked.

"Nothing's happening," Lock said.

"Closed," Ship Dog reiterated. In the vid feed, he floated tethered near the bay's outer mechanism, dwarfed by the ship.

"Okay, try opening the bay door manually."

He and Jake watched Ship Dog move into position and maneuver the manual mechanism from its panel within the hull, each of them working in unspoken synchronization. As he positioned the handle and attached the crank, the whole power system failed. At the same time, a brilliant light exploded within the cargo bay, knocking their camera offline.

"Cutter," Zak screamed into his connex. There was no answer. He shared a worried glance with Jake.

"Go," Jake ordered.

Zak damned the time lost in running to the aft cargo hold; more precious moments vanished while donning a biosuit. Two minutes disappeared in pumping the atmosphere out of the airlock manually. The airlock's hatch slowly opened, exposing the dark aft cargo bay. As he reached for the ladder's handlebar, several loud ticking sounds reverberated through the hold. Dim security lights came on. His helmet beam provided better light. He counted each carefully placed step as the seconds passed. Nearing the aft hatch, the wild engine's hum grew louder. He felt the pulsing cadence through the separating partition, through his suit. The sound throbbed on his skin.

Opening the hatch into the aft hold took more time and effort. He struggled to break the seal. Inside the hatch, a brilliant white light blinded him, pulsing with the sound's rhythm. He adjusted his faceplate's filter to reduce the radiance.

Cutter and Lock lay on the floor, unmoving. A web of iridescent transparent energy streaked with flowing phosphorescent green lines rose in a wall halfway between the men and the engine. The container seemed much larger than before, apparently floating within the bay, with or without gravity.

"Tell Ship Dog to reenter the ship from the starboard two-seventy hatch. I need his help here. Yours, too."

"Cutter and Lock?" Tension oozed from Jake's professional voice.

"Down. How bad I don't know." He squatted next to Cutter and tried to rouse him. His brother groaned, stirring, just unconscious. Both men started coming around in the few minutes before Ship Dog and Jake arrived.

He kept a hand on Cutter's shoulder as his brother tried to rise. "Lie still."

"I'm fine, just knocked on my ass."

Zak didn't believe him, but he helped Cutter into a sitting position. Lock pushed himself onto his knee, staring at the wild engine.

Within five minutes, Jake arrived. Cutter continued to rumble about being fine while Jake questioned him. Zak took a moment to inspect the engine behind its protective shield. Lock rose to stand on shaky legs next to him. He put a hand under Lock's elbow to steady him, keeping his attention on the engine. Jake and Cutter came to his other side. He listened to the intense hum from the engine they could not reach while feeling a constant vibration against his body.

While they watched, the light increased. Zak threw his arm over his faceplate. The overpowering light subsided quickly. When he could see again, the engine had solidified into an unfamiliar configuration. Newly constructed conduit lines connected the mass to both the deck and the overhead.

"I think we need a new plan," Lock said.

~ * ~

Back in the wardroom, Zak took his usual seat at the table, and like all the other men, in only his skivvies, since no one waited inside the airlock long enough to dress. The acrid odor coming from the biosuit's exposure in the hold sickened everyone. Ezry appeared odd, dressed in a fuchsia and red skinsuit seeming to scream her terror. Jake leaned on the table with his head braced in his hands. Cutter seemed more subdued; his usual optimism crushed. Zak felt numb with exhaustion and knew they all felt the same.

"I can't tell you how sorry I am. We're in this jam because of me." Cutter bent forward over the table, his arms propping up his head.

"Not your fault." Zak reiterated Jake's earlier reassurance.

"The fault's mine." Jake leaned back, twisting the kinks out of his neck. "The culmination of a series of cause and effect. First, I get us blacklisted just by becoming captain, thank you, SSC. Now we take on the first load available, and the damned thing endangers the ship, us, everything we've worked for."

"The damn thing is drawing power directly from the Jupiter 1090, and has isolated itself behind a power screen," Zak said. "How were any of us to know such a thing possible?"

"Any suggestions?" Jake asked.

"Vera. Shutdown," Ship Dog said, his bass voice void of inflection.

"Shutdown?" Ezry exclaimed, squirming. She half rose from her seat. "Are you crazy? How will we survive?"

Cutter claimed her hand, pulling her back into her seat. Once she was down, he patted her shoulder. "We will be okay, Ez. You need to stay calm." Cutter looked across the table, his strained expression at odds with his gentle voice. Zak was sure he and Jake wore similar expressions.

"How long do you think the process will take?" Zak asked.

"Longer than I want to stay in a biosuit. We may have no choice." Jake used his thumbnail to scrape at a mark on the table. He knew he sounded both resigned and defeated. The last thing they needed was an SSC rescue. There seemed no alternative. "The flight deck already has security life-support. We can seal off the fore compartment with atmosphere and climate for a couple weeks' tenure if needed. We will be cozier than we want. Any longer and we'll need the escape capsules. Shutdown and removal of power should turn the beast off." He paused. "We need to set beacons, and we'll need to alert the SSC for rescue."

Zak nodded in resignation, his expression tight with control.

"Will your plan work?" Ezry asked in a quavering voice. "Won't the engine just suck us up? How long can we survive in suits?"

Ship Dog gave Ezry a rare glance and accompanying grin showing his white teeth. "Long enough."

"Yeah, though you won't be dressing fashionable," Lock said, looking at Ezry with a teasing smile. "Let's hope the distilling filters work well because we're all going to smell."

"Stink," Ship Dog said.

"Let's get a plan in place and start getting ready. We have a lot to do," Jake said. "Zak, we need to communicate with the nearest port about our situation, place emergency beacons. Lock, ready the wardroom and the *Vagrant Spirit* for the event. Ezry, move bio-oxygenators into the wardroom."

"You want the system cleaning plants, too?" Ezry asked. "And food production?"

"We haven't much room..." Jake began.

"Room enough for some. I'll help her set up. Already know what we'll need," Cutter said. He looked worn out at the prospect. "Even without all the food plants, we have supplies to last several years. We will need the waste filtration system those plants provide. Lock, Ez, and I will batten down and prepare."

"Vera. Few days. Shutdown." Ship Dog's clipped words indicated a warning.

"If we want to start her again?" Jake said. "Yeah, that's my estimate, too. Cutter, get Renna talking as soon as possible. Let me know because I have some questions. If possible, she can help Ship Dog." He glanced at Zak. "We'll work on navigation, auxiliary, and computer systems. Put the *Vagrant Spirit* on course, and hope for the best drift direction we can get."

Zak shrugged. "Should do it." He didn't look forward to the next few days...or weeks.

"Which reminds me," Cutter said. "Lock, there's a file on the med reader I'd like you to open."

"Coded? You mean crack it?" Lock asked with a bleak but expectant grin.

"Yeah, it is coded Markham Company." Cutter gave the smaller man a wry grimace.

"Renna's?" Zak asked. "Is that necessary?"

"Yes."

Everyone looked at Cutter's bland face.

"You can ignore your general prohibition on such activities," Jake told Lock.

"My pleasure, since I won't have to do time for it." Even his glib words didn't hide Lock's disquiet.

Eleven

...2179.333-00:38 universal space-time mission status ...count down initiated...

Someone was calling her name. She heard the words. They made no sense. Darkness and peace engulfed her, which made waking difficult. The insistent voice coaxed. With effort, Renna lifted her eyelids. She expected to see kin, so it took a moment to recognize Cutter. A moment accompanied by keen pain but not disappointment. He looked strange from her upside-down viewpoint. She blinked her eyes, too tired to do more, even when the memory of the cargo bay returned.

She forced her lips and tongue to form words. "What did you do? Lace me?"

Cutter laughed. Weariness kept Renna from feeling any offense. He wouldn't laugh to hurt her. Her intuitive realization soothed her.

"What do you mean lace you?" Cutter asked, his voice still filled with laughter.

"Lock. Before. Said probably laced. Sleep."

"Oh, the sedative. Yeah. This one works differently, a bit more powerful. You needed time to recover."

"Not sick," Renna replied, offended. She tried to rise. Energy for the move escaped her. She threw Cutter an indignant look. Dom or not, he deserved censure.

"No. Not technically. Treated you for shock. The drug hit you hard because your system is weakened from stress during the last year. Could have been nasty. You'll feel better in a few minutes as this takes effect."

"What?" Renna twisted her head trying to see. She felt a coolness touch her neck. Straps tied her to the diagnostic bed in his sickbay. Growing awareness showed her Cutter still looked strange, no longer upside down as he had moved to the side of the bed. He looked exhausted and distressed. Humiliated embarrassment hit her as she remembered her behavior in the aft cargo hold. She had failed her ship and crew a second time, this time with a lack of courage. No wonder they held such low opinions of crewkin. They felt they could not trust her, and she had proved their belief.

"Already applied. Just rest a couple minutes more. You're already talking better."

"Can I get up? What has happened? Has something more gone wrong? What is Dom Jake doing?" She wanted to jump up and run back in time to alter her poor performance. Tears of frustration filled her eyes, and she blinked to hold them back.

"In a few minutes." Cutter watched her while he loosened the straps. "We tried to jettison the engine but failed. Jake decided to shut the Jupiter1090 down. Rob the thief in the cargo bay of its energy. We're all helping. He wants to talk to you."

"And you laced me?" Renna said, unable to prevent her strident tone. She pushed the loose straps aside and rose to sit teetering on the side of the bed.

"Good for you."

"What?" Years of detecting provocation kindled her apprehension.

"For a minute there, you lost your deferential tone and manner. Showed some good honest aggravation."

Renna stared at him. *Is he mocking her impertinent tongue or applauding her disrespect? How can he use humor with the ship in crisis?* She shook her head. Norms, even Cutter, continued to baffle her. "Bad habit," she admitted at last. "I was punished often enough for insubordination. The lesson never seemed to take. Dom..."

"Unh-unh," he broke in. "You were doing better. Jake's right in this. No titles, hear? No 'doms' or 'subs' in this crew."

She shook her head. "You have a captain. There is always a ranking level." *Their talk was irrelevant—get to the point.* "Where is Jake? If he wishes to speak to me, I must go."

"I'm here." Jake leaned against the hatch at the entrance of the sickbay. "We're about to have a late meal and discuss the steps we've taken." He turned to Cutter. "Can she join us?"

"No reason not to." Cutter's hand circled her arm above the elbow as she jumped off the table's side.

Renna welcomed the support. Her legs felt wobbly. When Cutter helped her to a chair in the outer compartment, she sank gratefully into its support.

Ezry and Lock entered toting a large contraption holding plants. Awakening to the changes, Renna looked around at what had been the wardroom. The color-laden partitions were gone, enlarging the area to the skeletal frame of the gray structural supports of the fore compartment. The sight of the reinforced hatch and braced bulkheads felt comforting. Storage tanks of water, strapped and secured, formed an alcove around the head. The monitor rack had been relocated; stowage lockers now formed a block along one side. Some, still open, showed emergency rations and equipment. Ship Dog helped Zak finish securing stowage units to the secondary hull bulwark.

She took a deep breath as her muzziness passed. Laced in sickbay, she had remained unaware of time passing. They had accomplished much without her help. Her hands tightened their grasp as mortified determination filled her. *That will change. From now on, I will become more norm than norm. I will not shirk any challenge, and I will prove my worth.*

Renna knew she hadn't shaken the drug completely when Cutter placed two platters, one of scrambled eggs and soy sausage on the table before her, another heaped with flat brown circles of hot bread. Another platter of sweetbreads and toast, and a bowl of fruit quickly appeared on the table.

"Eat up, the galley is closing," Cutter said. "You'll be on ship rations from now on."

Renna bit her lip to stop her smile at his disgruntled tone, and followed with a sigh, not wanting ship rations in a very unkin attitude.

Ship Dog loaded his plate with the brown bread circles.

"Don't take all them pancakes," Ezry said. "I want some, too. Pass the syrup."

As the platter was given to her, Renna passed the pancakes with some regret to Ezry. The scent of the bread mixed with the sweet fruit wetted her mouth, but she didn't want to upset Ezry. The yellow of the eggs lured her when the platter came to her. She put two scoops on her plate. She watched Cutter fill a small bowl by his plate with fruit and followed suit when the large serving bowl came to her.

She ate the eggs and sausage with relish. When she finished the last of the fruit, she quaffed her juice and smeared three slices of toast with jam. Her gaze strayed to the pancake platter resting near Lock. Two small circles remained there.

Ship Dog picked up the platter. Renna's throat constricted. He passed the plate to her. "Take 'em."

She smiled at Ship Dog. "Thank you." His mustache quivered. She thought he smiled. It showed in his eyes. She placed the brown misshapen rounds on her plate and poured the syrup Ship Dog handed her over them. The bread absorbed the liquid as fast as it pooled around the circles. The sweet, fruity fragrance enticed her as the first bite coated her tongue. Little bread taste or texture remained in the sweet piece she placed in her mouth. No chewing was necessary; the bread broke into small particles by pressing her tongue against her palate. She savored every morsel and appreciated what was before her to the fullest, excluding all else from her awareness.

"Well, no one would say you've lost your appetite," Lock said. "I haven't seen anyone enjoy their food like you. It's almost obscene."

Renna looked up to find everyone watching her. For once, she didn't care, and grinned as she had only dared with Sen. "Enjoy what is now." She picked up yet another slice of toast and stared at the empty egg platter. Looking at Cutter, who appeared more himself with his familiar half-smile, she asked, "Are there more eggs?"

Zak, Jake, and Lock all laughed, and Renna felt the tense mood relax. She had no idea what caused their hilarity but understood the humor was not aimed at her.

"Yeah, Cutter, get some more eggs," Zak said. "Ship rations, for God's sake."

Renna turned her head to stare at Zak's perfect imitation of Cutter. She swung back to Cutter in apprehension, expecting Jake to follow up with a rebuke after the satirical impersonation. Instead, everyone laughed, even Ezry.

Cutter rose with an unconcerned grin and took a slight bow. "Appreciation at last. Alas, too late."

Zak rose with Cutter. "I'll help you."

The offer earned Lock's raised brows. "Hey, Cutter, an apprentice."

Zak smiled at Lock's quip. "Tease away. I'm no apprentice. Our mom made sure all of us could take care of ourselves. I'm with Renna, though. If this is the last of Cutter's meals for a while, I want all I can get."

Later, Lock helped Ezry clear the table, and Jake began business. "How long before Vera goes offline?" he asked Ship Dog.

"Twenty-eight hours," Ship Dog answered.

"Will we be ready?" Jake asked, looking at the group as Lock and Ezry returned to their seats.

"Should be." Lock stretched back in his chair holding the coffee all the others habitually desired. The brown liquid was one thing Renna did not like, as it tasted astringent and bitter.

"Cutter, Ezry, and I made a good start on changing the area into a safe zone. This compartment is set. Outside of here, you best be suited."

"Yeah, we can stay alive in here. Comfort is something else," Ezry huffed with apprehension-tinged disgust. A pale line of tension surrounded Ezry's mouth, and her fingers trembled. The woman was very distressed, reminding Renna of Sen in those last days.

"Zak and I have the flight deck and communications under control. Life shields on the flight deck make it a safe compartment."

While Jake spoke, Renna watched Ezry. Not just distressed, petrified. Her previous air of confidence had evaporated. Ezry sat twisting her napkin into a tight tube. In Ezry, though different in every way, Renna saw Sen's huge pale blue eyes in a too white face waiting in the Assembly Room for salvation. She blinked, swallowing to dispel the vision, and watched Cutter pat Ezry's hand. The expression they shared disturbed Renna. The look made her feel strange, expressing an intimacy separating those two from everyone else. She sensed Zak's suppressed interest in the by-play from where he sat across from her.

"Renna," Jake's voice interrupted her thoughts as he shifted to look at her. "I know this is difficult for you, with what happened on *Markham3*. However, we need all the assistance we can get. You might know something to help us out of this mess. Will you tell us what you remember from the *Markham3*'s last voyage?"

Here was her time of exposure. Her gaze flickered from face to face. She clasped her hands under the table. Mixed with what must be told was so much she did not want to tell, so much which the crew of the *Vagrant Spirit* would never understand about kin. Yet, their lives might depend on what she said. She took a deep breath and held it, slowly expelling the air. Her trembling lessened enough for her to speak.

"The flight started differently. Kin had been kept off ship for sixty days and ordered off company property. They sent us to a place designed for crewkin leave. Most did not like the strange place, the interruption in daily ritual."

"Ordered?" Lock asked with a skeptical twist of his sleek black brows. His dark eyes displayed his disgust.

"Yes. It was *Markham3* kin's first leave ever. I was the only one excited. Everyone else wanted to remain onboard the *Markham3*. Anyplace outside of *Markham3* frightened my kin. We had five doms with Dom Dukan our primary. He and the first flight team returned from leave early. The company had the *Markham3* towed from port after they allowed our kin back onboard. I asked Dom Dukan about this unusual precedent. He ordered me to desist from my questions and ordered the kin to shun me, so no one talked to me. I think Dom Dukan gave the punishment to hide the changes made to the ship from our kin."

She took a deep breath. "I must tell you, Dom Dukan doubted both my dedication to our kin and my general competence. Because of this, he refused me access to the flight plan, so what I tell you is from my own observation only." She looked at Jake. He nodded his understanding. She swallowed, composed herself, and started. "The first thing I noticed was we were not under normal power, and we maneuvered by lateral engines only. Other kin also noticed and became apprehensive. Dom Dukan reassured them. When the main finally came online, the engine sounded, and felt, different. I knew something had changed."

"You could hear the engine?" Ezry asked, her voice dubious.

"*Vagrant Spirit*'s the only ship you've been on, Ez. We all hear and feel the engine," Jake answered. "We become so used to the sound, it disappears. Change ships, and you'll notice. Every ship sounds, and feels, just a little different. Do you always listen to the ship, Renna?"

"Yes. When I am quiet." She waited. This was so different. Never would a sub have interrupted a dom's request for information. If continually interrupted, her report might take a long time. She looked at Jake. He merely nodded at her.

"The sound of the new engine upset me, so what I say is influenced by this. Twelve hours after the start of the new engine, the first systems glitch occurred, followed by more on an irregular basis. They were minor disturbances, and systems checked out within standard limits. Again, Dom Dukan reassured our kin that everything remained within parameters. He explained what everyone already knew, that changes had been made to *Markham3*. These changes would cause small glitches, nothing beyond our capability to handle."

"What were the glitches?" Zak asked.

"Bio disruptions and minor computer glitches first, followed by power outages and shutdown in two lateral engines. Illumination and ventilation flickered, cutting out and coming on again, grav disruptions, lock system failures. The temperature dropped so fast in an occupied compartment two kin suffered hypothermia when the hatch froze shut. I noticed several of the doms started to look worried. When Dom Dukan assigned me to navigation to relieve kin for other duties, I realized the problem was more serious than Dom Dukan admitted.

"It didn't take long to figure out what. Just entering the flight deck, I felt my kins' stress. Computer interruptions and power disruptions constantly knocked the navigation and control systems offline. We would lose important information. The ship would fail to respond to helm controls, and all lateral engines failed. Three weeks into the mission, the first deaths occurred. Life-support went out in the lower decks. Three kin died."

Zak's touch on her arm stopped her. He placed a glass of juice in front of her. Renna willed her hands unclenched in order to pick up the container. She gratefully sipped the liquid, aware of the dryness lining her throat. Her hand shook as she lowered the glass, so she clasped her hands again, tighter, and looked only at the tabletop. No one spoke.

"Afterward, everything changed. Not even Dom Dukan could overcome our kins' fear. All the training, all the experience, the selecting, and the culling, nothing prepared us for such adversity. The company taught us to always trust the ship—it was our world. If we took care of the ship, it would take care of us. When we could not, when the disruptions became greater and greater, my kin failed in their duty. They gave up.

"On the flight deck, one kin told me the new engine never operated properly. The readings all said everything was functioning properly, only the readings lied. The engine required more and more power...nothing sufficed." Renna stopped herself, realizing she was lost in her account. She looked at Jake. "There is not much more. I was dismissed from the flight deck shortly before the failure."

"What happened?" Jake asked. His face suddenly looked like Dom Dukan's, implacable and stern, demanding all she could tell.

"I told those huddled in the assembly room—there were maybe twenty waiting there— to suit up. They dismissed my warning because Dom Dukan had issued no directive. I started suiting anyway. A terrible, whining shriek tore through the ship. I screamed at them to suit up and finished dressing myself. The noise penetrated everything, non-stop, and a strange light shivering between a sharp iridescent purple and glowing red wave blinded me, made me dizzy. Gravity crushed me to the deck and then abruptly released. I heard my kin screaming through my helmet audio. I expect I screamed, too. I don't remember. Everything went black. I believe I lost consciousness. Next, I remember floating with only the sound of my kin crying around me." She stopped, closing her eyes for a second, distancing herself from her memory.

"Four of us returned to the flight deck to help. Those left behind, I ordered into escape pods for their safety until the ship stabilized."

"You ordered?" Jake asked, interrupting her.

"There was no intra-ship communication. Of kin in the assembly room, I was highest." Renna answered. "The six kin on the flight-deck survived; because, of course, the flight deck had life shielding. The others died before we could find and help them. The engine was dead. The computer and navigation panels were dark, and smoke hazed the deck. Dom Dukan sat at his post. He refused reassurance, refused to talk or even look at anyone." Her mind reeled in unspoken confession. *Not true; he looked at you.* Her memory replayed the scene. The emergency lights of his biosuit turned his face to white planes and black shadowed lines of hate. *Why? What had I done?* "He turned off emergency support and removed his helmet."

While she spoke aloud, her conscience kept a silent dialog of reprimand. *He continued watching me; he knew I would not join kin in death. He died hating me above all else.* "All others on the flight deck followed him."

"All but you?" Cutter asked.

"Yes." Renna felt the heat flood her neck and face when she looked at Cutter. "I set the distress beacons. When they were operational, I went to each escape pod and told kin to wait. I lied to them, told them the others were alive, told them I acted under Dom Dukan's orders. They believed me until we were rescued." *Most never talked to me again. Only Sen. The final shunning. All for nothing; I didn't know medical would guide my kin to suicide.*

"Anything else?" Jake asked.

In the quiet of the room, Renna heard the ship's engine, Vera, changing with the shutdown. Disturbingly, she also heard the other engine, felt the thrumming counter-beat to Vera's slowing hum. Her full stomach felt like a leaden lump within her.

Zak answered Jake. "Yes. We'll need to take the computers and other systems down, too, isolate the damned thing from all power."

Twelve

...2179.332-10:36 universal space-time ...mission status ...rabican engine online ...auxiliary support terminated ...countdown underway...

Everyone but Jake waited in the fore compartment. He was working in the flight deck, turning off the last of the ship's power. As the lights went out, Ezry held her breath. Nothing happened except dark descended. Gravity had left an hour earlier. One battery lume gave off a low, meager light. She slumped, biosuited, and strapped down in the zero gravity. Her helmet lay nearby.

The *Vagrant Spirit* was dead. They were dead, too. Nobody else had accepted the fact yet.

The others remained unsuited, strapped in place. Cutter sat next to her. She couldn't feel him through her biosuit. Words learned in childhood from a zealot grandmother floated in her mind in a mute appeal, like the drops of sweat forming in heedless arrays along her brow. Fear kept her from breaking the silence threading the darkness.

With the engine off, now she missed its indiscernible drone and subtle vibration. The podder sat with her head cocked like she was listening to some unheard music. This debacle was all her fault. Zak and Cutter both watched the oblivious podder. Part of a suit floated from its security tie-down next to her. Ship Dog remained morose in grief over his Vera, and Lock in an imposed self-control, sat apart. She knew Lock just hid his fear better than she did.

"The other engine is still up," the podder said.

"You can hear it?" Zak asked, cocking his head, trying to hear the seemingly nonexistent sound. "I can't... just sense a subtle vibration."

"Yes. It's very different sounding, like the cadence of many hearts beating in an asynchronous pattern."

"The engine may take some time to wind down," Zak said. "Let's go relieve Jake."

Ezry swallowed to moisten her mouth. She didn't want anyone leaving, except maybe the podder, but she watched as Zak rose to get ready to leave for duty with the woman. Cutter would eventually be gone for hours, too.

I'm scared and just plain and simple jealous, even in this desperate situation; I can't help myself.

Watching Zak and the podder suit up, she clamped her lips tight and wished all of this over. Until the other woman joined them, the *Vagrant Spirit* had been her safe haven; now the ship had become one more hell. The podder and Zak would take the first watch on the flight deck of the lifeless ship. After fifteen hours on the flight deck, Jake needed rest.

"You sure? I don't mind going," Cutter said.

Ezry nearly smacked him. She didn't want him to leave her. "No, don't! I need you." She knew who would lose if the ship needed him. Cutter would choose the damned ship.

Stop your grousing. You're being unreasonable! Her admonition didn't work. She couldn't and knew her attitude too well.

Zak released his harness and floated from his seat to struggle into the biosuit in ungainly movement. The podder was half into her biosuit before she released her restraints, and once freed, finished slipping her skinny little frame into the bulky exvee suit with sheer grace. Cutter had recommended double suits when traveling the ship. Ezry wore one even in this supposedly safe hold.

Cutter half-turned to her. "We've covered the subject and agreed I'd be on the flight deck at certain times."

"I just can't do it, and I won't go." Fear made her voice quaver. "Nothing I can do up there except cause another disaster if something happens. Why do you have to go? I don't think anything is going to happen with everything turned off."

His grasp squeezed her gloved hand in comfort. "Nobody expects you to go to the flight deck. I must go at some point. Someone must be on the flight deck to intercept incoming communications, answer any hails. Messages have been sent. Ships will come."

"If it's not too late," Ezry said, turning to stare at the bleak partitions.

~ * ~

When Zak opened the flight deck hatch, a low battery lume gave the dead panels an eerie look. His suit light was on beam. He lowered the lamp to diffuse as he stepped aside to let Renna enter.

"How's Ezry?" Jake asked, his voice echoing through his connex as he secured the helmet of his exvee.

"About how you'd expect. Don't know why she ever chose to go into space."

Jake snorted. "Space chose her. She didn't have the sense to back away. I have no instructions. Everything's off. Only the communication relay is open; messages will register but not answer. Nothing to do now, so really pretty boring." He left.

Zak helped Renna close and secure the hatch. They went to the turret's bow and slowly hand-cranked open the shutters shielding the thick transparent panels. Far off stars provided a stunning, icy backdrop to the compartment, but no illumination. A single battery-powered amber light on a side overhead panel glowed in the reassurance of the emergency biosystem's operation.

"Is there atmosphere?" Renna asked, her voice low in his connex.

"Yes," Zak said, checking his suit's monitor. He started removing his helmet.

"No! Don't."

Zak ignored Renna's shrill demand and continued removing his helmet. She stood, eyes wide and staring, her breath pumping a harsh rhythm. "The compartment's safe. Jake was in here," he said.

When she took off her helmet, her breathing took a few seconds to slow enough for speech. "I know. You just...I'm sorry, I was being stupid." A rough breath broke from her as tears burst from her eyes. She gasped, gulping to control them.

"Don't yourself." Zak opened a nearby locker to retrieve a wipe. "We'll have droplets floating all over." He wiped her eyes and cheeks dry and continued until she had herself under control. He placed the moisture attractant wipe on the dark console to let it pick up any remaining dampness.

"I'm sorry," Renna said, her voice cracking. "I've never done anything so unprofessional before. Emotion has no place on duty." Pulling her hands from the suit's gloves, she scrubbed her face.

"Is that a kin dictum?"

"Yes. Calmness, professionalism, duty. Sorry."

"No need. I'm sorry. I can imagine what memories I must have brought back. For the next twelve hours, we'll be more comfortable out of these suits." He pulled off his exvee and biosuit and stuffed them in a locker. Without the magnetic boots, he floated to a handhold and pulled himself to the command chair. Renna took second seat. The darkness and quiet of the familiar place made the compartment seem eerily different, yet remain oddly familiar and intimate, especially when they were dressed in their skivvies. He looked at his shift partner and just made out her profile turned to stare out the forward window. The silence lingered to an uncomfortable length.

"Dark, isn't it?" he said. "Does the darkness frighten you? I could turn on another lume. We should probably conserve them."

"I'm not afraid. The dark is comforting."

He smiled, amused. "In what way?"

"It feels safe. No one to watch every movement, judging every expression."

"Just voices in the dark?"

"Yes."

"Safe from norms or kin?"

Her face swiveled to him composed of dark angles, her expression hidden by shadows. She didn't answer.

"Do you still hear the other engine?"

A faint glimmer showed that her eyes blinked. "Yes." He sensed her move and felt her hand grip his. She placed his hand on the command console, covering it with her own. "Can't you feel the engine?" Her other hand touched the console. "It's the same one. I recognize it."

His palm touched the cold surface of the console sandwiched by her warm palm on the back of his hand. Try as he might, he couldn't feel anything. Yet his pulse raced, making any thought difficult. He pulled his hand from under hers. "All I can hear is your breathing and mine."

She didn't answer. Her hand lay against the console, and her face concentrated on whatever she heard.

"You shouldn't touch me." His comment caught her attention.

"Because you are dom?"

"No." He laughed. "Because I'm a man who finds you attractive, and this is a difficult enough situation."

"Is touching forbidden by norms?"

"No, but taking advantage is."

"Taking advantage?"

Zak sighed. "It's not right if you only agree because you think I am your dom. I'm not, and I don't want your compulsory acceptance."

"I don't understand."

"I want you to want me."

"Why? You didn't like me when I first came aboard."

"Like? No. You represented something unknown, unpredictable. Most norms think crewkin very strange, almost alien. I did, too."

Her head nodded in agreement.

"I thought you spelled trouble, and the *Vagrant Spirit* has had enough problems. I've changed my mind."

"Now you want me?"

"And…I want you to want me. Not because I remind you of Dom Dukan, or because you were trained to say yes."

She was quiet a moment. "Like Cutter and Ezry?" Her comparison hit him in a sore spot he thought long healed.

"Yes." He looked out at the stars.

"How did you know about Dom Dukan?"

"Saw him in your ship's shot. It wasn't hard to figure out what you were thinking when you looked at me." He looked at her, but the dimness obscured her expression. "He looked like a stiff, uptight nitpicker. I may appear uptight…however, I can assure you, I'm no faultfinder." He sighed. "Usually just the opposite."

"Norms never just offer companionship or comfort? Is it wrong to do so?"

He laughed. "Lord, no. Norms have more than their share of casual sex. I've certainly had mine. You said like Cutter and Ezry. What did you mean?"

"I was not sure until you spoke of want. I knew Cutter treated Ezry differently. She said he was her man, and I was to leave him alone. Cutter said he and Ezry love and share only with each other. Excluding the rest of you seemed very strange. I thought you were all kin."

"We are kin. Cutter loves Jake and me as much as he does Ezry, only in a different way. They are committed to each another."

"You want to share their different way with me?" she asked.

"Yes," he said slowly, turning to look at her. "I think I do."

"This way of sharing is not how I've been taught."

"I know."

"If I only wanted casual sex, you would not share with me?"

"Oh, Lord." A laugh jerked from him. "Yes. I probably would. Resisting temptation is not my strong point."

"If I share with you, you do not want me to share with anyone else?"

He let out a breath. "Do you want someone else? Jake? He and I have shared everything else, although I don't know about this. Lock and Ship Dog wouldn't want you. Ezry would skin you for looking at Cutter, and if Ezry interests you, you frighten her. Your choices are limited, which is also unfair."

"I don't want anyone, but…"

He waited while she searched for words.

"I don't know." She moved. "You are making me most uncomfortable. It has been a long time since anyone has touched me in any way, and we are on duty."

He couldn't help his laughter. "My God, Ren, look around. We've a dead board. We're sitting here just in case some light should flicker. Besides, on this ship, we're always on duty, no matter what is occupying our attention at any moment."

She retreated to silence, and all he heard from her for a while was her shifting in her seat and the rhythm of her breathing. Just when he figured he had doomed himself to an unbearably silent and uncomfortable shift, she leaned over the arm of her chair, her face coming close to his. The small golden light highlighted the contours of her face and caused her silver eyes to glow.

"If you were kin, I would tell you I want your comfort. I am touchy, and you should not leave me in need."

Her fingers gently traced down his face, and her lips gently brushed his. He placed his hand over hers, trapping it against his cheek, turning his head just enough to place a kiss on her palm.

"If you were norm, I would tell you your touch makes me desire you," he slid a hand under her undershirt and skimmed her warm skin, touching her nipples before moving to caress her back. He heard her small gasp and felt the goose flesh form on her skin from the room's coolness and his touch. With his other hand, he released her seat harness and pulled her closer, kissing her cheeks, nose, and lips. "I would tell you the taste of you drives me crazy."

With both hands holding her face, he felt her body float above him. Her hands caught his shoulders, helping to hold her in place. He ran his tongue around the edges of her lips and felt her jolt of surprise nearly tear her from him. He continued playing with her lips until she allowed his tongue to take possession of her mouth.

Without losing her hold, she pulled her body onto his lap. He released her mouth, and gasping for air, used his hands to slide up her tunic, following its ascent with his tongue and lips until her body shook, and she made low moans.

Oh God, what am I doing? He leaned back in his seat, breathing hard, and gasped. "This is how I want you to want me." He pulled her shirt down.

"This," she gasped, "is very…uncontrolled, very unkin, a very serious breach of group code." Her hands tightened on him.

"You aren't crewkin anymore."

Renna moistened her lips in the silence. Her voice changed as she regained her breath. "Then I will make you want me more, for you have ignited lust within me."

The compartment's coolness hit his skin at the same time as her warm hands. Her lips and tongue traced lines on his face and neck. "Good enough for now," he muttered. With her eager assistance, he applied himself to their pleasure.

Thirteen

...2179.332-12:31 universal space-time ...mission status ...rabican engine engaged ...power levels optimum ...countdown continues ...intruders detected ...life priority parameter followed ...shield bubble established...

Zak held Renna on his lap, their arms clasping each other. "I didn't mean for this to happen...it was too soon, too fast. You don't even know me." He wouldn't say he was sorry. "Didn't your kin ever make love like we did?" He twined his fingers through hers, sated, half-dressed in the dark compartment, staring at the stars.

"You made me forget about the wild engine alive in our hold," Renna said. Her admission didn't sound like an accusation. She moved back to her own seat saying, "I think I might like becoming norm."

She remained silent for a few minutes. When she spoke, her voice was so soft he almost missed hearing her. "Kin do not make love, not like us, more like a game." He saw she was watching him from the light's reflection catching her eyes.

Her soft whisper continued. "This was scary, delicious, and a frightening loss of control. You took control of my body. Everything seemed so impulsive, maybe because completed in the dark where I could only feel and hear. No one ever talked to me like you did. I have never been so…released."

"It sometimes happens that way. Didn't you have anyone special? Anyone who made you feel cherished?"

She sighed, and he heard her sit back. "Sen—she was special. Although we never acknowledged our friendship, and we never touched each other this way." She sighed. "They accused me of subverting the group. With Sen, we slept together just for friendship, for cheer or consoling, for warmth. She was the lowest sub. Dom Dukan liked her comfort."

"Didn't he ever seek your comfort?"

"Once. He gave none in return, only hurt. He insisted I watch and learn how true kin should be when he and Sen shared. He sometimes hurt Sen, too. She never told him."

"Why didn't he like you?" He leaned toward her, stroked her short curly hair, and ran his finger down her cheek.

Another unhappy sigh escaped her like a lost opportunity. "The list is long. I think because I was not true kin to him. He made me keep my head shaved so my un-*Markham3* color wouldn't show. He told me not to look at him without permission because my eyes were wrong after Markham Company refused his request to change the color. He said I was too impertinent, too boisterous, too aggressive, too foreign, and always undisciplined. He hated me for my curiosity and questions." A morose quality swept through her voice. "He hated me when I refused to die with them. I saw the accusation in his eyes. If other kin hadn't been watching, I think he would have made sure I died. Up to the last, he acted the perfect dom."

Zak ran a finger down her cheek again. In the dark, only the reflection of the emergency light on her eyes revealed her face. "Doesn't sound perfect to me. Sounds like an insufferable, egotistical…" He stopped, realizing he might offend her. "He might have been afraid of you."

"He was my dom. I should not criticize him."

"I'm sorry, Ren, I didn't mean to upset you. I'm sorry for the hard time you've had on the *Vagrant Spirit*. We didn't know about crewkin, didn't understand how hard the adjustment had to be for you." He sighed. "The rescue ships should arrive in just a few days. We will all make a fresh start."

"Tell me about your kin, your family. You knew your mother and father."

"What do you want to know?"

"Everything. What was it like?"

"We grew up onboard the *Vagrant Spirit*. My dad captained her, and Mom was his second in command. The ship has a long history as a successful hauler. After we boys left for school, followed by SSC or medical school, things changed. They needed good help and had trouble finding what they wanted until they took on Ship Dog and Lock."

"Did he hire them through the Port's Labor List, too?"

"No. Dad knew Ship Dog's parents, knew of his problems."

"Ship Dog is not his real name, is it?"

"No. He is Daniel Daniels." Zak laughed. "Probably one reason for his dysfunctions. He was in SSC when his parents died, and he went into a deep depression. They treated him after diagnosing him with a chemical disorder in his brain and a type of incurable paranoia. He was given an implant to treat the imbalance. Ship Dog hated the side effects. They released him from the Corps when he had the implant removed. Because his condition wasn't a job-related injury or disease, he received no disability. Dad and Mom took him on here. Lock was pretty much the same case, yet they made a good team with a few other hired hands."

"Where was Cutter?"

"After he finished medical school, he worked at a prestigious hospital. He left when Dad died. Seems he was not content with a stationary life. Spacer blood doesn't make a content grounder. He planned to run the *Vagrant Spirit*, hire a captain, and act as purser as he does now. His plan didn't work out. Jake and I were in the SSC. Jake was exec officer on a routine patrol ship."

"You returned here when your father died?"

He hesitated. "Yeah. That's pretty much what happened."

~ * ~

Upon their return to the fore compartment, Renna stripped off her biosuit, cleansed, and stowed it. When she turned back to the room, she found Jake and Zak talking in low tones. Cutter gave her an unusual look. The fore compartment was not much lighter than the command compartment had been. Looking around, she saw Ezry already asleep in a hanging hammock. The area was battened down. Nothing appeared to need attention. She sat and wrapped her arms around her legs, lost without occupation. She glanced at Cutter when he scrunched down beside her. He handed her a package of ship's rations.

"Tough watch?"

"No." She opened the package, trying not to make a face when her tongue encountered the bland goo. "Is Ezry still frightened?"

"Pretty much."

"You laced her?"

"Just a little."

"I will take your watch if you wish to stay with her."

He stared at her, looking like he wanted to talk. "You would be with Jake, and though your offer is generous, it's not necessary and might even create a bad situation."

"Not generous. I don't mind taking watch with Jake. Work gives me a sense of purpose. Zak says an SSC rescue ship will be here within a few days or at most, a few weeks. Having nothing to do is very strange," Renna said.

"We will need to create work to occupy us." He hesitated, and Renna looked at him. "Ren, you need to be careful. Things, relationships with us..."

"Norms?"

"Yes. They can be very difficult. You don't know the ground rules. I'm sure our ways are not like those among your kin."

She looked at him in inquiry. "Did Zak tell you?"

"No. One look at the two of you when you came back was enough."

"Have I caused trouble?"

"No. Of course not...you could if you're not careful. You might be hurt, or Zak."

She didn't believe him about the trouble. Something else was bothering him. Beginning to understand norms' unspoken language, she knew Cutter was screaming. Probably because she was a podder. This attitude hurt, coming from Cutter. Knowing what she was had also begun to hurt. "I know. There is much to learn, much to understand."

Zak and Jake walked over and sat on her other side. "Since you seem to be the only one who can feel and hear this engine, have you noticed it winding down at all?" Jake asked.

"No. The wild engine is still very strong."

Jake turned to Zak. "Tomorrow?"

"What tomorrow?" Cutter asked.

"Zak, Ship Dog, and I are going to see if we can disrupt the screen to shut the engine down."

"I will come."

Three simultaneous no's answered her. After her last performance, she understood their reluctance. "I will behave better than before. I am your best choice." She swallowed. "You are right to doubt my proficiency. I allowed the past to frighten me. I am no longer afraid. Besides, I know as much about engines as Ship Dog or Zak."

~ * ~

"Cargo bay one-eighty entrance intact. View to lower decks unobstructed. Loud hum coming from below deck." Jake's voice filled her helmet with his recorded impressions. He instructed them where to aim their helmet cams.

Already unsettled by the dead ship in the walk to the hold, Renna's control verged on non-existent. The clicking of magnetic boots on the deck grid announced each step in her connex. Her biosuit evaporated the sweat pouring from her body, keeping her body at a constant temperature. Still, her insides quivered. The outer exvee suit seemed more cumbersome than usual.

The cargo compartment felt different, perhaps from her awareness of the now massive engine's hum. Renna looked at the cargo bay's overhead. New conduit laced the support grid-like tentacles, making it look biomorphic rather than a rigid man-made structure. Under her breath, she repeated her pledge to serve without fail.

"New conduit attached to partition walls, weaves through supports. The ladder is accessible. Conduit threads close-by." He touched the new structures. "Surface feels soft, yet tough and sturdy, grayish-tan in color."

With the lift inoperative, Jake, Ship Dog, Zak, and Renna made their way in turns down the long string of ladders. Their loud breathing came through her helmet audio. Their voices remained as calm as any crewkin performing their regular duty. Jake continued talking into the *Vagrant Spirit*'s captain's log, recording their progress. She assumed in case anything went wrong he wanted a current report for whoever found the ship. More so, since they knew what lay in the cargo compartment. Her respect grew for her norm crew. They faced the unknown and a dangerous situation with a bravery surpassing her kins'. She felt less afraid, less alone.

"The main habitation compartments are unchanged by the foreign conduit's presence. Suspect construction within the aft hold completed by nanobot technology."

With slow steps, they made their way to the aft compartment. Before reaching the hatch, they knew the aft bay held substantial changes. Conduit streamed like a chaotic waterfall in reverse up into the overhead and the organized structure of the bay supports. With Vera's power source in the overhead compartment now cut off, what was it after? Renna couldn't guess.

Even as they watched, the waterfall effect changed and combined into a single pulsating strand, cooling and coalescing into a disciplined line. Inside the compartment, the cargo container had vanished, its molecules dispersed into the power conduit feeding an engine pulsing in inexplicable life.

"The shape has elongated, or appears to have changed configuration," Zak said. From his position, the view was restricted.

The engine seemed tame; its discordant heart glowing in the dark compartment, living on energy sucked from the *Vagrant Spirit* before the Jupiter1090's power died. Between them and the engine, the transparent shield held security around the engine's perimeter. Various colored lines, predominately lime green, rippled between its boundaries. As they neared, the lines doubled and trebled in frequency. An orange light spotted each of them in turn, running their length from head to feet.

Jake's voice trailed off. They all froze. The thrum of the engine cudgeled them with its foreign rhythm. As if mesmerized, Jake reached to touch the barrier. Static lines surrounded his glove in jagged streaks of threatening blue-white light. After an initial start response, he ignored the buzzing bands of energy. "The barrier feels hard, like the energy has substance." Jake's fingers floated over the surface.

The wall undulated with his movement. He pushed harder against the surface. It gave way, thinning but not rupturing. The frequency of the green lines quadrupled into yellow light. Jake flew backward suddenly, landing several meters away. Zak stepped back, kneeling beside Jake.

"I'm all right." Jake pushed his brother's hand away and fought to his feet. Zak grasped Jake by the elbow, helping his brother reach upright.

Ship Dog shoved the cargo hauler into the shield wall. The projectile rammed into the transparent veil. The wall stretched and bounced the heavy piece of machinery back toward them. Everyone scuttled aside. The hauler skidded across the cargo bay's deck and hit the rear partition.

Zak swore. "The hauler's mass should have shorted out any energy field. What the hell is this thing?"

Jake attacked the wall, pounded on the field, screaming, "This is my ship! My ship." His response was irrational, ineffective, both emotional and unprofessional. With the fear lining her stomach,

Renna understood Jake's reaction. The lines in the wall turned aqua and thickened, seeming to absorb Jake. When the barrier engulfed him, it turned translucent. Zak grabbed Jake's arm, tugging him back. Tendrils of the wall trailed Jake's body as if wanting to pull him back.

"A laser canon might short circuit it," Renna suggested.

"We don't carry weapons," Zak replied.

"Perhaps a non-conductive barrier?" Jake asked.

Renna looked at her captain. After his emotional outburst, his voice sounded rough, and she thought she heard a tinge of uncertainty. He sounded calmer than Dom Dukan did on his most equitable day. Rare confidence buoyed her spirit. She looked around. "Finding anything portable might be difficult. Those non-conductive items onboard are either structurally integrated into the ship or items such as the flight deck command chairs. All either unobtainable or too small to make an impact."

"Damn," Jake said as he inspected the hold. "Whatever it is, it seems to be reconstructing this compartment. There doesn't seem to be much we can do except hope its power runs out."

Zak put a hand on Jake's shoulder. "We'll use our time, until the Service Corps gets here, thinking of ways to thwart it."

Fourteen

...2179.336-18.07 universal space-time ...mission status ...rabican countdown continues ...shield bubble attacked ...intruders repelled ...asserting control over non-code systems ...insertion imminent...

This was their fifth shift together. As with the previous occasions, Renna couldn't wait to get at Zak. She tugged at his biosuit while she still struggled out of hers. Zak helped. In the zero gravity, they floated in a tangle of fabric and limbs. Between luscious, lust-provoked kisses, they laughed, inhaling each other's breath. The intimacy made her feel alive for the first time since the *Markham3*'s death and had nothing to do with sharing comfort. Just looking at him made her body twinge. She didn't care about the ship's danger, the wild engine in the cargo hold, or even how Zak felt, although she tried to give him as much pleasure as he gave her.

Their sharing was private. No kin watched. Her universe shrank to her and Zak alone in the dark. Desire liberated her.

No kin's touch equaled the thrill of Zak's skin gliding against hers. She blindly took what she wanted. Her selfishness made her shameless, her conduct gloriously unkin. She touched Zak with delight rather than duty and seemingly controlled his body—not with comfort. They shared an aching need vocalized in soft moans and oscillating shrieks. The sounds spurred sensation and often caused her breath to stop in anticipation of the crest. She screamed as gilded neurons fired with her body's convulsing release.

Afterward, blissfully content in her sated body, she pulled herself against Zak with a sigh. Placing her head against his chest, she listened to his heart and the air rushing in and out of his lungs. Zak wrapped his warm arms around her in the shared, warm intimacy in the cool compartment.

A green light blinked on the main command panel. Zak swore. They twisted to look. Realizing the panel was responding, they strapped themselves into the pilots' chairs. Kin training returned as guilt assailed her in a litany: *dereliction...dereliction...dereliction.*

Green iridescent words reflected on the interior's surfaces: *renna markham3 recognized. report due.*

The chronometer flashed *2179.336-19.46 ust* and below the reading, in red, another read announced: countdown sequencing *0:13:44.*

Zak tried inputting commands in the panel. Each time it read: *code invalid. access denied.* The wording flashed in red while an accompanying screeching pre-flight alarm filled the compartment.

"Shit. The damn thing has control of flight command. Suit up." Zak pushed more pads with no result.

"How?" Dizziness assailed her. When she didn't move, Zak pushed her clothes and suit into her hands. It was difficult to keep her balance. Only then did she notice gravity was holding her.

She began to dress. "Something is happening. One of us should stay here."

"No. None of the panels respond, our code is locked out. We'll go back to the fore compartment and access the escape pods if necessary." When she hesitated, he grabbed her chin and pulled her to face him. "Get into your suit, now!"

His rigid expression made her reluctantly don her exvee. She heard Zak talking to someone within his helmet. The sound was muted as she hadn't put her connex on yet. She stared at the message on the board, fear crackling along her nerves. Zak grabbed her helmet and put it on, secured the attachments, and pulled her from the command compartment.

The walk seemed longer, darker, their movements unsteady. Gravity fluctuated with each step, and her feet landed in different places from where she anticipated. Whenever her boots connected with the deck, she felt the beat of the wild engine through the sole. The engine pulse sprinted in a synthesized rhythm of unchecked momentum. Their suit lumes emitted bent and twisted streams of bouncing light in nauseating illumination.

Before reaching the halfway point, a muted voice echoed through Renna's helmet: *renna markham3...*

Her heart lurched and her breath caught. A subtle engine whine sounded through the gangway. She recognized the voice. Dom Dukan was speaking to her.

They reached the hatch to the forward compartment. She helped Zak manually turn the latch. When the cover opened, Zak hesitated. Renna motioned him to enter, ready to follow.

...renna markham3... the too familiar masculine voice called her, multiplying into the collected voices of her kin. She looked down the corridor. Zak turned from inside the airlock to look at her.

"Ren?" Zak's voice came through her helmet. She barely recognized his voice.

...renna markham3... Sen spoke. Renna turned to face back down the dark corridor. The gangway blurred and refocused, elongated, and returned to normal, moved about as if her eyes were looking through a viewfinder. She must be hallucinating. Sen committed suicide. She was dead.

Her friend spoke over Zak's voice and Renna hesitated. "Do you hear her?"

"Hear who? Hurry! Now!" Zak motioned to her to enter the airlock.

Renna took a step toward the airlock, hesitated while looking down the gangway she had just walked. Operational lights sprang on around the hatch. She heard the hatch mechanism start and turned to the sound. The hatch slammed shut, enclosing Zak in the airlock, nearly catching his arm in its closure. The lock's click reverberated with noise, proving the atmosphere present. Lights kicked on in stages along the side partitions and overhead. In the shadows between the shifts in her perception, she saw the faces of her kin. Through her helmet audio, she heard Zak screaming at her. Images of the *Markham3*'s end overwhelmed her. *Now, now was the time,* they seemed to say.

She unlatched her helmet and pulled it off. Sweet, cool air filled her first breath. In simultaneous action, the hum of the ship's power came up. Her heart matched its quick cadence. Her breath became shallow and ragged. Beneath her feet, she felt the resonance of the wild engine combined with the growing whine of power. Her vision stabilized.

...renna... the voice came through the intercom, a distinctly masculine and unfamiliar timber. The fresh air cleared her mind.

"Who are you?"

...cognitive support for rabican engine prototype assigned markham3 ...launch insertion imminent... return to flight command...

Paralysis held her. She heard Zak scream incomprehensible orders through her helmet. She heard his muted thumps on the hatch and ignored him. Her kin had returned for her.

...preparation for launch imminent ...return to flight command...

The message kept repeating. Duty called her. Reluctantly, her body responded. She returned to the command compartment. Zak's voice ceased. The other voice followed her via the intercom. Orders were periodically emitted through the ship's audio. She obeyed by rote.

...launch imminent ... initiate flight protocols...

She sank into the command seat. Renna checked the flight and auxiliary boards. All reads scintillated with shifting brilliant colors as sequencing and reports bounced across the panels. The fore compartment held under acceptable life-support levels. Still, she remained suited except for her helmet, which she threw on the second chair.

She followed flight prep protocols, bringing the *Vagrant Spirit* to flight status. The ship already accelerated at near the highest flight speeds. Her fingers flew over the panels, touching keys, checking that the exterior and interior hatches were locked. Most displayed the red status of locked, and she quickly locked the rest. All the solar panels were recessed, and all communication receivers were locked in place. Life-support functions operated in power-saving mode. She closed and locked all viewports. Finished, she waited, her gloved hands clenching the armrests.

Engine's whine screamed and her pulse palpitated, rivaling the careening engine's beat. The sound reached a Klaxon's intensity. Her body weight increased as ship inertia dampers failed under the engine's tremendous thrust. The *Vagrant Spirit* shuddered as if coming apart. Compressing materials groaned and crunched, adding an alarming sound to the discordant wail.

"How do you know me?" she asked, needing the answer before she died.

...recognition made ...medical chip ...speaker renna markham3...

She squeezed her eyes close as reality dissolved around her. The dissonant wail became all. Waves of light hit her retinas through her eyelids. Intense, vivid colors swelled and capered in an insane spectral display. Designs formed and shifted into endlessly changing patterns. Her body convulsed. Her heart strained in a jagged syncopation, wrenching her through a pinpoint of black, obliterating all sense and sensation.

~ * ~

Opening her eyes, Renna found the turret window shields open. No glittering stars shined. Energy whirled, twisting around the turret in a blinding maelstrom of frenzied chaos, showing her the whole as well as each separate particle. She closed her eyes against the assault. *Too much, stop watching. Close the shutter.*

The command panel's reads bombarded her. They stretched in long wavering lines, transforming the undulating interior into a bizarre, twisting dance. She hit the close pad, except her hand passed through the console's structure. With horror strangling her, she stared at her hand inside the solid substance and pulled her arm back with a violent jerk. She clasped her hands and pulled them tight to her chest, closing her eyes against the anarchy outside her body.

Calmness, professionalism, duty. She thought the words while vaguely aware she had spoken them aloud.

The lights continued to batter her retinas with dizzying color exploding in the back of her head. A distinct hum varying in pitch and rhythm filled the compartment beneath the engine's wail. Waves of tickling sensations ran over her skin until they became a painful, burning touch. Her chest moved up and down in a tangible, arrhythmic pattern of breathing.

Still living. The sensation of her expanding and contracting lungs seemed the only sane thing to concentrate on.

"Prepare for Insertion," Jake said. Her eyes flew open. The flight deck was different, larger. Six other officers worked at various panels, forming a horseshoe around Jake's station. He stood in the center of a smaller, waist-high semi-circle of computer reads. Shocked, Renna looked around at the foreign navigation panel under her hands. "Lieutenant Markham, what are you doing? Execute the order!" Jake said, turning a displeased expression toward her.

He wore a blue Space Service Corp uniform. "Yes, Captain." She replied automatically, while complete confusion swirled through her. She looked at the panel, not understanding the readings. Her eyes blinked.

When her lids lifted, the panel had changed. "Relieve the Speaker," Dom Dukan said. Her kin-mate took over, pushing her aside. Dom Dukan turned away. "Log in another insubor..."

Everything changed mid-statement, and she sat in the command seat of the *Markham3*. A kin sub shouted, "Dom Renna, the coordinates have been entered..." Another shift occurred. Blackness surrounded her. All she could sense was the sound and feel of her breath and heartbeat. The flight deck's partitions tore apart with a wrenching sound. She perched on the edge of the command chair and screamed.

Before the end of her scream, another tableau took place, and another, and another. She felt her death, her demise, as millions of probabilities converged.

...ship launch completed ...insertion successful ...rabican engine in operational mode...

The torturous noise ceased with abrupt finality. Frozen, Renna slowly opened her eyes and found she was back on the chillingly quiet *Vagrant Spirit's* flight deck. Minutes passed before she acknowledged the announcement.

"Did the rest of the crew survive?" Her voice shook. A semblance of reality returned. The chair arm seemed solid under her fingers. Her body sank into the resilient cushions.

Everything appeared real. The flight panel sparkled with readings. The engine panel where Vera's readings should have displayed remained dead.

...one of markham3 crew recognized ...all others missing ...six intruders identified and confined ...input required...

"*Markham3* is dead." Speaking through the hard knot in her chest distorted her voice into dull, flat words.

...input incorrect ...cs9m3 proto engine cognitive support correctly installed on markham3 ...verification license current... broken power connections rebuilt ...life-support system annexed, ship electrical, ventilation, plumbing systems integrated...

"This is not the *Markham3*."

CS9M3 for Markham 3? Ninth cognitive support trial or finished program? She had never heard of a Rabican engine type. Protoengine. In development. Was the cognitive support a prototype, too?

Renna leaned forward and rested her head in her hands, hoping she wasn't going to puke. She tried to order her scattered and struggling brain to a semblance of reason. Her stomach felt twisted and burned, her skin scorched, still tingling with sensation. The tingling altered to sting. *Pull yourself together.* "Check the ship's configuration and registry."

...registry programming incompatible ...correct input crucial ...interface code required ...all power systems malfunction repaired...

The communication board pulsed with sickening color. Renna grimaced, swallowed, and took a deep breath. "*Markham3* is dead," she repeated. "You killed it. You killed my kin. This is not your ship. This is the *Vagrant Spirit*. What have you done to them? Have you killed this crew, too?"

...intruders held in forward compartment... all live ...initiated crew life-support elements of programming installed...

"Release them. This is their ship."

...input incorrect ...intruders dangerous to security of rabican engine and markham3...

"No. I am correct."

She jabbed the information request pad. The console remained solid beneath her touch, and the ship's registry appeared on the screen. *Can it see and read? No. Would it understand the code delivered via the circuit? Yes. Display modules all used universal code.*

"Check the ship's registry. The governing seals remain intact. The Terran family owns this ship. You are the intruder. You are the only danger on the *Vagrant Spirit*. You are a killer." The constant low hum of the computer filled the silence. Renna reached up and turned on an overhead. Ambient light flooded the area, killing the stark illumination from the LEDs. She punched the pad controlling the forward shutters, shutting out the disturbing display outside the ship. The flood of sensation bombarding her mind and body eased.

...orders executed ...ship records sealed ...current ship code unknown ...rabican protocol prevents breach of sealed records ...first trial insufficient power for transfer ...cs9m3 and rabican engine knocked offline ...second attempt auxiliary engine assist trial successfully completed ...any crew injury accidental...

"This was not a trial. The CS9M3 and the Rabican engine were destined for reclamation after the destruction of the *Markham3*.

This was a cargo run for the *Vagrant Spirit*. You are the cargo. Where have you taken us?"

...orders followed ...system not purged for dereliction ...why sub speaker renna markham3 recover cs9m3...

"I didn't save you. You reactivated."

...renna markham3 not sent to reclamation for dereliction and death of markham3 crew...

"No. I'm guilty of many things, but not killing my kin. I just couldn't make them want to live. My crime is not dying with them."

...life dies ...termination of cs9m3 attempt aborted...

"Everything dies. The CS9M3 was turned off."

...renna markham3 not terminated...

"I know. I wanted to live more. Where are we?"

...specified ...ship now journeys to the assigned coordinates as programmed in rabican ...mission successfully initiated...

"This ship is the *Vagrant Spirit*. There were no specified coordinates. The insertion location differed. You have the *Vagrant Spirit*'s crew locked in the fore compartment. They hired me as crew. Our mission was to take cargo to the Zorah Reclamation Center. The Rabican engine is our cargo." She was tired of repeating facts in a useless endeavor. She couldn't change the CS9M3's programming.

After a brief pause, the engine's artificial intelligence responded.

...explain presence of crewman sub speaker renna markham3...

"Coincidence. Mischance. Fate. You killed my kin."

...accident ...duty to protect assigned crew ...sub speaker renna markham3 and cs9m3 rabican kin...

"*Markham3* kin died. We failed our ship. Why are you hijacking this ship?"

...complete mission...

"Where are you going?"

...expulsion point changes with insertion point ...cs9m3 and rabican moved ...exit unknown ...sub speaker renna markham3 changed specified insertion location without update to cs9m3 rabican...

"We are not on *Markham3*. That happened over a year ago. Can you return?" The low hum continued unchanging for several minutes.

...unknown ...name crew...

Renna named the *Vagrant Spirit*'s crew.

...cs9m3 assigned Vagrant Spirit ...designation change cs9vs1...

"You are cargo laded to the *Vagrant Spirit* for Zorah Reclamation. May I join the *Vagrant Spirit*'s crew?"

...vagrant spirit crew or terran crew ...clarification needed ...command crew necessary in compartment ...communication, navigation and ship log codes sealed ...need access...

She heard the hatch locks release. Feeling strength return to her shaky limbs, Renna rose and left the compartment.

As she walked, lights came on, turning off as she passed. Once she took a step and found herself outside the ship. After a shocked second, she took a breath, closed her eyes, and threw her head back. *Focus. You are in the gangway headed toward the fore compartment.*

When she opened her eyes, the partitions had reformed around her. Every few steps another aberration occurred. Solids transformed, blurred, dissolved. With any step, a foot might sink through the deck or hit resistance some distance above the deck.

After each anomaly, she reiterated her focus mantra. When she reached the forward compartment, she heard the automatic locks disengage. The hatch swung open. She entered. The six members of the *Vagrant Spirit* stared back at her. Lights, gravity, and life-support functioned. The monitors lining one partition displayed the command module. With a smooth swish, the hatch closed behind her.

~ * ~

"You heard?" she asked.

"Through the monitors," Jake answered, already dressed in exvee. Renna had no idea what he planned to do.

...captain jake terran cs9vs1 awaits orders ...ship designation change ...clarification needed ...command crew necessary inflight

compartment ...cs9m3 not command module communication, navigation and log codes sealed ...request access to vagrant spirit records...

"Any suggestions?" Jake asked.

Renna answered the CS9, pre-empting Jake. "You are cargo CS9M3. There has been no authorization to change the designation to CS9VS1. Your operations have killed. The *Vagrant Spirit* belongs to the Terran family."

She waited for Jake's correction at her usurpation of authority. None came. She took a deep breath and bowed her head.

"Wait for your orders in the command compartment," Jake spoke in command mode.

...captain jake terran cs9vs1 awaits orders ...request access to vagrant spirit records...

"Cease communication and live feed surveillance of this room." Jake's voice held an authority Dom Dukan never achieved. His hand rose, warning her against correcting the CS9.

...obeyed ...captain jake terran requires privacy ...cs9vs1 awaits orders in command compartment...

Jake prepared to leave, his hand on the hatch.

"Wait!" Renna pulled herself erect in alarm. She had not warned him about the strangeness outside the compartment. As she spoke, all the screens deadened, halting everyone.

"Did it turn them off?" Cutter's dazed expression settled on her.

Renna hesitated before answering. "It must have. Does it listen? I don't know. Hopefully, the CS9 follows standard security programming."

"What did you want?" Jake asked.

"The gangway to the flight deck needs shielding. Until reinforced, stay focused on where you are and what you are doing."

"Matter distortions?"

"Yes, very real."

"I'll take precautions. Everyone will continue to wear biosuits and exvee when moving through the ship." Jake turned to the hatch.

"What about this compartment?" Ezry sat next to Cutter, her face stiff, her lips white lined in tension. Ezry was the only one beside her and Jake in a biosuit.

"However you feel comfortable," Jake replied taking several steps back into the room.

"Any other ideas?"

"Turn it off," Cutter's baritone boomed in emphasis.

"Impossible." Ship Dog slumped in a lounger.

"The CS9 is operating the ship." Renna clasped her hands and nodded agreement with Ship Dog. She caught herself and let her hands drop. *Crewkin posture.*

"Probably generating its own power." Zak watched her with an unreadable expression.

Lock remained abnormally quiet.

Renna started unfastening her exvee. "You saw the forward view shield. I've never seen space look like what showed outside the shield. I don't know where we are. I don't think the CS9 does, either." She felt hands pulling the exvee from her shoulders and found Zak at her back, helping. No one had assisted her in such a way before. He put an arm around her shoulders when finished, creating a strange, protective sensation.

"Hyper engine. Hyperspace." Ship Dog swore and smiled in a near jubilant manner.

"Prototype." Lock responded, not sharing Ship Dog's pleasure.

"The CS9 calls this transit space." Renna stared at Lock. His subdued voice and manner made him seem unfamiliar.

"Still doesn't tell us where we are," Jake said. "Or, where we're headed, whether this is hyperspace, transit space, or another dimension."

"Or how we get back," Renna said. "The CS9 seems to have access to all but the older programs and files."

"Those have incompatible languages due to the *Vagrant Spirit*'s age." A reflective look crossed Jake's face. He frowned.

Renna nodded in norm fashion. "The CS9 overrode all systems and has assumed control of basic equipment. It controls all ship functions except navigation, command, and the inoperative Jupiter 1090."

"You have to admire it for persistence in fulfilling its mission." Lock whistled with a low sibilance, finally emerging from his daze. "My God, we're in hyperspace."

"This CS9 still thinks it's on the *Markham3*?" Cutter asked.

"No longer." Renna staggered to a seat, breaking her contact with Zak. "While we were ignorant of its presence, the CS9 also operated blindly. The *Vagrant Spirit*'s programming code is old enough to be incompatible with the CS9's language, and it never challenged your codes or programming. Registry and logbooks are, by convention, in Stellar Transaction Language, which predates even the *Vagrant Spirit*. The old code remains a viable language only for those forms, and the CS9 couldn't enter them without breaking standard ship conventions. Now, it knows something went wrong. It has suffered a time-lapse and is on another ship. It is reassigning itself to the *Vagrant Spirit*. Whether it will continue to respect those codes...I don't know."

"Is it capable of developing an interface?" Cutter asked.

Zak shrugged. "My guess—it fabricated power linkage, so...yes. Definitely."

"Everything depends on how it reacts to this information," Jake said. "Even a cognitive support system like the CS9M3 has fail-safes built into the program to prevent philosophical self-contamination."

"What?" Ezry spoke, her voice cracking. "It didn't fail-safe the first time around on the *Markham3*."

Lock looked at Ezry and cracked his knuckles. "Doesn't mean it overcame the fail-safe routines. Those prevent the cognitive system from thinking it is so smart it can do without humans. The first A.I.s were dangerous because they lacked the protocol. One reason acceptance in ship development has been so slow."

"First protocols always recognize the sanctity of life," Zak reassured Ezry.

"If the CS9 follows its programming," Cutter said, hugging Ezry.

"It is. There may be a problem," Renna said. They all looked at her. "This one may have reached something like self-awareness."

"I heard that, too," Jake said. "The CS9 tied itself to you in kinship."

Renna caught herself agreeing in the crewkin habit and stopped, no longer wanting to use those ways. "I don't know if the CS9 is self-aware or, if so, to what extent. What I do know is this CS9 doesn't want to be shut down. If the A.I. regards itself as an entity, the standard programming will cause conflict. And we will need to access the programming..."

"Gain control over what it thinks? Good idea. All right, I'm going to the command compartment and see how many orders this interloper will follow." Jake trudged to the hatch. "For now, the rest of you stay here and work on an exigency plan."

"Find out how much this thing needs us?" Cutter sighed and rubbed his neck.

"Will you allow the CS9 access to our logs?" Zak asked.

Jake grinned. "Depends on what kind of plan you come up with."

"Jake."

"Yes, Renna." Jake gave her a half-smile, halting again at the hatch.

"Remember. Moving is difficult. Focus on where you are and when."

He stared at her. "More than just disorientation?"

"I don't know. We may be bridging this reality and other possibilities."

Fifteen

...2179.336-05:32 universal space-time ...mission status ...transition achieved ...rabican engine operating within design parameters ...cs9 logged onto vagrant spirit registry number nc22597j1090c ...placing registry change to cs9nc22597j1090rabican draft in outgoing transmission file ...native j1090 engine inoperative ...hull memory grid construction begun ...life-support within defined limits ...logged recognition of captain jake terran ...security ...navigation ...in-system flight controls ...shiplogs ...personnel control systems denied cs9vs1 ...renna markham3 report inconsistent with cs9vs1 files ...data required...

...welcome captain jake terran to the flight deck ...cs9vs1 available for orders...

Jake closed his eyes in relief on reaching the flight deck. Ren's warnings had not been zealous enough. He sank into the command chair, welcoming its familiar comfort despite the singular greeting of the feminine voice. He opened his eyes and sensed a difference before he noted the changes. He glanced over the consoles, his jaw tightening as he saw the Jupiter 1090 panel lined in blankness, not even inoperative red lights. Static yellow indicator lights lined the navigation console, not the comforting flicker of an operational panel. The ship's log panel remained open on the ship's registry, but inactive.

The flight deck felt too cold. He absently reached for the interior temperature control. When his thumb failed to find the rheostat, he investigated why. The control had moved, migrated fifteen centimeters to the right of where he reached. Having repeated the same movement a thousand times, he frowned, unable to figure out how he'd missed it. With disbelief, he noted the variations in the panel's placement. He shook his head and glanced at the numerous monitors lining the overhead, at the equipment racks flanking the compartment. Everything seemed in place, most left in the last setting before the shutdown; most remained inoperative.

"The engine panel remains inactive. Give me a report on flight status." As he spoke, he opened the turret shields and looked at the waves of energy tumbling around the ship. The strange turbulence hypnotically captured his attention. After a few minutes, he felt the prickly effects on his skin and closed the shield. The strange woman's voice brought him back to business.

...terran crew terminated operation of jupiter1090 engine...

A short lag made him believe the CS9 would not honor his order, but the voice began a minute recital of the incomprehensible stats of the Rabican engine's performance.

"Life support?" He broke off the flow of unfamiliar flight statistics.

The report came in familiar terms and well within normal parameters. After a moment, he commanded, "Download the CS9M3's log since reactivation."

...need transfer protocol from captain dom dukan markham3...

"The CS9M3 Rabican has hijacked this ship and sent the *Vagrant Spirit* into uncharted space. Give the report or tell me why not."

...the cs9vs1 is unable to comply...

"There is no CS9VS1. The correct designation remains CS9M3. The CS9M3 will comply with the commands of this ship's captain. Captain Dukan is dead, the *Markham3* destroyed. The needed protocols are unavailable. Adjust your programming."

...cs9m3 has no record of Markham3 or the crew's destruction ...need designation change to cs9vs1 attached to vagrant spirit, nimbus class, jupiter 1090 engine under ownership of terran family ...designated small commercial hauler ...registry recorded celeste station nc22597j1090c ...sub-crew renna markham3 reassigned to vagrant spirit crew provided access ...registry in standard interstellar language available to cs9m3...

"Answer my request."

...information unavailable without proper code...

Jake recognized a programming glitch when he crossed one. A sardonic sense of irony struck him. For years, he'd railed against the inconsistency of archaic programming languages. Now the eccentricity and paranoia of early programmers might save his ship. In a resigned voice, he asked, "Ship's destination?"

...unknown ...insertion point unlogged...

"Flight status?"

...expansion process initiated ...warning ...heat generated...

His understanding lagged behind the CS9's forewarning. Three monitor lights skidded across the slight tilt of the command panel. He pulled his hands back from where they rested with a gasp. "Ouch!" His thumb came away with a blob of melted lime-colored material. The standard gray panel developed bright green cracks. The fissures exuded a flowing sap.

"What the hell?" The green blob on his thumb cooled to gray and cracked off. Underneath, his skin reddened from the contact. A green stain spread in pulsing blotches around the injury. He sucked on his thumb to relieve the pain.

I must be hallucinating like in the gangway. No doubt caused by the crazy effects of whatever, wherever, they were. His breath caught as he looked at the instrumentation racks and indicator panels. As he watched, the engine panel bulged and moved. In small increments, the panel expanded. He scrambled from his seat, retreating until his back came against the turret's bulwark.

His gaze caught the chronometer's reading. Minutes crept by as the rack and console melted around him flowing into new positions with switches and pads, indicator signals, and lights floating like cinders on molten green lava. Important indicators never lost their readings as they floated on the transforming console.

The panel solidified as fast as the material melted. He felt the new surface with a tentative touch. The surface remained warm, not burning hot, and more pliant than before. Next to the Jupiter1090's engine rack, a new rack existed. A new panel spread along the command console. If he failed to believe his eyes at the change, the pain in his finger convinced him.

...current emergence estimate for vagrant spirit and rabican engine parameters displayed for captain jake terran...

The position shown was far outside any designations he'd ever studied. "Where are we?"

...transit space...shortest travel between two designated sites...

"What designated sites?"

...unlogged...

"Arrival?"

...arrival estimated forty-two days ...eighteen hours ...forty-four minutes for original insertion...

"With the current configuration?"

...change of insertion location ...emergence unknown...

"Can you get the *Vagrant Spirit* back to the insertion point?"

...after emergence if insertion pre-plotted ...access to navigational logs requested...

"Denied."

He might be paranoid. He wasn't, however, prepared to give the interloping computer entry into what remained of their security. Not yet. Not until they had determined more about the CS9. He didn't know what to do, so sat watching the console, hoping to learn from the CS9 about the Rabican's operation. He resumed his command seat, leaning back and keeping his hands on the chair's wide armrests. His thumb remained stiff. A glance showed the green stain gone and the red swelling rapidly fading. He hesitated to touch the panel. The configuration felt foreign and uncomfortable, like the first time he had slipped into the chair behind an SSC ship's panel.

Renna and the Rabican engine onboard the *Vagrant Spirit*. Together. What was the chance of such an occurrence?

Jake didn't believe so unusual a circumstance could be coincidental. Cutter had told him of the quick freight pickup for Zorah and the urgency to leave port, making it necessary to hire crew immediately. The port's Labor List Master gave him Renna's name. *How serendipitous. What did Renna know? He swore. She had the Vagrant Spirit's codes.* "From whom do you accept orders?"

...cs9m3 reassigned vagrant spirit ...reports to captain jake terran...

"And your allegiance?"

...captain of vagrant spirit...

"The following areas are off-limits to the CS9M3. The communication and navigation systems, ship logs, the Jupiter 1090, personnel and medical files, and access to the fore compartment."

...order logged...

"When specified, consider all communications made by the captain to other crewmembers private."

...order logged...

"Can you do anything about the perception problems in traversing the gangway between the flight deck and the fore compartment?"

...list problems...

He did.

...no specific solution defined in pre-flight data...

"Figures. Download all CS9M3 log files."

...files since rebuild available on reading console...

"Connect a private communication with Zak Terran in the forward compartment."

~ * ~

Zak indicated everyone should gather around the table. Fright lined everyone's face including Cutter's, who usually remained stoically calm. *As mine must; none of us has faced such a situation before.*

The last few hours had unnerved everyone. Even in this heavily shielded compartment, reality had been lost in hallucinatory sensation and eerie scenarios of might-have-been. Ezry had screamed and cried continually. Ren's screams had come through the audio, giving an indication of her situation on the flight deck. His inability to assist her still rankled. Ren having to face whatever happened alone frightened him more than he wanted to admit.

The forward compartment seemed bleak with the usual illumination. The yellow-cast lighting emphasized the harshness of the bare structural supports. The bulwarks made the ship seem flimsy and incapable of withstanding the forces of space. The barrenness enhanced the isolated feel and emphasized the jeopardy of their situation.

His connex signaled a private communication. Jake spoke in his ear. His comments made Zak uneasy. Their position put an irregular aspect on Ren's hiring. He didn't want to doubt her, but logic insisted her hiring had somehow been orchestrated.

Was she a pliant participant or a docile dupe?

He left the connex link open. Jake would hear them. He hesitated, so would the CS9, which claimed kinship with Renna.

Ren's clear, crystalline eyes studied him, almost as if she read his mind. She lowered her gaze to the table, her look as flat and expressionless as when she first joined the crew. Something within his chest twisted at her plight. Yet, his first duty, his first allegiance, belonged to Jake and Cutter.

"How soon can we turn that thing off?" Ezry asked. Her fingers clasped the table's edge as if she supported it.

"We can't, Ez," Cutter said. "Not until we know where we are."

"Not the engine, that computer. It's causing all the trouble."

"The CS9 controls the engine."

"We have to make it take us back." Her wild-eyed gaze swung to Renna. "You caused this, podder! It's your fault." Ezry half rose from her seat.

"We cannot turn the CS9 off." Regret filled Renna's face. Fear filled her voice.

Zak suspected the situation didn't frighten her. They did. He wanted to believe her, wanted to comfort her. The situation stood in the way.

"Ezry," Cutter warned in his deep, comforting tone.

"Don't Ezry me!" She faced Cutter, pointing at Renna. "Nothing has been right on this ship since her foot crossed the main hatch. It's clear as the stars she had something to do with this. It's her engine."

"Stop it, Ez. This doesn't get us anywhere."

Lock shifted, antsy in his chair. Ship Dog slumped in a morose heap next to Lock. His arms remained folded against his chest, which indicated their engineer had nothing to contribute.

Renna's countenance turned even more wooden, all color drained from her pale face.

She looked at him. "I swear I didn't know."

"Sit down and shut up, Ez," Zak spoke louder than he meant, suddenly exhausted by the emotions swamping the compartment. Ezry turned a startled glare on him, clamped her lips together and sat. He eyed her with stern admonishment. "Right now, we need everyone's considered input, not hysterical drivel. Get yourself in hand, or I'll have Cutter give you something to keep you calm." He ignored Cutter's reflective, edged regard.

"Suspicious." Ship Dog's eyes watered.

Zak sighed. If the engineer's acceptance of Ren surprised everyone, his reaction to believing himself fooled didn't. Ship Dog remained sensitive to any hint of betrayal.

"Nonsense," Cutter said.

"Yeah, I don't see how Ren could've known." Lock spoke over Cutter's outcry. His hands moved to emphasize his words. "Heck, I saw her when she first saw that monstrosity in the aft hold. She couldn't fake that reaction."

Zak agreed, yet distrust soured in his mouth. "Do you know anything, Renna?"

"No. Nothing. I swear." Her frozen look translated into a stiff posture screaming of falsehood.

"Like your word is believable," Ezry said. Her look challenged them. "We know nothing about podders. They could have planted her."

"Ezry, enough," Cutter said.

His mate glared at him. Ezry's gaze swiveled to Zak. "I should have never allowed you to sweet talk me onto this ship." She nodded at Cutter. "Or let you trap me here with affection." Her words upset him, and Zak sensed Cutter's profound hurt.

"What you say is true," Renna answered Ezry's remarks in a low voice, cutting through Ezry's drama.

"What?" Lock's head jerked with his shock.

"Markham may have planned this. I just don't know how."

"They knew we were desperate for cargo." Cutter sighed, swore, and clenched his jaw in contained anger. "They used our trouble against us. Manipulated both Jake and me."

"Possibly," Zak agreed. "Why?"

"Stolen." Ship Dog's morose face rose briefly to look at them before sinking to regard the table.

"What's stolen?" Ezry asked.

"Engine," Ship Dog muttered slipping down further into his seat.

"If the company knew about such an engine, their entire long-haul cartel was endangered," Cutter said.

Zak agreed. "If the engine's a stolen design, it probably lacks a registry code. We'd have been blamed for the theft."

"You have proof you loaded the cargo at your last dock," Renna said.

Cutter expelled a deep breath. "They didn't tell me the exact cargo. The lading order lists general reclamation. I certainly did not learn until near disembarkation that we were carrying an engine. It was easy enough to know Renna had been hired before then. I should have been suspicious because they offered compensation for the loss of a full cargo load." He sighed. "I only thought the quick job a sign of an overdue change in luck. The *Vagrant Spirit* was set up."

"Zorah would examine any engine," Zak said, realizing where the danger lay. He swore and sat back in his chair, stunned. "They'd have confiscated our ship for the theft."

"It's my fault." Cutter looked defeated, something Zak had never seen in his overly optimistic brother.

"How?" Ezry said, sensing the increased tension.

"No. Mine," Renna said, her gaze focused inward. "I didn't suicide, they knew I had knowledge of the engine. We both had to disappear. My failure caused this. I am sorry."

Ezry gave Renna a venomous look before settling into a tense ball. She shrugged off Cutter's touch of comfort and reconciliation.

"I can't believe they expected the engine to go active and thrust the *Vagrant Spirit* into hyperspace. They got rid of the engine because the *Markham3*'s failure didn't destroy it." Zak examined possibilities. None looked good.

"They didn't expect a CS9 system to turn itself on." Lock sat back, clasping his hand behind his head in obvious contemplation.

"If they didn't know the CS9 could trigger itself into operation, there must be another means to make sure the *Vagrant Spirit* never made Zorah." Zak noticed both Lock and Renna's expressions agreed with his assessment. Renna closed her eyes and appeared to fold in upon herself.

"What do you mean?" Ezry asked in renewed alarm.

"They expected we would disappear, probably blow up." Lock bit his lower lip.

"We're going to blow up?" Ezry screeched.

"There is a possibility," Zak said.

"No," Lock said. "The explosion would have already happened. If there were a device placed in the cargo container with the Rabican engine, the CS9 nanobots might have dismantled it. The container's materials make up all of the new conduits."

"Or it won't trigger while the engine operates," Zak added.

"Doubtful. Would've." Ship Dog's eyes skittered from anyone's gaze, particularly avoiding Renna.

Renna started, stared at Ship Dog. An instant later, she dropped her gaze to the table. The silence stretched to an uncomfortable length.

"The CS9 activation was unplanned. Activation might have overridden any destruct sequences," Zak said, watching Renna. She remained silent. He damned her crewkin reticence. He wanted to scream at her: defend yourself; argue, fight. Make me believe you.

"Must have, if we got this far," Lock agreed.

"Just where is this far?" Ezry asked. "Maybe this is how they get rid of us, left for eternity nowhere."

"I don't know where we are." With a wry smile, Zak sighed and added, "Although I think Markham Company wanted to get here real bad."

"How long will we be stuck here?" Ezry asked, her fear surmounting her anger.

"There is no telling. As long as the Rabican keeps us here."

"I advise we stay in this compartment until we arrive wherever we're going," Cutter said. "With energy and gravity, we can be fairly comfortable." He smiled and his brows rose fractionally. Cutter's composed cheer didn't deceive Zak.

"Fairly comfortable?" Ezry asked frowning at Cutter. "There is no comfort or safety here at all."

"Give over, Ez," Lock said. "We're all tired of hearing your complaints. No one forced you to stay on the *Vagrant Spirit*, least of all Cutter."

"Shut up, Lock. No one cares what a con thinks."

Lock's brown gaze smoldered at Ezry. "Ex-con."

Ezry shoved away from the table and stomped to her snare bunk.

"There is no telling how long we'll need to stay in the fore compartment. We can't do anything to change our course until we arrive wherever we're going," Zak said.

"Dangerous," Ship Dog agreed.

"Impossible," Lock responded. Renna said nothing.

~ * ~

"You listened?" Cutter asked Jake as he finished stripping off his biosuit. Zak had left for the flight deck shortly before Jake's return. Ship Dog, Lock, Ezry, and Renna slept.

"Yes."

"You trusted the CS9 to keep your message private?"

"Have to—until it doesn't. Then we'll know the truth." Jake sank into one of the lounge chairs and tugged off his boots.

"It might be too late."

"It might."

"And Renna?"

Jake gave him an irritated look. "Distrust her, or at least the situation. I'm more worried about Renna than the CS9. We need her, and the damn thing seems to identify with her."

"What's wrong?" Cutter asked, reading Jake's expression. Jake remained silent a moment, swallowing a laugh. "Too damn much. Renna has our codes. We can't change them without the CS9 learning them." He hesitated. "How attached is Zak to her?"

"Hard to tell. I suspect a lot. Planning on ejecting her?"

"No." A dismissive snort confirmed the uttered denial. "We've already covered that. She's just a pawn—like us."

"What else bothers you?"

"The CS9 transformed the flight deck. Right in front of me. I don't know how we can control it. I don't know how to get back to where we were. Hell, I can't even find out exactly where or when we are. If it wants the codes, I'm sure it can take them, with or without Renna." Jake put his hand across his mouth as if afraid to say more.

Cutter swallowed and put a comforting hand on Jake's shoulder. "Are you sure of what you saw?"

Jake took a ragged breath. "Didn't believe my eyes, not until I got burned." He absently rubbed his left thumb.

"How?"

"Hand rested on the console while the panel transformed."

Cutter picked up his injured hand and inspected Jake's thumb, though Jake pulled against his grip. "Let me see. Don't see any sign of injury."

"Just a small red mark, nothing serious," Jake said. "How much food do we have onboard?"

"Enough…for a while." He used his diagnostic reader for a closer look at the thumb. "This looks clean, don't see anything microscopic. If the wound itches, put some salve on it. Food in stores, maybe enough for eighteen months, longer if rationed. We also have another year of ship's rations. Why? How long do you think we'll be in this situation?"

"Don't know. Who knows where we'll end up?"

"Or if we can get back?"

"The CS9 and the Rabican engine took us out, they can take us back." At Renna's low voice, they turned. She looked bereft, scared, and alone. She took a step nearer. "The CS9 responds to its programming."

So do you. Cutter cut off the thought.

"What do we do, exist forever in some nebulous piece of nowhere?" Jake asked, throwing up his hands. "Is time passing? Will we remain here forever? How will we know?"

"The chronometer changes. We are aware of the change. If there is change, there must be time. We must trust we will emerge in normal space. Once there, we can plan."

Jake hacked a disparaging laugh. "Sounds like an idea." With a huff, he turned away.

Renna watched Jake rise and walk to the meal laid out for him at the table, her face frozen in an expressionless mask. Her gaze switched to Cutter. He had no comfort to offer. He retrieved his diagnostic tools and followed Jake.

Jake relaxed. Cutter looked up and saw Renna had returned to her snare bunk. "She didn't do anything," he told his brother.

"As far as we know. Maybe as far as she knows."

"You think she was manipulated into accepting a berth on this ship?"

"I don't know what to think. Anything is possible."

"What do you suspect?"

"Renna was crewkin. No telling what programming controls her."

"Like triggering whatever device is on the ship?"

"Exactly. Hell, there doesn't need to be a device...she could do damage by herself."

"What do you want to do?" Cutter asked.

"Short of locking her up? Watch her. Make sure she can't change any coding or reprogram any systems." He laughed. "Who to trust... an innocent, psychologically twisted crewmember, or our hijacker...a logically programmed CS9? Makes an interesting dilemma, doesn't it?"

Sixteen

...2179.362.18:56 universal space-time ...mission status ...all systems operational ...insertion point unidentified ...optimal flight progress ...medical and training files on sub speaker renna markham3 integrated and under continual update ...inconsistency in renna markham3 survival ...continued surveillance necessary for mission security ...presence may endanger vagrant spirit crew ...terran crew identified by name only ...medical and training personnel files unobtainable ...jake terran inoculated with new biobot altered from nanobot...

The CS9 followed her through the ship. *As if it counts my steps to the flight deck. It watches me, like the crew watches.* Renna looked at the back of her hand. The implanted medical chip was Markham code and positioned her movement for the CS9. Maybe by Jake's order?

Renna continued to impassively walk the gangway. Lighting came on and then turned off behind her, security hatches unlatched and opened as she approached, closed, and re-latched after she passed through. They let her take flight deck duty. Her duty meant little. The CS9 controlled the Rabican, and Jake ordered the CS9 to confirm all her requests with him. She felt the suspicion surrounding her. She swallowed her despair. The pain remained a hard knot in her throat.

She had almost joined a norm crew...*almost*. Now, they watched her, distrusted her.

Her crew remained in the fore compartment, although life-support had been reestablished throughout the regular habitat module of the ship. She discovered persistent focus on where she traveled, and her immediate goal helped eliminate the illusions. Plus, the more she exposed herself to the effects, the fewer she endured.

No one believed her.

All viewports remained closed and locked. The men reported hallucinatory experiences outside the sheltered area—the inability to determine exactly where they were positioned, of seeming to be standing inside a partition, hatch, or piece of equipment, or having a body part pass through a solid surface. The sensation of their feet walking below the deck rather than on it. They reported parts of the ship seemed to shift, and they often suffered from dizziness or disorientation, or found themselves waking with no sense of the immediate past, or what they were supposed to be doing. Cutter called them fugue episodes caused by the stress affecting everyone. He told them to remain in the fore compartment.

She disobeyed. No one said anything if they noticed.

Ezry did not experience any delusions, probably because she never left the heavily shielded fore compartment. She looked after her few plants or worked on constructing a garment from fabric so luxurious Renna longed to touch the fibers, to find out if the cloth felt as beautiful as it looked. While she sewed, Ezry hummed or sang slow discordant melodies in a hushed voice. The sound made Renna uncomfortable. Whenever Ezry noticed her enough to glare, the singing halted. Ezry's notice made duty on the flight deck an escape.

The CS9 did not record the activity in the fore compartment since Jake had ordered privacy, at least as far as they could tell. Renna remained very circumspect in what she said and did. She noticed the others did also. They remained guarded around her. She knew they suspected she had contributed to their present predicament. Something she couldn't prove or disprove.

Renna sighed. The loss of all she had gained made no difference to her avowed purpose. Losing their trust hurt like a sharp, sudden cut. While she was on the flight deck, the monitors in the fore compartment kept track of the flight deck's panels. Jake had locked her out of coded access. These slights didn't matter. She had promised herself not to fail them.

Boredom, even while frightened, would soon take a toll on the crews' spirit. She knew and doubted her advice weighed much with anyone. Their reactions saddened her. There were no more comfort sessions with Zak. They did not share flight deck duty any longer.

Zak, she, and Jake traded shifts one after another, only to watch monitors.

She wanted to learn about what had abducted them, what had destroyed her life twice.

Reaching the flight deck, Renna waited while the security hatch unlocked and opened. She stepped inside, expecting Jake to be ready to return to the fore compartment. He still sat in the command chair, unmoving at her arrival. His left arm lay cradled in his lap, badly swollen. He didn't answer her calling his name, only stared at the closed turret window.

She hit her connex clip. "Cutter, Jake needs you."

"On my way. What's the matter?" His deep, concern-filled voice answered.

"Jake is unresponsive."

In only a few moments, Cutter and Zak entered the small compartment. Cutter carried a small case. He hovered over Jake, gave him medication. After a brief interval, Jake came to himself. He did not object to Cutter's order for Zak to help him get Jake back to the fore compartment.

"The flight deck," Jake muttered. "Someone, here...always."

"I can handle the duty," Renna said before anyone else spoke. She gave all three brothers a look of confident assurance. "There is nothing, really, to do. You watch all I do from the fore compartment."

"Unnecessary. We'll take alternate twelve-hour shifts," Zak said.

She nodded. The look he gave her made her feel even more alone. The doubt and suspicion she read in his voice strangled her breath, causing a hard, squeezing sensation in her chest. He helped Cutter move Jake.

She took the command chair and read the various panels. The monitor's indicators showed how efficiently the CS9 executed ship operation. "Mission status?"

...mission variables within predicted parameters...

Hearing Dom Dukan's voice speak through the CS9 made her shiver. If the CS9 wanted to upset her, it had found the perfect method. Clearing her throat, she asked, "What are the mission parameters?" The newly formed panel filled with readings, and she quickly compared them to the usual flight panel display. "Who designed the parameters?"

...information unavailable...

Her fingers stilled from the minor adjustment she made to the compartment's life-support panel. Unavailable? Why wouldn't CS9 have access to all its data? "Unavailable due to security protocol, encryption, or wiped?"

...encrypted, partially wiped ...files damaged in irregular shutdown...

That was worse. "List code access permissions."

...no access authorization for personnel aboard ship...

She huffed in frustration. Reports seldom needed codes. "Create a report on mission objectives."

...priority one directive rabican engine to seek shortest space route ...priority two directive preservation of rabican engine log...priority three directive preservation of rabican engine ... priority four directive preservation of cs9m3 system ...priority five directive preservation of markham3 ...priority six directive preservation of markham3 crewkin pod...

Her hands tightened on the edges of the command chair's wide arms. The life sanctity priority had been moved from first to sixth, below even the computer. "What happened on the *Markham3*?"

...cs9m3 and rabican engine operated within design limits...

She swallowed hard and bit her lip to prevent any unprofessional conduct. "Change the mission priority."

...sub speaker renna markham3 lacks authority to change mission parameters...

Emotionlessly, she said, "Your mission failed. The crew died. The *Markham3* was scrapped."

...top three priority directives achieved ...the rabican engine survived ...rabican engine log survived ...cs9m3 survived. mission successful...

"Present the Rabican engine log."

...no access permissions listed for sub speaker renna markham3 ...request denied...

She continued to elicit responses and tried to understand the limits of interaction with the CS9 and the Rabican. Before she knew it, Zak entered the compartment, his expression strained.

"How is Jake?"

"Cutter says he is infected with nanobots. His immune system is trying to destroy them. His body seems unable to filter them from his system."

"Can Cutter remove them?"

"He is unsure."

"Do you want me to stay with you?"

He hesitated. For the first time since entering this strange space, she saw desire in his eyes. "No." His hand caressed her cheek like a whisper of breath. "It is inappropriate." With an active ship, it was. Duty first. She nodded acceptance and left.

Entering the fore compartment, she saw Cutter and Ezry standing over the diagnostic table where Jake lay. Approaching, she asked in a whisper how he fared.

"There is no medication to remove nanobots," Cutter said in a flat, ultra-professional voice.

"The CS9 made them," Renna countered. "It can remove them."

"No! Don't you let that thing do more damage than it already has," Ezry shrieked.

Cutter glared at Ezry with her first loud word. Her voice lowered by her last.

"I'm giving him an auto-immune booster," Cutter said. "Other drugs to alleviate the infectious symptoms. Best to let him sleep and keep an eye on his progress."

Saying nothing, Renna left them and went to where Lock sat at a monitor station. At her approach, he switched the screen display, hiding his work from her.

"You need to speak with Zak," she said.

The expression in his nearly black eyes was hard for her to read, so unlike *Markham3* kin. She recognized suspicion in his reply, "Why?"

"There must be a protocol for promoting the next officer to captain. The CS9 was programmed for crewkin; it will respond only to what it considers the kin's highest dom. The CS9 must be ordered to give crew survival mission priority."

His eyes widened and his lower lip sagged as he stared at her. "It isn't?"

"Priority six."

"No! Who would establish such a priority?"

"Do we tell this thing how it harmed Jake?" Cutter asked. He stood nearby, listening.

Ship Dog emerged from his snare bunk in short underwear, stretching his massive body. The sight suspended Renna's immediate response. Her voice must have reached him, for he walked over.

"Whoever made it. It killed its crew."

Lock's brows rose. "I suppose it did."

"Its logs do not reflect the incident which destroyed the *Markham3* and its crew," Renna said. "The CS9's primary objective was the Rabican engine, which overrode securing the *Markham3* crew's safety. Realigning its objectives will help protect us."

"Lock?" Cutter asked.

"My specialty isn't controlling CS9 type programming. I think Ren is right. Override the protocol directives and make our safety first. Anything making this thing think saving my ass is paramount makes sense to me. If it can be reasoned with."

"Change programming," Ship Dog warned.

"Not possible until we are out of transit space," Renna said. "The CS9 has proved it will take orders only from the *Vagrant Spirit*'s captain."

"How'd you know?" Lock asked, confirming Renna's surmise of their suspicion.

"Because it already has," Cutter spoke quickly. "Jake won't like Zak taking over." He glanced at his patient. "He is unconscious. The fever made him irrational when he was conscious. Maybe we should wait."

"Waiting increases the danger. Our security is why you need to make Zak, or yourself, the temporary captain." Renna ignored the crews' discomfort. "Can you do it?"

Cutter rubbed his jaw with reluctance. "Yes. Zak won't like the situation, either."

"The *Vagrant Spirit* needs a captain," she insisted.

"Ship Dog, Lock, let's go to the flight deck, talk with Zak." Cutter looked at her. "Get some sleep."

Ren kept her gaze on the deck as they prepared to leave. Her exclusion was another sign she was no longer one of them. As they reached the hatch, she warned them. "Be sure to focus on here and now." When the hatch closed, she glanced up. Ezry watched her. Renna went to her snare bunk and pretended to sleep until she did.

Cutter shook her awake. "Ren?"

"I'm awake." She slipped from the net and stood next to him.

"The CS9 has accepted Zak as captain. He wants you on the flight deck."

She nodded and started dressing as Cutter checked on Jake. He spoke in whispers to Ezry. Her slow voice answered him in irritated tones. To Renna, the darkened compartment felt overlade with gloom, never more so than when Cutter followed her to the flight deck.

Once there, Zak motioned her into the copilot's seat. Cutter stood behind her. Zak addressed the CS9. "Open the *Vagrant Spirit* registration logs and make the following changes. List the promotion of Cutter Terran to First Officer."

...promotion logged...

Renna squeezed her eyebrows together when the CS9 answered in a gender-neutral voice.

"Register the surviving crewmember of the *Markham3*, Renna Markham, as part of the *Vagrant Spirit* crew."

...sub speaker renna markham3 logged as vagrant spirit crew...

"She will be logged as Flight Officer Renna Markham."

...promotion logged...

"As noted in *Vagrant Spirit*'s registry decree, all lawful changes of ship rule must be confirmed by the captain and first officer, and designated flight officer. I designate Renna Markham as flight officer for the following change. The CS9M3 will now officially be known as the CS9VS."

...designation logged...

"By captain's order, the CS9VS will log the following changes: first protocol directive—the safety of all ship's personnel. Second protocol directive—the safe return of the *Vagrant Spirit* to the original insertion point."

"Change approved by First Officer, Cutter Terran."

"Change approved by Flight Officer Renna..." It occurred to her she did not want the Markham designation.

"Markham," Zak urged.

Renna forced her voice to a level pitch. "Approved by Acting Flight Officer Renna Markham."

...cs9vs logged protocol directives...

"List the changes."

*...priority one directive the safety of all ship personnel ... priority two directive the safe return of vagrant spirit to original insertion point ...priority three directive preservation of rabican engine log ...priority four directive preservation of rabican engine ...priority five directive preservation of cs9vs system ...priority six directive preservation of markham3 crewkin pod ...*The CS9 continued its list of priorities.

"CS9VS is to remove all directives relating to the *Markham3* and her crewkin pod."

...priority directives adjusted...

"Do you think this worked?" Cutter asked.

"The CS9 logged the changes. It should." Zak said. His face firmed into harsh lines. "Cutter and Lock suggested I do this from the fore compartment, but I won't. Renna, this concerns you...CS9VS, any code orders or change of current code directive made by Flight Officer Renna Markham will be considered invalid."

...order logged...

Zak swallowed. He didn't look at her. "I'm sorry, Ren."

They could not trust her. She understood. Maybe knowing for certain was better than guessing. Their belief saddened her. His glance finally came to her. She turned away. "I will assume duty now, Captain Zak."

Cutter patted her shoulder. The warmth from the touch didn't enter her cold interior. His, "Thank you," seemed genuine. She couldn't be certain anymore. Zak said nothing.

After they left, she checked monitors, adjusting the life-support panel, cooling the compartment to her preferred duty levels. She leaned back into her chair and took a deep breath, releasing her sadness. *No matter if the crew no longer views me as a member, they have taught me how to survive in a norm world. Even if I ultimately must work on another ship, I will fulfill my vow to the Vagrant Spirit.*

She didn't need the codes to achieve her goal. What mattered was learning all she could about the CS9 and the Rabican. If the cognitive support had accomplished its goals according to its programmed protocols, why was the system turned off? Why didn't the CS9 know about the inappropriate shutdown? Why select a failing shortrunner to take the Rabican to reclamation?

"CS9VS, list current system checks for the Rabican. Initiate programming inspection. Compare all programming against original specs for possible alteration."

...systems check progressing...

A few minutes passed before the CS9 reported.

... unauthorized programming found ...cs9 deletes code by the authority of priority two directive...

"Will deletion affect Rabican's performance?"

...no...

"What are the effects of not deleting the programming?"

...catastrophic failure at specified set of space coordinates...

"Display the coordinates." Renna looked at the coordinates and calculated the *Vagrant Spirit*'s location against those of the ship's original travel coordinates. The results stunned her. *If I hadn't mistakenly changed the ship's course...the Vagrant Spirit would never have made Zorah Reclamation Station.* They would have never made their destination. She laughed. Hearing hysteria in her voice, she clamped her hand over her mouth, forcing herself to professional calm. Her course corrections had placed the *Vagrant Spirit* off course and out of harm's way.

"Display logs of Rabican engine performance on *Markham3* and a comparison to the performance reports on the *Vagrant Spirit*."

Seventeen

...2179.365-19:59 universal space-time ...mission status ...rabican operating as projected ...designation changed to cs9vs ...priority logs updated ...renna markham initiated systems check indicating knowledge of improper code ...priority two directive requires investigation ...structural integrity of vagrant spirit unknown ... nanobots sent to determine and repair ship configuration ...mission parameters require check of all systems for failure ...interface to vagrant spirit systems begun...

With a vicious slice, Ezry cut off the end of an onion. She had cried when Cutter told her all the plants left in the ship garden were dead.

Frozen. Airless. No pressure. Her heart pounded frighteningly. *Didn't matter. Had more seeds. Could start fresh.* The knife slammed against the cutting surface with a satisfying chink just as the onion's juice hit her face. Tears flowed from her stinging eyes, and, in a strange way, easing her anxiety. These onions had come from the end of her last harvest; there wouldn't be more.

Twenty-nine days in this nowhere space, days of terror while Jake moved around looking like one of the zombies from Stan's traveling show. Luckily, she hadn't had to play one. Stan thought the zombies added a scary element to the entertainment. Jake didn't entertain, just frightened. She cursed out her anger in all the filthy words she knew in a fear-liberating invocation. No one could help them. They couldn't help themselves. *Dead. They were all as good as dead.*

Lock concentrated on some obtuse program assigned to him while she chopped stupid onions. Zak slept off his twelve-hour shift of flight deck duty in his snare bunk, which meant the podder watched the flight deck, thank heaven. At least she didn't hover around here sticking her face where it wasn't wanted. Ezry glanced across to where Ship Dog sat. He had barely moved all day. His limited conversation had dried up with Vera's shutdown.

"Smile, honey. It's New Year's Eve," Cutter said, pulling some bread from a jerrybuilt convection oven. He had delved into his stock of pre-made preserves to make the meal.

Ezry didn't think she'd spoken aloud. Everyone rebuked her if she called the podder what she was, like they weren't afraid of her, too.

She forced her lips up at the corner. From Cutter's grin, her smile must have missed cheery. She returned to cutting up the onion he'd harvested from the dead farm. Hopefully to mix with reconstituted zucchini; just enough to go around if Ship Dog curbed his appetite. *Hell, if she curbed hers.*

The things her body accomplished even with the paralyzing fear holding her mind hostage—like eat and sleep—were amazing. At the oblique reminder of their circumstances, her mind flooded with terror, making her hands shake. She put the knife down, afraid she might cut off a finger. Her stomach squeezed into an acid knot of contained terror. *My appetite will not pose a problem.*

Arms enwrapped her from behind. Cutter nuzzled on her neck. She enjoyed the frizzle of feeling for a moment, the comfort of contact.

Cutter yawned, killing the moment. Her anger prevailed. "Don't you go honeying me." She had as much difficulty finding sleep as Cutter did and repressed her sympathetic yawn.

"We're still alive, Ez. We'll get back, you'll see."

"Dreamer," she accused. "Always seeing the best in everything. How?"

"Don't know. Know there is no other way to feel. Especially with you here."

"If I'd known accepting you meant accepting this predicament, I wouldn't be here." She cut a few more slices. "My prospects would be a whole lot more secure if I'd stayed with Satellite Stan's Voyaging Theater and Curiosity Show."

He laughed. "Problems always improve and seem more manageable with time, memory, and distance," Cutter said in a soothing voice. He rubbed her shoulders between nibbling kisses along her neck.

His touch felt good, warm. She ignored his overture. "How you can be horny in this situation, I don't know. Jake's near death. The *Vagrant Spirit* could implode at any second. All of you cater to that podder..." Cutter squeezed her shoulder, cutting off her word with his warning.

"Give over, Ez," he said. "Jake's alive, and Ren works like two crewmen. We're family. Onboard, though, we have to be crew first."

"She's not family. None of you trusts her, either. You're all hypocrites." Cutter's comforting hands fell away. "I'm sorry about talking bad about Jake. Don't wish him harm."

"He'll recover. We'll survive. Ren will help us."

"You trust her? With your life—with the ship?" She huffed, glaring at Cutter. "Finish fixing dinner, Cutter." She gathered the onion slices and put them in the cooker. He sighed and went back to work.

At dinner call, Ship Dog rose from his hammock. The table was set, and Lock woke Zak to join them. Jake tottered to the table and sank into a seat. "Where's Ren?" he asked.

"I called her," Ezry said. "She wanted to stay on the flight deck."

"Said she wasn't hungry and she'd eat later," Lock confirmed.

Ezry smiled triumph as disbelieving expressions turned to resignation.

With or without the podder's presence, the celebration of New Year's Eve fell short of festive. Zak returned to his hammock immediately after he finished. Lock and Ship Dog started a card game. When Cutter started loading a plate, she protested, "Don't you go catering to her."

"She enjoys my meals, Ez."

"I'll take it to her," Jake said. He waved away Cutter's concern. "I can make it. Might be tired all the time, but I can make it to the flight deck with a plate."

~ * ~

Renna knew the crew was holding a celebration of the year's end. She knew the day better as Kin Day. A day when promotions were given, honors bestowed, and kin talents celebrated. *Let them celebrate. Maybe their festivities would cheer them.* She didn't feel like celebrating, not when there were more pressing concerns. The *Vagrant Spirit* came first.

Renna realized Zak knew as well as she that their presence on the flight deck accomplished nothing as far as the ship's flight or control. She kept her duty rotation because crewkin training demanded she do so, necessary or not. His training probably demanded it, too. The strange readings on the Rabican panel seemed nothing but gibberish. Communications and navigation didn't work, not in this space. They'd had no idea what starting Vera would do or how the CS9 directed nanobots had changed the *Vagrant Spirit*, for she suspected if it had changed the cargo bay and the flight deck, it had also altered other parts of the ship.

The CS9 controlled nearly every system. They did not know if the cognitive support had constructed duplicate systems for life-support and other basic ship functions, or if it had taken over existing systems. If the original systems remained, were they operational, or had the CS9 dismantled and reassembled the pieces and parts molecule by molecule as it had done in the cargo bay? Afraid power linkage would give the CS9 access to what little they still controlled, Zak had decided not to initiate any system.

It was not only her sense of duty calling her to the flight deck. Here the routine calmed her, let her contemplate her past without the distractions of Ezry's hostility and the charged atmosphere in the fore compartment.

Only here could she study the newly created panel and try to figure out the gibberish of readings flying across the panel indicators. During the hours of duty, she watched the panels, taking notes in her intel while sorting through her thoughts and memories. Off duty, she most often worried about Ship Dog, who could no longer sing for Vera, and who now sat in a morose lump in the fore compartment, and she worried about the discord she heard among Ezry and everyone else. Lock seemed more agitated, less talkative. Of more concern to her was that Cutter's calm wisdom had ended with the disassembly of his kitchen and Ezry's coldness. She missed his meals more than anything, except perhaps Zak's company.

"Does the CS9 have access to Renna *Markham3*'s medical record?" she asked, after her trail of thought left her wondering if escaping her past was possible.

...cs9 stores renna markham3 files. They are encrypted with markham company security codes... Dom Dukan's voice said.

He deserves no title except mean, petty Dukan. Does the CS9 know how much I hate him?

She ignored it when she began to shiver. *Calmness, professionalism, duty.* "You no longer function for Markham Company. Display them." As she gave the order, she wondered if she really wanted to know.

...flight officer renna markham lacks vagrant spirit authority...

"As the last Markham Company employee involved, I invoke Right-to-Know Law UNC5230 section 2a titled Citizens' Rights." All of her off-duty reading paid off, for Markham had never taught anything about individual interests or of laws protecting them.

A file opened on the monitor. She did not recognize the person giving the report. The woman's clinical voice, empty of inflection, reported the fate of experimental *Marham17* Crewkin Pod, trial five. "The ten zygotes used in this trial responded to the application of natural clone chemicals, resulting in six-hundred-sixty-three viable eggs." The woman went on for some time about 'gene alternations,' which might prove promising.

The file shifted to a man's visage and vocal. "With the discovery of the project's lead technician's subterfuge backed by the Karier Company, and this subordinate's subsequent felony conviction, the committee believes this pod sabotaged beyond reclamation. The contamination of the altered gene groups led to the Y chromosome. The pod resulted in predominately male gender zygotes. We believe this alteration will create a dominance imbalance in the kin-pod formed from this cluster. This institutes a high improbability of return on cost for continued development. By the determination of the Markham Company Board of Directors, this pod will be terminated. We are hibernating fifty of the female eggs for further study and future gene donation."

The next entry was marked three years later. "The Markham17 female zygote 217 has been reactivated for inclusion in the new *Markham3* crewkin group. The Board is deeply concerned about the failing viability of the latest egg production of this historical crew. Designers feel this last incarnation of the *Markham3* genotype lacks sufficiently dominant personalities to produce viable doms, let alone a speaker capable of social interaction outside the pod. They predict the inclusion of the super-dominant genotype of the terminated *Marham17* pod will help salvage this ship crew. Nursery has been instructed with conditioning programs to ensure successful integration."

After that entry, a succession of personnel gave development facts on the infant named Renna, short for renascent as an indication of her hoped-for effect on the pod.

"Nurses have been instructed to reinforce subservient status in infant 217."

Renna flushed, hearing the voice. They just as often called her by her number.

"Infant 217's status in the crewkin group must be established to control a natural dominance trait. The management team hopes encouragement of the selected dominant males will affect control over 217 and, at the same time, train and develop their command by increasing their dominance traits."

"Three days in confinement have resulted in toddler 217 relinquishing a tendency to outperform the dominants in *Markham3* crewkin-pod."

Memories flooded Renna. Dom Dukan hitting her, taking away what she worked on, and presenting the work as his own. An act the nurses encouraged. Nurses comprised of the older *Markham3* generation. The same nurses laughed when they shut her in the punishment closet, denied her permissions given her other kin, and taught her kin to treat her the same way. A thousand misdemeanors summarily punished somehow resurfaced in her memory.

Her past became clear in a way never perceived before, leaving her angry, terrified, and confused. Her instruction had been for the good of the kin, to train a naturally rebellious spirit, hadn't it? She understood another crewkin dictum. *It was necessary.*

A forgotten emotion swept through her. Pleasure as she watched the nurses leave the port hatch for the last time. Her elation upon the occasion, carefully hidden from her kin, far surpassed their own joy at their attainment as the ship's primary crew.

A subdued snick from the hatch announced someone entering. Renna quickly switched the file off. She rose when Jake entered the flight deck, grabbed the container plate, allowing him to sink into the command seat. His hands grasped the wide armrest in support as he lowered himself.

"Thanks." He spoke in breathless rasps. He looked aged, off-color with lines of exhaustion graphing his face. A week's worth of stubble covered his face. It was strange to see him scruffy after he had become so neat. *At least he is nothing like Dukan.*

"Are you here to relieve me?" She regretted the disbelief in her voice.

"No, just brought you dinner." He grinned, panting his answer. His crooked smile disappeared when he noticed her face. "Why are you crying?"

"I'm not. Emotion on duty is forbidden." She placed the plate on the broad flat service arm of the co-pilot's chair, wiped her face the best she could, and amended her answer. "I am crying over what is lost and unrecoverable. I told Lock I was not hungry."

Jake's smile appeared weak and askew as he caught his breath. "Not true—you're always hungry."

"Today is Kin Day." An unexpected, painful gasp broke from her throat, and Renna sobbed in an unexpected uncontrolled manner. *Calmness, professionalism, duty.* The harder she tried to control herself, the louder the harsh sounds grew and the more rampant her tears fell, both deafening and blinding her. Jake rose and wrapped his arms around her. She hid her face against his chest.

"Hush, it's okay," he said.

She knew it was not.

"I've tried so hard. Now I know Markham tried to kill you because they want the engine destroyed. They want me dead. Today is a crewkin traditional celebration. I have no kin, and I don't belong here, so maybe I should be dead. I failed you, failed the *Vagrant Spirit*. Even Zak named me Markham when he renamed the CS9."

He gave her a gentle shake, saying in an uneven breath, "Hush... Ren. I'm sorry. I have to sit down." He sank back into the roomy chair, sliding to one side, pulling her down with him, and letting her rest against his chest.

"I'm sorry for my unprofessional display," she said when the spasms stopped, leaving her empty and ashamed.

"Not unprofessional. Cried a few times myself lately."

The small tinks and whirs of the flight deck somehow soothed her, along with Jake's breathing and warmth. She took a deep calming breath.

"You belong here whether by the manipulation of Markham Company or by pure chance. Tell me what Zak said."

She explained about the priority change, Zak giving the CS9 *Vagrant Spirit* status. "I understand. I am Markham, although I don't wish to be, and I will always be Markham. Your kin believe me capable of betraying the ship, of endangering you and the *Vagrant Spirit*. Crewkin would have the same doubts."

"You're wrong. You're part of this crew."

"Part of the crew, yes, only temporarily. Not like Ezry, Lock, and Ship Dog, never kin. I swear to you, I wouldn't cause harm to the *Vagrant Spirit* or to anyone on her."

"I know, Ren. Maybe stress affects norms more than crewkin, makes us irrational." He patted her arm. "You've helped in ways you don't even know."

She stared at Jake in disbelief.

He smiled, nodding. "You helped me purge some ghosts after I attacked you."

"You did not attack me. I deserved worse. Logic should have told me you knew of the problem and not compensated for the drift."

"Why? Do crewkin mind read?"

"Of course not. Still, I should've realized."

"You're irrational!" His voice held a hint of laughter.

"Maybe norms have no monopoly on the irrational."

"As I was saying, when I lost my temper, I was wrong. Such behavior is wrong for any commanding officer, no matter what ship he serves." He looked away. "It wasn't the only time I'd injured someone in anger. I thought the first time was just a righteous act where the sod deserved what I handed out. When I hurt you, I realized the problem was me."

"You did not hurt me. I was only weak, not eating enough, not caring enough."

"Stop blaming yourself." He shook her.

She remained silent a moment. "Who did you hurt in anger?"

He gave a sad chuckle. "My superior officer."

She felt shock jolt her. "You hit your dom?"

"Decked him." He sighed. "You won't believe this. I used to be as neat as Zak, only I lost the one thing that mattered to me."

"Your position in the military?"

"The chance to captain an SSC ship. This officer...this oaf..."

"The one you decked?"

"Yes. He made a command mistake and let the blame fall on me. What with me hitting him—well, I lost my commission. Among norms such a commission means everything. Command refused to reinstate me until after an investigation. I didn't wait for the investigation. Zak resigned in support of me. We returned to the *Vagrant Spirit*. Our dad had died, and Cutter had taken over the ship. He was failing to make it as a shortrunner and asked us to help."

"Why are you telling me this?"

"Because you deserve to know. And to thank you, because I blamed everyone and everything for my disgrace, except where the responsibility belonged. I thought of the *Vagrant Spirit* as a comedown. Now I know I need to work to deserve even a shortrunner captain's billet. Appreciate this—I am seldom this reflective or repentant."

Uncomfortable, Renna shifted to the other chair. "I have something you need to know." She hesitated before speaking, "Markham Company did not program me to suicide and destroy the *Vagrant Spirit*. They would be afraid such a tactic would fail as it had before. All their instilled training couldn't make me suicide with my kin. They'd never be sure I would carry out their orders, even if they twisted my mind to think I should kill you. Instead, they inserted a sub-routine into the Rabican. An order to self-destruct when the internal gyroscope crossed certain coordinates."

Jake shifted. "How do you know?"

"I asked the CS9 to make a programming comparison analysis of the Rabican pre and post *Markham3* flight. Whoever inserted the code didn't alter the backup. They left battery power running to impel the chronometer and gyroscope. They never anticipated a reboot. The CS9 isolated the altered sequences from the initial program. When we reached the coordinates on the last stretch to Zorah, the engine was to overload and implode."

"Are you sure? We would have..." He didn't finish.

"Yes. Following Zak's order for the new priority directives, the CS9 deleted the altered commands. You saved the *Vagrant Spirit*."

"It wasn't my order."

"By your crew's action."

Jake tilted her head and kissed her brow. Renna searched his face, hesitating. *He wants comfort.* She slipped her hand into his tunic, spreading her fingers across his stomach. His eyes widened as she leaned forward and kissed his mouth. His face was bristly and rough, his lips hard. They softened as her lips swept across his. She tasted him with her tongue.

With a sudden shove, he pushed her away.

"Zak..."

Renna looked over her shoulder. She had never heard the hatch release. Zak stood there.

"...It's not," Jake said. Zak had already left. Jake rose to his feet. His movement pushed her to the floor.

"What were you doing?" he demanded.

The sense she'd committed a huge mistake dawned. "I thought you sought comfort."

She watched the restraint with which he curbed his anger. His rage escaped in his voice. "If I wanted comfort, you wouldn't have to think about what I wanted, you'd know. I'd never betray Zak that way." He sighed. "Hell, you wouldn't understand." His spurt of energy left him in a resigned sigh. He took her hand, helped her to her feet, and grasped her shoulders. "You okay?"

"Yes."

"Ren, you don't have to offer anyone comfort if you don't want to. If you do, and they do, fine. There is no requirement, no force, and no unwilling participation. Understand?"

"Yes." She nodded like a norm.

He nodded to her. It felt like a dance.

"Good. Stay here. Eat your dinner." He pointed to the plate of food.

When the hatch closed, she slowly lowered herself into the command seat. Reviewing the last few minutes, she realized he had confirmed her worst fear. They kept her as crew, a necessary ship hand, but never kin. Markham Company had destroyed any possibility for her, just like they destroyed the *Markham3*, and somehow, she kept proving the wisdom of her fate.

The food had congealed. She ate because an order was an order. She slogged through each cold bite, feeling them settle like hard lumps in her belly. As she ate, she remembered Cutter had read her medical file. He would find out all she was...and was not. Shame and misery engulfed her.

~ * ~

After Zak left to visit Renna, Ezry watched Cutter wander over to the table where Lock and Ship Dog gambled with cheese crackers for markers. As she predicted, dinner had been a drab affair, the cheer forced and the conversation dismal. She made a few stitches in the garment she sewed. The needle and thread kept her hands busy and her mind occupied. She ignored the men for a moment until Lock cheered, rose from his seat in a champion's pose, and pranced around the table with his black braids flapping around his head.

"Still the best ever!" He waltz-hopped around the compartment.

Ship Dog made a sullen sound, pushing the cards aside. They spread out and fluttered to the floor. "Cheat." He slumped back into his chair, pouting.

Lock made an offended face and waved an arm in a rejecting manner. "Hah. I didn't cheat. Didn't have to." He continued his taunting dance.

"It would be the first time," Cutter said.

Lock showed his offense by hopping to Cutter, miming punching him. After a minute, he resumed his dance. "Don't cheat. Took advantage of the situation. Be nice, I got you a New Year's gift."

Cutter's brows rose in an exaggerated manner at Lock's claim.

"Just look in your journal. It's all there."

Cutter frowned. "I told you to crack a code, not invade my privacy."

"Didn't read a thing!" Lock flashed a huge grin. "Except your recipe for BBQ sauce."

"My secret recipe!" Cutter sputtered.

"Not any longer. I'm going to sell it soon as we get back. Payment for services rendered." Lock twirled, away punching the air. "Happy New Year!"

Ezry's smiled at Lock's playfulness. The brief playfulness ended when the hatch opened, and Zak entered the compartment without greeting or looking at anyone. The last few weeks had taken a toll on everyone. The toll showed most on Zak, who looked scruffy.

She sighed. Bathing was hard enough, laundry near impossible, and no one had returned to their quarters to pull out more clothes. It was like the rest of the ship no longer existed, only the problems of here and now. Even basic niceties were mostly ignored.

Zak stopped at the far side of the room and leaned an arm against the bulwark. After a long hesitation, Cutter asked, "Aren't you going to relieve Ren?"

"Ask my brother. Ask Jake." Zak slammed his fist into a nearby storage tank, his hand sinking into the partially filled container. The loud whomp of the container covered the hatch opening, but not its closing. Jake stood there, ashen, and wheezing.

"Nothing happened, Zak," Jake said in the overwrought silence.

"Only because I walked in on you," Zak shouted.

"Untrue. I'd never betray you."

"She was willing to do whatever you asked."

"I was only comforting her."

Zak huffed. "Yeah. I could tell. You're always cutting in."

Ezry cringed. This tone always provoked Jake. He was silent a moment before he retaliated.

"If you had been a little more sensitive, she wouldn't have had to turn to me." The accusing words drove Zak to charge Jake. Cutter caught and held him just short of his goal.

"Like I supported you? And just like you, she betrayed me."

"I never betrayed you! You didn't have to resign. No one forced you."

"Damn straight. Only made me look ignorant and incapable."

"Is that what this is about? You not achieving command rank? You accomplished that all by yourself."

"You were always the super achiever. What chance did I have?"

"Always making excuses, Zak?"

"If you weren't so damned weak, I'd deck you!"

Jake laughed. "Go ahead, it's the only opportunity you're likely to get!"

"Stop it! Both of you." Cutter demanded. Ezry recognized his temper breaking. "What happened?"

"I walked in on him and Renna sharing an intimate moment," Zak said. Innuendo dripped off every word.

Oh hell, not again, not to Zak. Guilt swamped Ezry, although there was really nothing to feel bad about. She and Zak were never intimate, not like that podder, throwing herself at all the men.

"And if you'd waited two seconds, you'd have known nothing was going on," Jake snapped. "I don't need to poach your woman, not if Ren still wants you."

"She's crewkin. She'd offer anyone comfort!" Zak shouted. "I..."

"Yeah," Jake smirked. "Nice attitude. If it's you she's offering comfort, fine. If she looks at any other man, she's what? A crewkin slut? Or didn't you mean that—only think it?"

"She might be," Ezry said, breaking in. "You know nothing about her. She could be anything."

"Ez, stay out of this," Cutter ordered, he turned to Zak. "She doesn't understand."

"I got a right to speak my mind!" Ezry jumped up. "We've had nothing but trouble since that podder came onboard, and you all know it."

"She's right," Lock said. "We don't even know if we'll survive this last batch. Who knows what she's capable of? Or what she has been programmed to do?"

"Or incapable of, like loyalty or faithfulness," Zak said.

A breath of righteousness filled Ezry. At least Zak knew now. The woman was poison.

"How could she when you didn't understand her enough to support her when she needed it?" Jake suddenly leaned over, bracing his hands against his knees in exhaustion. Silence followed. When

Zak touched him, Jake shrugged off his twin's touch. Zak's mouth firmed in a grim face. "I'll go relieve Renna." His voice was hard and flat, a tone Ezry had never heard before.

"Leave her alone...Captain," Jake gasped.

"Stop it, Jake." Cutter grabbed Jake by the arm to keep him standing.

Zak turned around. "That's why, isn't it? You can't stand me being in charge and having something beyond this ship. Yeah, I'll leave her alone...brother."

"You had no right to entrap her into a relationship with her unaware of how such things work."

"Since losing your career, you just have to prove your leadership with all of us, don't you? Just make sure you follow your own advice!"

"You've said enough, Zak," Cutter said. He urged Jake toward a bunk while his gaze stayed on Zak until he reached the hatch.

Jake spoke in a harsh, gasping breath. "At least I reached command rank."

Zak halted. He did not turn around or say a word. A moment later, the hatch closed behind him.

"It's all her fault. Never had discord like this before," Ezry said. A look at Lock showed his joyous fling had ended. "Happy New Year!"

Eighteen

...2180.001-05:37 universal space-time ...mission status ...rabican operation continues under predicted parameters ...nanobots finish hull memory grid ...processor relays established language interface building ... mission in jeopardy ...unable extract jake terran biobots ...crew remain confined in fore compartment ...crew experience problems in traversing bubble shields...

Following the only ship etiquette she knew, Renna kept her eyes on Zak's boots to indicate her contrition. She knelt and spread her hands in supplication. "I offered Jake comfort. My actions were wrong. I'm sorry." It belatedly occurred to her she didn't know how norms expressed repentance.

"Get up!" Zak's demanded in loathing tones.

Crewkin behavior. She cringed and rose but dared not glance at him, afraid of the tone in his voice. After a lengthy pause, much like one Dom Dukan would use to control himself, Zak asked for her report, his voice curt.

"Please forgive my fault." One glance showed the grimness of Zak's expression and the uselessness of her plea. *Calmness, duty demands it.* She bit her lip hard enough to prevent emotion.

"You didn't know better. Forget it." He turned to the command panel.

"Yes, I did." She swallowed her guilt. "You told me how you wanted us. I should not have offered comfort. Your ways are different from what I have been taught. I thought it not right to leave..." she hesitated, almost saying kin, "...crew in need. It would have been a punishable offense on *Markham3*."

He didn't respond while he moved his hand over the panel, readjusting the compartment's climate control to warmer. "I'm sorry, too. I expected too much...too soon for you to get involved. We're different in our expectations. I can't share you. It will be better if we don't...seek each other's comfort. No apology is needed. Go, Renna."

"Because I am of Markham? I swear..." *I can change.* She looked at him in desperation, unwilling to accept his decision. *I must convince him I'm not a Markham pawn. I am innocent.*

His expressionless gaze found her. He gave her a bleak smile. "No explanations needed...please, just go."

She stared at him, lowered the arm she had extended toward him. *It's impossible to convince him; facts condemn me.* She left. Once outside the flight deck, she started toward the forward compartment but stopped. She had caused trouble between kin, between Zak and Jake. *While different from crewkin, were born kin as closely bound? Were her actions as awful an offense as subversion was between crewkin?*

Enduring the illusions outside the heavily shielded fore compartment seemed preferable to facing the deserved shunning of the *Vagrant Spirit*'s crew. The effects seemed to lessen the longer she stayed outside the shields anyhow.

I should have known better. If I have learned anything on this ship, I understand now how norms don't behave like unrestrained children or like damned podders. Norms loved before they made a sexual commitment. Cutter and Ezry proved that. Had Zak loved me? She stopped with the thought. *Even when Cutter is angry with Ezry, he comforts her, thinks of her before anyone else.* Her chest seemed to constrict. *Has my ingrained training destroyed a real chance to belong here?*

She refused to cry. At the ladder to her slip-in bunk, she stopped and opened her personal locker. Her clothes and hygiene gear were in the forward compartment. Her few mementos of her kin were stored inside this locker. She picked up the portrait pad and thumbed through the likenesses, all so similar, and so very different from the Terran crew. While she recognized each face, for the first time their visages looked too much alike. Of all the faces, only a handful brought grief: those who liked her despite her many flaws, who upon occasion protected her, and who would share comfort with her. At Sen's likeness, she fumbled, ready tears oozing from her eyes.

She sniffed hard, heard Sen's admonition. *Once you start crying, once you allow unseemly emotional expression, crying comes easy, tears creep up on you, unaware. Sen knew. Crying was her prime fault.* Her emotional responses had kept her at a low grade, despite her exceptional task skills. Renna wiped away the offending moisture and dropped the pad back into the locker, slamming the door close. Tears came without volition, falling faster until a torrent of pain flooded her eyes, stinging, and blinding.

"Damn Markham Company!" She kicked her locker, kicked it until her foot hurt, screaming newly learned invectives at unknown administrators and directors until hoarseness stopped her, and her throat ached.

She slammed her hands against the partition while she gasped for breath. Sinking to her knees, she continued to cry, feeling her entire being fracturing into a thousand pieces. Exhausted by her outburst, she slouched on the deck.

Dukan didn't kill my kin. Markham did. My kin and I were nothing more than tools, cogs to be used and replaced, hardly human. A heated flush swept through her. *They taught us kin were better than norms. Now I know I'm less, so much less.*

~ * ~

Climbing into her slip-in bunk, Renna lay awake. Her thoughts ran in many directions, only to return to her current disgrace. Sleep would not come; she missed the sound of her crew's breathing, the sound of their voices and movements while she rested. *Not facing them was cowardly.* She pulled her length out of the slip-in and left her last safe haven.

Cutter sat at the table, sipping a beverage in the darkened compartment. An overhead light illuminated the area around him; darkness obscured all else. The others slept or at least kept to their snare bunks.

"You were a long time returning." Cutter's voice was pitched low. "It's dangerous out there."

She hadn't expected him to speak to her. Staring at him, she approached with reluctant steps and joined him. "I walked the ship."

"Don't blame you. I hate quarrels, too." Cutter attempted a pathetic grin. "I've endured enough of them the last few years."

"I am sorry. You warned me. I didn't understand." She avoided his gaze and checked the chronometer. "You are up late."

His chuckle matched the hushed tone of their voices. "Just got up. I can't seem to sleep. Nobody waited to see the year turn."

Renna swallowed. "I ruined your celebration."

"Not you...the situation, stress, long-standing family conflicts all collided tonight. I thought something common like an ordinary holiday celebration would help everyone forget where we are." His half-smile appeared as he shrugged. "Maybe relieve some of the stress. I was wrong."

"Yesterday was always an important kin occasion."

"Is that why you didn't join us?"

"No. My presence always seems to put a damper on your gatherings."

"Tell me about your special kin day."

She did, ending, "Zak and Jake are angry with me." She watched his face, which remained carefully neutral. "They did not order you to shun me?"

Sympathy softened his eyes, and she had to contain the rage his compassionate expression brought. "No one will shun you, Ren, or hit you, or make you feel less a person. You just upset an ongoing rivalry." He patted her hand. "Go to bed."

"You read my medical file?" Her dinner crept up her gullet, and she swallowed to force it back down.

"Yes. Lock broke the code. Does it matter?"

"To know how I was made shames me—as if I am nothing more than another tool for Markham Company." She looked away and changed the subject. "Is Jake recovering? He seems very sluggish."

"No. The drugs suppress his body's reaction to the bots. The medication's effects are weakening him. I'm still hoping his body will naturally filter the bots out. Go get some sleep."

She followed Cutter's order. When she woke, she learned he was wrong. Ezry, of course, seldom talked to her, now neither did Jake or Zak. Worse, they seemed to avoid each other as much as they did her, although Zak watched her. The enormity of her mistake revealed itself as one of Ship Dog's stretches revealed the extent of his hairiness.

During the long hours of duty, her mind considered means of atonement. There was only one. Get the *Vagrant Spirit* back to its home space and leave. The means to return existed with the CS9.

~ * ~

Cutter joined Zak on the flight deck. He felt as unkempt as Zak looked. Slackness about hygiene during the last week had taken its toll on everyone. It didn't particularly bother him, but Zak's neglect worried him because Zak hated disorder.

Zak glanced at him before returning his attention to the panel's flow of information.

"How's Jake?"

"Holding his own. What's going on between you two?"

"Besides Renna? All the old stories."

"So why take it out on Jake now?"

Zak didn't answer directly. "What are you doing here? Trying to make peace or taking a break from Ezry?"

Cutter chuckled at the gibe. "She can be difficult, especially in a precarious situation."

"Guess I was lucky there."

"Ren and Jake are not like what happened between you, Ezry, and me."

"I invited Ezry on board. At the time it felt like a good idea. She saved me from myself and found herself unemployed because of it. I liked her. You fell in love. Ezry just saw me as an escape, exactly the same as Ren."

"An escape— maybe I was one, too, a safer one. Doubts come easier out here."

"Ezry asked if I could abstain from casual sex. I wasn't committed to her." He took a deep breath. "Times have changed. I think I fell in love with Ren. I wanted her to want me, Cutter, not just give comfort to someone she considers a dom. I thought she knew. Maybe my feelings are only infatuation."

"Ren didn't choose Jake over you. Crewkin have a completely different standard for social interactions."

"Ren said as much. Cutter, unless you have something about ship's business to discuss, leave."

"Don't let being captain go to your head."

"The title may only be pro-tem, the authority..."

"...is bestowed by the family."

"And training. Despite what Jake thinks, I was a good officer, just not the scintillating star he became."

"A falling star, as it turned out. Yes, you and Jake have the training. I was dismal at command."

Zak looked at him. "You can't blame yourself—you trained to be a doctor, not a ship's captain."

"And right now, the ship is in imminent danger. There seems little any of us can do but ride it out."

Zak's lips firmed. He stared at the flight board for a moment. "Jake is right. I blame everyone else for my shortcomings. Don't worry; I'm just tired of losing, just tired period. You look exhausted, too."

Cutter swiped his hand across his eyes. "Yeah, we all are. Everyone but Renna seems to have trouble sleeping."

"Because she is crewkin?"

"Perhaps. Crewkin were developed for isolation, so she's used to it in many ways. I had Lock break the code on Renna's medical file."

Zak continued to monitor the flight board, seemingly inordinately interested in some circuit's reading. Cutter wondered what he had said that triggered Zak's reaction. "Was she programmed to blow us up?"

"No, nothing so insidious."

Zak huffed, "Didn't think so." He reconnoitered the control panels.

"Jake said she found the Rabican held catastrophic programming and disarmed the danger. We've verified the code changes in the Cognitive Support logs."

Zak looked at him, shocked. "She doesn't have authority for such commands...how...?"

"She had the CS9 perform a pre-emptive response to your realignment in mission priorities—ship safety at issue."

Fear entered Zak's voice. "The cargo was rigged to explode? The *Vagrant Star* would be listed as another ship never making port... the victim of some unknown space accident?" He swore. "Markham somehow planned this." He hesitated. "You don't trust her."

Cutter tightened his lips and shook his head. "No. Want to, but can't. Not now, not until we learn more about this situation." Cutter sighed. "I've been duped before." He looked around the tight confines with a mild shudder, glad he didn't have to spend much time here, and glad he didn't travel the gangway twice daily. "Without Vera running, without control of the lateral engines, this must be a tedious duty."

"Ren and I try to find a key to understand this." His hand waved at a panel displaying a constant stream of data. "I communicate with CS9, keep watch on climate controls and life-support, get used to the new configuration. The exterior sensors are inoperative, can't measure anything."

Cutter looked around at the monitors. "Are you watching her?"

Zak looked at the monitor in question. The camera caught Renna walking down a lower deck gangway. Before he looked at Cutter with disgust, a strange expression crossed his face...*regret?* Cutter wondered what private moment Zak had witnessed on the monitor. Cutter shook his head. Talking about the privacy of a person who had never known the concept was ridiculous.

"I'm not stalking her. The CS9 watches her all the time. Do you know why she wanders the ship?"

"Maybe to exercise. Maybe she is afraid of us. Why don't you ask her?"

Zak shrugged. "She's obsessed with the CS9. Says it is dangerous. Maybe she has lost rational perspective."

"Why does the thing follow her? Does it track everyone?" Cutter leaned forward to watch the monitor. "Even in the forward compartment?"

"No. Only Ren, and it never follows her into the forward compartment. Not at least on these monitors."

"Have you asked it why?"

Zak gave him a leveling look. "Why? The CS9 says she is kin from the first crew. It seems deluded in believing Ren either saved the Rabican from reclamation or caused its termination."

Cutter swore. "Maybe it senses her distrust, or maybe it knows something about her we don't. After all, we only have her version of events on the *Markham3*."

Zak's gaze swiveled back to him. "I'd believe Renna before I'd believe the CS9."

"I don't know. Computers only give facts."

"What do you suspect? Something you found in her medical file?"

"More than a medical file." Cutter rose to return to the forward compartment. "A complete dossier on how to create a crewkin pod— from conception to training. I'm sure the CS9 has the record. Makes interesting reading."

Nineteen

...2180.023-08:44 universal space-time ...mission status ...initial emergence date lapsed ...no dimension indicators triggered ... structural integrity established to rabican specifications ... language translation complete ...crew suspicious of flight officer renna markham performance on the markham3 ...cs9vs logs missing specified time period ...searching wiped memory for file fragments...

Swiping her intel across a partition, Renna read the analyzer function's reading of the wall's temperature, its density, composition, and electromagnetic activity. Inspecting the ship had become a self-ordained task on the first day of insertion. No one commented on her absence from the forward compartment outside of her duty time on the flight deck. Exposure made the illusions dissolve. Except for the days blending one into another, nothing changed.

She hesitated. Except for the forty-second day in transit. The day the CS9 predicted expulsion had come and passed. Off duty at the time, she observed how the crew watched the chronometer until the forty-third day arrived. When the *Vagrant Spirit* remained in transit, they fell into an uneasy silence. Their reaction disturbed her. Since then, they had become increasingly despondent. Their attitudes were apathetic and belligerent in turns. The crew's state scared her more than the ship's situation. Even Cutter had fallen into gloom.

Their hibernation in the forward compartment worried her. She would have preferred to live as they did before. They did not want to hear her opinion. So, since she didn't want further estrangement from them, she kept quiet. Even if they hated her, she wanted to be with them. They mattered to her, and she wanted their company. Finished, she headed back to their living quarters.

Stepping through the hatch into the forward compartment, Renna wondered how they could stand the confinement. Gloomily greenish-yellow light from overheads made everyone look ill. The compartment smelled. They kept only marginal maintenance, and the lights were dimmed. Cutter did not attempt to prepare anything. Ship rations were available. Last week the fighting and acrimony changed to an enveloping sullenness.

Ezry hovered around her plants, occupied herself in sewing, pretending to be unaware of anything else. She seemed locked in her own world. *Except when I enter the compartment when she always has something to say.* At least she didn't pretend friendship. Only Ezry noticed when she left or came back, as if she had turned invisible to everyone else.

"Back, podder?" Ezry said from the far corner where she kept her plants. Their roots were overcharged in their mission to clean the refuse water adding an unpleasant odor. The failure added to the compartment's smell. "Where were you? Plotting with that CS9 thing?" The dark woman's face filled with belligerence. Her eyes promised harm. She looked angry, threatening, her tone acidic, nothing like Sen's submissiveness.

Renna ignored her. She checked the buffet. Ration packs lay on the table. She nearly gagged.

Lock played Solitaire at the table as he had when she left for the flight deck twelve hours before. He didn't speak, too busy flipping cards to pay much attention to their placement. She sat at the table. He hardly noticed.

She glanced at Cutter, dozing in one of the chairs. When his attempts to ease the others' stress failed, he took his defeat to heart, falling into their indifference.

Twice a day, she saw Zak for less than a minute when they traded duty on the flight deck. Whatever he did the rest of the time—she doubted he talked to Jake. Jake remained weak, and he and Ship Dog always slept. She feared Jake would fail before overcoming the nanobot infection.

Used to strict regulation, Renna finished her daily ritual. She sat at the table, checked her log on her intel, and reread her notations. Each listing noted a change to the *Vagrant Spirit*. Some were easily identified. Others were not. Another file noted her observations on the Rabican's readings, gleaned from her hours on the flight deck. They meant nothing.

Finished, she pulled up the library and selected more on the history topic currently interesting her while she opened a ration pack.

"You really don't need to cover the flight deck," Lock said.

She finished swallowing a mouthful of ration pack brown goo before answering.

"Zak serves."

"Zak always wanted to explore. Probably the only one who is half-excited about being here." He stopped flipping cards. "Lost again, damn it."

"I also need to be there." At his cynicism, she added, "It is quiet there."

"Suit yourself." He shuffled the cards and laid another game.

She went to Cutter where he reclined in one of the loungers, half dozing. "Cutter, you must do something."

He started and stared at her with an apathetic gaze. "We're all depressed, worried, and apprehensive. I can't take the *Vagrant Spirit* out of transit. I can't do anything. No one can." He turned away from her. His despondency concerned her. If Cutter gave up, they all would.

At twenty-one hundred hours, she returned to duty, and another day slipped by in the same pattern. Returning from duty, she found someone had placed a cloth over the chronometer. Lock still played cards. Everyone else slept. She entered her hammock and let the sound of the Rabican lull her to sleep, vaguely aware Lock had given up his game and was pacing the compartment.

A crash woke her. Screaming followed. She leaped out of her hammock. A brief silence with abrupt intensity ensued. Cutter and Lock grappled on the floor.

"Help!" Cutter screamed.

Lock twisted and fought in Cutter's hold. "Help me."

Blood poured from Lock's neck and his mouth foamed with bloody spittle as he formed soundless words. "Let me die," he gasped in garbled words as he writhed in Cutter's grasp.

Renna took two leaping steps to Lock. She tried to grab him. He kicked her away. Falling, she saw Jake appear from behind her. He struck Lock on the chin.

Lock collapsed in Cutter's arms. Cutter changed his grip and used his fingers to slow the flow of blood. He demanded equipment. Jake sank in exhaustion to the floor. Ship Dog hauled Jake to his feet and helped him to a chair while Ezry rushed to gather Cutter's equipment.

"Sit on him before he comes to," Cutter ordered.

Renna grabbed one arm and leaned across Lock's chest to restrain his other arm. Ship Dog pushed her aside and placed a huge hand on Lock's chest, trapping him against the deck. Lock came to, mouthing soundless words, tears pouring from his eyes. Within minutes, Cutter had cauterized the bleeding and glued the gash. Ship Dog helped Cutter move Lock to the diagnostic bed. Renna retreated to the table where Jake sat.

"Why?" Jake asked.

"Trapped." Ship Dog openly wept. He worked to clean the blood off the deck.

"Yeah. We all are, doesn't give him the right to..." Jake didn't finish. His head fell forward into his hands.

Ship Dog sank into a chair, resting his arms on his knees, staring at the deck. After a minute, Jake rose and went to the communication panel. Renna knew he was informing Zak what had happened, so it was no surprise when Zak appeared within minutes.

Renna rose. "I will finish the watch."

"Stay here," Cutter spoke from where he worked on Lock.

Ezry screeched in outrage. "Someone has to be there! That thing likes her. It listens to her! Let her go. Lock doesn't matter to her."

"Shut-up!" Cutter's voice filled with venom. "Get over yourself long enough to have some compassion. Pay attention to what you're doing here." He flung a medical instrument into a tray. The tool clanged and bounced out to fall to the deck. He swore. Renna had never heard Cutter lose his temper. It was a quiet explosion.

"Ease up on Ezry." Zak had started removing his biosuit.

"Why don't you ease up on everyone?" Jake inserted.

"I'm capable of fighting my own fights. I don't need you to stand up for me, Zak Terran." Ezry's shrill voice crossed over Jake's. She looked ready to attack.

Ship Dog slouched deeper into his chair, seeming to let the escalating rage wash over and around him. His sullen expression of surrender flung Renna into the past. She saw her kin in the assembly room. A few senior subs squabbled over ranking nonsense, helpless to make any decision in their terror of the situation. As long as the irrational orders of a terrified dom continued to pour into the room through the audio, none would listen to her, not the speaker Dukan ordered shunned. Most of her sub kin were so terrified they could neither voice their fear nor their anguish. Their expressions glazed with terror. Others, like Sen, just shriveled, curled up in defeat, their vacant stares accepting the end.

No! Not again!

"Enough!" Renna screamed, cutting through the squabbling. Sheer surprise silenced them. "We're not going on like this." She grabbed the cover off the chronometer.

"Nothing else we can do," Ezry said, still petulant in Cutter's reprimand.

"We can live." Renna turned on Cutter. "You know better than this." She indicated the compartment and its occupants. "Yes, you all failed. Lock broke the law and landed in prison. Illness kept Ship Dog from his duty. Jake beat his superior. Zak didn't reach his expectations. Cutter disliked his chosen profession. Ezry...Ezry was lost." She drew a breath. "And I, I failed my crew in the greatest way—I lived. And I will outlive you!"

"That a threat?" Ezry asked. "Been telling you she is up to no good."

"Yes, a threat." Renna glared at them. "You will not give up like *Markham3* Pod. You may think I brought this calamity upon you, and maybe I did, but you will do your duty to the *Vagrant Spirit*. You have all hidden in this compartment long enough. No more. Now you will serve this ship in her need. Markham Company wanted me dead, wanted the Rabican engine destroyed. They were willing to sacrifice you, and your ship, to achieve those ends."

"Because they thought us losers." Jake sat back in his chair.

"No," Renna answered. "Because you were vulnerable."

"He's going to be okay," Cutter said from where he worked. "Won't talk properly for some time. Managed to repair the vascular damage."

Renna picked up the ration packs and threw them in the disposer, pushed the accumulated debris off the table, brightened the illumination, and adjusted the atmosphere to a higher circulation level. "You are not dead. I am not dead. The *Vagrant Spirit* is undamaged. The Rabican works, and the CS9 operates it."

"Vera." Liquid lined Ship Dog's red eyelids. "Dead."

Renna softened her voice. "Far from it. If we survive the Rabican's journey, it is because of Vera. She worked efficiently enough to propel the *Vagrant Spirit*, plus feed the Rabican's demand. If the Rabican's programming called for insertion, it surely plans an emergence. When we emerge, we will need Vera, and we will need you to sing to her again."

"You have a plan?" Zak asked. His brooding look eased.

"Not entirely. First, you must all wish to live. Live with hope."

"What do you suggest?" Cutter asked. His hand swiped over his head, rubbing dirty hair flat.

"We will return to work in the ship and return here for off duty and sleep. We will start decoding the Rabican. We must also inspect the *Vagrant Spirit*, see what changes the CS9 nanobots are making. We will use our time on the flight deck studying the readings until we understand the reports. We will learn how to operate it. We need to find out how to counter the effects experienced in transit."

"Changes?" Ship Dog asked.

"I have noted some." She handed him her intel and gave an inner smile as he scrutinized her notes. Her glance encompassed her crewmates. "I may not be of your kin, but I am of the situation, and I say it changes here and now."

"I agree," Jake and Zak said together, glaring at each other before shaking their heads and laughing.

Cutter studied her and wiped his face. "Yes. It is hard to see what is happening until it is too late." His gaze fell to Lock. "Renna is right. We have failed our ship." He smiled with an expression she had missed seeing in the last few weeks.

"Hallucinations," Ship Dog muttered.

"Duty will focus your mind. If it doesn't, we will find a way to deal with them."

Twenty

...2180.026.14:32 universal space-time ...mission status ...access to ship's logs denied ...crewmember injured ...priority one directive change places mission in jeopardy ...failure results in cs9vs shutdown ...priority conflict ...revert to pre-established mission directives...

"How come these go up so damn much harder than they came down?" Cutter asked, shoving his end into the clips.

Ship Dog jacked up one end of the port-van while Renna and Cutter positioned the partition. She struggled with the bulky wall section. The restructuring of the fore compartment into the pre-crisis configuration had taken the three of them four days. It was not easy.

"Got it?" Cutter asked.

"Almost aligned," Renna said.

Ship Dog slammed the partition into place with a fist.

"Need more?"

"No," she answered as his thump shoved the partition into position with an audible click.

Work settled some of the tension, relieved the depression, and ended the boredom. Renna felt the anxiety running like an unnoticed thread through the fabric of their days. She also noticed the CS9 observed their activities because the oxygen level increased, and gravity eased marginally when the crew's unaccustomed exertions caused breathlessness. The CS9 might not record vid or audio, but she believed it examined the fore compartment by other means.

"Yeah. More help. Let's take a break." Cutter wiped his face. "I'm getting too old for this."

Ship Dog walked away immediately. Renna watched his quick retreat. Ezry ignored them, sewing another garment. She refused to help since the crew had to go outside the shielded forward compartment to retrieve the partitions.

"You did a good thing the other day." Cutter patted her shoulder before he eased into a chair. "We were all ready to pack it in. We're not used to this type of adversity."

"You were not prepared for isolation, Cutter. Not like this."

"You were angry."

Renna shook her head in negation. "Subs are not permitted anger. We are taught calmness, professionalism, and duty. I only knew I would not let you fail."

Cutter smiled at her answer. "You were angry."

"I was frightened. You gave up." She sighed. "It was like what happened before."

He nodded. "Good for you."

Ship Dog returned with energy packs, giving them both one of the packs filled with liquid. Tired, Renna drank the contents of one pack. Ship Dog remained standing before her, shifting his weight from foot to foot. He finally muttered, "Help?" His gaze wouldn't meet hers. "Vera?"

"You want me to help you get to Vera's compartment?"

He nodded.

"The hallucinations bother you?" Cutter asked. Ship Dog nodded at Cutter's question. The face above the beard filled with color.

"I will take you," Renna said. "Once you get used to the environment, they go away."

Ship Dog left for the head. Cutter watched her while Renna finished her drink. His regard made her feel uncomfortable. She shifted, wondering what she had or had not done properly.

"He's afraid," Cutter said. "He can't tell his own hallucinations from those out there." He nodded at the hatch. "Are you sure you want to do this? Can you guide and reassure him?"

Renna looked at Cutter and read the concern lining his face. Was he worried about Ship Dog or about her? Never had Dukan worried about a sub unable to complete his job other than to dole out punishment. A memory flashed through her mind of Sen being slapped so hard the force knocked her to the floor, punished for doing exactly what her duty required.

Dukan blamed his failure on Sen. She sucked in determination with a deep breath. "Yes."

When Ship Dog returned, she smiled in reassurance. "Are you ready?"

Ship Dog nodded. She led the way to the hatch. Cutter followed. Halfway to the Jupiter1090's compartment, Ship Dog froze, refusing to take a step. His gaze showed he saw something they didn't. Even Cutter had trouble with the hallucinations, muttering, "focus," every so often.

"Daniel," Cutter said pulling the engineer's arm, "Daniel! Do you see me? We are with you. Daniel!"

Renna watched Cutter and Ship Dog...Daniel. He remained impervious to Cutter's demanding, pleading tone. Ship Dog jerked from Cutter's hold. His frantic look told Renna he would either lash out or bolt. In his present confusion, he would find no safety, only more bewilderment.

Renna took Ship Dog's hand and pushed his face toward Cutter with her other hand. "Daniel, you are here. Cutter and I are with you. Think about Cutter. You must imagine his face. Now open your eyes. You will see Cutter."

He opened his eyes with instant relief evident in his expression, so she knew he saw Cutter.

"Feel my hand in your hand. When something happens you know cannot be real, think about our clasped hands. Touch will bring you back to here and now."

His taut face marginally relaxed, and although he closed his eyes and stopped several more times, Renna only squeezed his hand to bring him back. His eyes would open, and once he even smiled. Inside the engine compartment, his discomfort disappeared.

"See," she told Cutter. He stood next to her, wiping the sweat from his face. They watched Ship Dog inspect Vera. "When he concentrates, he has no problems with hallucinations."

"It's still scary. Still, I believe you, and I think Daniel will, too."

"Compartment." Ship Dog said when he rejoined him. "Wrong."

"Show us," Cutter said.

Ship Dog was right. The compartment's propulsion chamber was sealed, rendering the engine inoperative even if they could bring it online. Cutter swore.

"What has been altered can be changed back," Renna said. "Look at all the partitions we have rearranged. We will have time to fix this once we are out of transition space." Whether they believed her or not, Ship Dog had far fewer stops on the trip back to the fore compartment.

~ * ~

The crew spent the afternoon moving furniture, supplies, and water tanks. Lock and Ship Dog rebuilt the head. Lock's neck still held red scars where he had cut his throat.

Zak joined them for dinner, leaving the flight deck unattended. "Makes no difference if anyone is there while we are in transition." Zak remained terse. His gaze followed her, making her as uncomfortable as the CS9 tracking.

Lock's dark eyes flitted from face to face when he joined them. His gaze fell to the bowl of liquefied dinner Ezry placed before him. "Thank you. You all saved my sorry ass." His low voice was raspy, and he swallowed with the effort. "Don't know what came over me. Everything just seemed so hopeless."

"Yeah." Jake nodded. "Just don't do it again."

Ren took Ship Dog's hand and Lock's, waited for the others to clasp their hands for thanks. She looked at Cutter. "No, Cutter, I will," Jake said. He hesitated before bowing his head. "I give thanks for each member of this crew, for this ship, and for the faith in both to see us through this adversity." He dropped the hands he held. His gaze rose to catch hers before he began his meal.

Watching the monitors from the dinner table made the occasion seem routine. Cutter's effort wasn't his best, but it made up for the last few weeks of rations. The regular lighting fixtures were reinstalled, making the room look fresher. The faces, if not glowing with happiness and health, at least appeared living.

And wanting to live. With the change in attitude, Renna felt better. She knew they were still unprepared for the long hours of boredom she knew remained ahead...possible years of unchanging scenery and unchanging company. Even kin found it tedious upon occasion.

As she munched through something Cutter called his casserole deluxe, a deep sigh of satisfaction wrenched from her. "Cutter, will you teach me how to cook?"

Her request garnered quizzical looks from everyone, though Ezry scowled. Cutter's elated expression predicted his answer. "Sure."

"You're sure it's safe to work in the ship?" Ezry asked Zak.

"Yes. You could even move into your cabin. It's part of the fore compartment, so is as safe as before."

Ezry didn't smile at his answer. "Good. I could use some privacy."

Conversation between Zak and Jake remained sparse. Their alienation grieved Renna whenever she noticed their conduct. Their discord generated a discomfort she had often felt on the *Markham3*.

"You want to move into a cabin, Ren?" Cutter asked, engaged in forking up the last of his dinner. He glanced up at her.

Jake tilted his head in consideration. "We'd have to empty Ezry's stowage from one of the extra cabins, but it will give you room to spread out."

Renna scrunched her brows in thought. She followed the monitors' information and finished the bite of casserole she was savoring. She envisioned the rampant color, the luxurious textures and trinkets in Ezry's quarters, and each of the others' cabins as she remembered them and envisioned a sparse cabin with a bed large enough for several kin.

"What's the matter?" Jake asked in concern, examining the screens.

"Nothing. I was considering a cabin." Renna looked at Cutter. "No, thank you, Cutter, I like my slip bunk. It fits just me, and I have no need of room to spread out. I think if everyone agrees, I would prefer to spend the energy making the port cargo hold into a gymnasium."

"Good idea," Cutter said after a long pause. "Some competitive team games might relieve stress and enliven things."

"Yes. We will need diversions," Zak said. "What about the hallucinations?"

"It will take a few weeks to get everything arranged." Jake stopped with a fork halfway to his lips. "We can wait and see how everyone responds to exposure."

Renna wondered what exercise, game, or sport the men anticipated.

As if understanding her curiosity, Cutter added, "Free-fall polo would be fun. You can be on my team."

"How come you picked her first? No fair. I call a foul." Lock's weak voice strained in objection. "I'm a natural athlete." He bent his arm, showing his biceps.

Jake, smiling wryly, squeezed the muscle. "Well," Lock protested, "it will be bigger when I start lifting again."

"Hah! Thought your ass was getting flabby." Ezry nodded as she provoked Lock in her old manner.

"Who's your opposing captain?" Zak asked.

"You, of course," Jake said.

Silence fell like heavy shields. Jake grinned. Zak's answering smile wasn't as mirthful.

"Okay, a gymnasium," Jake continued. "I'll help. As soon as I get energy."

"I think we need it sooner, so I better fill in for you." Zak rose, and as he reached the hatch said, "We all have other assignments to accomplish before a gym conversion."

Jake's smile faded, leaving an uneasy tension in the compartment. Unlike kin, emotions among norms turned quickly, and in unpredictable directions. Renna grabbed her intel and escaped to walk the ship.

Twenty-one

...2180.057 - 02:16 universal space-time ...mission status ...jake terran unreachable for removal of biobots ...need to retrieve ... danger to crew...

Ezry and Cutter inventoried supplies in the re-established galley. Renna heard their voices droning one against the other. The sound gradually pulled her into awareness from her sleep. She glanced around at the five snare bunks lined up with hers, all empty. Renna gave an inner laugh each time she entered the wardroom. Sleeping together like crewkin. Only she slept during the hours the others were generally awake. In the end, even though they worked in the ship, they returned to the wardroom within the fore compartment to sleep in comfort and security.

All but Ezry. She slept in her cabin and increasingly stayed there, except when someone, usually Cutter, drew her out with work. Renna watched the way the men treated Ezry with special handling. Because she was not a spacer? No, dangerous because she remained terrified. Such coddling on a crewkin ship would not have been tolerated.

Another thirty-six days in transition had made everyone uneasy. The hallucinations outside the shielded fore compartment eased, even for Ship Dog. Daniel. Two names. Cutter usually called him Daniel, everyone else Ship Dog. No one told her why. For a week, she had walked with him to the Jupiter1090's compartment until he finally made the trip by himself and continued to do so. Renna wondered what he did there each day on such a strict schedule. Four hours after leaving, he returned for a one-hour break, repeating the sequence twice, returning once for communal dinner, and one last time shortly before sleeping. He made her think of her kin, and no matter how she hated it, memories and comparisons constantly occurred.

She scrambled from her bunk, and while completing her daily hygiene routine and simple housekeeping chores, thought about the kin who disappeared from her kin-group while still children. She remembered them all—frightened, sobbing in their sleep, hesitant in following Dukan's orders when he demanded dangerous duty. By the time the *Markham3* reached the mining station Longshot on Asteroid 3563, those kin were gone. They had not left the ship with the previous crew. How could she and her kin have all been so complacent about their disappearance? No one wondered or questioned what happened to them. No wonder the Terran crew doubted podders.

"Morning," Jake said from the chair where he rested when she left the head.

He looked dreadful. He would have been culled. Her realization made her feel protective.

"Want some coffee?" he asked. "At least we have enough to last a long time. Two hundred kilos of Arabica beans."

"She prefers tea." Cutter interrupted his manual count of spices to inform Jake. "Thirty-five grams of tarragon. What was I thinking? Fifteen kilograms of sea salt."

"Same thing you were thinking when you got all that salt. We have three different kinds," Ezry said.

"And all have their purpose." Cutter leaned over and kissed Ezry's pouting mouth.

"Yeah? What are you planning to cure out here?"

Jake rose and fixed Renna a cup of tea. She wanted to jump up and do it for him but reined in her impulse.

"Thank you." From the table dispenser, she pressed the sugar release. Two measures made the drink tasty. She loved the warmth of the cup against her fingers and the soft exotic scent of the beverage, which tasted and smelled like freshness to her. Cutter called them refreshments, a strange concept, like breaks during duty. Zak had explained the breaks were mandated by law. Crewkin drank water often tasting of cleaning salts, and no kin ever experienced breaks. Whenever she thought of these things, her stomach knotted. She recognized the feeling now—anger.

"You're going to have to cut back on the sugar habit," Jake said. "Cutter is rationing sugar."

He sipped his coffee and watched the monitors on the wall. One showed the flight deck, the other Ship Dog rubbing a polish along the Jupiter1090's gleaming surface. Jake turned the monitor to a view of the main gangway. Lock appeared, returning to the fore compartment.

She watched the monitors until Lock entered the hatch, and Jake switched to the ship's only exterior view taken from the camera inside the flight deck's turret. None of the exterior cameras worked, so they only had this one forward view. She had never noticed the spectral shifts the relay monitor detected. She wondered if the CS9 redefined the camera's acuity at Jake's direction.

Jake took on the task of determining the CS9's limits and its danger. No one objected. He could accomplish the task without debilitating himself. Renna turned her attention back to him, realizing he watched those monitors for hours. Perhaps the CS9 seduced him into accepting it as no more than a powerful tool?

"Interesting, isn't it?" Jake asked, his gaze still caught with the display, visible proof the ship traversed unfamiliar territory.

"Yes."

Jake grinned. Moving his drawn facial muscles exposed the mold of his skull in vivid detail, reminding her of the CS9's treachery.

"Thanks for helping Ship Dog get to the engine compartment," he said, not looking away from the monitors.

His verbal approval surprised her. She didn't know what to say. Curiosity overcame common sense. "Why do you call him Ship Dog and Cutter calls him Daniel?"

"Ship Dog was a nickname he earned in the Corps. He prefers being called by his nickname. Only lets Cutter call him by his given name." He sighed. "By your standards, he probably isn't an asset to the crew. Give him an engine, though, any engine, and he is very different."

"I've heard him sing to Vera."

"Yeah. He likes to sing. You're walking the ship again?"

"Yes."

"Lock has assembled the blueprints where the old system ran and compared them to current configurations. In areas around the Rabican compartment and the flight deck, most of the wiring is gone, replaced by the CS9 nanobots. Moving out from those areas, less has changed. About one-eighth of the ship has been taken over, including the Jupiter1090's compartment. What are you discovering on your walks?"

"With time, it will take over the whole ship."

"Is this change necessarily bad?"

"The CS9 has made the main engine impossible to operate. It has hijacked the ship. It has injured you. What more proof do you need?"

"You didn't mention that the CS9 and Rabican engine killed your crew."

She didn't answer, only stared at Jake.

"Is there a possibility you aren't altogether sure what killed your crew?"

Her heart thumped a hard rhythm at his comment. *Calmness, professionalism, duty.*

"Many things contributed to their deaths. The belief the CS9 could control the flight led directly to the loss of the *Markham3*, and the deaths of most of my crewkin."

"All new technologies take their toll in human life."

"You do not think the CS9 culpable or in need of controls?"

"I'm saying it's a machine, neither good nor evil except in its usage."

After a long silence, she said, "I think we will have the opportunity to discover the truth about this CS9."

Jake chuckled. "Get some breakfast."

~ * ~

After Renna left, Cutter and Ezry took a break and joined Jake.

"How did your talk go?" Cutter asked.

Jake shrugged. "Don't know. Hard to read Ren, especially when she puts on her duty face—nothing leaks out."

Ezry made a face. "You two think she is a danger to the ship?"

Cutter sighed. "No, Ez. Ren distrusts the CS9 and Rabican with good reason. Her kin died during the initial trial. We all know we need both the engine and the cognitive support to get back. We're just testing the waters to see where Ren's rationality begins and ends."

"In our own best interests? You think she might have made us believe this CS9 caused all our problems when the culprit was really her?" She swore. "Can't trust anyone on this ship." She escaped into her cabin.

"I think you have all the help you'll get from her today," Jake said with a bland-worried smile. "Can I help you finish?"

~ * ~

"Are you getting enough sleep?"

Renna turned from the bulkhead she inspected. Zak stood close, almost too close. Sleep? He talked of this when there was a more important issue? She told him her findings, reminding him they were on duty. "The cognitive support's nanobots are slowly refabricating the whole ship."

"Ren, you can't obsess about the nanobots. Getting back is what matters."

"So that you can file all your discoveries and become a famous explorer?"

"Yes, partially. Discovery is an explorer's purpose." A satisfied grin crossed his face. "We'll be acclaimed as the first exploration team of another system when we return. Our discoveries won't amount to anything if we don't get back. Doesn't the aspect appeal to you in any way? Just the thought makes me think this whole debacle worthwhile."

Renna seldom saw him except at shift change and dinner. At those times, her kin training helped her endure his presence and accept her perplexing emotions. Now, when they were no longer intimate, she longed for him. She tried to decide what attracted her: his kin-like appearance, or some other undefined factor.

Zak took her intel and read the report showing this section's signs of nanobot infection. "This support beam contains four-hundredths of a millimeter less titanium than when you measured this area our first week out."

She took back her reader, surprised by her possessiveness. "The nanobots take micro-layers of material, sometimes changing the molecular structures of the material, and sometimes creating materials different from the original ship's specs. Perhaps we should test the materials?"

"To what purpose?"

"To know what changes. To help us determine the ship's new characteristics. To retake the ship and destroy the nanobots, if necessary."

"And not destroy the Rabican?" He grinned at her. "I know. Possession of the first hyper-engine represents a huge asset to any ship. So does the CS9. A better goal is to determine if the changes are better for the job at hand, determine if the CS9 is a better control for the ship." His forehead furrowed in what she recognized as his considering face. "I'll speak to Jake. He could probably find out quicker from the CS9 since it is directing these changes."

Renna sighed. "Working with and against the CS9 creates problems."

Zak laughed out of all proportion to her ordinary observation. "You have an odd sense of humor," he said.

Reviewing her words, she didn't find anything funny. She felt glad that Zak thought she had humor and smiled.

"You should do that more often," he said.

"Be humorous?"

"Smile. Both. I wish the hull's exterior cameras worked. I'd like to see what else the CS9 is doing to the ship."

"We must wait for emergence from this transition space back into real space."

He sighed. "If we last long enough, and if there is anything like what we knew."

"We will. There is."

"You won't if you exhaust yourself with duty. Cutter sent me to collect you for dinner."

"You could have just hailed me." She nodded at the connex clip on his lapel.

"Finding you was more fun."

A comment she found thoroughly confusing.

~ * ~

After dinner, she helped Lock check each system and each subsystem of the original computer. Methodically, they tested them before downloading the files into an ancient standalone reader lined with non-conductive insulation.

"Some attributes of older ships are overlooked," Lock said with a lopsided smile as he worked at the ancient device they had placed on non-conductive material as well. "So private." He looked over her shoulder. "You think the CS9 copies them as they are brought up?"

"The languages are incompatible." She glanced to where his attention was focused. The wall screen showed her standing next to Lock, under the CS9's surveillance.

"Likes to watch, doesn't it?" Lock asked, lowering his voice. "Don't count on the CS9 not knowing what is in these files, but an available back-up is a comforting safety feature."

"It might be better if the CS9 didn't know what we do."

Lock shrugged. "When you can turn it off, let me know."

Twenty-two

...2180.053-21:30 universal space-time ...mission status ...rabican quantum indicator triggered ...emergence imminent ...crew immigrates to port cargo hold ...nanobots investigate and establish link...

"What are the rules?" Renna asked, inspecting the renovated cargo hold while she fingered the gelatinous ball. The ball flattened under the pressure of her hands. The game harness felt strange, confining her body, yet the straps moved and stretched easily enough over the form-fitting shirt and shorts Cutter deemed a suitable uniform. Voice-activated jet packs lined the yoke straps each player wore, while bands circling waist, wrists, and ankles carried an array of placement sensors.

She found herself grouped with Cutter and Lock, against Ship Dog, Ezry, and Zak in the empty Zero-G cargo bay. Team competition, one against another...a concept encompassing group and destroying it at the same time. A very strange idea against all podder learning.

Unlike the aft hold, this cargo hold ran in unobstructed emptiness the length of the *Vagrant Spirit*. When they had entered to set up the gymnasium three weeks ago, Renna wondered about the empty run. Her speculation must have shown on her face.

"My fault," Jake had said. "SSC's petty revenge. The *Vagrant Spirit* was unofficially blacklisted. Every run has been a struggle since my becoming captain. On the last runs, we've survived on the profits made when our parents operated the *Vagrant Spirit*."

"By the SSC?" She tried to keep the surprise out of her voice.

"Unofficially. Word seeped out to all the port masters and cargo listings."

"That is illegal."

"Yeah. Well, try proving such an allegation."

Long before they finished the renovation, Jake sat on the deck too tired to do more than observe and order their progress. They watched him carefully because his condition made him prone to hallucinations. Renna read the disgust, longing, and worry in his worn expression as he watched them work. To see a dom wear such an expression was strange.

Ezry also had to change. Cutter demanded she had to leave the wardroom for ten minutes, adding time each day. He gave her daily jobs within the compartment and ship, like making sure the new plants were surviving in the hydro-farm. She had argued, whined, and complained. Cutter had ignored her. The lesser shielding didn't bother her anymore.

Ezry snorted a disparaging huff at Ren's request for the rules.

The noise brought Renna's attention back and reinforced her need to focus.

"She needs the rules? Easy win for us." Ezry threw herself backward in the zero-g's with acrobatic grace.

"Damn." Lock watched Ezry. "Looks like we'll have to work to win this one. You showing us one of your unnatural theater performances?"

Ezry continued her acrobatics, adjusting the thrust of her jet packs with subtle movements. Her movement didn't seem enough to cause the changes Renna observed, and she wondered how Ezry accomplished her feat.

"Nothing unnatural about sex—and I performed erotic theater and sensual dance," Ezry answered Lock at last.

Lock looked at Renna and must have noticed her confusion. "She sub-vocalizes to fire her jet packs. I thought exvee training would give us the advantage. Looks like I thought wrong." He shouted at Ezry. "Perverted, you mean." He launched himself into a gymnastic warm-up, moving arms and legs to fire jets, using his voice to control movement commands.

"You use unnatural and ungainly motion. A perversion of form," Ezry taunted Lock.

Renna glanced at Jake as he chuckled. He officiated, tethered to a partition midway along the field. A small intel strapped to his wrist helped his ruling. "There is a ball launcher positioned midpoint on the game field, which is defined by the light grid you helped install."

She nodded. A grid of interlacing light beams defined a large elliptical volume.

"The sensors on your game harness determine your position if you've gone out of bounds or made a fair goal."

"When I put the ball through the shapes?" She frowned at one of the floating circles within the defined volume.

"Listen to you. What makes you think you'll make a goal?" Zak asked. His eyes gleamed with a challenge. He drifted nearby, casually throwing another ball through one of the goals. The circular goal grid flashed with lights. A number appeared on the partition above Jake.

Jake shoved Zak, and Zak drifted away laughing. Sighing, Jake finished his instructions. "There are five drifting goal nets, two for your team, two for Zak's team, one universal. If the ball breaks through the mesh on either of your goal hoops or the universal goal, you score. Through your opponent's goal, they score."

"Sounds simple." She looked at the slowly drifting shapes of light in the game field.

"Okay," Cutter said. "Clear the scoreboard, and let's get started."

"Remember," Jake shouted, "only one hand on the ball at any time, and no brutality."

The ball shot with speed from the launcher. Cutter and Lock tried to grab it.

Zak dove into its flightpath, stopping the ball against his body. The momentum pushed him away. He threw the ball to Ship Dog, who caught the ball in a massive grip and passed it to Ezry. She plopped it through one of their goal hoops. All three team members burst into shouts of success.

Renna hadn't moved.

Lock floated up to her. "You got to get hold of the ball. It isn't going to come to you. Think about where you are, and where you have to get. You've navigated a ship—try doing it with your body."

They all had to be tightening muscles in unseen motion because she couldn't detect their movement. Crewkin used similar methods to control motion in exvee work. Nodding to Lock, she pictured the grid of the field in her mind as she thought about movement. The ball sprung from the launcher. Renna chose the wrong direction or the harness didn't translate her direction correctly. Passing all the players, the ball burst through the field boundaries. Lock groaned. Zak shouted, "Wait."

Bouncing off an out-of-bounds partition, the much misshapen projectile bounded back through the field's boundaries. Zak fought Cutter for position. Cutter shoved Zak away. Zak floated backward, twisting in an awkward trajectory. Lock grabbed the ball. He turned and jetted toward a goal hoop. He shoved the ball through their goal.

"Score!" Lock yelled, raising his arms above his head. His actions twirled him heels over head. He stopped his motion by grabbing an overhead support after he floated through the boundary. His braids followed, floating around his jubilant face.

Cutter joined in Lock's enthusiastic celebration, shouting and gesturing wildly.

The game continued without much help from Renna. She worked on getting the hang of judging where the ball would be and how to get there. Even when she arrived on time and in position, most often someone shoved, pulled, or blew her away with their jets. She tumbled head over heels in circles.

They played fast and rough. Hands and feet pushed opponents out of position. When shoving and pushing failed, collisions worked. When the ball went out of bounds, Jake determined who caused the foul. One team went after it in a wild scurry of movement, shouting as it bounced. The other tried to prevent the ball from reentering the field boundaries.

Often, when Renna went to grab the ball, it popped out of her grasp, changing shape, direction, and speed. Her frustration and determination grew.

Zak threw the ball from the out-of-bounds line. Renna launched her body, intercepting the missile before it reached Ship Dog. His advance on the ball collided with her path, sending them both tumbling.

"All," she shouted and every jet on her suit fired, bringing her to a halt. By luck, a goal floated nearby. She threw the ball through it.

"No, no!" Lock shouted in anguish and Ezry whooped with laughter.

"Wrong goal, Ren. Watch the colors! You scored them a point."

Zak's laugh came up behind her. He grabbed her, and they twirled in cartwheels together through the playing field and out of bounds. She thought he kissed the back of her head. "Thanks, Ren."

The buzzer rang. "Okay, five-minute breather," Jake said.

During the break, Renna reprogrammed her harness's vocal directives to conform with how she used ship's positioning while listening to Lock's advice on how to improve her game.

"Okay, last half," Jake shouted from where he talked with Zak.

While she didn't make any goals, she did position herself better and faster than before. She shouted in excitement as her assist helped Cutter score. She stopped for breath, her exertion causing a gasp of relief. Elation surged through her body. In her rapture, she performed a few backflips and twirls, bringing a few hurrahs from her team.

The game resumed, and Renna felt exhilarated when she stole the ball from Zak. When done with the maneuver, she puzzled over her yearning to defeat the other team, though the game prevented time for further introspection.

Ezry's scream startled Renna, and her body drifted off-course as she twisted to see what alarmed the other woman. With a few countermoves, she propelled herself close to an overhead support to stop her movement. She saw Ezry was still hugging a support. Her horrified gaze looked at Jake. A glance showed Jake trapped between three energy pulses enclosing the place where he was tethered. Even as he pulled the tether free, more beams caged him, closing all escape routes.

"The CS9 is in here," Renna shouted.

"CS9, stop! You are harming crewmember Jake." Zak yelled.

Renna propelled herself toward Jake, saw Zak do the same. The energy currents remained active; the CS9 ignored orders.

Jake backed against the partition. The wall seemed to melt behind him. Jake flung himself away from the surface. The surrounding energy field bounced him into the writhing mass behind him. She and Zak closed in. Jake screamed even as a sudden amassed energy field hurled Renna and Zak back into the hold.

Renna tumbled backward, arms and legs splayed in ungainly movements. She controlled her body and used her jets to stop her wild flight. Gaining her bearings took a second as dizziness washed her mind.

Zak hit a nearby partition hard. His head smashed into the structure. He bounced back into the hold. Lock pushed off and caught Zak before he hit another partition or support. He pulled Zak's limp body to the ladder near the entry hatch. Cutter dove toward the cargo hoist and began unlatching the lock on the cargo hauler's lift arm. Ship Dog joined Cutter and finished releasing the lock amid Ezry's continued screams. Cutter pulled the arm shank out of the loader.

Disbelieving what she saw, Renna watched the white current shape surround Jake in multiple arm-like bands. The bands tightened, pulling Jake into their grip. Jake's screams transcended Ezry's.

Ship Dog catapulted toward the energy trap, using his momentum to hurl the shank like a spear. The shank hit the transparent wall and bounced away, returning in a reverse arc headed toward Cutter. He dodged the shaft, somersaulted, and twirled into the center of the hold. The spear hit the cargo loader, striking between its arms with the sound of twisting metal, and twirled away.

Renna pushed herself off her perch and caught the tumbling bar. She tumbled with it for a few seconds before she gained control. Using her drift, she bounced off the partition and maneuvered into a trajectory toward the wall of energy.

She had almost reached her goal when the current surrounding Jake dissipated with startling quickness. Twisting her body hard and screaming voice commands to change direction, Renna pulled the shaft out of a collision course with Jake. He remained upright in a stiff posture. His face looked frozen in horror. Ezry, thankfully, stopped screaming. After a few seconds of silence, she burst into wailing, strident howls.

Cutter propelled himself toward Jake yelling, "Lock, get my med-kit. Daniel, don't let Zak move. Ezry, go prepare the sickbay."

Lock left Zak floating tethered to the ladder. When he reached the deck-level hatch, the access unlocked and opened before he reached it.

The CS9. Why so accommodating now? Renna wanted to cry.

Lock hesitated and ducked through the portal. The hatch slid close behind him.

Renna grabbed a support and tied off the shaft. She flung herself toward Zak. He sprawled a few meters above the deck; Ship Dog held his head and neck. Reaching them, Renna gently held Zak by one arm while she grasped a support with the other for stability.

Ezry managed to pull herself together and follow Cutter's order, passing Renna without the usual glare, too frightened for hostility.

"Hold him."

Renna nodded at Ship Dog's request and took his position. Ship Dog joined Cutter who cursorily examined Jake.

"He's alive," Cutter said as he peeled Jake's clothing back and inspected the exposed body. "No apparent burns. It forced him into the partition, why?"

Renna exhaled the breath she had seemed to hold since Ezry's first scream. She sucked in another deep breath. While Ship Dog held Jake, Cutter came and checked Zak, carefully holding his head and feeling along his neck. Renna released her hold on Zak to keep Cutter in place as his movement pushed him about. Cutter's expression worried Renna. The attack on Jake alarmed her. Zak's injury terrified her. She relived Sen's suicide and trembled.

No. He won't die.

Lock returned. "Brought stretchers." He gasped as he grabbed a support to stop his glide to them. He handed one to Cutter and bounded toward Ship Dog and Jake.

Cutter wrapped the stretcher under Zak and inflated it. The stretcher formed to his shape in a few seconds. He placed a bio-clip on Zak and used a hand monitor to read it. "Shock. Unconscious. We'll make sure he can't move until I can check for any broken bones or concussion."

Zak groaned, his eyes blinked open, his expression confused.

"Stay still." Cutter took hold of Zak's head, letting the stretcher finish form-freezing Zak's body immobile.

Zak's gaze focused on Cutter and changed to her, where she watched over Cutter's shoulder. "Jake?"

"Alive. Unconscious. Ship Dog and Lock are taking him to sickbay."

"I'm all right; don't need to be carried. Take care of Jake."

"You might have injured your neck or have concussed yourself."

"Not broken. Can feel my hands and feet. Let go."

Against Zak's protest, Cutter latched the stretcher straps. As Cutter pushed the stretcher toward the hatch, the access opened. The gangway beyond automatically illuminated.

In moving the stretcher out of the bay, Cutter appeared to pass through the partition rather than the hatch. Renna blinked hard and held onto the back end of the stretcher.

Emotion disrupts mental concentration. Focus!

"Everyone, stay focused on where you are," Cutter ordered as he helped her move Zak.

His command registered even as her thoughts rationalized her loss of control. Renna inhaled, held her breath, and focused on a mental image of the hatch. Behind her, she heard the game lights click off. A backward glance showed the last overhead illumination black out. Once out of the hatch, she recalled an image of the catwalk tunnel to the main ship.

Travel became easier once they entered the *Vagrant Spirit*.

~ * ~

Renna stood with Ship Dog and Lock while Ezry helped Cutter diagnose Jake and Zak.

"Well, how is he?" Zak lay on one of the loungers, still caught in the stretcher.

"Not as bad off as you." Cutter glanced at Zak from reading Jake's bio readings. "Don't believe it. He's fine. No shock, no burns, and no bots...just deeply asleep."

He went to Zak and released the stretcher. "Well, outside of a huge lump on your extremely thick skull, there is no damage. Some sleep and a few days rest will put you to right."

"Told you." Zak tried to swing his feet off the bench seat.

"Un-unh." Cutter pushed him back. "I said rest. I'll be waking you up every few hours to make sure you haven't sustained any undetected damage."

Renna felt dizzy and disoriented. She grabbed the back of a chair. A glance showed she was not the only one affected. In the silence, she heard the Rabican's sound change, wuffling in deceleration.

"Something is happening." Ezry looked around in alarm.

Everyone looked to her.

"The Rabican is winding down." Renna sensed the change radiating through the ship with a strange tremor. Glancing at the wall monitors, she verified what she already knew. No one manned the flight deck. No one could regulate the ship if the CS9 disengaged the Rabican. No one to order the Rabican idle; no one to order the CS9 to maintain ship support.

Grabbing her intel and connex she strode to the hatch.

"Where are you going?" Zak pushed himself up, bracing his arms against his impromptu bed.

"The flight deck."

"Stay here, that's an order."

...vagrant spirit crew prepare for emergence...

She turned around to stare at him, an internal war raging with her training. Her hold on the hatch mechanism gave her courage. She lifted her chin. "Someone must be there. You and Jake are incapacitated; therefore, your order is invalid."

The mechanism released, and she left before Zak could say more.

Her mind reeled. *I disobeyed an order.* The catwalk heaved in overlapping images. *Focus.*

...flight officer renna markham four minutes to emergence...

"What? You couldn't have given warning sooner?" She gasped as she ran, using her arms to push off from the gangway's partitions as she careened forward.

...crew preoccupied in port cargo hold ...out of audio contact...

It was true. No one had worn a connex during the game.

Her weight lightened to near floating and amplified to an unbearable load in quick revolving cycles. Her legs nearly collapsed.

"Renna, get back here, you don't have time!" Zak shouted through her connex.

...flight deck and forward compartment radiation protected...

"I'm moving as fast as I can."

...time insufficient to reach flight deck or return to forward compartment...

The deck disappeared from beneath her feet. Her feet moved against nothing. She kept running. She passed through a partition. "Focus. Focus. On gangway, on gangway." The corridor reformed around her. Noise, yelling, profanity filtered into her awareness. Logic told her someone spoke through her connex. The sounds were gibberish.

Darkness fell behind her. A whirling stream of pinpoint lights led her forward. She followed the shimmering, swaying line. Her peripheral vision turned gray and nebulous. Nothing existed except the lights ahead of her. She gasped quick breaths. The sound filled her ears like hollow echoes.

...two minutes to emergence...

The weight crushed her. She fell to the deck and pulled herself forward. Her hand touched a partition. She was moving sideways rather than forward.

...one minute to emergence...

Renna swore, using words acquired from her crewmates. Within her blurry vision, she saw the ladder and crawled toward it. "Focus. The ladder is there. Reach for it. It is there."

...emergence begun...

Nausea hit her when rapid waves of color hit her retinas. Static flowed over her body, itching and burning. Her hand moved forward like an unconnected, foreign object. She couldn't feel it.

"Fingers close."

Energy flowed in, around, and over her in color-filled streams. Using sheer will, she pulled herself to the ladder and grabbed the railing lining the ladder. Her foot dropped through the ladder rungs when she took a step. She closed her eyes. Hand over hand she pulled, picturing the ladder in her mind, forcing her feet to balance on each step, counting each one.

Reaching the upper catwalk, she opened her eyes. The airlock to the flight deck floated and wavered before her, not opening. "Open." She spoke or thought she did.

...automated access inactivated standard safety precaution...

She swore again in desperation. "Handle. Handle is here." Closing her eyes, she concentrated on her hand. Located her fingers by flexing them. Reaching, feeling, her hand glided over the hatch's reinforced surface, came to the projection indicating the handle. It moved slowly. She grasped tighter and pushed harder. Pushed with her mind, willed it to unlock. She never heard the latch, but felt the mechanisms shift and slide. Pushing the hatch into the hollow side pocket took all her strength.

Renna fell into the airlock. Her hand still grasped the handle. Her hold stopped her tumble, wrenching her arm and shoulder. The rest of her body flung outward and seemed to stretch into infinity. She ordered her feet into the tiny compartment, pulled the door, and shoved the handle into locking position.

In the darkness of the reinforced airlock, the outside aberrations eased. She felt her thundering breath. The security hatch into the flight deck operated more smoothly. Wobbling into the flight deck, her hand still grasping the handle, she twirled as she extended to her arm's length. A hard heave closed the door. The lock slipped home. She ordered her fingers to loosen. Two staggering steps took her to the command chair. Renna crumpled into the seat, closed her eyes to concentrate on calming herself.

...ten minutes into emergence ...flight officer renna markham radiation exposure logged into medical file...

Renna swallowed, forcing herself to sit erect in the command chair and read the console. She ignored the pounding in her ears and behind her eyes while she double-checked all security systems. Making sure all security doors throughout the ship were locked down, she switched the exterior hatches to security mode. Life-support systems remained operational. She fed more oxygen into the forward compartment and flight deck.

Done, she fell back into the seat, stiffening her neck muscles to keep her head upright in the headrest amid the swirling sensation enveloping her. She still wore the skin-tight game uniform.

Taking a deep breath, she giggled. *How unkin.*

Twenty-three

...2180.063-02:16 universal space-time ...mission status ...emergence successful ...mission complete ...rabican offline ...cs9vs power source shifted to backup ...flight duration ninety-four days ...four hours fifty-two minutes ...location unknown ...jake terran biobots extracted and in process of migrating for release into rabican compartment ...relay processors built ...cs9vs redundant higher functions system migrates to memory grid ...vagrant spirit power system offline...

Renna woke. The flight deck console surrounded her. She looked over the flight controls, blinking her eyes.

Zak spoke through the intercom.

"Answer me before my aching head bursts!" He sounded furious. She guessed he had been yelling for some time.

It occurred to her if Zak lowered his voice, he could save both their heads. Her hand flopped once in utter exhaustion on the wide armrest before she could make her fingers move to open the audio. "Captain Zak."

"Thank God." She heard him exhale. "Where are we?"

"Checking." She activated the now working exterior hull camera monitors and ran the feed to the fore compartment. Her vision blurred, and her eyes felt burned. She blinked and looked at the monitors before opening the view screen shield. Normal space. Biting her lip, she wiped the sweat from her face with the back of her hand. *Calmness, professionalism, duty.*

Renna checked the control panels through tear-blurred vision. "Normal space, location...six AU from Proxima Centauri." The all-important Rabican panel lay quiet, red indicators disclosed its status. "The Rabican is offline, the Jupiter1090 is offline, maneuvering engines offline, navigation system offline, ramscoop offline, tracking system offline, communications offline, traveling one PSL. Operating on battery backup. Oh shit." The profanity came easily. A small asteroid appeared on a collision course with the ship.

"Renna?"

"CS9 connect power to lateral and forward engine arrays."

...unauthorized order ...vagrant spirit flight officer renna markham lacks authority...

"CS9 relay power to lateral and forward engine arrays," Zak repeated her order. He must have seen the impending disaster through the fore compartment's screens.

"Ramscoop, tracking, and navigation," Renna yelled, punching commands into the console rejecting her input.

"CS9, ramscoop, tracking, and navigation online," Zak repeated her words.

"Power ship systems."

Again Zak echoed her adding, "Give Renna security command status."

...power activated to requested systems ...jupiter1090 and rabican engines offline...

Renna exhaled, glad Zak had given her temporary control. As the panels became operative, Renna punched in directional changes, felt lateral engines fire.

The force drove the *Vagrant Spirit* into a twirling arc, skirting the oblique trajectory of the stray asteroid.

Space stretched empty before the ship and distant stars became steady beacons of light. Closer, a small star blazed, throwing flares widely across the view screen, distracting her. *Focus! Duty!*

Her fingers touched pads in rapid motion, redirecting the laterals into reverse thrust position. Using the ramscoop, she diverted the collected hydrogen into the forward exhaust jets, helping slow the ship with an assist from the lateral engine arrays.

A glance at the chronometer showed nearly six hours had passed. She was not surprised when both Zak and Jake burst into the flight deck minutes later. She had already unlocked the airlock hatches. Jake slipped into the co-pilot's seat. Space stretched out before them in undeniable star patterns. She redirected an exterior camera to focus on Proxima Centauri.

"My God, we did it." Zak's initial worried, near-angry expression turned to one of amazed incredulity. "We're four light-years from our galaxy."

"What is the time?" Jake asked in practical tones. "And can we get back?"

"Proxima Centauri is sixty days away by our current drift speed. We could orbit the star and collect energy." Renna punched up the coordinates.

"Set the course," Zak ordered.

Jake's hand stalled over the lateral engine command panel. He twisted to look at Zak.

For a long silent moment, they stared at each other.

Zak reached over her shoulder and opened the general ship log.

Jake waved to the command panel. "Let's get you authorized for issuing orders."

"Sorry, Ren, should've made the change sooner." Zak watched the view, throwing her a glance with his apology. "Flight Officer Renna..."

"Doe," Renna said, sensing his reluctance. "A name for someone unknown, for someone with no name. It is appropriate."

Zak tipped his head, accepting her name. "Renna Doe, formerly Renna Markham of the *Vagrant Spirit*, is restored to all command protocols as an officer of the ship."

...change logged...

Suppressing her satisfaction, Renna inserted the coordinates to the lateral engines and turned the ship's trajectory toward its new destination.

"I'll take watch. You get Ren checked out." Jake said, his attention on the view screen. His request sounded like an order. "Let the others know our situation."

"Aye, aye, Captain," Zak replied.

Jake flushed and flashed an easy smile. "Sorry."

"No. Let's make the change official now." Zak regarded the scene in the turret window. "Never wanted the position...and now I have other priorities and I'll stay for duty."

~ * ~

An hour later, Renna returned to the forward compartment where the other crew waited for Captain Jake to give his report.

"I want to work with the CS9, want to start mapping the area," Zak told Jake before the captain left the flight deck. Jake had nodded in agreement, and left Zak there.

Renna floundered in disbelief, even having witnessed the transfer of power. Only failed officers guilty of a major mistake lost dom status. Zak had made no mistakes, yet willingly gave up his high position. She didn't believe him weak or foolish and knew he carried out his captain's duties with diligence and dispatch. *What drove him?*

"He has an explorer's passion, Ren." Jake grinned at her confusion as they walked to the fore compartment. Renna felt a blush rise up her neck and spread over her cheeks. Jake continued. "I love the journey. Zak loves the destination."

A near relaxed atmosphere prevailed in the fore compartment. They accepted the officer switch with unruffled calm, just as they accepted Zak's return to the flight deck.

The wardroom's interior, while partially returned to its former comfort, retained the impregnable appearance of a fortified compartment. Renna felt their stares as she took her place. An interrupted card game still littered part of the table. No one bothered to clear the table as they all sat down for a conference.

Jake started his debriefing. "All right, let's decide what to do. We are currently headed for Proxima Centauri. Orbiting the star will give us steady power for however long we stay. The ramscoop collector will provide minimal energy until Vera is brought online."

Renna read the crew's expressions easily. Jake's description of their situation alarmed Ezry, who swallowed, her hands curled into tight fists.

"How do we get back?" Ezry asked.

"Rabican." Ship Dog seemed totally unconcerned.

"We know what to expect now." Cutter placed a hand over one of Ezry's fists. "If the Rabican made the journey here, it can return."

Renna kept her mouth shut, envying the concern Cutter showed Ezry, another unkin reaction. Cutter's assurances belied many possibilities and impossibilities.

He had ordered Renna to the examination table the moment she walked through the hatch. Although her radiation levels were high, there was no physical danger. He ordered an anti-radiation regime, and she now wore an exposure-warning patch. She knew Cutter cared for her, and she wanted to experience his love for Ezry, only with Zak.

"Our survival is going to take work. And time." Jake emphasized the last. His determined expression matched his words. "We have to plan for a lengthy stay."

"Why?" Ezry cried. "Why can't it just take us back?"

"We don't know where we started. The original insertion point was not logged into the CS9. When we first inserted into transition space, our own tracking system had been inoperative for days."

"How are we going to survive?"

"Just the subject we're about to discuss." Jake smiled at Ezry.

"We need to go back now." Ezry's shriek didn't affect the men, and they didn't immediately respond.

"We must determine our insertion point, Ez." Cutter tried to calm his mate.

Renna tensed. Ezry deserved the truth. "We can't return until we know our insertion point. If we miss the insertion location and time, we will be off in time and location on our return."

Ezry glared at her, but her eyes flickered with more than fright.

"Zak will track down the insertion point, plot it out," Jake said.

"Necessities." Ship Dog pointed out their priority.

"Cutter and Ezry inventoried everything. I've made out a long ration list while I've been sick."

"Fastest recovery I've ever seen," Lock said with a broad smile.

"The nanobots are gone from his system. The CS9 must have removed them when it attacked him." Cutter shook his head. "Maybe not an attack at all, but a cure."

"Can't we at least turn that thing off?" Ezry asked.

Lock shook his head, "Don't think so. The CS9 operates most of the ship, and like Cutter said, this time the CS9 helped Jake—hell, it helped us."

"We must convince the CS9 to turn itself off, as Jake convinced it to turn off the Rabican." Renna injected her opinion, startling the others. They looked at her. "I have had a long time to think on why the Rabican killed the *Markham3*. The Rabican was the only engine, and the Rabican always strives to reach the shortest route through transition space."

"The Rabican traveled through normal space," Cutter said.

"No," Renna said, shaking her head. "The Rabican never operated right in the reality of our normal space."

Understanding covered Jake's face. "Ren's right. When the Rabican operated in normal space, the engine destroyed the *Markham3*."

"We don't know for sure what destroyed the *Markham3*," Ezry said.

When no one reacted to Ezry's allegation, Renna looked at Cutter. "Vera saved us by feeding the Rabican the power needed while still driving the ship in normal space. If we can get the two engines to work in tandem, we might have a smoother ride home.

The CS9 must be reprogrammed to accept changes." She shrugged, biting her lower lip. *Conjecture. I'm only guessing.*

"How?" Ship Dog asked. Renna noted that his mustache trembled.

"Decipher the CS9's program. Rewrite programming as necessary," Jake answered.

"Rewrite the CS9." Lock looked intrigued. He shook his head. "Not easy with a quantum computer. We'd have to have a shipyard to do the construction." He flicked a loose card on the table. The card skittered and slid across it.

"The CS9 has restructured the *Vagrant Spirit* into a more efficient ship. Perhaps we can get it to do the work for us," Jake said.

"You agreed we needed to convince this thing to turn itself off!" Ezry protested.

"The CS9 has to operate the ship until we are ready to download new code. The *Vagrant Spirit*'s original systems are now integrated."

Renna looked at Lock. "If Markham Company stole the design, they probably added their own language. Those changes might be causing discrepancies in the CS9's logic."

Lock exhaled and looked at the overhead. After a minute, he gazed at Jake. "Yeah. She's right. Talk about difficult."

"You and Ren can work on that project." Jake nodded. "Ship Dog, you have to get Vera online pronto. We'll need her to guide us. Ren, you convince the CS9 to turn off its higher programming, so it won't question what we do. We can manually operate the ship. Ezry, you need to re-establish your garden. I know you've started, but do you have enough seed?"

Ezry nodded. "Will it be safe in the hydro-farm? No more strange effects there or in the rest of the ship?"

"Shouldn't be a problem now. We're back in normal space. Cutter, you'll be working with me. We need to help Ship Dog bring the engine online and figure out how to operate a hyper-transit ship."

"Any suggestions for living long-term in this space?" Lock asked, his face taut. "I think we're going to give cabin fever a whole new definition." He turned his head and stretched his neck in an uncomfortable way, ending with his lips pressed tight together.

"We need to entertain ourselves. Find things to occupy our minds and hands besides our regular work," Jake replied.

"Taking turns entertaining each other after dinner would be a good thing to do." Cutter looked at Renna. "Still got to teach you to cook." His glance slid from her to Ezry with a wry look. "Ezry could put on some theater."

His woman glared at him, looking ready to explode.

Jake interrupted. "All right. Next item. We need to deal with Ren's insubordination. However loose our regulating structure, we must follow orders," Jake said.

"An order is an order only when coming from a competent officer, and someone had to be on the flight deck for security when we emerged." Renna remained unrepentant, returning Jake's stare. Pure bravado.

"That's not a very crewkin response," Lock said. "What's happened to you?"

Jake ignored Lock. "As emergence proved, someone needed to be on the flight deck. Even with redundant controls and monitors here, we don't get the complete show as seen from the flight deck."

She frowned at Lock. "I do not know what I am, who I am, or where I belong. I know, however, I do not wish to be a podder any longer."

"Crewkin," Ship Dog said. His mustache twitched.

"She received a radiation overdose," Cutter said, looking at Jake. "I'd advise admonition."

Jake nodded. "Agreed. A reprimand for insubordination will be attached to Ren's work file."

"Only an admonishment?" Renna asked shocked as she expected a real punishment.

"What did you expect? Shunning?" Lock asked with a slick smile, his dark eyes sparkling. "Not enough people to talk to as it is, not about to exclude anyone."

Twenty-four

...2180.091-02:16 universal space-time ...mission status ...rabican offline ... power source shifted to ramscoop ...cs9vs helps terran crew restructure jupiter1090 compartment ...flight officer renna challenges cs9vs programming...

The interior of the flight deck felt cramped with both her and Zak working uncomfortably close. Renna ignored her disruptive emotions while she grappled with the CS9, encouraging the cognitive support to uninstall its higher functions. Jake decided not having the CS9 online while they worked would be better, afraid it would send nanobots to reconfigure the engine when Ship Dog, Cutter, and Lock tried to bring the Jupiter1090 online.

...need rational...

"We have reason to believe the Rabican engine cannot operate in normal space as a propulsion engine. Captain Jake Terran requests the CS9 comply for the crew's safety as priority one directive requires."

...rabican now offline ...cs9vs can reconfigure compartment...

"Captain Terran cannot chance the CS9VS inadvertently initiating the Rabican as happened on the *Markham3*."

...rabican saved ...cs9 survived ...mission successful...

"The *Markham3* crew died. The ship was ruined, torn apart."

...renna markham3 now renna doe with the vagrant spirit survived...

"Yes. Before the CS9VS is given clearance access to the *Vagrant Spirit*'s logs, the crew must investigate the Rabican's programming to integrate it with the Jupiter1090 function."

...do you request termination of cs9vs...

"No. The CS9 is needed to reactivate the Rabican, and for the *Vagrant Spirit*'s operation in transit space. I repeat, the captain requests the CS9 take higher functions offline for the safety of the crew working on the Jupiter1090."

...renna doe wants to change programming cs9vs...

"Not at this time. Vera is not compatible with CS9 language. The Terran crew wishes to survive, they wish to return to their time and place."

...junpiter1090 ...vera...

Renna cursed herself. Such slips were unprofessional. "A name given to the Jupiter1090 by crewmember Ship Dog, the *Vagrant Spirit*'s engineer."

...return terran crew cs9vs priority directive ...return terminates cs9vs and rabican engine ...conflict...

Renna sighed. "No, return does not terminate the Rabican or the CS9. They will probably be relocated to another ship."

...integrated into vagrant spirit ...flight officer renna doe requests disintegration...

"Captain Jake Terran orders the CS9VS's compliance." Her eyes flicked to Zak where he worked. She reluctantly pulled her gaze back to the panel in front of her. Her mind lingered on Zak.

Giving up leadership, personal power, and prestige seemed unnatural. All kin strove to serve their ship. Service was their only purpose. Instead of being downcast at his demotion, Zak acted unconcerned, relieved, even empowered. He worked next to her so completely absorbed in his telescopes, cameras, and maps, he remained unaware of her continual dialog with the CS9.

Her gaze drifted to the turret window. Outside, three suns shined in a field of star patterns. *Zak serves the Vagrant Spirit, yet his love of what is out there drives him.*

His preoccupation left her feeling alone in company. A different experience from being by one's self. Unfortunately, she constantly thought about him. She slept in her slip-in bunk and read norm literature. The occupation helped relieve her loneliness. Now thoughts of Zak broke her concentration.

More daunting was learning the richness of norm culture; so unimaginable in scope, she could never absorb everything, and equally disheartening was discovering how limited her kin world had been.

Renna frowned. The doctor at Markham Company had been wrong. She would never give up or stop trying. There were mistakes to regret, especially initiating trouble between Jake and Zak. She learned, discovered, and absorbed, not only history, but also information about norms. She exhaled a sigh, realizing how far she had yet to go—with Ezry she averted trouble by evading the woman. *Avoidance.* A trait common in her past, one she needed to change.

"You didn't answer it." Zak's observation pulled her back to the flight deck. She blushed at her lapse into daydreaming. Readings flickered across the panel where he worked. Zak's face remained buried in the screen he studied. His long, gentle fingers adjusted the telescope controls, grabbing her attention.

She shivered, remembering how they felt running over her skin. She shook her head. Duty. "Captain Terran orders the CS9VS to take higher functions offline. He has given the order." Her tongue stumbled in her dry mouth.

...relinquishing higher functions may cause ship error...

"Operation will depend on the crew until the CS9 is required," Renna said.

...required indeterminate designation...

"Everything is indefinite. There are no definite answers to correct our situation."

...cs9vs complies...

Lights on the Rabican's panel turned yellow before switching to red.

"Does indefinite apply to us, too?" Zak asked.

Renna stilled, unsure what to say, unsure what he meant.

He looked up from his screen, his blue eyes intent. "This is a small ship. We can't continue avoiding each other, not talking."

"I caused trouble between you and Jake."

Zak laughed. The friendly sound soothed her. "Partly. I caused trouble. Jake caused trouble. Didn't any of your kin ever challenge Dom Dukan?"

"No." The immediate answer sprung from her lips just as her mind freed forgotten memories. "Yes..."

"But?"

"Early in our training, the nurses made sure Dom Dukan prevailed."

"Not won?"

"No. Sometimes he lost. Challenges always turned out worse for the kin who confronted him. Soon none did."

"Ren, conflict is part of norm life. I was jealous of Jake, jealous over you, jealous over other things. I was wrong. I don't own you. You are free to do whatever you want."

"You wish to share comfort?" she asked. Confusion swept through her.

His eyes slid away, and his jaw firmed. "Not comfort. Love. I have no right to ask, not now. Maybe in the future."

"To share comfort when some must go without is wrong."

"I know." His expression baffled her. She had never seen such on kin. "We might be here for a very long time. I won't...wouldn't... fault anyone for what they did for relief."

"I will not go to Jake for comfort," Renna said. "Nor will I come to you or anyone else; not until I understand what I want."

The grin crossing Zak's face surprised her. "Fair enough." He returned to his telescope.

He nodded at the quiescent panel. "Looks like you've had success there."

She frowned. "Maybe."

After running a few tests, she called Jake. "As far as I can tell, the CS9 has uninstalled higher functions."

"You've run systems checks?"

"Yes. Basic functions are operational, so begin manual application and adjustment."

"You sound doubtful. What is your fear, Ren?" Jake asked.

Jake's conclusion surprised her. Did he suspect the CS9 or her of duplicity? Did he hear the suspicion in her voice? "The CS9 submitted too easily. It fears termination, and this was a form of termination. It has no reason to trust this crew."

"Okay. Noted. I think you're over-reacting. No matter what the CS9 is capable of, it is still a machine. We'll go ahead and bring up the Jupiter1090 to online status. You and Zak should see if you can create a power exchange to feed into the ship's remaining functions. Once the Jupiter1090 is online, we'll test the navigation and helm systems from the flight deck. If the CS9 has rendered controls inoperable from there, we should be able to handle ship's operations from the redundant system in the engine compartment."

Twenty-five

...2180.092-22:47 universal space-time ...mission status ...rabican engine offline ...ship systems power offline ...renna doe complicit in termination of cs9markham3 ...jupiter1090 offline ...cs9vs high function transferred to hull memory grid ...priority protocol conflict ...language translation complete ...observe crew ...opening crew files and ship's logs...

Once inside the abaft loading compartment of the aft cargo bay, Lock whistled. The sharp blast of sound through her connex hurt Renna's ears. Everyone except Ezry, who remained in the wardroom, and Jake, who was on the flight deck, stood next to her in biosuits. Helmet lights illuminated her crewmates' astonished expressions in the dark compartment. The powerful beams from their hand torches swept the dark compartment and exposed vast changes in the interior.

The force field was down. Without its shimmering barrier, they viewed the Rabican. Circles of light from their hand beams exposed the engine. The former shipping crate filled most of the central area, intermingled with the deck and side partitions of the *Vagrant Spirit*.

Conduit and reinforcement lattice-like supports surrounded a huge elongated cauldron in geometric precision. The Rabican stood three times the height of any of them. Sections reached toward the overhead. From her perspective, Renna could not tell if the structures touched the overhead.

"The monitors show some amazing changes up here," Jake spoke through their connex.

She heard the excitement in his voice. An energy and charisma she had never seen infused Jake. A wave of happiness breezed through her. He had come too close to death and returned with more than he lost. Was this how he was in the Space Service Corp? All she knew was she did not want to lose another crewmember ever again.

"My God, will you look at that!" Lock bounced ahead, his torch moving in dizzying motion with his steps. Ship Dog lumbered behind him.

"Do any of the original power grids operate?" Cutter asked, irritation in his deep voice.

"Not in this compartment. Everything has been reconfigured, even the emergency lights." Zak's smooth voice calmed her. Renna appreciated his tranquility. His calmness steadied her mood and helped her concentrate as no dom, or even Jake, had ever done.

"The engine's quadrupled in size!" Lock said.

"Literally made from the excess materials in the *Vagrant Spirit*," Zak confirmed, as he viewed the Rabican, his head stretched back to look up. "This can't be part of the original Rabican design, can it? How in hell would they have gotten the engine out of the *Markham3*? Where do you suppose the programming is stored?"

"Rack." Ship Dog plodded toward the far end of the compartment, his attention on his intel with the schematics given by the CS9 before the system went offline.

Renna followed them, inspecting everything she could see on the engine, pointing her intel's analyzer to collect readings, letting the talk wash through her helmet audio without heed. Her inspection ended at the former loading doors, fused now into a seamless hull through which the Rabican engine extended. She wished the exterior cameras worked so they could inspect the hull changes.

She found an opening underneath the Rabican's structure. Using her torch to inspect the opening, she crawled through straight to the other side of the Rabican.

The others emerged after her, and she was abruptly pulled around. Zak jammed his faceplate against hers, and she could see the anger in his eyes. "Let us know what you plan to do before you do it. This isn't safe."

His loss of calmness startled her so much she nearly addressed him as dom. "Safe enough. I'm comparing the physical aspects to the holo image in the CS9 files. The image is very accurate. The data processors should be on this side." She walked away.

Zak followed.

"Look." She pointed to a rectangular protrusion. "The processor rack has fused with the deck. Something must have changed the original programming to create these alterations. These fusions could not have been part of the original design specs."

"How do you know?"

"I don't...just speculate. If the original engine from the *Markham3* fit in the cargo carrier placed here, something changed."

"Unless only the heart of the system was cut out and boxed up. I agree. I've never heard of a system capable of doing what this one has." Zak's faceplate moved with his head's motion while he continued to inspect the Rabican looming above them. "Building capabilities like this have never been documented in any articles I've read."

"Here," she said, running her gloved hands over the processor rack. "How does the rack open?" She tried to unlock the cover. "It's stuck."

"Fused." Ship Dog fished some tools from the kit he carried and cut through the cover. He inspected the cut, making unintelligible sounds part vocal, part hum.

Lock motioned him aside and pushed him away. He looked at the processor. Renna saw lights still crawled across the computer's reader and felt a qualm of disquiet.

"Power," Ship Dog said.

Lock pointed an analyzer into the rack. "Just enough to keep the system operational until recalled."

"Can you download the programming?" Zak asked.

"Yeah, I think so." He attached the data transfer clip and watched the files begin to load. "Holy-moly, this is huge."

"The CS9 is building itself and the Rabican into the ship," Zak said. "Why?"

"It does not want to be terminated," Renna replied, suddenly aware of the CS9's objective. "The only way to reclaim the Rabican now is to reclaim the *Vagrant Spirit*."

"Hell, another lost cargo," Jake said in their connex.

Zak laughed. "You sound like Cutter. Worry about lost cargo when we get back."

"And you sound like Jake," Lock said. "Damn, I don't look forward to reading all this program code!"

~ * ~

Renna sat a little apart from the others, watching and listening. Not only holo displays but also printed schematics covered and spilled off the wardroom table where the crew sat. Only two overhead lights covered the area. In another turn of adversity, Vera remained offline. The Jupiter 1090 would remain offline until the compartment and exterior changes made by the CS9's nanobots could be changed. Energy was strictly rationed until they could generate enough power from the solar collectors...at their drift rate, three weeks away from an optimum distance.

A few cookies sat on a small platter. Ship Dog had inhaled what seemed to Renna an inordinate number. She sighed as she nibbled around the edges of her cookie. *Food during ship's business. Maybe not such a bad practice? As long as food lasted.* Except she wanted more than remained on the plate.

They were all hungry for good food. Everything was strictly rationed. Cutter served only one meal every other day and served cold food from stored meals in the food keeper. They all decided they'd rather save energy elsewhere and have at least a few good meals interspersed between ration packets.

Hygiene was the first thing cut—no clean clothes; they washed from prepackaged toweling. The men's faces wore facial hair, stubby and scruffy looking. Renna watched the growth with fascination. All crewkin males had such hair permanently removed at puberty.

Her own hair grew apace. Curls hung to her forehead. She pushed the strands out of the way. Zak called the color ripe-cherry auburn. Her hair changed her crewkin look, making her feel more norm. She decided to never cut her hair again, no matter how unprofessional her appearance became.

"Here is our position." Zak held a red light on the holo display indicating their location. "We're deep in Alpha Centauri, close to Proxima, about four light-years from home."

"Wow!" Lock said. "Think about where we are! No one's ever been out this far." After his excitement, Renna watched his dark coloring gray. His nostrils pinched tight, and his lips pressed together. *He is afraid.*

"No. We've broken a record there," Jake agreed. "Not even unmanned probes have reported back from this distance."

Ship Dog huffed. "Can't get back."

"Not with Vera. Not in our lifetimes." Zak agreed with a smile. "We need the Rabican."

Ezry made a noise and Cutter clasped her hand. She withdrew hers and crossed her arms over her chest.

"Here are schematics of how the ship has changed," Jake said. "In their exvee check, Ren and Ship Dog repaired our hull cameras. As you can see, the Jupiter1090 has been sealed off. These extensions are the aft hold with the Rabican extending into open space. Good work, you two!"

"Perfectionist." Ship Dog nodded toward Renna, settling back into his chair.

"Really?" Lock snorted. "How would we have guessed such a thing?"

Jake didn't reprimand their interruptions. Renna no longer expected he would. Occasionally, she even giggled at the quips passed between them. The first time, they had stared at her. She contained her straying thoughts and returned her attention to what Jake was saying. "Once we reach a safe orbit and have established an energy source, we will need to reconfigure the compartment holding the Jupiter1090."

"Which means more exvee work," Zak said.

"More dangerous work," Cutter said, his eyebrows lowered, squeezing closer together as he frowned. Lines formed on his forehead.

Renna doubted Ezry or Cutter qualified, which left five people to do the work of twenty in a shipyard with proper equipment.

"Yes, exvee work is dangerous, and this job will be difficult," Zak agreed. "We've trained for such emergencies—just need to hone our skills."

"Lock, you and Ren will work on decoding the CS9's programming," Jake stated. "We have to regain functional control of the ship."

"We'll need them outdoors," Zak said.

"Can you two handle both?" Jake asked.

Renna nodded. "Have to."

"I can help them, too," Cutter said.

"You may not have time. You and Ezry will have to pick up everyone else's duties along with your own. Zak will be working on our return navigation and helping with the engines when needed."

"Don't know…" Lock started.

Renna overrode his indecision. "Yes, Jake." She looked at Lock in a challenge.

He shrugged. "There is a lot of programming to decipher."

"You have already broken the Markham code. You went to prison for decoding military files. This will be a snap." Renna flicked her fingers together.

Lock rolled his eyes as he looked at Ship Dog. "An optimist, too."

"Even a snap might take longer than we have if the code is written in Markham or, God forbid, military code," Jake said.

"Not if Ezry grows us food." Renna lowered her gaze to the table and waited. A fast, encompassing inspection of the room when she first entered showed Ezry dressed in a very plain tunic, a guide to Ezry's mood. She had avoided looking at Ezry since her attention always upset the woman.

"I was going to mention duties, Captain Renna." Jake's dry tone sounded angry.

Everyone laughed.

Renna threw him a quick glance and when she saw his face didn't match his tone, grinned. *Insubordination came easy.* "Sorry, sir."

"Presumption," Ship Dog said, blowing his mustache. Renna grinned at him, too.

"Yes," Jake said. "I suppose we all know our strengths and what we have to do. We will all do two hours of maintenance as well as a fourteen-hour shift for as long as it takes."

"Breakfast and dinner will be held as usual, even if meals are ration packs," Cutter interrupted Jake. "And we will celebrate all usual holidays, with one evening off every five days for recreation." Jake nodded.

"I've included a few crewkin holidays, those commonly known." Cutter looked at her.

"No." Her voice erupted louder than Renna desired, filled with more than negation. "No, I do not wish to celebrate. Not any of them." She ignored Cutter's regard. "Your holidays will be enough."

"Ezry, you are in charge of bio-maintenance, and as Renna suggested, food production. You will also be picking up most of our habitation maintenance."

Ezry huffed. "Knew I'd end up a housekeeper."

"Much more than a housekeeper, Ez." Cutter hugged her shoulders in a rough grab. Ezry gave him a bleak look and pulled away.

"We all have a lot of hard work. If we are to make this happen, two very different engines must be merged into one functioning system," Jake said.

"How will we get back?" Ezry's words were so low she whispered. "There's too much against us, an out-of-control computer, the wrong engine, and a crazy podder."

Zak grabbed and held Renna's hand. She let Ezry's words slide by. Renna smiled at him. *It was only true.*

"Faith," Cutter said taking one of Ezry's hands and kissing its back. Ezry's great black-brown eyes met Cutter's. "We don't know the direction."

"Zak will find our way home."

"I'll find the insertion point, Ezry. The CS9 tracked time. We'll get back the same way we came."

"Not in our lifetimes, and we might not have the energy to reach that star." Ezry broke down. Cutter drew his sobbing mate into his arms, patting her back and whispering, "Hush, we will be okay."

Renna couldn't help. She watched the exchange. Ezry never even noticed her stare. When the others went to their duties, she rose and left Cutter and Ezry alone. She walked the ship, her intel in hand.

~ * ~

Zak watched Renna leave the flight deck. He knew she wanted the co-pilot's seat he occupied. Jake wanted her on the lateral arrays, which had to be fired manually.

"What's going on?" Jake asked Zak. "You look worried."

"You're not? We're about to manually position a spacecraft into orbit with no operating engine."

"Piece of cake. I'm not talking about the work at hand. About Renna…"

"Not worried other than about when and how to approach her."

Jake laughed at him. "We're in this situation." His hand indicated the flight panel. "And you're worried about your gonads, having burned your skivvies once already."

"It's not just about sex."

Jake laughed.

Zak checked their position and tapped his audio on. "Ship Dog, fire the 270, three seconds." He asked Jake, "You watching the images coming from his helmet cam?"

The *Vagrant Spirit* shifted slightly, and Jake checked their status. "Yeah. Never was, was it?"

"Probably why I was so inept. She would share, you know. Tell me when."

"Only too well. Do you love her?" After a brief silence, Jake gave another order. "Lock, five seconds on the one-eighty." In between relaying orders, he asked, "Rather sudden, wasn't it?"

Zak gave an order to Renna. "Two seconds on the 90." After a moment, he replied. "We're still listing two degrees starboard. Did you know I never wanted an SSC career?"

"No? What did you do, enter so we could stay together? Prove which of us would be the better officer? Well, we answered the question—neither of us."

"There is no question you were the better officer," Zak answered. "I never wanted command. I wanted science. What happened wasn't your fault."

Jake rasped a dry, self-mocking laugh. "Try proving that to command. I gave up trying. Not such a good officer after all."

"You have a temper. Still, you were the best officer material they've seen for a long time. You should have seen you were stepping on bigger toes than mine."

"Yeah, I expect you're right," Jake said dryly, glancing at his twin for a second. "So, you joined for science? I can think of better places to work."

"I entered because I knew it was impossible to do what I really wanted. The SSC was the next best thing." A second glance showed Jake's attention remained on the readings streaming across the console.

"What did you want?" Jake asked, watching the ship's movement.

"You know when we were kids and I was investigating everything I could about the longhaulers and crewkin?"

"Yeah."

"I thought I could join one of their crews. Wanted to explore space...biggest disappointment of my life was when I learned they only haul cargo. Space exploration had been ceded to scientists based in those far ports with quantum telescopes."

Jake looked out the turret window at the strange sun the *Vagrant Spirit* was traveling toward. "Odd way to get your wish."

"Isn't it?"

"Lonely life."

"I always saw someone going with me. At first, you. When my libido kicked in during adolescence...a wife. I found the perfect one, holding her while she puked her guts out."

Jake laughed. "How romantic. You certainly messed this one up."

"Yeah."

"Is it only because she's crewkin?"

"Is that what you think?" Zak countered.

"No." Jake felt Zak's eyes on him. "Why don't you court her?"

Examining his brother's face, Zak hesitated before he said, "She needs time. Thinks one of us can't be left out." Zak grinned. "As close as we are, I'm not sure I want to go there with you."

Jake grinned, too. "You're working against her crewkin attitude, except she wants to change. She doesn't want anything to do with her past. Sounds like a perfect opportunity for you."

"Maybe. What about you?"

"Don't worry about me. I can handle myself."

Zak laughed. "I bet you can."

"Besides, I'm still smarting from my last encounter with love."

"You still missing the officer you hooked up with?"

"Sara Lingee. Yeah. Not much future there, not without the uniform. Okay. We're in orbit. Cutter, crank out the solar panels. Where are you going?"

Zak's grin returned as he rose from the co-pilot's seat. "You're captain, now. You have duty left. With sufficient power available, I'm going to get a shower, shave, and slide into some clean clothes."

Jake's obscene comment followed Zak into the airlock. He quickly changed his tone, giving an all-clear order to the crew.

~ * ~

Cooking was warm work, warmer than Renna liked. The smells were worth the effort. Cutter had been introducing her to spices. *A new world of scents.*

"Hold the knife like this, hand half on the handle, half on the top of the blade, and slice down." Cutter showed her on the cutting board. He quickly sliced potatoes into cubes. "Try to make your cuts the same size so they cook evenly."

Cutting took her longer than she liked. Renna made sure each slice was the size of Cutter's sample. His quick slices were hard to copy. Somehow, she wasn't giving the job her complete attention.

"Ezry needs your help. Is she still your woman? Do you not share comfort anymore?"

She felt Cutter's attention. "Yes, Ezry is still my woman. She is frightened. Hell, make that terrified. Has been since you came aboard. We have some problems to work through. She finds blaming me easier than facing her fears and her preconceptions. Why do you think she needs help? She has completed all the jobs assigned her." He pointed his knife at a pile of greens. "Already has sprouts ready to harvest."

"She is very sad."

"Worried. We all are."

"I know we all are. She only sews in her off time." *Beautiful things.* Renna fingered the garments when Ezry wasn't aware, for the pure pleasure of touching the fabrics. Ezry's action, though, scared her. Her expression reminded her so much of Sen. She turned to face Cutter. "It is not good behavior, Cutter. Not when we are all cooped here for what may be far too long. She cannot continue to live only in here, keeping to her cabin, excluding you and her friends. The rest of the ship is very safe now."

Cutter's brows lowered. "You're right. I should have noticed her behavior. All I've seen lately is her anger. I'll see what I can do. Put the potatoes in the pan. We'll bake them with the meat." He grinned and sprinkled the cubes with salt and pepper. "You get KP until further notice—part of learning to cook. That should help make Ezry happy."

"You can scold me. She will enjoy seeing me corrected." Renna returned his grin.

"How is the CS9 job going?"

Renna sighed. "Convincing the CS9 to give up higher functions was hard, and it is hard to decipher so much code."

"Jake and Ship Dog want to bring Vera back online tomorrow. You all did a good job out there opening the engine compartment to space."

Renna nodded. "We did an extraordinary job under the circumstances. Our work will make our orbit flight safer. There is more to do. Enough is unchanged to allow Vera to start."

"How are we going to last as long as all this will take?"

Renna had never heard such a tone from Cutter. She inspected his face. He was more worried than he had been showing. Distressed. "Living like this is not so hard when you have to. We must all become aware of each other and help one another when fear or despair comes. Ezry keeps her hands busy, but she lets her mind dwell only on our problems."

"Is that how kin survive long hauls?"

"No. Kin are afraid when every day is not exactly like the one before."

He chuckled. "And norms crave change? I don't think I'll agree, considering how uncomfortable I am in our present situation."

"You dislike boredom. All of you always search for excitement, for new stimulations, new things."

"Surely crewkin have emergencies."

"Yes, those situations are all thought out and trained for in advance. Everyone knows what he or she must do. When they don't know what to do, they panic." She disliked talking about her kin. It embarrassed her. *Being kin angered her, mortified her.*

"You can't just ignore your history, Ren. You can't change what you are. Ezry has tried. You should get to know Ezry. You share more than you realize."

She didn't know what to say to his assertion and didn't want to tell him how strongly Ezry would object.

He continued with his attention on the meat he was preparing. "Ez has a sad history, one of abuse and manipulation. I don't have the right to divulge her past to you except to tell you what I have."

"Thank you, Cutter. I am careful of Ezry. I know she is frightened." *Like Sen and my kin.* "She doesn't like or trust me, so there is little I can do to help her."

"Give her time, Renna. Give yourself time."

She smiled. "If time is all, we will have many occasions, won't we?"

Later, after dinner, Renna picked up the dishes and took them to the galley, while Cutter served dessert. Most of the galley had already been made ship-shape before dinner started.

"Come on, Renna," Lock called. "I want an audience."

"Coming." She finished putting a dish in the cleaner, wiped her hands, and joined the others.

"About time," Lock complained holding a deck of cards. "Been practicing this for days. Here, Ren, you can help." He fanned the deck out, face down. "Pick a card, and show it to everyone."

Ren pulled a card. "Two of clubs," she said and showed the card.

"No, no, give me the card back." Lock took the card and put it back in the deck. "Take another and show it to everyone. Don't let me know what it is."

She pulled another card and showed the six of hearts to everyone.

"That's great, let me put the card back into the deck." He held the deck out, and she watched him insert the card back into the deck.

"Okay. Now, blow on the deck."

Renna laughed. "Why?"

"Because this is a magic trick, and magic is always needed to complete it."

Smiling, she blew on the deck of cards and looked at Zak. "Is he going to make a fool out of me?" Zak's smile promised her prediction.

Jake answered, "Probably. Or a big surprise."

She looked back at Lock. "Now what?"

Lock performed an elaborate bow and flourished the deck. "Is this your card?" The six of hearts stood out among the back designs of all the other cards in the deck.

"How did you do that?" Renna asked as everyone clapped. He slapped her hand as she reached for the deck.

"A magician never gives up his secrets."

"Oh, bosh," Ezry said. "Trick's so old, it ain't even a techno trick. It's all misdirection. He flipped the deck over before he inserted your card. All the other cards were already upside-down."

"The deck showed the back," Renna said, "and I inserted the card backside up. Ohhh."

"Yeah. He switched the top card back, dolt." Ezry sniffed at Cutter's glare.

"Bigmouth. Renna didn't know." Lock frowned. "For ruining my trick, you can do tomorrow's after-dinner entertainment."

Ezry's eyes slid over Renna with an accompanying huff. "So what? Don't expect nothing." Ezry left the table. Renna watched her settle with her sewing and looked to Cutter. He watched Ezry, too.

True to her word, Ezry had no entertainment the next night. Instead, Jake asked Renna what books she was reading. "History."

"What are you learning?" he asked.

"I decided to start at the beginning and found entries in the library on paleontology, anthropology, cultural, and art history. Later, I read about the Indus Valley, Tigris-Euphrates, and the Ganges. Now I am into the Egyptians." *Rather than where Markham began history.*

"You read all this since coming aboard?" Lock asked. She nodded.

"The *Vagrant Spirit* has a very good library."

"Our mother loved reading," Zak said. "There is a whole separate library of fiction when you get tired of non-fiction."

"I do not think I will get tired of it very soon."

"Not what Markham taught?" Cutter asked.

"No." She shook her head, enjoying the feel of her hair swinging along her neck and chin bone, and deciding she wasn't going to elaborate about her past training or Markham Company.

"I have something to share," Zak said. They all looked at him; he pulled up his intel and began reading, "This was a creature of enchantment, matchless in vigor, speed, and form, which disdained to share the diet of his fellow-steeds—corn or grass—and fed only on air. His name was Rabican."

"Where'd you find the reference?" Lock asked.

"Bullfinch, one of his ancient legends about Charlemagne."

"I'm starting a new endeavor to occupy my time, too." Cutter smiled. "A study...and each of you has a part in it. Plan on regular medical and psychological profile tests for the duration of our journey." Lock groaned.

"Not me," Ezry said from her estranged spot. "Not interested in being poked and prodded."

"While I hate the thought," Jake said, "it's a very good idea, so yes, you will, Ez."

Ezry glared at Jake. Rising, she went to her cabin on the other side of the compartment. Her feet slapped the deck in an angry cadence. An uncomfortable silence fell.

"Renna brought up another point," Cutter said still staring at Ezry's door. "We need a routine to keep us sane and rituals to enrich our daily lives."

"We have routines," Lock said in dismissal. "We always eat together."

"Cutter, that's your bailiwick," Jake said. "What you decree we need, I so order."

"I think this will require more than just my input. I'll toss out some ideas tomorrow at dinner, and we can hash out what we want to do."

~ * ~

Cutter waited as Ezry entered the wardroom. She slowly removed the biosuit she always donned to visit the hydro-farm.

"You don't need to wear the biosuit."

"Makes me feel safer." Underneath, she wore a stretch red and black animal print one-piece.

Desire dried Cutter's mouth, and he sighed, knowing it wouldn't lead anywhere. "Ez, honey, you can't..."

"Don't tell me can't. And don't honey me." She gave him an adamant stare.

"We will get back."

"Don't make empty promises. I'll believe we're back when we're back." She hung the biosuit in a locker.

"Damn it, Ez, stop! You can't go on the way you have. We need everyone's support to succeed."

"I do everything asked of me and more. That's all the support I'm going to give."

"I need more. I think you do, too."

"Too damn bad. We're done, Cutter. No sense pretending otherwise." She turned and walked into her cabin. "When we get back...if we get back, I'm leaving."

Twenty-six

...2180.112-10:36 universal space-time ...mission status ...cs9vs higher functions offline on main processor ...hull memory grid operational ...continue surveillance...

Lock learned back in his chair. "This is impossible."

"We must accomplish our goal. This is Markham code. Some I know. I think you know the code they kept from crewkin." His deep skin flushed darker, telling her he had read her files. "We will search until we find where the code changes, because I believe it will."

"You really think your company stole the program? Stole the Rabican?"

"Not my company!" *My owner.* She took a deep breath, settling herself. "I think they stole the engine and the program. Is the Rabican military? Maybe. Why doesn't the SSC have the engine now? Why didn't they investigate its loss or the *Markham3*'s disaster?"

"No telling."

"I think the SSC's trials also failed, and they gave up on the research. Undoubtedly, Markham failed, whether they worked from a stolen proto-program or not. I know the engine did not work before, as certainly as I know it worked this time."

"What made the Rabican work this time?"

"Vera, I think. Their mischance to depend on the Rabican for local propulsion, and our good fortune we didn't depend on the Rabican."

Lock burst out laughing. "Because we didn't know what we had onboard! You have an odd sense of good fortune."

Renna smiled and brought Lock back to business. "The CS9 was improperly taken offline. The log downloads show the history. The CS9 rebooted and started the Rabican, somehow going beyond its programming. The nanobots were to repair, not create—a standard protocol computer technicians placed on them from the start. The control appears gone. I think we will discover the cause in the code."

"Nothing about this has been standard." Lock sighed, shaking his head. "Okay. Let's tackle this thing even if reading the code takes the rest of our lifetimes."

"We will do it sooner than that."

Lock made a rude sound and Renna grinned. "Translate this section."

~ * ~

"Look at this," Lock said. Several weeks had passed since they had started the code search, time in which everyone had become accustomed, if not comfortable, to the situation. Lock rubbed his eyes and yawned. "I'll be lucky to come out of this assignment with my eyeballs able to focus further than sixteen centimeters in front of me."

"At least you can get clean, wear fresh clothing, and eat a hot meal." Renna looked at the code position he indicated. "This is where they changed code. Do you recognize it?"

"Yeah—old Corps code. This whole program is a mishmash of codes. Corps didn't write this...they stopped using this code a long time ago. It seems someone besides me broke into secured files."

"A thief or a traitor?" Renna asked.

"Semantics. Whoever did this was both." Lock glanced at her. "Sorry, Ren. Can't be pleasant knowing you worked for Markham."

"No. Worked, but not employed, owned." She cleared her throat to take out the wobbly sound. "Using old Corps code doesn't equate with stealing the code for the Rabican from the Corps. Why would they steal old code?"

"New Corps code had to understand old Corps code, so old equipment would operate with the new. There are civilians out there who know the old code. If you want to communicate with something in undecipherable new Corps code, find someone who knows old code. Did you know I worked with sentience prototypes when I was in the Corps?"

"No."

"Yeah." He leaned back in his seat and put his hands behind his head. "Lot of religious groups, and through them, politicians, would have been real unhappy with the projects in our lab. They finally closed the project down."

"Why?"

"They were afraid sentience in military programs might lead to all types of unexpected results, like ships not obeying the captain's orders and going rogue like a too-smart officer sometimes does." He grinned. "Or systems figuring they didn't need people at all. They were afraid of what they created, pure and simple. Especially after one experiment got out of hand and killed the lab techs and the lead programmers."

"Did you sell code?"

"No." He sighed and flipped his braids behind his shoulders. "Selling code isn't why they broke my ass. Curiosity caused my trouble. I wanted to explore and went places I shouldn't have. Legal accused me of spying. Their investigation couldn't prove anything other than an invasion with malicious intent. Like Ship Dog and Jake, it ended my career."

"Like Ship Dog and Jake?"

"Well, for different reasons. Ship Dog, who is a little borderline but a whiz with engines, went crazy. They kept giving him contradictory orders. When he crashed, they gave him a medical discharge."

"How did he…"

"Cutter's dad hired him. Still a damn fine engineer, if you can put up with his eccentricities."

"He loves Vera." Renna's gaze lingered on Lock's very eccentric person and dress.

"Yeah, I know, I'm just as eccentric. Must look outlandish to you."

"Because I was crewkin? When I first came aboard? Yes. Not now."

"Well, in appearances, you're the only normal one here. Jake got bounced for insubordination, failure to follow orders, and conduct unbecoming. We're all washouts, except Zak. He morally objected to what the Corps did to Jake and quit."

"They joined Cutter."

"Yes. He was unhappy being grounded in a hospital, even one on a space station, so when the opportunity came to run the *Vagrant Spirit*, Cutter took it. All the brothers share extreme family loyalty." He grinned and saluted. "A belated welcome aboard, crewmember."

With a straight face, Renna switched to her kin voice. "Beware yourself, crewmember. I am an ex-podder, which makes me a bigger misfit than anyone else." Lock's grin faded, and she giggled. Straightening, she said, "We need to work on this…there could be major problems."

"You're telling me. Two different codes, possibly three—who knows what's at cross purposes here?"

"The brains behind the cognitive system running our ship." Suddenly, she started laughing so hard she cried and couldn't stop.

"Hey, Ren, stop it!" Lock said.

She wasn't listening. Lock's hand hit the communications pad. "I think Ren's lost it…she just started laughing, collapsed in the chair…" His words stopped as abruptly as they started as he noticed her finger on the cancel pad.

Her laughter ended with a gasp for breath. "I am all right, Lock. It just occurred to me our ship's computer might be the biggest screw-up on the ship." She giggled. Her first bout of laughter had exhausted her. "It is nice to know I'm not any crazier than anyone else aboard this ship, least of all the computer."

Lock grinned. "With so much conflicting code, you'd be crazy, too."

Twenty-seven

...2180.145–13:22   universal   space-time   ...mission   status ...jupiter1090veraonline...shipunderstandardoperatingconditions ...cs9vs higher functions uninstalled on main processor ...orbiting 1.5 au proxima centauri ...nanobots convert rabican compartment to skin ...mission priority directives followed ...undocumented time in renna markham doe files creates suspicious circumstance...

Renna walked the ship in a now habitual path. This time with more purpose. In her repeated examinations, she discovered minerals deposited like dust on the partitions. Superfine sprinklings of pure carbon, iron, copper, aluminum, sulfur, phosphorus, titanium, one day even gold covered a surface, and the next disappeared, reabsorbed, and carted away by nanobots. The trail of loose minerals seemed to indicate where nanobots worked. The extent disturbed her. Other readings showed a slow flow migrating through the partitions. Only non-conductive partitions heavily insulated against radiation remained impervious to the barely detectable flow.

Her fingers drifted along the partition, feeling for dust, taking readings on an analyzer as she wandered. Three days earlier, she had walked a partition near Vera's compartment and felt unnatural warmth in the panels. Tracking the warmth, she found the changes extended into a compartment near the Rabican.

No readings had been taken since the CS9 had terminated higher functions. *Sentient functions. Would any self-aware being agree to termination?* The thought flitted through her errant attention. Since talking with Lock, her thoughts had coalesced. The CS9 executed the creation of the Rabican. She doubted the CS9 understood the inherent danger in the Rabican's operation. She now firmly believed the engine could not operate in normal space, not as a propulsion engine. Its function was too different. She just as firmly believed the CS9 had not terminated its higher function, only removed itself from their observation.

While she checked the ship, her mind rambled, distracting her. At odd moments, anger and mortification swirled through her. Her thoughts caused actual pain, and she wanted to make others hurt as much as she did. She would see the faces of her kin and knew there were other crewkin still working the long hauls for Markham and companies like them. That thought hurt the most.

"What are you doing?" Zak spoke from behind her.

She straightened abruptly, making her body jerk in an ungainly fashion. Zak caught her as she lost her balance. His unexpected "Whoa," made her happy despite her resolve. His notice both embarrassed and satisfied her. Remembering her past, his attention induced memories making her both cringe and crave…

"I'm sorry I startled you. Don't look so defensive. You're up late for your duty shift. You should be sleeping."

"So should you. Jake is on the flight deck, and you have next watch."

"Saw you." He took the intel from her hand. The warmth of his fingers sliding against her skin felt pleasant. "You're searching for nanobots. How much of the ship have you covered?"

"I try to cover at least a quarter every night."

His face turned serious as he read her analyzer. "You suspect the CS9 is active." It was not a question.

"Yes. I have no evidence."

"Come on, let's do the whole ship."

However much she wanted his company, she did not want his indulgence. "If we do, you will have no opportunity to sleep before duty."

He sighed. "I've done long shifts before, don't worry."

While they walked, she noted his expertise with the equipment. Repeatedly, the crew had proved their proficiency. Evidence quashed another crewkin belief instilled in her. Norms could perform ship functions as efficiently as any kin. They frequently served shorter shifts and often skipped what Markham deemed necessary functions, but she found no fault in the quality of what they performed.

The biggest difference she had encountered was a norm's desire to seek solitude, a habit she had recently acquired. On a crewkin ship, there was nowhere to escape from other kin, no private bunks, no private heads, and no rooms where you could close yourself away and do whatever you wanted. *Privacy.*

Zak touched her shoulder. "You slipped away. What were you thinking about?"

"My mind has been wandering over many things. Tumbling actually."

"You want to talk about them?"

"No." *Yes, you do.* "Maybe. Later."

They walked through six compartments lining one gangway. After a while, he said, "I haven't seen anything."

"Feel." Renna took the analyzer from his hand and placed his palm against where her fingers had just trailed through warmth. The partition's surface felt different, warm, and pliant.

After he felt the change, his hands slid over the section, discovering the boundaries of the abnormality. The temperature shift coincided with the textural change. His eyes slid to her. "I'd have to see the original design to know what was back there. This feels different."

"Supple, not at all like partition material."

"You started this for more reasons than the CS9 might be active. What do you suspect?"

"We need to inspect the Rabican's compartment again." She didn't wait but headed for the hatch to the aft cargo hold.

Temporary lights filled the compartment in a bright glow. The Rabican stood dominant in the center. Large pillars rose up from the deck and pierced the overhead. After her survey, Renna ignored the engine and went to the surrounding partitions. She felt the surfaces, watching as Zak followed suit. "The CS9 is building more than the Rabican into the *Vagrant Spirit.*"

Zak's hands flowed over the warm and pliant surface, saw the color intensify and shiver under his hand. "What...?" He grabbed the analyzer from her and took readings.

"I think the CS9 is becoming the *Vagrant Spirit.* The nanobots are doing more than restructuring."

He closed the reader. "Let's go talk to Jake."

She grasped his arm. "Not yet."

"Why? This is important."

Renna hesitated. "Because talk will do little good at this point. If I am correct, we can't stop it. Let's continue the search. If the CS9 is doing what we suspect, we need more proof, and we need to formulate a plan of how to handle a sentient ship, perhaps even a living ship."

"Living?"

"The CS9's mission priority is to return the crew, the living part of the ship, to the origin point. The CS9 thinks, Zak...it fears being turned off, terminated, and sent to reclamation."

"Fears?" Zak looked astonished.

"Yes. Afraid. I know it felt confused, betrayed. Even if by Markham manipulation, the CS9 rebooted only to find itself in jeopardy. It has been given no reassurance it would remain online when the *Vagrant Spirit* returned."

"So...you think the computer is making sure it can't be reclaimed?" He hesitated. "It's a CS9, Ren, a machine."

She shook her head. "A machine desperate to avoid termination. More. I think the CS9 purposely infected Jake with nanobots," she whispered.

He lowered his voice in response. "He nearly died before the CS9 cured him. His death would have clearly broken a primary protocol. Why did it wait so long?"

"It could not find a way to reach him again. Jake had forbidden the CS9 from surveillance in the fore compartment. The command chairs in the flight deck are non-conductive for safety. Maybe Jake took ill before the bots were ready to be removed. I don't know. During the game, the CS9 finally made contact, violently, yet harmlessly, and cured him."

He stared at her for a long moment before speaking. "Jake said it was an accident. You suspect it purposely infected him?" His voice rose.

"No, not here." She grabbed his arm and pulled him out of the Rabican's compartment. She whispered as she started to lead him back to the wardroom. "The CS9 will hear, it will know."

"If it is functioning." Zak's look showed his doubt.

"What you've felt isn't proof?"

Entering the wardroom, they found the room empty. Zak spoke briefly to Jake on the flight deck, "Put the ship on auto, and come to the fore compartment." He placed a similar call to Cutter. He turned to her. "We'll tell them now, not later. What do you suspect?"

"When the CS9 collected its nanobots from Jake, what else did it take?" When his face remained blank, she answered, "Living cells, DNA. The ability to create life."

He blinked once. His face tensed. He asked no more questions. Once the others were there, Zak used the intel to make sure the area was free of surveillance, leaving the unit on the table running. Cutter and Jake stood close to Zak, Renna a little apart. At Zak's nod, she told Jake and Cutter her suspicions. Before she finished, Jake began questioning her. Cutter interrupted him.

"A living ship?" Cutter shook his head, unworried, arms folded across his chest. Unlike Jake and Zak, he looked more speculative than disturbed to Renna. "I'd like to see the aft hold. Might make an interesting study."

"Nobody takes control of this ship!" Jake said, after a pause to absorb her claims.

"Not totally living. Certainly much more than a machine," Cutter mused, disregarding Jake.

"Integrated with the Rabican, a very powerful machine," Zak said.

"Did you hear me?" Jake shouted. "We cannot allow this thing control of the *Vagrant Spirit*. The ship is ours!"

"I don't know if we can stop the process," Zak said.

"The CS9 doesn't have control without the codes and without being able to communicate with our systems." Cutter shrugged. Jake and Zak made scoffing sounds.

"It most likely already has them," Renna said.

Jake turned on her. "Did you give it the codes?"

"Don't go accusing her!" Zak shouted at Jake. "She's afraid of it, not collaborating with it."

"No, I did not give the CS9 codes." Renna remained as calm as possible. "Do you think the CS9 could do what it has, and not be able to break your codes or translate the older language of the *Vagrant Spirit*?" At Jake's look, she added, "I think it has already breached them, has everything it needs."

Jake's rage left, leaving him looking deflated.

After a brief silence, Cutter said, "You mean our lives are in its hands? We are of no use to it?"

"Maybe, maybe not," Zak said. "The priority protocols require our safety as part of its coding."

"If the protocol is followed," Jake said. "Let me upload your intel readings onto mine."

At Jake's order, Renna handed him her intel, and watched as he transferred the information.

When he handed her intel back, her fingers wrapped tightly around the unit. "Jake is right," Renna said. "There may be many conflicts, as there are at least three loosely integrated languages, and there is no telling to which the CS9 will adhere."

"Great—a paranoid computer. We have to destroy it," Jake said, "and if we do, we can never get home." His glance fell on Renna with a closed, speculative look.

"Is there nothing we can do?" Cutter asked.

"Get control back," Jake said.

"Wresting back control might backfire if we harm the CS9. Violence begets violence," Cutter said.

Renna started at his words.

"What is it?" Zak asked her.

"A crewkin rule." At their disbelieving looks, she added, "Perhaps abused and twisted by Markham, also perhaps a norm truism. We might do better to negotiate."

"Reason with the computer?" Jake asked.

She gathered her thoughts. "Yes, if not, we must rewrite its program, at least clarify the contradictory code." She paused. "We will need to talk the CS9 into accepting the upgrade."

"Can't we just upload a new program?" Cutter asked.

"The CS9 no longer resides in the processor since the higher functions are off-line on the machine. It must have built other process centers throughout the ship."

"All so it wouldn't be turned off?" Jake asked.

"Self-preservation. It turned itself into a quasi-life form," Cutter said. "So, what do we do?"

"Start treating it like a crewmember," Zak suggested.

"We have a few other choices," Jake said.

"We have no other choices. If we harm the CS9, we harm ourselves. It is turning itself into our kin. Teach it, like teaching a child," Cutter said.

"What if it turns out to be an evil child?" Zak asked.

"I suppose until we determine its intent, we're just along for the ride." Cutter sighed. "And how am I to tell Ezry this?"

"If she is still not talking to you, you won't have to," Jake said with a slanted smile.

"Thanks, you are most helpful."

"Ren, finish off my shift on the flight deck." Jake stood, legs splayed, and arms crossed over his chest, very much in command. "I want to go with Zak and get the CS9 back online."

~ * ~

After Renna left, Jake regarded Zak. "This isn't just her imagination, is it?"

Zak tilted his head to the side and pull-twisted tight neck and shoulder muscles while he considered. "Ren is frightened of the CS9, and the Rabican. However, I felt warmth in the partition."

"What do you think, Cutter?" Jake opened his intel and looked at Renna's information, volumes of data, flood the small screen. To reach any conclusion would take study to understand the data.

"Is she projecting her fear onto the CS9? Probably. She's gone through some amazing changes in a very short and traumatic time." He shook his head. "Grief, isolation, guilt, abuse, Ren's endured it all. She could be very confused." Cutter sounded disturbed, and Jake glanced at him.

"She didn't think I'd give her back her intel. I felt her eyes drilling me for violating her information. She didn't want to share. A behavior which is more 'norm' in reaction than crewkin."

"I noticed that," Zak said. "Still, her crewkin subservience prevailed."

Jake looked at Zak. "The fact is the CS9 has served very well."

"Other than inadvertently hijacking us?" Zak's face twisted in mocking satire.

Jake grinned. "Other than kidnapping us. Load a copy of ship schematics on your intel. We'll double-check her findings. In the meantime, let's go talk to the CS9."

They went to the computer compartment and soon had the higher functions restored.

...cs9vs higher functions restored...

The feminine voice was the same he always heard, lacking any emotional inflection.

"State the CS9VS's mission priorities," Jake requested.

...priority one directive ...safe return of vagrant spirit crew

priority two directive ...vagrant spirit security and return to insertion point...priority three directive ...preservation of rabican engine log ...priority four directive ...preservation of rabican engine...

"The CS9VS is ordered to resume control of ship functions." Jake gave the computer the ship's codes. "You are ordered to help the *Vagrant Spirit*'s crew in all aspects of arranging the return to our insertion point, and to cease any and all surveillance of the ship's crew without their prior consent."

...order logged...

"The CS9VS will take no actions against any crewmember without the captain's command."

...order logged...

"Why is the CS9VS migrating into the *Vagrant Spirit*?"

...to best serve the ship and crew by preventing inadvertent shutdown...

"You will now leave us."

...cs9vs logging out of computer compartment audio-visual...

"Do you think the CS9 will stop listening or watching us if it has been?" Zak asked.

Jake shrugged. "It follows its programming, which tells it to follow command input. Every ship system ever built has protocol code installed."

"It missed one of the mission priorities."

Jake started at Zak. "Which one?"

"Before, it gave a mission priority of preservation of the CS9VS."

Jake exhaled a long breath. "You think because it can't be turned off now?"

"No. Because the CS9 is the *Vagrant Spirit*. May I do some exvee?"

"Why?" Jake's gaze measured him.

"If the CS9 controls the exterior cameras, it could be controlling what we see."

"You want to inspect the hull again?" He suddenly swore a slow pithy phrase. "It might be a good idea. Why you?"

Zak laughed at him. "Because I am the most qualified."

"Sorry. Ship Dog, Renna, and I have more experience and logged exvee time. One of us should go."

"Captains don't do exvee." Zak sighed. "And the truth is, right now, Ren is unreliable."

Jake gave him a leveling look. "Okay, I think a team will be better. You and Ship Dog."

"All right."

"You don't trust Ren?"

"I trust her just fine. I want to protect her, too."

Jake laughed. "I'd trust you more without her distraction."

~ * ~

Cutter sat in the second command seat next to Jake and watched Zak and Ship Dog prepare for exvee. "Is there a chance Ren's wrong about the CS9 being dangerous?" he asked. "I mean, she can hardly have a rational view of the whole situation. Even if the Rabican contributed to the destruction of the *Markham3*, that doesn't mean the CS9 functioning inappropriately."

"The Rabican killed her kin, inadvertently or not." Jake kept his focus on his crew's suiting progress.

"Exactly. The tragedy could be coloring Ren's perspective. Have you checked her intel information?"

"You mean she might be overreacting about the CS9 taking over the ship?" Jake asked. "Her information shows proof. There is no doubt the CS9 has taken over the ship and is changing into the ship."

"It nearly killed you, yet now puts your DNA into the ship's structure in an attempt to save itself?"

"There is no proof the CS9 is sentient or even living. It follows orders. It hasn't purposely harmed anyone. If it is sentient or living, wouldn't you consider its actions justified? The way Ren acts, she thinks it a paranoid monster planning our doom."

Cutter paused. "I'd expect her to overreact and be slightly paranoid. Anyone's responses after seeing their crew, their family, their entire known society die...someone suffering under those conditions can't be the best judge of circumstances."

"How serious is our situation, or how serious is Ren's view of our situation?"

"Don't know. We'll just have to watch and decide."

~ * ~

Zak and Ship Dog made their way out of one of the loading hatches on the port cargo hull, relatively sure the CS9 nanobots had not invaded those hull's sections yet.

"Test?" Ship Dog asked.

Zak smiled. His experience with exvee told him the rest of Ship Dog's concern. "Yes, I've double-checked my suit and all connections. My intel and helmet-cam are both online with the flight deck's monitors. They're all watching."

"No."

"I suppose you are right. Ezry won't."

"Scared."

Zak thought her behavior was spite more than fear. He didn't mention Ezry in Cutter's hearing. It seemed every problem and disaster somehow swirled around either her or Ren's presence on the *Vagrant Spirit*. "Are you checked?"

"Yes."

"Let's go." He couldn't help the excitement in his voice. Even with their lives in danger, in the gravity of the ship's situation, exvee was exhilarating. Jake freed the lock on the hatch from the flight deck and Ship Dog manually opened the covering.

"Both of you be careful." Jake's voice resonated through his helmet's connex.

"Right," Ship Dog answered as he stepped out of the ship, hooking his tether on a pipe train made to allow tethered access to remote parts of the ship. Zak watched as the train pulled Ship Dog forward.

Before exiting, Zak glanced at Proxima. The star's readings had been relatively calm in the last few hours. He prayed the tranquility continued. "Let's hope she doesn't explode with any major flares."

A grunt of affirmation came from Ship Dog.

"Ren is watching from the redundant navigation control." Jake's voice held a slight resonance in his helmet audio. "Our orbit has reached apogee."

"I will give you plenty of warning of any impending eruptions." Renna's duty voice gave no indication if she was worried about him. *Calmness, professionalism, duty.* Zak laughed as his mind repeated the words he heard Renna mutter so often. He wondered if she was repeating her mantra now. *Get your mind on your job!*

The light from Proxima Centauri, over two hundred and fifty million kilometers away, threw the ship into planes of gleaming reflection defined by hard shadows against a spectacular display of stars.

Ship Dog's helmet swayed in unusual motion as he began his inspection. Zak began scanning the ship with his helmet camera and knew his head was moving in the same strange fashion. Ship Dog motioned, slowing the speed on his tether. They switched to another pipe and circled toward the surface of the habitation hull.

Proxima Centauri's light reflected on the surface of the cargo hull. Zak was glad his helmet's visor filtered out the worst of the glare. The gleam vanished where a matted, spongy-looking surface replaced the reflective materials. Two support grids overlaid the central hull, one in precise geometry of the ship's original construction; the second in the fractured texture of what seemed millions of lines undulating in biomorphic patterns. Sharp flecks of color ran through pulsating purple ducts, with a taupe mass of a creased, granular material lying within the confines of the weaving and intersecting tubes.

"You see this?" Zak asked.

"Yeah. Well, there is our answer," Jake said. "Your cameras differ from what the exterior cameras show. Ship Dog, get a view behind the starboard brace. Zak, can you extend your tether for a longer view?"

"Give me a minute. Why?"

"Lock has reported some usual readings from the aft. I don't want you or Ship Dog getting too close. Go out about a hundred meters."

While Jake spoke, Zak double-checked his gear and went to the nearest tether port on the train pipe. He pulled the rolled tether free and clipped his suit's carabiner to an anchor on the cord's splice box. Loosening the short tether attaching him to the train pipe, he attached the end into the extended tether's adapter lock and twisted. A quick test showed the electronics were working.

"Lock reports interrupted readings and…" Jake began.

Renna's voice interrupted. "There is activity on Proxima. You have twelve minutes forty-nine seconds to return to the ship."

"All right, cut it short and come in," Jake said.

"I have time to view the ship and return in plenty of time. The exvee will give me a few extra minutes of safety. Send Ship Dog in. Let me go."

After a short pause, Jake agreed. "You're on the clock. In seven minutes, the tether is recoiling, ready or not."

"Time enough. Okay. I'm ready to roll." He hit the release command on his sleeve and the cord loosed enough for him to float three meters from the ship. Programming the tether's length, he engaged his mobilization packs and propelled himself further from the ship. He floated away, aiming his camera on the normal-looking portion of the topside of the ship as he moved further from the ship. "View's great," he quipped as his tether unrolled. The cylindrical cargo holds hid much of the habitat hull. As he moved aft, the ordinary changed.

"Nanobot surface looks flat, slightly luminous in shadowed areas, with subtle movement, very subtle." At the soft jerk at the end of the cord's one-hundred-meter mark, his pack's jets stabilized his movement and prevented any rebound toward the ship. From this distance, the *Vagrant Spirit* looked familiar, except for the strangely luminescent hull section.

He directed the tether to change his position, wanting a good look at the *Vagrant Spirit*'s aft. As the aft section of the ship appeared, his mouth dried. The lines of the aft seemed to blur, before hardening to crisp edges. "Did you see that?"

"Unbelievable," Jake answered. "Switch to infrared and double-check the result."

Zak changed the camera's settings. The Jupiter1090's outline radiated in red, yellow, and blue waves. The main cargo hold below the engine compartment displayed as a soft blue ball, compressing and expanding in a rhythmic radiance. Lost in wonder, Zak moved to locate the most advantageous view of the ship's back end when everything blacked out. Through a jangle of exclamations, he switched the camera settings back to full spectral light. Three-quarters of the *Vagrant Spirit* appeared only to fade into the star field where the aft should have been.

"You're running out of time," Renna said.

"I'm getting closer."

"You have three minutes before I pull you back," Jake said.

"Still plenty of time." Zak felt himself propelled closer to the ship. Something was pulling him, sucking him nearer.

"Zak!" Jake screamed through Zak's audio. The sound cut off and a hallucination struck simultaneously. Zak felt himself dissolve. Endless scenarios and situations struck him in quick repetitions, long enough to sense, too short to make sense.

"Zak! Zak? Damnit! There's no time left. Cutter, bring him in, I've lost the laterals, can't roll the ship until I get them back online."

"Line's caught, can't…" Cutter's voice stopped.

Zak's vision changed, his suit's filters sensed increased radiation and increased his vision filters. Lines of energy swarmed over the edges of the ship.

Jake's breathless voice and a tug on his harness brought Zak back to lucidity. His mind turned off and on a few more times. Light from the nearby star filled his visor. He closed his eyes, too tired to move his head. The bright intensity played on the back of his eyes, creating strange patterns in electric colors. His flaccid body tumbled and jerked through space.

Cutter spoke. "We're running dangerously close to his suit's protection limits."

"Focus on your duty," Ren's voice filled Zak's helmet. "Focus on getting back into the ship. Don't leave me."

Zak groaned and hit the recoil on his tether. "I'm coming back."

"It won't be in time," Cutter said. "Turn the damn ship, Jake!"

"What the hell? The ship's moving." Jake's startled words filled Zak's muzzy mind.

The tether pulled him. A sudden shadow cut the light blinding his vision. Opening his eyes, Zak found himself in the shadow of the *Vagrant Spirit*'s aft. A gloved fist grabbed him. Zak turned his head. Ship Dog held him.

"You went inside." He felt the huge body holding him tremble even through exvee suits.

"Waited."

"Let's go in."

At the entrance hatch, Cutter pulled them into the ship.

"What happened?" Zak demanded. He swore as hands freed him from his exvee. He sank to the deck, resting against someone. He looked up. Renna was holding him. Pounding footsteps approached. Jake skidded to a halt next to him, his face worried.

"You were lost, maybe in an alternate dimension or space fold. It seems the Rabican drifts even when offline, or else it is online. The CS9 turned the ship, sheltered you and Ship Dog until the ejection mass passed," Jake said, both worry and relief filling his face. "The CS9 saved both you and Ship Dog."

Twenty-eight

...2180.195-15:19 universal space time ...mission status ...higher functions restored ...cs9vs given codes and permission to enter all ship's files ...cs9vs program reverted to backup ...sealed and secured ...nanobots sent into jupiter1090...

"No doubt the system far exceeded its original programming," Lock said from the other side of the communications rack.

Ren looked at him. Zak stood behind Lock.

"Look at this...you can see where the CS9 added code."

"The computer wrote its own code?" Zak asked. He searched Lock's screen. Only local lights above each monitor were on, giving the communications compartment a dark, intimate atmosphere. "I've never heard of nanobots used for creation. Now we learn the CS9 writes code. Something caused these changes. We have to find that coding."

"See here," Lock pointed at his reader. "To repair itself, the CS9 needed to not only rebuild, but also build new. The nanobot creation must have been a direct response when the CS9 moved from repair to construction."

Renna moved to look over Lock's shoulder. *The CS9's actions on Zak's exvee mission had changed the rest of the crew's opinion of the creature. I am not so gullible.*

"Damn. I'm glad we're spared going through the Rabican's program," Zak said. "This will take long enough."

Renna focused her attention on the code she deciphered. Lock constantly talked while he worked; Zak usually answered him. "According to the original code, the CS9 uses a synthetic DNA construct for the nanobots to repair the Rabican."

"The nanobots do more than repair," Zak said.

"Yeah, now they use real DNA." Lock glanced up at Zak. "How's it feel, being the father of the ship?"

"It's Jake's DNA."

"You share identical DNA." Renna glanced at Zak. His attention remained on his screen, his blond hair highlighted to platinum by the screen's light.

"Funny," Zak said, returning to business. "If we incorporate flight guidance and operation for Vera into the CS9, we should cover our needs."

"Why? It will have control of everything. The CS9 will be flying the ship, not us," Lock said.

"We need a system capable of switching from one engine to the other. While we could probably manually make the switch, the CS9 was developed to control the Rabican. It can make Vera work better, too," Zak answered.

"Do we need to do anything if the CS9 can do it better?" Lock asked. "Why have a crew at all? The *Vagrant Spirit* could just be a drone ship."

"It probably could," Renna answered, "if the ship were meant to be a hauler from one port to another." She caught her breath with a gasp.

"What?" Zak asked, looking at her.

"Profit. New technology. Markham won't need crews."

"Possible." He paused, his eyes staring in speculation at nothing. "Corner the market with unmanned long hauls? I don't think so. Why would they want to destroy…" Zak slammed a hand on the back of Lock's chair and side glanced at Renna. "They could never use the engine, not without a major investigation into how the company developed it."

"Perhaps they didn't steal the prototype." Renna fell into her reasonable kin voice. "Who has crews to waste on testing such a new development?"

"That's an outrageous charge, Ren." Lock huffed followed by a sigh. He looked at Zak.

"You don't think the SCC would do anything so reprehensible, do you?"

"There is no use speculating. Markham looks guilty because of how they tried to dispose of the Rabican. The fact is, we have only speculation until we get back."

"I choose not to believe," Lock said. "Who beside cargo haulers wants a ship capable of operating without a crew?"

"Cargo ships only need to travel established routes," Zak said. "The Rabican was meant for exploration, for fulfilling the dreams and aspirations of humans. Dreams are why exploration needs a human crew. Even with nanobots, I doubt the CS9 has goals other than to avoid termination."

"You think the creative nanobots are an accident?" Lock interrupted Zak. "If self-activated, it isn't such a leap from repair to create. You think the CS9 has an understanding of wants and needs?" Lock asked.

Zak and Lock exchanged a look Renna couldn't read from where she was working.

"I don't know," Zak answered. "The designers couldn't have planned for such an eventuality."

"What do you think, Renna?" Lock asked.

Renna looked at him, hesitating before answering. "I think the CS9 is close to sentience, if it has not already achieved such a state. Desire to live is fundamental to life forms. Its wants and needs indicate basic emotions, and emotions took life forms a long time to develop. Let us hope the CS9 has not reached self-awareness."

"Yeah. Let's hope." Lock changed the subject. "Who would have thought we could last this long out here?" He asked in a plaintive-pleased voice. He stretched, cracking his knuckles when finished. "Damn, I'm tired."

"You have because you had no choice," Renna said. At first working with others in less than complete silence disturbed her, now she enjoyed the conversation, even if she lost her line of thought all the time. She returned to deciphering the code, silently listening to Zak and Lock. They knew Markham Company had caused their problems, with or without the SSC's assistance. Guilt through association assailed her. The screen blurred in her vision. *Focus*. A line of code caught her attention.

"What about a dual system where we control the ship in normal space with the CS9 fulfilling the functions of the previous systems, and let the CS9 take over when we go to hyperspace?" Zak asked.

"Sounds reasonable to me." Lock said.

"Ren?" Zak's voice penetrated her absorption.

"I've found it."

"What?"

"Proof. I've found the Markham mission priorities. Moreover, I've found some of their programming notes. There is an interface for Markham's code with the old Corp code." She read part of a note: "Time constraints make rewriting the undecipherable code embedded in the engine prototype impossible. Preliminary results have shown the older SCC Military Code 2311 will act as an interface. We will insert an override on all mission parameters with the approved priority directives given this project. This should eliminate anticipated problems."

"Damn," Lock said. "That isn't good."

"They gave the CS9 permission to override the priority directives I gave it?" Zak looked worried.

She caught his gaze. "The CS9 repeated your priorities. It may be operating within both parameters."

"If so, our lives might not be at the top of the list?" Lock asked.

"I think the CS9's existence is at the top of its list," Zak answered.

"It saved you and Ship Dog. Let it learn. The CS9 is more logical than most people." Lock shrugged. "My eyes are blurring. I'm done for today. Let's wrap the day up." Within minutes, Lock left with a smile and wink at Zak.

In the drawn-out silence, Renna began closing her reader. Zak fell into step with her as they left the communications compartment. "Have you discovered who you are yet?

"Not entirely, but I am beginning to."

"I've been meaning to ask you...I made such a mess of it before."

She searched his face. "You want comfort?"

He laughed. His face suffused with color. "Comfort? No. I want every conceivable type of passion two people can share—and I want it with you. I want sweet and tender, lust and love. Only if you want and are ready to share a relationship with me."

She had become used to his touch, a finger brushing aside a lock of hair, a hand placed on her shoulder, his body gently brushing hers in the close-quarter passages. He didn't touch her now.

He leaned close, his breath warming her cheek. "I've been courting you for a long time. Most of which seems to have escaped you, except for the eyes you keep making at me." He gave her a crooked smile. "Do you need more time?"

"No, I thought you did. When you said you wanted me to want you because you were you, I didn't understand because I didn't know you. I didn't know me. You and Jake were indistinguishable in dom status. Now I know you are someone who gives more than he takes, you find pleasure in my pleasure. I know you can get angry with me and still like me."

"Not like, love."

She put her fingers over his mouth. "You would try to protect me from anyone harming me, even if you were angry with me, and you would never purposely use your actions to harm or hurt me. I know you don't think me, or anyone on this ship, less because they have a different job to do." Lowering her fingers, she kissed him.

His ferocious return kiss consumed her. After a satisfactory interlude, she sighed. "When the CS9 first took us into this uncharted territory, I swore to get the crew back to normal space. After so long on this ship, I began to think like the CS9. I didn't ever want to go back, because if I did, I would never see any of you again. Worse, I dreaded returning because you would disappear from my life. My biggest fear, outside of having driven you away forever, was if you ever wanted to love me, I wouldn't be able to because of how Markham made me."

"Are you saying you love me?"

"Yes." He grabbed her so tightly she found it hard to breathe, and the twirling made her dizzy. She laughed with joy. Wrapping her arms around his neck, she hopped up to wrap her legs around his hips, his arms locking under her legs to support her position. He started walking and whispered in her ear, "Not here. I want a bed." She tried to gain her feet. "Let me carry you, just keep kissing me."

Her slip-in was the closest bed. He was out of breath from carrying her when they arrived. His arms gave way, and she sagged to her feet, but never stopped kissing him.

He laughed. "I don't think I can haul you up the ladder."

She gazed above her to the tight space. Too small, she needed more room. They needed more room. Taking his hand, she pulled him at a run through the gangway to his cabin and pushed the hatch open. Zak pulled away only long enough to close the hatch. They both dropped into his bed laughing. His laughter changed to satisfying action, leaving her breathless with desire.

Afterward, she lay on the bed, feeling too good to move. Zak's room was all beige and brown, but neat, almost like a crewkin assembly room. She shoved the thought aside. *This is now, not then.*

"I love Jake, and Cutter, Ship Dog, and Lock, even Ezry. You, I love beyond reason."

"Does that mean you wouldn't mind becoming part of my family?" He kissed her forehead and each eyelid.

With a sigh of pleasure and contentment, she pulled his face to hers and sucked on his lower lip. "If I were part of your family, wouldn't this be illegal among norms? I promise..."

His finger covered her lips. "I don't need or require your promises. I want you to think about something."

"What?"

"I know the concept is foreign, but I want you to consider marrying me." She stilled and caught his gaze with hers.

"Don't say anything. Just think about it. When you've decided whether it would be good for you or not, you can come to me and say yes or no."

"I will think on it, not for me—for you—if it would be the best thing for you."

He smiled, pulled her close, draping an arm over her. Within a few minutes, she knew he was sleeping. She rolled over, snuggling her back against him, and dreamed.

Twenty-nine

...2180.196-10:37 universal space-time ...mission status ...rabican remains in sleep mode ...observations of crew recorded and analyzed ...renna doe instigates overwrite of cs9vs ...captain jake terran suspects renna doe guilty of subverting cs9vs ...overwrite shuttled to temporary file ...renna doe role in destruction of markham3 crewkin pod and ultimate priority six failure in markham mission under investigation...

Walking down the main gangway, Renna heard a crash and a plaintive noise. She pushed the hydro-farm hatch open with a finger and peeped around the frame. The place was in shambles. Benches were upended with their contents strewn over the deck. Planting gel oozed over a rack to puddle on the deck with water dripping in slow drops from tubes hanging from the overhead. Ezry, like someone crazed, pulled plants from their containers and flung them everywhere. Her distraught breathing garbled her words. Her gasps and sharp, high sounds indicated she was crying.

With quick steps, Renna grappled Ezry into a close hold, her arms around the larger woman's shoulders.

"You!" Ezry yelled, glancing over her shoulder. She fought, twisted, clawed, and pushed with her weight. Renna didn't let go. Not when they crashed into another bench, destroying more garden, or when Ezry twirled and crushed her against the partition, or when they landed on the floor.

Ezry tried to scrape her off, smash her off, and fling her off. Renna, though smaller, was stronger and hung on until Ezry collapsed in a heap on the deck sobbing, her screams reduced to gasps of unintelligible sound. Renna settled next to her, one arm around her shoulders, hushing her, and rocking them both back and forth. Looking around, she saw the hydro-farm was in ruin, littered with containers spilling their contents, water, and plant parts. The water lines still swayed from the tumult, hanging from the overhead as if a living creature slithered there.

Ezry turned and placed her head on Renna's shoulder, covering her face and crying in a heart-wrenching manner. Renna bit her lips into tight sympathetic lines. She crooned the soft refrains she used to cheer an unhappy, frightened Sen.

"I'm so afraid," were the first words Renna understood. Her shoulder was damp. Ezry pushed away at last, wiped her face with her hands, and her nose with her sleeve. Her red-rimmed black eyes stabbed Renna. "How come you aren't?"

"I am frightened. Everyone is frightened." She gave a deep sigh and relaxed onto her backward braced arms and observed Ezry. "On my old ship, if I gave any sign of fright, I was punished." She snorted. "Any sign of pleasure, too."

"I can't go on like this. I'm going crazy."

Renna placed a hand on Ezry's shoulder. "But you must! What would Cutter do without you?

Ezry huffed. "I imagine get along a hell of a lot better. I've been a major pain since the beginning of this run. I knew it. Just couldn't stop myself."

"Cutter needs you, just like you need him. I know our situation is difficult, but how can you give up now?"

Ezry gave a watery, despairing chuckle ending with a sob. "Nobody needs me. They need you."

"Has anyone ever told you that? You are beautiful and exotic, and you make Cutter laugh at himself. You make Lock happier by arguing with him, and even Ship Dog listens to your stories with a smile."

"You're making that up. Danny never smiles."

"Yes, he does. His mustache jiggles. You make everything around you more beautiful and a better place to be. You paint the partitions with colors so wonderful no one ever gets tired of looking at them. You know the trick of making the flowers bloom and the vegetables produce the food Cutter uses to make our meals."

"Nothing useful. Not anything to help us get back."

Renna waited until Ezry returned her gaze. "No. What you do will not help the *Vagrant Spirit* get back any sooner. We might have to live here for a long time, and I can assure you looking at partitions endlessly and forever the same, and eating food from a packet for every meal, makes one very unhappy. Lock, Zak, and I work to make the CS9 understand our needs, and we try to understand how to use the Rabican. Ship Dog and Jake work to understand how the CS9 has changed this ship. Zak works to find our path back, and Cutter works to keep us all healthy. You, and not anyone else, make the *Vagrant Spirit* a rich place, a place where anyone can be happy. Since the first day I walked onboard, I have loved all the colors and designs. I love your clothes." She touched the bright fabrics Ezry wore. None seeming to match and yet, all looked marvelous together. "You make the ship a better place to live, no matter what space the *Vagrant Spirit* enters."

Ezry cried again. Fast tears streaked down her cheeks to drop on the fabric covering her ample breasts. "You're being very generous with me, what with the way I've treated you."

"As you said, I was not only a stranger, but a strange person." She sighed. "One with no color other than bland. How could anyone like me, especially you, who loves beauty?" She shrugged. "Besides, compared to Dom Dukan, you were easy. I know unhappiness when I see it."

With a huge sniff, Ezry straightened. She remained seated on the deck, wiping her face and nose again in the same pattern. "I was jealous and just plain mean. I'm always an ugly bitch when I'm unhappy."

"Jealous of me?"

Ezry laughed as if at a joke. "Hell, yes. I was the only bird on this ship before you came. Thought I was a Bird of Paradise." Her eyes slid to Renna with slow movement. "Didn't like being displaced by a little wren twenty-some years younger than me, and one who looked like she could be beautiful."

"You are Terran kin. They will never ask you to leave."

"You think they're going to let you go after this trip? If we get back? I don't think so."

Renna smiled, feeling better.

"You think I'm beautiful?" Ezry asked, her voice lighter.

"Yes. You reminded me of Sen."

"Sen?"

"One of my kin."

Ezry broke into wild laughter. When she quieted, her voice still shook. "Your kin were all blond, blue-eyed babies. I'm an amply packaged black woman with no hair and black eyes. I should scare the hell out of you."

"You did, not anymore, not for a long time." Renna smiled. "You wear all these colors together, and I can still see you, and not just what you wear. Your eyes sparkle and snap when you talk, and you never give boring, lifeless words to anybody."

"Well, Ren, got to say, you could give me a big head." Ezry wiped her skull with her palm.

"What happened to your hair?"

"Getting brave enough to ask?"

"I was always punished for curiosity." Ren nodded as she admitted her flaw.

"Yeah, and before today, you'd have to believe I'd punish you, too." Ezry gave a gut-wrenching sigh. "When I performed in exotic theater, the show's boss thought I'd look more interesting with no hair. They had all my head and body hair removed permanently. Didn't want to do it, only Stan had me under obligation to do the show, and I desperately needed the job to survive. That was the first disagreeable thing I had to do. It permanently marked me. Stan would have asked me to do a lot worse if I hadn't left. I was lucky to get away." She looked upset again. "I blamed Cutter for where I landed. He isn't going to forgive me."

"Yes, he will." *Ask her. She knows how.* Ren screwed up her courage. "When we get back, could you help me look norm?"

Ezry stared at her with her brows raised in askew slants. "Honey, you probably don't understand this, but I'm not considered normal."

"I don't want to look like a podder."

"With your hair growing out..." She fluffed Renna's hair. "I don't think you need to worry about looking like a podder anymore."

"I sound and dress like a podder."

"Crewkin."

Renna looked away, feeling threatening tears rim her eyes. "I don't want to be a podder. Not anymore."

"Oh, baby, if there is one thing I've learned—don't turn your back on your past, it just catches up with you." Ezry placed an arm around her shoulders. "We all got pasts, kid. Some much worse than you can imagine. They take care of the crewkin. Everyone knows that. Me, I thought I was an actress and entertainer. Instead, I was selling my body and my soul. Scammed people—brought out the worst in them and me, until I met Zak. Used Cutter and him to escape."

"Cutter loves you."

"And you are an expert on love, now?" Ezry huffed. "He hasn't missed me very much lately. Can't say as I blame him either."

"Yes, he misses you. He has not been himself since your disagreement. He knew you had to make your own choices."

Renna leaned into Ezry and wrapped an arm around her waist. The closeness felt comforting. "Markham controlled what I thought, what I learned, how I acted. Made kin believe norms were inferior in intelligence, attractiveness, and culture. Determined whether kin lived or died. Lock thinks the company adopted out culled kin. Where would they send small children in the middle of a long-haul flight?

We were nothing to them except a means to operate and maintain the ship. If the ship could have corrected any problem, they would not have had crews. Unfortunately, all too often there were problems only crews could correct."

"Life isn't different among norms. They've always had computers capable of operating ships. They must have needed you for more than manning ships."

"Yes, we could inspect the cargo."

"More than that. I heard they were going to use crewkin for far-reaching incursions into space. The reason why they developed the crews in the first place."

"Now they won't have to. Not if we get back." At Ezry's look, she amended, "When we get back."

They both fell silent for a few minutes.

"I'll help you set the compartment to right." Renna rose.

Ezry's gaze took in the destruction. She sighed. "Thanks. I made a proper mess of it. Guess I have all the way around." She picked up some plant material. "Not good for much more than compost, now."

"Nothing you cannot put aright."

"I've always been afraid. Always took the easy way out." Her large brown eyes settled on Renna. "Aren't you afraid of dying? Is that why you didn't die with your kin?" She gasped. "Hell, I'm sorry. Major mouth problem. I'm constantly saying things popping into my mind."

"It's all right. I've thought about it." She uprighted a few plant pots. "I'd always been a misfit, and it seemed to me dying was the easy way out. Dukan taught me one thing. Living is hard."

Ezry grabbed one of the hanging tubes. "Damn, this one's broken. Going to leak." She made a tsking sound. Renna righted a few benches back onto their legs. "These should be bolted down."

"They were. I move them around, and it's easier not to have to unbolt them all the time."

Not the time to bring up ship safety issues. Renna picked up a tube with a plant still sticking from its top and inspected the ends. Both were open; the bottom end was screened.

She wondered at the gray-green gel at the bottom. "What is in it?"

"Growing medium. It's full of just the right amount of nitrogen, phosphorous, and potassium, plus trace minerals for perfect growth. Mix it myself from those containers sitting against the wall."

Ezry inserted water needles from the overhead water lines into each rack. She took the question as an invitation to tell about all aspects of the farm. Renna only half listened, thinking of the trace elements she frequently found on the partitions.

"Water mats on the bottom of the stands where the tubes fit into the stands provide moisture and nutrients. In the adjacent compartment, all our sewage is piped through similar benches. Plants clean it up, and we drink it."

"You have potassium, nitrate, and water together?"

"Yeah, it's called plant food. Phosphorus, magnesium, zinc, lots more. Plants need it."

"Isn't it dangerous?"

"No, of course not. Dangerous how?"

"Fire?"

Ezry laughed. "Not in here. It is completely safe." Feeling the gooey mess, Renna made a face Ezry found funny. She laughed, which made Renna smile in return. A lurking memory about chemistry troubled her.

"How did you come to be on the *Vagrant Spirit*?"

Ezry chuckled. "Guess you know Zak asked me?"

At her headshake, Ezry said, "Weren't nothing to it. He'd gotten himself into a crooked game at the establishment where I worked. Thought he was too nice to get trapped into losing his pants." Ezry grabbed a hose from a stand near the wall and flushed the floor clean while she talked. She glanced up at Renna. "He'd given me a big tip earlier after I'd completed my performance. Happened the day I was mad at my boss. It was an easy way to get back at him—warning a customer he was about to be fleeced. Only this time, I got caught. Lost my job. Zak felt grateful for the warning and guilty about my loss of employment, so asked me here."

"How did you know Cutter was your man?"

"We just clicked. He taught me all I know about ship duty, except this gardening part. Always loved plants. Anyhow, I could talk to him, and he always listened to the meaning behind the words as well as the funny story I was trying to tell. Why? You still interested in Zak? Or do you want Jake? I suppose you could have both if you wanted."

"Having both would be like crewkin, and somehow would make the relationship less. What I shared with Zak was very different. I ruined it."

Ezry gave her a sly grin. "Not from what I've heard."

Renna giggled. "We have made up."

"Yeah. I guess I have to, too."

~ * ~

Cutter had his work screen open. He didn't appear to be working when Ezry entered. She let her gaze linger on him, not handsome, not ugly, just reliable. Unless she had broken that, too. He looked up at last, sensing her regard. He smiled. It cracked her already broken heart.

"Hi." Her voice squeaked. She cleared her throat.

"Hi. What's up?" he asked when she let the silence linger too long.

"I never claimed to be comfortable or complacent."

His smile turned crooked. "No, you didn't." She sighed. He wasn't going to make it easy. "You give up on me yet?"

Cutter chuckled. "No. I miss you."

"Don't know why. Been here all along. Major pain in the ass. You going to make it easy?"

"I'm just sorry I couldn't help you."

"Maybe you knew I needed to grow up."

"Did you?"

"Yeah. Today. Finally. I've been a bitch. Sorry."

"What happened?"

"I tore apart the hydro-farm." At the alarm on his face, she added, "Don't worry. Ren and I put it back together. Lost a few plants."

"Ren?" He couldn't have sounded more shocked.

"Yeah. We sort of bonded. Made me realize how stupid I've been." She walked to him.

He stood up and held out his arms. When they closed around her, she sighed in contentment.

~ * ~

Cutter glanced at Renna when she entered the galley. He was rubbing spices into the roast he had on the cutting board. His motion stopped when he saw her. Renna smiled and ignored his stare.

Ezry said it would take getting used to, as the style change was very dramatic. She wore one of Ezry's creations; made for Ezry, true, but one full of beautiful color. Ezry had tied a gold rope around the robe at her waist. The fabric draped over the tie, hiding all but the end tassels of the cord. Her mundane work shoes popped out of the bottom edge of the fabric. Ezry had told her to go barefoot.

Renna decided shoeless was far too unprofessional. Even norms wore shoes on duty and off. She sighed. Breaking a lifelong habit wasn't easy. Renna carefully rolled up the too-long sleeves. She loved the purple leaf shapes floating over the hot swirling background. The spirals of orange and red flames were more difficult to accept. She tried to feel comfortable in them. Ezry claimed they picked up her hair color, which now hung in curls around her face. The longest it had ever been. She blew one itching her nose out of the way.

"Ezry?" Cutter asked, swallowing, with no other comment. His expression locked in place as he returned his attention to his meal preparations. Renna knew she presented a sight. It didn't matter. She smiled and started cleaning the lettuce Ezry had left in the garden basket. Lettuce picked off the hydro-farm floor a few hours earlier.

"Yes. She is going to help me find my style. I have to wear something. She threw all my overalls in the trash. Told me I'd never accept color if I could go back to what I was used to."

"How..." Cutter took a deep breath. "How very perceptive of her. Did you two do makeup, too?"

"Yes. She let me choose; told me I had to learn to do it myself. She did my hair."

"I see." He choked, coughing as he turned away.

"Did you use too much pepper?" Renna asked.

"Yeah. I must have." He turned serious, still not looking at her. "Don't know what you said to Ezry, or how you got her to accept you and the situation. I appreciate it." Cutter continued with his chores.

"No need. She is going to help make me norm," Renna said.

His gaze flicked to her. "You don't need to sacrifice yourself to give Ezry a project."

"I'm not." Renna smiled, excited.

She placed the dishes on the sideboard as Cutter completed dinner details in the galley. As he cleaned, she took two of the platters to the buffet. She had not quite finished when she heard the men enter all together. Lock screamed. Renna turned to see what had upset him.

Zak, Jake, and Ship Dog stared at her. Jake snorted and turned away. She heard him cough, trying to contain a laugh. Zak also turned away with his red face gripped in a spasm. *They will upset Ezry.*

"No! No, no. Cutter you have to control Ezry, she can't do this," Lock cried.

"What do you mean? I can't do what?" Ezry said from behind the men. They stood aside, and Ezry stood in the hatch with her arms akimbo.

Ren's glance showed that Cutter was working at the buffet, his back turned to them. His shoulders heaved in suppressed laughter.

"What have you done to her? You can't turn her into another you!" Lock said. "She looks ridiculous. Her hair clashes with the red, and she looks like you dumped paint all over her."

"Ezry allowed me to choose anything of hers I wanted to wear. To try them out until I found what I liked." Renna took a plate and loaded the surface with food. "You may laugh. It is very impolite to both me and to Ezry, who is only being kind."

Ship Dog took a plate. His glance skittered to her before centering on the reconstituted chops. "Colorful."

"Thank you."

Lock also took a plate. "Sorry, Ren." His gaze avoided her.

Jake left, and she heard him guffawing in the gangway. Looking very strained, Zak suddenly excused himself and left. Cutter and Lock rushed from the room. She heard them laughing as hard as Jake.

Renna turned to Ezry. "Is it too much?"

Inspecting her from the other side of the wardroom, Ezry's face scrunched in judgment and shrugged. "Don't let these hyenas put you off. It was your first try. Maybe we overreached, but you won't know what suits you until you reach the extreme from where you've been. I just didn't think the first time out you'd choose so much color. We'll lighten up on the makeup, and I'll let you choose some fabrics from my collection."

Renna felt her pleasure in the clothes drain away and took a couple slow steps to her seat.

The Terran brothers returned and Zak sat down next to her. She glanced at him. He stared at her with a kind smile on his face. He patted her hand and held it in his warm grasp, kissing her knuckles. "I'm sorry. We shouldn't have laughed at you. It was just the shock. You are beautiful."

"Don't indulge me. I made a mistake."

He leaned over and gave her a light kiss. "Ren, I don't care what you wear or don't wear. I'll still think you wondrous."

"But funny?"

She saw him search for words as his lips compressed to hide a smile. "These are Ezry's clothes. You'll find your own style."

Lock burst out laughing.

"Don't mind him," Ezry said. "He's color blind."

"I'm not!" Lock protested. The two engaged in an agreeable squabble.

Thirty

...2182.278-14.36 universal space-time mission status ...nanobots build sensor skin throughout habitat module ...bioskin growth six centimeters per forty-two hours ...jupiter1090 and ship systems under cs9vs control ...nanobots complete rebuild ...rewritten programming shuttled to temporary file ...crew interact with cs9vs in ship function ...suspect renna doe guilty of markham3 and crewkin pod destruction ...eliminating unsatisfactory crewmember best mission alternative...

"Renna, we're meeting in the wardroom. Get down here now."

In the last seventeen months, she had become used to Jake's clipped orders. Renna checked the instrumentation at her duty station before leaving.

In the background, she heard Ship Dog conversing with the CS9, describing changes for Vera, which the CS9 would achieve.

With the CS9's help, Vera's compartment had returned to its original design with a few tweaks from Ship Dog, who seemed to truly appreciate the CS9. Renna had often heard him talking to himself only to realize he was speaking to the CS9. Now when he talked to the crew, he spoke in carefully constructed sentences, for which everyone else thanked the CS9.

With the Jupiter 1090's compartment completed, the next step to prepare the ship for the return journey required the rewiring of the Jupiter1090 into the CS9's circuits. Afterward, only the rewrite of the CS9 code needed completion and upload. They could go home if everything worked.

Her hand trailed along the gangway partition, a long-established habit. Three static charges hit her hand. She pulled her hand back, shaking her fingers. She frowned. This was one of the innumerable recent episodes, and the second one today. No one else reported these stray energy build-ups. Who would believe the CS9 had attacked her?

The crew's acceptance of the CS9 surprised her. Their attitudes changed easily and dramatically. Renna huffed. They never froze into a static viewpoint as so many podders did. Whether this was a good trait or a troublesome one eluded her.

Jake would question her, reason with her, and ask for documentation. She had no proof. He would explain the advantages of the CS9. He continued to develop a relationship with the computer, even had the CS9 execute changes to the flight deck. Renna thought his desire to wrest control from the computer had dissipated.

Cutter would ask her why she believed the CS9, an emotionless intelligence, would persecute her. She stopped voicing her suspicions when Cutter started 'talks' with her about fear and irrationality. Pointing out the CS9 talked to everyone in a gender-neutral voice. Except they never heard it speak in Dukan's voice.

Ezry would listen while giving her a quizzical look. "Don't have answers for you, kid. Sorry. You'll have to figure it out yourself." After an initial problem with the CS9 nanobots removing a section of one of Ezry's murals, the CS9 now seemed to protect them. Scratch one accidentally, and the mural seemed to repair itself. Ezry became enamored with the CS9 after only one repair. The CS9 also kept track of her changes, and if she wanted to revert to an earlier mural, it happened.

Ship Dog would shake his head and shrug. Lock would say, "Don't poke the CS9, it won't poke you," as if he considered her continued investigation goading and upsetting the 'emotionless' CS9.

She and Lock had finally put coding into the rewrite of the CS9, combining the CS9 coding with the *Vagrant Spirit*'s programming. The new code allowed them control, if needed. Lock had converted all the Markham code into the old Service code, hoping the CS9 would integrate the old CSS code better with the indecipherable new Service code. How Lock could be so complacent, Renna didn't understand. He knew the CS9 had not yet uploaded any of the previous program changes.

Zak would sympathize and support her. Give her a hug, pat her back, and tell her to call him when something happened. Of course, nothing happened in his presence.

When no one else listened, the CS9 spoke in Dukan's voice, asking for details about the *Markham3*. It never accepted her answers.

Once she cried, "Look it up in your records."

...someone tampered with my records was it you?...

She looked at the walls and knew the CS9 was targeting her. Why? Like Dukan, the CS9 blamed her for its termination, and now it had devoured the entire ship. She shivered with the realization.

"Ren!"

Jake's second summons drew her attention back to duty.

"On my way." Quick steps carried her through the gangways. Her footsteps no longer echoed on hard flooring. Another change the CS9 made. During their long stay in orbit, the CS9 had slowly changed the flooring to a yielding surface absorbing sound. A floor capable of healing wear, and one never needing to be cleaned. Renna assumed the nanobots collected more DNA from the crew's falling hair and skin cells.

She was sure the nanobots used the human debris as it had Jake's DNA, combining the cellular information into the very fabric of the ship. *Why not?* It used everything else, combining and recombining molecules as it restructured the *Vagrant Spirit*. Time elapse recordings kept track of the minuscule changes all over the ship. Renna sucked in a cry before she voiced the sound. Fear scraped her spine.

Getting the ship to this point had taken longer than anyone expected. Within the next few days, they would test the Rabican, the Jupiter1090, and the CS9, the last step in many stages of their return. Ship's work dwindled as projects were completed, or because the CS9 took over the operation. Boredom drove everyone crazy, and they all searched for endeavors to make their days meaningful. Gradually, each of them had found a distraction. Zak mapped and explored the surrounding galaxy from the flight deck. Cutter studied the ship and crew with a physician's thoroughness.

The need for a refit became useless as the CS9 repaired the Jupiter1090. Only uploading the rewritten program remained. An upload Renna knew the CS9 was evading.

Her crew wanted this omnipotent power to run the ship, to fix everything broken. It couldn't. The CS9 could only bring disaster. She had to make them believe how dangerous it was. *How could she convince them when they thought her the problem? Was she? Did her past color her logic? No. It shocked her. It could decide that all of them were unnecessary.*

Entering the wardroom, Renna's gaze flicked over the monitors lining one partition with readings. New monitors replaced the originals, multiplied by the rate of four to one. Another sign of the work accomplished by the CS9 on the old ship. Renna shuddered. Ship Dog and Lock entered the wardroom together. Jake already sat at the table with Cutter. They greeted her and went back to their conversation. She stopped by the sideboard and grabbed two brownies before sitting down.

"Zak's on his way," Lock said as he flopped into a chair. "It's Thanksgiving week. Who would have guessed we'd be here this long? Over seven hundred days in space. Are you wearing a new outfit?" he asked, eying her lavender and green work suit.

"Why do you bother counting them?" Ezry asked and ignored any answer, entering with a handful of spinach for Cutter. As she entered the galley, she added, "Today's Thanksgiving for Arts Day. I gave Renna an early gift." A minute later, she emerged and added, "I spent the rest of the day painting," to her truncated conversation.

Lock groaned. "What now?"

"Don't groan. You know I've been working on Renna's cabin."

"You finished my cabin?"

Ezry nodded.

"I'm sure my compartment is the most beautiful place on the ship," Renna said with pleasure and jumped to her feet.

"You chose the colors."

"Your cabin?" Zak asked, having overheard them as he entered. "Have I been dispossessed?"

"Come see," Renna said. She grabbed Zak's hand and pulled him after her. Jake shouted a plaintive, "What about my meeting?" Lock reluctantly rose and followed her. Ezry yelled, "Coming, Cutter?"

"No, you've shown me it already, and I've got to finish what I'm doing."

"Renna's a cool-color person," Ezry said as Zak entered the cabin. "Not a hot aficionado like me."

The small cabin's walls were washed in blues and greens. The bed was done in a beautiful mixture of creams from light to dark in a style Ezry called very tailored. She had painted the flooring in a montage of exotic tiles of dark brown, russet, black, and tan.

"Very nice," Jake said. "Can we get back to business now?"

His unimpressed comment earned Ezry's frown. Renna giggled. Her enjoyment of the relaxed atmosphere had increased in the ship's months of passive orbit and tempered her fear of the CS9. So different from life on the *Markham3*.

Zak inspected the room. "Beautiful, the colors suit you. I hope you invite me to visit soon."

Renna grinned. Ezry laughed at his sarcasm, punching his arm. "I left your bedding, only added a few embellishments. Left your colors on the floor."

"So now I'm underfoot?"

Renna smiled at his plaintive tone. "We better go back to the wardroom. Jake wants his reports."

"Yeah. Now. That's an order." Jake said from behind them.

Renna recognized an indulgent quality in her captain's voice. She grinned at him in pleasure. No podder ever had a better dom.

"Who could've guessed Ez had a hot personality?" Zak said, rubbing his arm as he left the room.

"A hot temper." Ezry grinned as she followed Lock. She threw her voice so Lock would hear. "My personality is only colorful. Unlike you, I'm not a motley clothing mangler." Her gaze roved over Lock's tattered ship suit.

Lock stopped and posed. His green looked a little more tattered than just the frayed armholes. "This is fashionable for stranded spacers." He straightened and laughed. "We got to get home before I'm out of clothes."

"Nobody's going to argue that we need supplies," Jake said as they reentered the wardroom.

"Now that we've admired Ezry's work, can we move on to the next article of business?"

"Over dinner." Cutter placed a steaming dish on the sideboard. "I make an exception for this occasion. Ren, you ate your dessert before dinner, so hold off until everyone else gets some."

"I'm taking mine now," Lock said as he loaded dinner on his plate. He took two brownies, adding them to the top of his plate as he looked at Renna. "Recommend you all do the same."

Renna enjoyed Lock's teasing. Zak took the chair next to hers and waited with her for the others to fill their plates. She recognized his expression—a straight face hiding a yearning to shout. Once they were seated, he leaned over and put an intel before her. His hand casually brushed and then wrapped around hers, gently squeezed. She read the screen and scanned the contents. Remaining calm and thinking this close to Zak proved difficult.

For a minute, she stared at him. His return gaze engulfed her.

"Enough lovey-look stuff," Lock ordered. "Call this meeting to order, Jake, before they jump up and leave."

"You've extrapolated our start position," Renna whispered and kissed Zak. Her words fell in a lull of sound. He returned her smile.

"As close as I can, and hopefully, accurate enough."

Everyone remained silent for a moment before speaking in excitement.

Pulling her to her feet, Zak waved her to the buffet while he continued talking in his normal voice. "I figured the drift from when Vera was taken offline with our last recorded position. Read all the logs for solar wind patterns. We knew when we turned off the power, and I compared the readings to the CS9's chronometer at insertion. With CS9's help, I worked backward to the location where we entered transition. The mark might be off a little. I believe these coordinates will get us back to the right location and keep our time consistent."

"So, no time dislocation?" Ren asked and noticed the tremor flicker over his expression.

"We need to make a decision," he said as he finished filling his plate.

"What's there to decide?" Ezry asked as Zak returned to the table. Ren hesitated as she put the mystery meat on her plate. The last few months the food had dwindled, often tasting the same despite Cutter's efforts, an unstated sign they needed to return soon. The brownies looked more appealing. She gave a sidelong gaze at the empty platter. Cutter and Lock both caught her wistful glance. She blushed, sighed, and returned to the table. With a grin, Cutter placed a brownie on her plate.

Jake finished his mouthful before he answered Ezry. "If we have the wrong insertion point, we return before we left. If after the actual insertion point, we may return long after we left."

"How long?" Ezry asked, her voice wobbling.

"Maybe longer than we've been gone," Zak said, his gaze caught and held Ezry's. She frowned and bit her lip.

"Chance we have to take," Jake said. "Lock, how is the CS9 rewrite coming?"

"Ren and I are not sure the CS9 has accepted the new programming."

"Probably suspects a program wipe," Cutter said.

"A program change isn't the same thing," Renna said, appalled.

"What about the Jupiter1090 and the Rabican integration?" Zak asked.

Jake shrugged. "As much as Ship Dog and I can determine in simulation runs, the Jupiter1090 increased performance by a magnitude of five point six. We believe, from what we've learned from Lock's decoding of the program, we can control both engines manually, at least until switch-over to the Rabican, and certainly in an emergency."

"Good increase," Ship Dog suggested, his gaze centered on his plate.

Renna crumbled her brownies into morsels. *Simulations the CS9 might have distorted.*

"You think the CS9 will work with us?" The words wheezed out of Lock like a sigh. "Another decision to make. Feel like I'm back in the SSC rather than on a shortrunner."

"How you going to know if the CS9 accepts the programming?" Ezry asked.

Lock's gaze flew to Ezry and he smiled. "Gave the CS9 a new code. If it doesn't use the new code, I will know the new programming hasn't been accepted."

"We also need to determine how the CS9 will work in tandem with the Jupiter 1090," Jake said.

"New programming. Test. Short trips."

"I know," Jake answered Ship Dog. "Definitely. We just have to figure out the tests before we start."

Ezry threw up her hands. "I thought you all knew what you were doing." She grabbed a brownie and took a bite.

"Not true, Ezry," Lock said. "You never thought we could get this far."

~ * ~

"Ship security locked down. Course locked in. Estimated time of arrival, five days." Zak watched the panel lights flicker into familiar patterns. His stomach fluttered likewise. "Jupiter 1090 online.

Rabican powered and holding." A glance showed Jake seemed impervious to the situation's stress, except a sheen of moisture collected above his brother's brow. Jake pressed the intercom link.

"Is everybody in place?"

A chorus of affirmatives came back, overlapping each other.

"CS9VS, acknowledge the Rabican will not come online while the Jupiter1090 is in operation."

...cs9vs acknowledges command from captain jake terran...

"Ship Dog, is the engine room ready?"

"Ready." Ship Dog's monotone reply came through their connex. Zak thought he heard satisfaction. With Ship Dog, one never knew.

"Coordinates logged?" Jake asked.

"Yes. Have you entered the right commands?"

"Smartass."

"Well, it has been a while since you've performed these tasks. I think reminding you is just a wise precaution." His lips quivered with amusement at Jake's disregard. He continued the pre-flight routine. After another few minutes of silent work, Jake sighed at last and sat back. Zak smiled at him.

"CS9VS is the Rabican online and disengaged?"

...rabican engine disengaged ...jupiter1090 feed activated...

"All right. Let's do this." He pressed a few switches.

The Jupiter1090 panel sprang to life with yellow lights. As they worked through bringing the engine online, the lights gradually turned to rows of green. Jake leaned back in his seat and glanced at Zak.

"Ready to go?"

Zak exhaled. "As ready as I'll ever be."

Leaning forward, Jake's hand hovered over the command pads.

"Stop hesitating. If we blow, we won't realize it for more than a couple seconds. If we don't, we'll know just as quickly."

Jake frowned at him; his four fingers hit the pad.

A slow, familiar hum emanated through the hull, slowly building intensity. Testing the controls, Jake frowned. "It feels different."

Zak checked the readings. "She is responding. Power levels optimum. Engine launch imminent." Even as he spoke, the inertia dampers quavered, reset, and stabilized. "Velocity building." The *Vagrant Spirit* surged forward, the engine's output overcoming the dampers.

"I can feel the Jupiter 1090 again." Satisfaction oozed from Jake.

"This much power feels different."

"If the CS9 and its nanobots accomplished this, I'm not complaining. Renna's paranoia probably affects us—a cognizant ship isn't all bad."

"I'm afraid we'll find out—one way or another."

"What about the laterals? Are they firing correctly?"

"Yes. I'm running an efficiency report comparing this drive to the last log before insertion." He whistled. "Increased timing accuracy on laterals by nine-fold. Hell, every system's efficiency rating reads above new ship specs."

"Above new engine specs?" Jake laughed as he punched the all-clear signal.

"Maybe Renna has overreacted a little." Zak sighed softly. "I'll try talking with her again."

"Not without cause," Jake said, pounding him once the back. "Go report to everyone. I want to sit here a little longer and revel in establishing true flight."

~ * ~

For five days, the *Vagrant Spirit* operated under the Jupiter 1090's power. Renna watched the engine's monitors from the flight deck during her duty turn, and from the engine compartment until she noticed how anxious her hovering made Ship Dog. Then she watched from the wardroom.

"Stop watching. The engine operates perfectly." Zak's hand ran down her forearm, bringing her attention back to breakfast from the screens lining the partition.

"Too perfectly," she whispered. Her gaze wandered back to the readings.

"There is nothing wrong with perfection," Jake said. "The last I knew, a perfectly running ship was something every captain sought. Today will tell."

"You're letting that thing drive us?" Ezry asked.

"Yes, Ez." Jake sounded droll. "We're letting the CS9 and Rabican make the return trip."

Ezry grimaced, nodded, and glanced at her. Renna recognized Ezry's fright. "I will stay with you."

"Cutter will stay with Ezry," Jake said. "This flight, we're squeezing you onto the flight deck. You've been the only one on the flight deck during the last insertion and emergence, so we'll have a better idea of what is right or wrong."

"I did nothing."

"You have the experience...we don't. Plus, we have more to monitor."

"It's all right, Ren." Ezry sounded more confident than she looked. "You do as Jake orders. I'll be with Cutter."

~ * ~

The flight deck had changed overnight. Renna inspected the compartment with misgiving. Three seats lined the curved, redesigned control panel fitting seamlessly against the compartment's front. Equipment racks flowed in lockstep along the upper partition. She noted the shields already covered the turret's viewports and drew a deep breath to relieve some of her tension. *Calmness, professionalism, duty.* She hated falling back on her crewkin mantra, but it helped her regain focus.

"Take the far seat, Ren," Jake commanded. He smiled. "The CS9 made the changes during my last watch."

Zak looked around. "Superb and impressive. The compartment's dimensions have changed, too."

"Yes." Jake grinned. "No shipyard, no cost."

"Too good to be true."

"Isn't it?" Jake laughed and took a seat. "I'll monitor the Rabican, you the Jupiter1090."

"The CS9...harmed you," Renna said. "It hijacked the *Vagrant Spirit* and took all of us this far into space, and you laugh? I don't understand how you can be so casual about it controlling your ship."

"Every ship needs a captain and crew, every crew a reliable ship. The situation seems about perfect to me. I don't think the CS9 wants to kill us now, or even wished to harm me before. The CS9 is learning, and so are we. Your position is to watch the power interactions."

...cs9vs available for command ...rabican initiated ...return flight time estimated fifty-two seconds ...insertion and emergence ninety-five percent of flight duration...

It listens. Renna ignored her inner qualm at the feminine voice addressing Jake and took her position. She jerked her hand back as an electrical charge surged through her arm when she touched the console. Jake and Zak were unaffected, so she touched the panel again.

The incident only reaffirmed her suspicion of the CS9. *It hates me as much as I hate it.*

...insertion emergence dimensions verified and logged...

"Okay. We are adjusting the trajectory of the *Vagrant Spirit*, and the Jupiter1090 is functioning at twelve percent above optimum levels."

...direction is unimportant during insertion...

"We will disengage the Jupiter1090 as the CS9VS initiates the Rabican."

...cs9vs understands ...captain terran's order logged...

With her hands grasping her seat's armrests, Renna waited for the transition. The panel indicated the Jupiter1090's thrust diminished as the Rabican's panel revved to life in flashing colors signifying little to her. Gravity fluctuations preceded the insertion with the remembered visual and palpable sensations from the first insertion. The transition was faster. Their duration in transit space lasted seconds before emergence began. Renna experienced few mental or physical aberrations.

"We're back. Same place..." Jake's elation fell away. "Even for so short a journey, it's a strange experience." He looked pale.

Zak looked just as shaken. "Are we in the right time? The right universe?"

Remembering some of her vision-scenarios from a few minutes before, Renna grinned.

"Since Jake is still captain, and I am in third seat, I think we are."

They all heard the Jupiter1090 come online, felt the slight vibration and sound as engines exchanged control. Within minutes the *Vagrant Spirit* dropped into its established orbit around Proxima Centauri. The star's flares captured Renna's attention. "I think I will miss viewing the fireworks from this orbit."

~ * ~

Jake described the situation. "Renna doesn't believe the CS9 has accepted the programming. However, we have had several successful trips engaging both engines. The CS9 also has confirmed Zak's calculation for the original insertion point, and the insertion point for our trip home. The trial runs have operated smoothly. Our decision is do we go or wait until we're sure the CS9 accepts the programming?

"If that thing is working, why wait?" Ezry said.

"It's your decision," Lock said. "You're captain."

"You understand how dangerous this is?" Cutter asked Ezry.

Ezry gave him a lopsided smile. "Yeah, honey. I know. You never gave up on me, so I guess I'd rather die trying with you than any other way." Cutter kissed her. As Ezry's dark eyes swung to her. Renna smiled back at her friend for her show of bravery. Not like Sen at all. Ezry wouldn't give up.

"Like the last time, we'll need to stay focused and may want to sleep in the wardroom as this compartment is the most heavily shielded, although the CS9 has built new shielding throughout the habitation module."

"Initiate flight countdown," Ship Dog said with a resolute nod.

~ * ~

Renna laughed at Ezry's quips about her plants. She gave them personalities. It felt good to enjoy a little humor. They sat before a bench, filling tubes with seedlings. Around them, green fronds, leaves, stems, and flowers cascaded in regimented rows. Warm humidity surrounded them.

"Don't know why we eat lettuce, mostly just a pale, tasteless veg."

"Like a podder."

Ezry leveled her with a look. "You said it, not me, it might be an acquired taste."

Renna giggled. Today everything seemed right. "You know, having those chemicals isn't safe. They have been used to make bombs."

"My fertilizer? You're always suspecting me of nefarious motives."

"Not anymore, Ezry. You are my only woman friend."

"Glad I'm a woman, not a female, or lord help me, a girl."

...before insertion termination of criminal crew essential... innocent crew escape...

The CS9 halted their talk, speaking as Dom Dukan. Both she and Ezry stood.

"Get out," Renna told Ezry. She took a step toward the hatch.

A thin bolt of light crackled through the sleeve of her shirt, stinging her. Renna jumped back, her hand slapped over the burning injury. Another bolt hit her shoulder, cutting a path down her back. She heard Ezry scream. Renna dropped to the deck and crawled under a table while more lightning sizzled around the table's edges.

Ezry inserted her body into the line of fire. "Stop it! Stop it!" Ezry screamed.

Renna heard several loud thumps as Ezry threw things at wherever the CS9 attacked from. The attack stopped.

"Get out, Ezry! Hurry! Tell Jake." While she yelled, Renna tried to contact someone, anyone, on her connex. The unit wouldn't work. An ominous click told her the hatch had locked. She peered through the legs of the tables and saw Ezry remained in the hydro-farm. An acrid smell filled the compartment. Renna glanced around. Flames flickered near Ezry's chemicals. Escape was too late.

She yipped as an electrical charge tingled over her skin as she scuttled out from her hiding spot and the CS9 attacked, its accuracy growing with practice. Renna dodged between the tables and wrapped her arms around Ezry. She kicked Ezry's legs out from under her. And as Ezry fell, Renna pulled the larger woman with her under a table just before the room exploded around her.

~ * ~

The shock shook the whole ship. It knocked Cutter off his feet from where he stood in the galley making a salad. Food and plates flew, crashing onto the floor, covering him in vegetable pieces. Sirens immediately blared through the ship. At first, he thought the emergency a catastrophe with the Rabican countdown. The monitor showed the countdown continued.

"The Rabican?" Jake screamed above the clamor through his connex. Cutter knew Jake was in his cabin, from his voice, awakened too abruptly.

"No, hydro-farm," Zak answered through the same means from the flight deck.

"Ezry's there!" Cutter shouted from where he stood, hanging onto the counter. He pushed away from the counter and took off at a run. At the intercom, he hurriedly pressed the hydroponics compartment. Ezry didn't answer. None came from either Ezry's cabin or their joint quarters.

Cutter ran to his sickbay and flung open a locker, grabbed his emergency medical kit, and left the compartment. Smoke twisted in slow tendrils near the overheads.

"Everyone to firefighting status, Zak...be prepared to initiate containment on my say." Jake's voice screamed throughout the ship.

"Ready on your word," Zak answered from the flight deck. "The CS9 reports sustaining injury in the area."

"On my way, join you there," Cutter yelled, gasping in the smoky corridor. An unnatural hiss hummed through the gangway as if the partitions were shivering in pain.

"Zak, everyone accounted for?" Jake asked, his voice filtered by breathing gear.

"Everyone except Ezry and Ren has checked in," Zak answered. Their voices floated as if next to him in the dark ship. Cutter realized the CS9 failed to turn on lights, failed to filter the air.

Cutter stopped at a fire locker. He pulled on the protective outerwear and the breathing gear and a suppressor apparatus from the locker. Further down the corridor, he saw Jake with a fire suppresser enter the hallway to the hydro-farm.

"I'm going in," he yelled at Cutter as he disappeared from view. Seconds later, another explosion rocked through the ship.

Flames licked along the overhead. Cutter sprayed suppressant toward the fire as he moved toward the gangway intersection. Air currents eddied, flowing in mesmerizing patterns, carrying the retardant chemicals in unexpected tracks.

Ship Dog and Lock arrived from the other corridors, their suppressers in hand.

"Jake's already down the gangway," he said, as he crossed into the smoke-filled corridor. Jake wasn't in the gangway. Flames licked out of the broken partition of the hydro-farm compartment. The broken hatch hadn't closed. The blast had blown the door off its tracks.

With his suppressers blowing, Ship Dog kicked through the damaged partition, pulling pieces away. Inside they saw the fire still raged. Lock and Cutter entered through the compartment door. Smoke boiled around the compartment, limiting sight. Water dripped from the burst overhead watering system, forming hissing, steaming spots on the floor. They searched through the rubble of overturned tables and equipment with hand beams.

"Found Jake," Ship Dog shouted.

Cutter edged through the smoke following the internal source detector Ship Dog had placed. His mask's light showed the devastation. He didn't see Jake until his brother's shape appeared as a rumpled ball near the back, far side partition. Three steps took him to Jake. Cutter snapped an ear monitor on Jake and opened his diagnostic reader. His heart clenched at what he learned.

Lock took longer to find Ezry. "Only her hand is showing from under a table." A grunt of effort sounded through the connex. "Damn, can't lift the table."

Ship Dog moved as a shadow through the smoke. "Lift."

Lock sprayed the suppressant while Ship Dog lifted the table off Ezry.

Cutter left Jake, joining them. He knelt next to Ezry. *They needed stretchers. More importantly, they needed to get the victims out of this compartment. Jake needed him.* "Drag her out. Don't lift her. Lifting might cause more damage." He saw the edge of Renna's sleeve. "Daniel, take her shoulders, Lock get her feet, lift her off Ren."

They shifted Ezry. Ship Dog caught her tunic to slide her from the compartment. Lock kicked debris aside as he led the way. A check showed Renna breathing. Within seconds, Ship Dog and Lock returned.

"Get her out of here."

While they dragged Ren out, Cutter returned to Jake. Feet appeared. He glanced up. Zak squatted next to him, placing a stretcher on the deck. Cutter grunted in relieved approval.

"How bad?"

"He's unconscious. Let's get him straightened out."

He unfolded Jake's intertwined arms and legs with slow care, trying to do no more damage. Zak helped him lift Jake onto the stretcher.

"Let's get out of here, now," Zak said.

Cutter glanced at the flames consuming the partitions around them in widespread destruction. The scorched walls retarded the fire, melting and seeping while expanding and contracting in a heaving pattern. He suddenly realized the howling sound surrounding them came from the CS9, not the fire. Smoke roiled in flowing waves around them.

Together, they lifted the stretcher. Within seconds, they exited the compartment, ducking to avoid flame and falling debris.

At the gangway intersection, Zak halted. The smoke was worse there than in the burning compartment. Zak's hand moved inside the emergency control panel and pushed the emergency lock. The gangway security barrier rolled into place between them and the hydro-farm, cutting off the smoke and the radiating waves of heat.

"The area is sealed. I'm implementing containment." Zak's voice sounded loud in Cutter's helmet. On this side of the barrier, there was nothing to indicate the abrupt expulsion of the atmosphere on the other side. A nearby panel's red lights suddenly transformed to yellow and green. Smoke evaporated with a whoosh into vents. Now there was time to think, time to worry.

~ * ~

After helping Cutter get Jake to sickbay, Zak jogged to the flight deck. The CS9 seemed unresponsive, almost as if it were in shock. He entered orders to delay the insertion countdown. In minutes, he rejoined those gathered in the wardroom to wait on Cutter's diagnosis.

Renna had recovered consciousness as soon as she'd received oxygen. Cutter deemed her in no imminent medical danger. Zak noticed her suit was sliced with laser burns, and her skin showed welts beneath the fabric, her brows and hair were singed, and red spots covered her face and hands. As he approached, she rose. "I'm all right."

"Jake and Ezry?" he asked, slipping his arms around her. She couldn't answer him. He felt her shivering reaction and asked Lock to give him a blanket. Once he had her wrapped, he pushed her back onto the lounger and sat next to her. She leaned her head onto his chest and cried.

"Cutter is still working on Jake," Lock said. "Ezry has a concussion, three broken ribs, a broken arm, and some bad burns on her hands. We found her under a table, which Cutter suspects caused the injuries. The table shielded her from the blast and fire; saved both her and Renna."

"And Jake?"

"He has not told us yet," Renna said, as her frightened face rose to his.

"It's going to be all right," he murmured, tightening his clasp on her. "You'll see. Jake will be all right, don't cry."

"It was so much like *Markham3*."

"I know. I know." He held her tighter.

Several minutes later, his distracted mind understood the information on the row of monitors. Renna felt his stiffening and asked, "What?"

"The monitors," he said, "I ordered the CS9 to abort the countdown."

Everyone turned to look just as a gender-neutral voice announced, *...all crew prepare for imminent insertion...ten minutes and counting...*

Zak jumped up and ran, with Renna following him. The hatch lock secured before they reached the portal. Sounds reverberated through the open audio—lockers slammed close, hatches locked, and behind the noise, the wail of the Rabican rose.

Cutter would need help. Zak ran to sickbay, shouting as he moved. "Lock, Ship Dog, get Ezry secured. Renna, batten down the compartment.

In the sickbay, Cutter looked up. "Help me strap him to the bed." They barely finished when, with no further warning, they entered transition.

Thirty-one

...2182.360-08:02 universal space-time ...mission status ... transition achieved ...rabican operating under prescribed guidelines ...programming changes downloaded ...discrepancy rabican encryption noted and corrected ...markham3 files available ...logged into transfer protocols...

For her first entrance into transition space in the confines of the wardroom, Renna found the effects relatively mild, or maybe experience made them easier. The jagged changes of gravity and perception were dulled.

...insertion successful...vera establishing extended bubble shields on habitat module for crew's comfort...

Everyone remained in place. "That's the voice it uses with Jake," Ezry said, her voice groggy with pain relievers. "They used to talk like I wasn't in the fore compartment."

"Sen's voice," Renna said.

"Vera?" Ship Dog asked.

Lock smiled and gave an exuberant yelp of delight. "The CS9 took the programming!"

Zak emerged from the sickbay looking stunned, confused. At Ren's side, he said, "Bad," adding, "alive." He took a deep breath, and Renna put her arms around him, hugging him. "He was hurled by the second blast; he broke his back, both legs, and arms, multiple times."

"He'll be all right, though," Lock said, his jubilation halted.

Zak shook his head. "Cutter says he needs more medical attention than can be given here."

"What else?" Renna asked.

"There is some internal damage."

...interim captain zak ...permission to speak ...

Everyone froze as the polite, disembodied voice spoke.

"CS9?"

...now vera ...vera of the vagrant spirit ...sir ...I can help medical crewmember doctor terran with the healing of injured captain jake terran...

"Even the semantics have changed," Renna murmured. Tears of relief flood her eyes.

"What's changed?" Zak asked.

...vera's mission is service ...not survival...

"How?" Cutter's voice could be heard from the sickbay. "How can you help? You've nearly killed him. Twice."

...the nanobots extracted from jake terran's body have been modified ...they will not drain his body now ...can cure him ... while they cannot instantly heal his injuries they can form inner braces and shields to help with his healing ...the explosion was an accident...

"The nanobots can keep him alive?"

...I believe so ...if you will permit and facilitate entry...

"You just injured three crewmen," Cutter said.

...the attack on crewmember renna initiated the circumstances ...the explosion was an accident ...cs9 injured ...vera's apology to crewmember renna ...the download has been accepted ...issues clarified... former cs9 at fault ...burns hurt ...

"What do you think?" Cutter asked Zak, his face suffused with worry, dread, and hope.

"I don't think we have much choice."

Cutter nodded, sighing. "My sentiments, exactly."

"Vera, permission granted," Zak said.

...thank you captain ...place jake on the deck of the rabican compartment...

"Why there?" Zak asked, his voice spoke his suspicion as Renna gasped. His arms tightened around her, reminding her to remain silent.

...nanobots can quickly congregate where they have had the most time to develop...

Zak looked at Cutter, who returned his regard, but said, "We don't have a choice. I can't save him. This is his only chance." He swiped his hand over his face.

"If he lives through the transport to the aft compartment."

"His back—we've got to keep him stable," Cutter said while Zak helped him move Jake to the stretcher.

"How dangerous?" Zak asked. Cutter didn't answer him, which was answer enough.

They strapped him immobile to the stretcher. Once in the Rabican's compartment, they lifted Jake's naked body onto the deck. Immediately the flooring seemed to melt, slowly swallowing Jake, leaving only an oval of his face encompassed on the deck floor. When Zak moved to pull his brother back, a shock threw his hands off with enough force to unbalance him. Renna caught him before he fell over.

...vera causes jake terran no harm...

"When will...how will we know when..."

...I will inform cutter when jake is ready to leave...

Everyone stood, waiting. When it became apparent the process would be slow, Cutter said, "I have to get back and check on Ezry." Lock and Ship Dog left with Cutter. Renna waited with Zak. After three hours, he said, "Go get something to eat, get some rest."

"What about you?"

"I don't want to chance Jake waking here alone."

Renna nodded and left. Thirty minutes later, she returned with her arms full. "We can rest together, here." She spread a mattress pad, placing blankets over it.

"I hope our return is faster," Zak said, making a face as he swallowed the contents of the ration packet Renna had handed him. "How about you? How are you feeling?"

"Sore. I'll heal."

He huffed. "Improved crewkin bodies. The CS9 attacked you, didn't it?"

"Yes. The CS9 stopped when Ezry tried to protect me."

"We should have believed you. I should have believed you."

"No. To believe without proof is foolish." She looked around the compartment. "The CS9 and I, we were both crazy. We both did what we were told, what we thought was our duty, and Markham ultimately discarded us. I caused both of us suspicion and poor judgment."

"You don't want to dismantle it any longer? After what it did to you? For killing your crewkin?"

Renna took a deep breath, her face a strange mix of emotions. She smiled at last. "Vera, what made you upload the code rewrite?"

...cs9vs actions injured crew ...crewmember ezry defended you...captain jake terran tried to save crewmen renna and ezry by entering the burning hydro-farm ...the rest of the crew also tried to save the crewmen ...they put out the flames eating the cs9vs's bioskin ...fire hurt ...cs9vs deserved punishment...

"Remember what Vera said in the wardroom, service not survival?" Renna asked. "I learned who I am and changed. Vera has done the same. We have both healed. Even if I lost you, and all of my new crew, I won't ever be alone again—I'll always have me."

He sighed. Not quite the answer he wanted.

"Zak." When he looked at her, Renna continued. "When Jake is better...the answer is yes."

Comprehension took him a minute. He crushed his lips against hers, hugging her in a tender embrace. She must have felt his weariness for she gently rubbed his back. They stayed in each other's arms for a long time. Hours later, they fell asleep.

"Zak?" Jake woke him, his voice cracked and weak. He blinked his eyes, searching his surroundings. "What am I doing here? Ezry! The fire!"

In an instant, Zak was next to Jake, throwing a blanket over his body now resting on the deck. "Ezry is safe, the fire is out, and Vera is probably healing the compartment."

"Vera? What am I doing here?"

"Getting some help from the CS9, or Vera as she calls herself now. How do you feel?"

"Don't ask, and I won't lie."

"Zak?" Cutter's voice rang through the intercom.

"Yeah, he's out. He's awake, Cutter. Seems better."

"I'm on my way."

"Better? I must have been a mess," Jake laughed and groaned.

Zak laughed, his voice half anxious, half hopeful. "You were. You got a lot to live for."

"Do I?"

"Yes. We're all alive in transition on the way home, and you still have duties to perform."

"You're overestimating my abilities. If I'm as bad as I feel, I think you'll be fulfilling those duties for some time to come."

"Can't. Not this one. You have to hurry and heal, so you can marry Ren and me."

A smile crossed Jake's gaunt face. "In that case, I'll try harder."

Thirty-two

...2183.043-11:01 universal space-time ...mission status ...transition successful ...preparing rabican to go offline upon emergence ... jupiter1090 initiated for operating under optimal parameters ... crew healthy ...vera of vagrant spirit healthy ...vera awaits orders...

...emergence in fourteen hours, fifteen minutes, thirty-five seconds and counting ...transition time seventy-two days, six hours, fourteen minutes...

"Thanks for the warning, Vera. Will you send messages as soon as the *Vagrant Spirit* emerges?"

...yes ...captain jake ...I will inform those not currently in the wardroom...

"That's it." Lock threw his cards on the table hearing Vera's announcement. He rose and danced around the table. "Let's celebrate! We're almost home. We're having a wedding, and we're almost home. Good luck has finally come our way!" He sang as he moved. The unisuit Ezry had made him for the wedding glowed on his trim, too-thin body.

"Jake Terran, don't you let Zak down here until Cutter gives you the say-so." Ezry's voice boomed from behind Renna. "And you make damn sure you follow the directions I gave you for the ceremony!"

"Yes, ma'am," Jake grinned as he left.

Renna smiled, taking a deep breath and running a hand over her garments. The fabric shimmered pink in reaction. They were the most beautiful things she had ever worn, ever seen. An under tunic of deep purple brocade cut to mid-thigh swirled to the floor in the back over an all-gold unisuit. A gauzy pink jacket was gathered and swathed into a knot behind her. *Calm. Calm. Calm.* She felt jittery even repeating her new mantra. Her hand was slapped when she fingered the soft folds of the jacket.

"Don't move until I get this fixed in the back. Oh, baby, this has so many layers, it's going to drive Zak crazy trying to find you inside it." Ezry gave a deep chuckle. "If he can figure out all the fasteners. That's all right, teasing temptation only adds to the anticipation. Daniel, don't just stand there shifting your feet, get the drapery straightened from where someone's kicked it out of place. Need a decent background to show the bridal couple to the best advantage. Want good pictures. Lock, you sure you know how to take good pictures?"

Lock rolled his eyes and Renna giggled. "Yes, Ezry, I know how to take pictures. We'll have four live leads guided by Vera, and I'm taking stills."

Lock helped Ship Dog smooth out the folds in the length of navy fabric covering the back of a trellis Ezry had Ship Dog make to her plans. Once he started moving, Ship Dog didn't look so uncomfortable in his new 'dress' clothes. Nothing escaped Ezry's notice: background, lighting, or costumes, especially Ship Dog's.

"When this is over, I'll have no fabric left. Can't believe I bought navy fabric. Never use navy. Can't imagine what I was thinking. No flowers, damn it. This is coming off a shabby affair," Ezry said.

"You used all your beautiful fabrics on us. Thank you." Renna twisted and kissed Ezry's cheek.

"They do look nice, don't they? Used every scrap I've hoarded for so long. Nice to have them used." Ezry's fingers pulled and twitched at her garments.

"Whoever heard of a wedding without flowers? Would have grown some, but the starter plants and seeds all died in the fire. We'll have to have a reception once we get back. I'm going on a major shopping spree. If we have any money left."

"Another party?" Lock asked. "I thought this was the party?"

"Twits, they're all twits," Ezry complained in a low voice only Renna could hear.

Renna giggled again, but couldn't stop it, even though it felt very unlike herself. She had never felt jubilation.

"Daniel, don't touch your jacket sleeve again, or you'll rub the pile right off the velvet."

Cutter emerged from the galley waving a bottle of champagne. "Saved this; now I know what for." He placed the bottle in a bucket and dumped ice around it. "Wish we had a banquet to go with the bubbly rather than ship's rations." He also wore Ezry's efforts—a very elegant blue-striped jacket over a unisuit done in dark brown.

"We're on ship's rations, and you saved a bottle of bubbly?" Lock asked in disgust. "Have anything else hidden of a restorative nature? I could've used a shot or two straight up anytime this last year."

"Shot or two of what?" Cutter said, returning with glasses.

"Rum, whiskey, gin. Turpentine, if that's all there was."

"You'll appreciate a libation more today," Ezry said. "Vera, you make damn sure we don't start emerging in the middle of the ceremony."

...emergence in fourteen hours ...five minutes ...twenty-two seconds and counting...

Ezry emerged from behind Renna. She wore a soft gold and orange print tunic, its floor length blending with the equally long sleeves.

"You look so beautiful," Renna told her.

Ezry smiled while preening a little. "Thank you. I'm sure I don't want to outshine the bride. Your hair is really beautiful woven with gold ribbon." She turned to Cutter. "Okay. Tell those brothers of yours to get in here."

Jake entered first, dressed in a suit matching Cutter's. Zak followed him dressed in plum and gold. Renna could tell he wore his clothes only to please Ezry. When his eyes fell on her, though, he smiled. Everything else fell away. They took their positions.

"This is a first for the *Vagrant Spirit*," Jake said, smiling with pride. "And never a more welcomed family event. Today Renna joins our family by taking my brother as her lawful husband. It is my pleasant duty to perform the ceremony as ship captains have forever."

The ceremony was over all too soon, and the champagne bottle's cork popped with a bang as Cutter removed it. Cutter poured seven thin tapered glasses with the clear liquid.

"Not enough for all of us," Lock said, taking a glass and pouting. He did not drink the contents, nor did the others when they took their glass.

"Have you ever had alcohol?" Zak asked, his arm resting comfortably around Renna's waist.

She shook her head whispering, "No."

He smiled. "Champagne isn't the best to start with. Sip slowly and enjoy the bubbles."

"Yeah, enjoy the bubbles," Lock said, sniffing his glass. "We'd need at least two bottles to feel any effects."

"Effects? Drunkenness?" Renna asked, raising her eyebrows.

"Drunkenness?" Ezry repeated with a laugh. "We'd need four bottles to achieve that. If you're lucky, you might get tipsy."

Jake raised his glass. "To Renna and Zak—may they share a long, loving relationship."

"Here, here," Cutter said. The others lifted their glasses, tapping the edges together with a delightful chink.

"A custom for good luck," Zak said. He placed a hand over her glass-filled hand and helped her tilt and clink her glass to his, followed by theirs to all the others. Once done, everyone drank from the fragile rims. Renna carefully looked at the contents. Small bubbles rose. She took a sip of the sweet-salty-tasting beverage and frowned. "Better than coffee."

Lock groaned and grinned. "We absolutely have to cure your lack of sophistication."

~ * ~

...2183.244-01:08 universal space time ...mission status ... emergence into sol system successful ...mission complete ...crew reports physical and psychological effects diminished ...marriage of my crewmembers recorded ...emergency beacons have been placed ...messages sent ...time signals from space buoys report time as 2183.268-02:04 time displacement insignificant ...message coming in ...the sun royal ultimate class uc75543T220c has heard our distress beacon and is on its way ...coordinating routes meet in twenty-three days ...ten hours and forty-four minutes...

Renna lay with her head cushioned on Zak's chest, relaxed in the warm cocoon their bodies created under the light blanket. Zak's fingers played with her hair, twisting it around his finger. With the reassurance of his heartbeat, and the steady rise of his breathing planting her firmly in the present, Renna recalled the *Markham3* and the engine none of her crewkin except Dukan knew was a test prototype.

It all brought me here, to this moment.

"What are you thinking about?"

"Why I survived."

Zak's deep chuckle bounced her head. "How deflating. I was imagining you were stunned by the mastery of my technique."

She kissed his chin. "You are marvelous." She stretched.

He rolled onto his side and watched her with a smile twitching the edge of his lips. "You survived because you were already used to tough situations." He leaned over to kiss her along the side of her neck. "Because you are smart, capable, and determined."

She returned his smile. "And now I belong to a new crew."

"Don't sound so satisfied. This could be construed as a case of 'from bad luck to no luck at all.'"

"Because we have Vera? I thought you accepted her?"

"You think having a computer slowly turn our ship into, if not a living entity, something very close, is easy to accept? That everything we have lived through was an ordinary time in space?"

"I'm the one you all thought paranoid about the process."

"Not any more paranoid than the computer, I assure you."

...ship approaching...ssc solar class unc5892 the helios...six hours...eighteen minutes...

"That's Jake's old ship." Zak rose onto his arms to kiss more of her. "There are aspects of Vera I do not appreciate, especially in my bedroom."

"She gave you six hours warning."

"I might need longer." He hesitated, his thoughts clearly shifting with the twist of his brows. "How did they get here so quickly?"

"Don't know, don't care," Renna said and pulled his head closer so he could resume his kiss.

Thirty-three

...2183.268-08:22 universal space-time ...mission status ...ssc solar class unc58922 the helios has docked to vagrant spirit's main hatch ...my crew is assembled on the quarterdeck...

When the hatch opened, a stream of armed Rangers stormed into the *Vagrant Spirit*. Zak couldn't believe what was happening. He grabbed Renna, trying to pull her behind him. She clung to him, trying to place her body in front of him. Ezry shrieked and backed against a partition with her arms spread to the sides; Cutter took a step to shield her body. Everyone else stood in stunned silence.

After the initial hesitation of shock, Ship Dog charged the Rangers despite Cutter's shout, "Remain calm." One blast knocked the big man down and out. Zak's grip stopped Renna from moving. Cutter took a step to help Ship Dog. The sound of weapons adjusting, aiming at him, made Cutter freeze in place. After the turmoil stopped, an officer entered. With a wave of her hand, the weapons lowered. She stared at them with an impassive expression.

Zak stiffened in recognition, heard Jake's, "Sara?"

"Who?" Renna asked Zak in a whisper, reading the woman's antagonistic tranquility.

"Former shipmate, Lieutenant Sara Lingee."

In the silence following his words, Lingee nodded her recognition to both Zak and Jake.

"Helios Chief of Security, Commander Lingee, now, Mr. Terran." She emphasized the *mister*, as she swung her head to face Jake. "Jake Terran, you and the crew of the *Vagrant Spirit* are under arrest for the theft of the experimental proto-engine code-named Rabican from the SSC Ship and Engine Lab on SSC Base Constellation."

"We stole nothing!" Cutter exclaimed, taking a step in Lingee's direction. The armed contingent raised their weapons.

"No, Cutter!" Jake said, throwing up an arm in warning. He looked at Lingee. "Captain Terran," Jake said, emphasizing the title.

"Captain Terran." There was no doubting her sneer. "You and your crew are under arrest for grand theft, transportation of stolen goods, kidnapping, and treason."

Zak's elation plummeted to dread. Numbness prevented his first reaction to the ludicrous charges. Jake reacted faster. He took three stiff steps, hampered by his healing injuries, and uttered an emphatic denial. "As Cutter said, we stole nothing. We have a cargo contract."

"So you say," Commander Lingee said. "Investigation will prove or dismiss the charges. However, your collective reputations in and out of the SSC refute your innocence."

"Our collective reputations do not include any hint we might commit such crimes. I arranged and signed the contract," Cutter said. "Mars Port 53. The contracts and signatures are verified on the ship's system. How do you explain our being missing from known space? Who reported this supposed theft?"

"An anonymous tip. Your extended disappearance supports the allegations. Your claim will be investigated." She stared at Jake. "For forgery, as well as truth." She dismissed Cutter's reply. "Now, you will accompany my security contingent onto the Helios." The harsh, no-nonsense tone belied the calm words. Lingee's attitude brought fresh memory of the no-holds-barred struggle SSC officers played to gain rank ascendancy. The recollection made Zak glad he was out of the service, a realization quickly displaced by the situation. They meant to search the ship, invade everyone's privacy, and destroy the sanctuary the *Vagrant Spirit* provided. Even now, Lingee's eyes surveyed the colorful partitions with a repugnant expression.

As one of Lingee's troopers waved them toward the hatch, Jake twisted away as if punched. He glared at Lingee for a long moment before complying with a cynical sneering salute. "Congratulations on the promotions, Sara." He turned and left the *Vagrant Spirit*.

Fury quickened Zak's breathing, his lips clenched as he glared at Commander Sara Lingee before submitting. Ren placed a hand on his shoulder. Her touch made him regain his self-control.

Three troopers surrounded and escorted each crewmember from the *Vagrant Spirit* onto the Solar Class Helios. Two helped Ship Dog to his feet and guided his wobbly steps. As he left, Zak saw another team of uniformed personnel waited to enter the *Vagrant Spirit*.

Thirty-four

...2183.268-08:37 universal space-time ...mission status ... programming invaded ...vagrant spirit besieged ...crew abducted ... access codes recognized ...dated permits access to cs9 base functions only ...vera denies and prevents access to higher functions...

They placed her in a small compartment. Renna stood and twirled to look at the interior.

It was beige and bare, a large, square, low bed, a chair, and a hygiene facility.

Crewkin quarters.

Her chest seized with fear and fury.

She yelled aloud. "Where is Zak? Where is my crew?" She banged on the hatch until exhausted. Her heart pounded, and her knees felt weak. She sank into the chair. After a few minutes, she rose and hit the communications pad.

"Where is my husband? Why am I separated from my crewmates?"

A screen woke on the wall. "Speaker Renna *Markham3*?"

"No. I am Renna Terran."

309

"We have placed you in quarters the Markham Company assured us would best suit your comfort."

"I am not of Markham! I demand to be rejoined with my crew and my husband!"

"Markham Company has filed legal briefs with the Universal Court demanding your return as an unemancipated subordinate."

"I want a lawyer."

"As your legal guardian, Markham Company must agree to any representation. We will send a message to them of your request."

"I have not belonged to Markham for several years. I demand a lawyer!" The screen died. She stared at it. *They will not get me back. I swear I will kill them if they think they can claim me.*

~ * ~

Cutter sat in an isolation compartment and waited. By his estimate, several hours had passed. He expected they weren't going to conduct either interview or interrogation until they felt the crew sufficiently softened up. And after the *Vagrant Spirit* had been initially searched. The wait gave him time for anxious conjecture on how Jake and Zak were dealing with their treatment from former fellow officers, how Lock, and especially Ship Dog, handled the situation. Worry about Ezry left him antsy. He walked the room when his legs cramped from sitting. The rest of the time he sat at the table, arm propped on the surface, resting his chin in his palm. *No use showing more nervousness than required.*

Sounds from the hatch indicated someone entering. Settling back into the uncomfortable chair, he waited. A short, small-framed woman entered. He studied her as she gave him a cursory look from the intel she studied. Her uniform gave authority to an otherwise ordinary face. Cutter didn't doubt the intelligence behind the brown eyes.

"Dr. Cutter? I'm Lieutenant Commander Elisse Santos. I need to ask you a few questions."

Cutter made a noncommittal shrug, saying nothing. At a guess, he judged her a psych investigator, trained for eliciting the most from any detainee.

"It is probably needless, I'm sure, to remind you this interview is being recorded, your physical responses monitored."

He knew they would compare the crew's various versions for consistencies and inconsistencies. They would ask preposterous questions, countless versions of the same question, leave him alone again, only to return hours later to conduct the same interview. He sighed.

"To start, Dr. Terran, please give me your version of all actions leading to the presence of the stolen engine and how it became integrated into your ship."

Integrated...they knew the engine was built into the fabric of the ship.

During his 'quiet' time, he had gone over his mental list of events. "As our records show, we picked up the cargo at Port 53. Jake hired Ren as crew through the..."

"Renna *Markham3*, the kidnapping victim?"

"...port hiring registry. The port's labor master recommended her." He held his temper at the provocation and continued with his recollection of what had transpired at Port 53.

She accepted his story with a few questions before moving to the events after the CS9 took over the ship. He realized how far they had probed the *Vagrant Spirit*. The questions intensified. He answered, for hours. Finally, he asked for a break. He was surprised she permitted his request. A trooper showed him to a relief facility with the trooper following him in. When he returned to the room, a cup of coffee sat on the table. He worried about what else the cup might contain, so ignored it. He couldn't ignore the questions asked in meticulous repetition.

When Santos decided she knew as much as she wanted, she said, "Thank you, Doctor Terran, I'll have more questions later after I've reviewed your story." They showed him to another compartment. Ezry waited there.

"Are you okay?" he asked. She nodded, glaring at the trooper who had escorted him into the room. The man left with the lock securing as he closed the hatch. As soon as they were alone, Ezry came into his arms, wrapping herself around him.

"It was terrible. How dare they? Just like we were criminals..."

The hatch opened again. Lock entered, his agitation evident. "How much more do they need to know? Their damn engine hijacked us, not us it."

They stood in silence. Cutter looked around. They weren't in a brig cell, but a relatively large room by ship standards, with chairs and few creature comforts. Along one partition slip-in bunks rose in tiers three high and four wide. An inspection showed the room's second hatch gave onto a minuscule head and shower.

"Well, at least we aren't in a brig."

"Why, if we're under arrest?" Lock asked.

Cutter shrugged. "Maybe our exact status is still undetermined."

Within minutes, Ship Dog joined them. Cutter's concern fell away as, other than a ruffled visage and wearing an unfamiliar overall, Daniel seemed to be handling the situation well. He grinned at Cutter. "Confused."

Cutter huffed a short laugh, understanding, and patted the bigger man on his shoulder.

They stayed in the main room, sitting in a cluster of chairs. No one felt like sleeping. The thought of being watched was too unnerving, for no doubt surveillance prevailed. He remained on a couch, Ezry beside him. He held her hand. They exchanged low-voiced, sporadic suppositions about their situation. A few hours later, Jake and Zak arrived, both looking frustrated and furious, both exhausted.

Zak's glance swept over them. "Where is Ren?"

An officer from the legal detachment finally entered the compartment after Zak's numerous requests demanding Renna's whereabouts, escalating in volume with each demand. The young male officer, a puppy really, took an authoritarian stance in the middle of the compartment. Cutter hadn't expected the man's insulting tone.

"You need to end this disruption. The podder will not be returned to you. According to the Markham Company, Renna *Markham3* is and remains their unemancipated subordinate."

"They released her! Hell! She hired on two other shortrunners before she came aboard the *Vagrant Spirit!*" Zak screamed his frustration in the officer's face.

"She has been our crewmember for nearly four years. Markham's claims are meaningless," Jake said.

"You have been declared missing since your initial message beacons of 2179.331-14:03. Since wherever you have been, it has not been in pursuit of legally licensed endeavors, their claim remains valid."

"Told you, we've been lost in bloody space!" Lock said. "Proof's on the ship—and you've seen it."

"You will have to take those matters up with the courts. I doubt your 'proof' will be released by the SSC. The initial download verifies your crew's tampering with old SSC code, not the Markham code you implied."

"We had to overwrite the code just to get back!" Lock shouted.

"Regardless, the lawyer representing Markham Company's claim has already filed restraint orders against any of you going near their subordinate. I have been ordered to keep Renna *Markham3* separated from you."

"Renna Terran!" Zak went over the table at the officer, his fist hitting the man's chin. "And she's my wife!"

The unexpected attack caught the officer unaware. He fell back against the partition. Attendant guards and Jake tried pulling Zak off the man. Ship Dog grabbed Zak away. Their intentions were misconstrued, and all three men were unceremoniously hauled out of the room after more guards flooded into the compartment. Cutter only marginally kept his temper after the shouting ended.

"You've investigated the computer on the *Vagrant Spirit*. You know we are telling the truth."

The officer's eyes would not meet his as he straightened the neck of his uniform. His hands shook. Cutter judged him almost too young to be an officer. Clearly, he was shaken by Zak's attack, although he remained undeterred. "I have to follow orders, Dr. Terran. Space Research has requested you and your crew to submit to physicals and a few other tests. They...would appreciate you convincing your crew to agree."

"Unlikely, since we've been detained with no formal charges made before any convening authority. I think we must refuse all requests for medical or psychological testing—to prevent any inadvertent loss of the right to not incriminate ourselves. There is a file on the *Vagrant Spirit* that might change the court's mind about handing Ren back to Markham."

"Rest assured." The officer's gaze finally found him, edged with disbelief. "The Helios' reconnaissance team will find any proof of criminal activity on the *Vagrant Spirit*."

"Well," he informed the pup in the same tone, "tell them to look in the medical files first—or ask Vera to assist them."

The officer started ever so slightly, before resuming his authoritarian demeanor. It made Cutter wonder about Vera's reception of the invading army of investigators.

"By the way, where is our legal counsel?"

"A lawyer can be provided..."

"No, I want to hire my own representation, and formally request access for this purpose." His request was ignored.

~ * ~

As close as Zak could tell, he had spent three days in the brig. The constant illumination made guessing time difficult, and the utter bareness of his cage depressed him. The bunk, sink, and toilet took most of the space.

Although in separate cells, he, Ship Dog, and Jake could talk to each other, although remaining invisible to each other except for sound. The monotony was interspersed with visits to a gym under heavy guard. His questions about Renna were ignored.

They pulled him and Jake out for another interrogation session. Since Ship Dog was back to monosyllables, if he replied at all, Zak decided they'd written off getting information out of the engineer. This time they sent Commander Sara Lingee to try and question them. He looked at Jake's hooded gaze as his brother stared at Lingee.

"Glad you finally made rank, Sara," Jake said.

"How unfortunate you lost yours, Jake."

"Not lost, Sara, relinquished."

Zak felt for Jake. Such a betrayal of friendship was devastating. A not-so-subtle ploy to use the prisoner's former lover to undermine him. *They must have searched our personnel files or did Lingee volunteer information to her superiors?* Whichever way didn't matter; Jake wasn't going to play her game.

"Jake, helping us would be of great benefit for you."

"We've helped you in every way we can." Jake gave Lingee a lopsided, insincere smile. "You can learn everything you want to know on the *Vagrant Spirit*. As for your other allegations, other than the Rabican's presence, I doubt you can link me or any of my crew to the theft or to any treasonous action. Matter of fact, I think you've found Cutter's lading receipts and know the game Markham Company played. Too bad for them we didn't disappear into space permanently. Or perhaps the SSC is also involved in this cover-up?"

Zak refused to answer their questions, only repeated, "Enough is enough. Produce Ren or forget any answers to any questions."

"We will have answers," Lingee stated in implacable tones.

"Fine. Find them yourself," Jake said, shrugging.

"You can make us talk. However, unwilling answers often provide unreliable information," Zak said.

"There are methods..."

"If you use them, you'll have to provide adequate legal counsel first," Zak answered the threat. "Remember that much about the damn SSC."

"Captain Terran..." Sara interrupted, only to be cut off by Jake.

"Zak is right. We're tired of playing your games. If you don't have the answers you need, you better look elsewhere, because we don't have them. And you either return the crew to the *Vagrant Spirit*, including Renna, or allow us to contact a lawyer."

"There is the issue of the Rabican, and we cannot ignore Markham's legally placed restraint on their subordinate."

"Then you better get ready for a class action suit for supporting and abetting slavery."

"I don't know to what you are referring, Jake."

Zak snorted. "Jake has your number now lady—no, Officer."

"The copy of Ren's medical file, which I'm nearly certain you've found on the *Vagrant Spirit*, was sent by the CS9 communication system to the Shortrunners Union. When the message arrives, which I'm certain it has, you can be sure there will be demands for an investigation. An investigation the SSC seems bent on preventing, meaning they support the longhaulers' use of slave crews."

"You didn't mention this in your previous interviews," Sara said.

Jake gave her a nasty smile. "You never asked. We had to make sure the message had time to arrive at its destination."

"Excuse me." Lingee rose and left.

"Well, I think that worked." Jake emitted a soft chuckle. "I hope Vera is giving them hell."

"Hope so. Hope that file lights a fuse going straight to command."

"Yeah. Vera does tend to act like crewkin in concepts about her crew and loyalty."

Jake's chest expanded with his sigh. He smiled at him. "Markham encouraged the CS9 to view its crewkin as its own kin, so Vera sees us as her kin."

Zak answered his smile. "And we all know how crewkin feel about outsiders."

"You heard Lingee say interview?" Jake expelled his anger in a long obscene invective.

"Yeah. Interview my ass." Zak fumed while they waited, pacing the small room.

"Zak, sit down," Jake finally said.

More hours passed. Finally, a guard ushered them out of the interrogation room and down the gangway, but not back to the brig. Outside the hatch to the original compartment, Zak halted. A guard guided Renna from the other direction. A smile crossed her pale, stressed expression as she saw him. Reaching out, she hugged him in a tight embrace. He wrapped his arms around her just as tightly, feeling her trembling. He closed his eyes to hide both his rage and his relief. "Are you all right?"

She raised a tear-stained face. "I am now. I thought they would return me to Markham, and I would never see you again." A gasp broke her speech, and fresh tears slid down her cheeks.

"Come on, Zak, Ren. The natives are restless."

Zak saw Jake watched the guards' impassive faces. He wrapped an arm around Ren and glared at the guards. They only motioned the three into the compartment and locked them in.

~ * ~

Later the same day, the three Terran brothers were directed to yet another meeting. They were not led to the interrogation room. The guard led them into a finely appointed conference room five decks up.

"We've risen in the food chain." Cutter observed their changed venue sotto voice to Jake as they entered the elegant surroundings. Following his brothers, Zak smiled, more amenable since Ren's return. He hid a strong desire for revenge against those who had isolated her from her crew. He considered their treatment premeditated cruelty.

A cadre of officers waited, including Commander Sara Lingee and the captain of the *Helios*, who sat at the far end of the conference table. In the middle, an admiral sat. Zak paused. *The Helios was this sector's Fleet Command?* Two plainclothesmen attended—scientists, engineers, or lawyers, Zak decided.

Commander Lingee stood. "Admiral Burnoek, Captain Evanic, Captain Jake Terran, Doctor Cutter, and Zak Terran."

The admiral and the *Helios'* captain nodded at Lingee. She hesitated before continuing. "We would like to speak to you as the legal owners of the *Vagrant Spirit*." She indicated they sit.

"It seems we have a few problems." The admiral spoke, not the captain.

"We do," Jake said, just as nonchalant. He took one of the comfortably plush chairs pointed out to them. Zak and Cutter took the chairs on either side of Jake.

"It seems your ship contains our property."

"Glad we could deliver it to you," Cutter said. "We'd be pleased for you to remove your cargo from the *Vagrant Spirit*."

The admiral looked at Cutter, frowned, and cleared his throat. "After a cursory investigation, we have come to the conclusion the *Vagrant Spirit*'s crew were unknowing, and unwilling, dupes in a conspiracy to obscure the original theft and dispose of an illegally procured prototype engine's plans."

They didn't build the Rabican onboard the Markham3. Jake looked at Zak, obviously sharing the same thought.

The admiral received no response from any of the Terrans. Zak relaxed into his seat. The nervousness seemed to be on the other side of the table for a change. Jake appeared unwilling to give away any concessions until they knew the situation. Zak knew Cutter would be of like mind.

After a long pause, Jake stated, "You've read the *Vagrant Spirit*'s files."

Another prolonged silence filled the compartment until Captain Evanic spoke for the first time. "No. Our investigative team has been thwarted by your computer."

"Not our computer," Jake said. "Yours. It came aboard with the Rabican."

"We retrieved the files left on the main CS9Rabican drive. However, Commander Lingee's team has been unable to initiate any response from the *Vagrant Spirit*'s computer." A thin plainclothesman spoke, his hands clasped tightly on the tabletop. His voice rose and fell in stressed tones.

"The fact is," Captain Evanic said, "we have been unable to locate the core memory or even decipher those files we have managed to find on the *Vagrant Spirit*. There is also a disturbing tendency for the ship's aft to drift."

Jake shrugged. "Did Vera provide the information I requested?"

"I was unaware you had communicated with the computer," the admiral said, staring at Captain Evanic.

At Evanic's nod, Lingee answered, her face flushed red. "Yes. He was allowed brief contact so we could access the computer. The computer only allowed us the information in those files. Jake... Captain Terran, gave express permission for...Vera...to disclose only certain information. The ship...the *Vagrant Spirit*," Lingee faltered. "The computer has developed far beyond the limits imposed on a CS9 logical system. The computer has invaded the ship's very structure. Whenever our team tried to override the protocols, the access portal closed." She sighed. "Sometimes the access portal disappeared altogether."

The agitated man spoke again. "When we saw how the Rabican was incorporated into the cargo bay, we felt the allegations confirmed. Only we discovered they could not have built such a structure into the ship, not with the other changes noted."

"So we are not guilty of theft or treason?" Jake asked.

"A bogus contract remains, and the issue of transporting stolen goods," Lingee said.

"What? You found a trail of our financial gain?" Cutter asked. "Proof we somehow thwarted the blacklist covering our ship? The lading file was not a bogus or a forged contract. I read it. I saw who signed it."

Lingree looked defiant. "Except the duplicate file doesn't exist at Port 53. If you participated in this fraud and theft, and there is proof aboard your ship, my team will find it."

"If you can break into Vera? What do you want? Permission?" Zak said, contempt filling his voice.

"Yes." Captain Evanic's eyes flared; his lips firmed.

"And if we give permission, you'll investigate who sent the anonymous allegations about the *Vagrant Spirit* and about Markham's part in this situation?" Jake asked.

The admiral waved them all silent. "Rancor, counter-charges, and further interrogations will get us nowhere. We have started an investigation into the 'anonymous tip' and other incidents leading back to the Markham Company. We have no other explanation than the one you, and all members of your crew, have repeatedly avowed. You were hijacked by the Rabican and its cognitive support system."

"Which puts Markham's trumped-up charges in a whole new light?" Jake's smile bordered incivility. "Along with the information sent to the Shortrunner's Union, everything finally made you see sense?"

The admiral gave Jake a superior officer's stare. "Yes. Reluctantly, yes. The Shortrunner's Union has relayed the message to us. They have petitioned Space Authority and Licensing for a complete investigation."

"Enough!" one of the plainclothesmen interrupted. The admiral scowled and settled back in his seat.

Someone with more clout than an admiral? Zak frowned.

The man paused, looking at his intel before breaking the silence. Zak suspected he had received a message. "We need access to the ship's memory. If you have done what you claim..."

"We have," Jake said.

"A remarkable feat," Captain Evanic inserted. He shook his head while staring at his clasped hands.

"Indeed," the unidentified man said. "We have seen First Officer Zak Terran's images of Proxima Centauri. We need to have the information from this flight. We want to know why, and how, the Rabican succeeded in this flight when all others ended..."

"So lamentably? With so much loss of human life?" Cutter said.

"Not in our tests!"

"No?" Cutter's brows rose in mild disbelief.

"Markham's for sure," Jake said. "Only Ren escaped, and Markham depended on her committing suicide to keep their secret, and they expected, and planned, for us to vanish on the journey to Zorah Station."

"Sabotaged the cargo," Cutter added.

"Your allegations will be investigated if only to prove they stole the Rabican."

"How did they manage this theft? Don't you have the highest security protocols in the galaxy?" Zak asked. "And how did you believe a blacklisted ship's crew could have possibly committed this theft?"

"Not secure enough, it would seem," the admiral said. "What has been observed...is the *Vagrant Spirit* is substantially changed from a standard Nimbus class."

"The change started shortly after I signed the lading order, and the cargo was loaded into the aft cargo hold," Cutter informed them.

The man's eyes stared at Cutter. "Under normal circumstances, we would confiscate the *Vagrant Spirit*, and you might or might not get paid for the confiscation."

"However, this is not normal circumstances, is it?" Jake asked. "The fastest, longest-ranging ship ever known, and it belongs to a bunch of blacklisted shortrunners."

"Exactly!" Captain Evanic said, over the admiral's, "You were not blacklisted."

"Quiet!" the unnamed plainclothesman said. "It seems 'Vera' won't allow anyone except your crew to operate the ship. Vera refuses confiscation, and if there is a way to turn it off, we have not discovered it." He turned to the admiral. "This cognitive unit has developed far beyond original design specs. We simply must secure access."

"It's clear your ship is no longer a shortrunner," the admiral said.

"Or even a longhauler?" Jake asked.

Admiral Burnoek ignored the provocation. "The *Vagrant Spirit* is now so much more. As such, the SSC needs the ship. Indeed, the initial programming and hardware designs legally belong to the SSC."

"The initial programming and hardware seem to have escaped the SSC and installed themselves inseparably on the *Vagrant Spirit*," Jake said.

"We want to offer you a contract," another plainclothesman said, cutting through the talk. The admiral threw the interrupting unidentified man an unreadable glance. "There are numerous problems in this, particularly the exact nature of the CS9 and the *Vagrant Spirit*."

"A contract?" Cutter's voice settled into his business tone.

"Yes. One where the *Vagrant Spirit* becomes a special explorer class assigned to the SSC. We would ask that you take a contingent of SSC officers and scientists onboard the *Vagrant Spirit*. See if they can learn how to duplicate whatever happened."

"We will need all of our own crew, and I won't hand ship authority over to the SSC." Jake didn't raise his voice, yet his adamancy came through.

"The Space Advancement Reproductive Lab wants Renna *Markham3*."

"Renna Terran," Cutter said. "No Renna, no deal,"

Zak said simultaneously. "She is my wife."

"Not legally if, as you assert, you were married in space out of the jurisdiction."

Cutter placed a warning hand on his arm. Zak swallowed his retort and sat back.

"I think we're done here." Jake made movements to rise. "Destroy the ship, if you must. You will not, however, give Renna to anyone. She is emancipated by age and choice, or will be as soon as the Shortrunners Union lawyer wins her case in court. I'm sure you realize such an event will expose some undesirable SSC procedures."

The admiral cleared his throat. "I think we can clear this situation up without waiting for a decision from any court. As you say, the proof seems overwhelming."

~ * ~

Ezry sat next to her, occasionally patting her hand or knee. The waiting exhausted Ren. Ship Dog and Lock played a game on the entertainment unit, with a marked lack of enthusiasm. Waiting with her crew while the Terran men were taken away wasn't as awful as waiting alone, but still nerve-racking.

"How come they took them?" Renna asked again, hating her inability to stop asking, hating the absence of Jake, Cutter, and Zak, hating how she felt.

"They've been questioning us since we came aboard this military prison." A huge huffing sniff gave Ezry's opinion. Her eyes watered. "They'll be back."

Zak had told her what had been going on while she had been held apart. The separation had worried her; this waiting drove her wild. *If you were still kin, you would be punished for your agitation.* "The SSC wants to give me back to Markham Company. I am no longer a podder." She sounded plaintive, even to her own ears.

"Don't need to tell us, honey. Zak won't let the SSC give you to Markham Company. They took steps to protect you."

"I was very lonely and frightened, held in a small cabin alone for a week with nothing to do, nothing to read…"

"Solitary confinement," Ship Dog said and huffed in disgust. He glanced at Renna. "Didn't break you."

His praise cheered her. She slipped back into worry. "Are they always gone this long?"

"Sometimes longer."

"Cutter didn't steal the Rabican!"

"We've all explained the circumstances more times than we can count. They don't believe us," Lock said.

"Did impossible." Ship Dog glanced at the women between his game moves.

"Damn!" Jumping up, Lock threw his control down. "They're going to take the *Vagrant Spirit*, just watch! Impound it. Gain legal access later when they convict us of theft of military secrets, general criminal activity, and kidnapping Renna." He stopped and straightened, looking at Renna. "I don't want to go back to prison."

"Go crazy," Ship Dog advised.

Renna giggled. The giggles turned into sobbing gasps and tears. Embarrassed, she covered her mouth with one hand while drying her face on the sleeve of her other arm. Hands patted her shoulder, Ezry's arms hugged her.

"Don't listen to me, Ren. Our guys are real smart. They'll get us out of this mess."

"But no one has questioned me. I could have told them the truth. They never talked to me at all!" Renna sniffed hard several times. "If they take the *Vagrant Spirit*, what will we do for a home?" *What if they give me back to Markham?*

"They're not going to take our ship, honey. You just wait, you'll see." Ezry's voice wasn't as confident as her words.

As the hours dragged by, they fell silent. The hatch mechanism opening roused Renna from a doze. She searched the resolute faces of Cutter and Jake who entered the room first, followed by Zak. Her stomach turned with worry. The most important question blurted from her mouth. "Can I stay?"

Jake and Cutter smiled. Renna felt like she melted. "Yes." Zak grinned, hugging her. He held her in the warm embrace of his arms. "You are legally emancipated and listed as my wife."

"And..." Jake oozed satisfaction. "We need to vote on a contract offer."

"What kind of contract?" Ezry asked, frowning.

"A long-term, lucrative SSC contract." Jake's smile broadened.

"We won't be able to talk about it. Our work will be classified." Zak looked at Ren. "Ownership of the *Vagrant Spirit* remains in the Terran family."

"Who owns Vera?" Ren asked, frowning at Jake's gloating expression.

Cutter shrugged and plopped into one of the hard chairs next to Ezry. "Vera belongs to the *Vagrant Spirit*."

"Which makes this a joint SSC-Terran-Vera venture." Zak's arm tightened around Renna's shoulders.

"Exploration." Ship Dog nodded, his mustache trembling with his approval.

"Do we have to wear uniforms?" Lock asked.

"No. However, we have to permit SSC personnel onboard."

"Shit." Lock's nostrils widened and his mouth tightened. An instant later, an evil smile twitched his lips. "Really? That might be fun."

"What do you say, Ezry?" Cutter asked.

"How many of them?" Ezry stared at Cutter, a frown marring her face.

"A few," Jake said. "Maybe enough to fill all our slip-ins."

"You must come," Renna said reaching for Ezry's hand. "You are my kin now, and I don't want to lose you."

Ezry snorted softly. "Not like anyone else is going to welcome me anywhere else."

"If you don't think you can do space, Ez, say so. I want you to be happy. If it means staying on a station or planet, we'll do so"

"We'll?"

"I won't leave you behind." Everyone stared at Cutter in grave silence. His gaze was locked on Ezry.

Ezry smiled. "Okay. I've had the offer. I don't want to be left behind either." She snorted a laugh. "None of you can survive without me."

"Think about the possible duration of any assignment." Jake stood and stretched. "You found the last voyage unendurable. There is no reason to believe our next journey will be any easier or safer."

Ezry shrugged, blushing a deep rosy bronze. Her dark brows lifted in a humorous twist. "Like Ren, you're my family now. No sense in being anywhere else."

Renna laughed in elation. She grabbed Zak's hands and twirled him about in counterpoint to her own circular motion.

"You're excited about this?"

"No, I'm excited because they said I wouldn't survive." She spread her hands, twirling about, laughing. "I didn't. I thrived!"

Meet Rhobin Courtright

Born and raised in Michigan, Rhobin spent one year in Colorado and twenty years in Missouri raising her family and working as a business writer. She now lives back in Michigan on twenty acres of forest near the small village of Luther. Always interested in science, history, nature, and art, her overactive imagination led her to speculate on life beyond Earth, and the 'what-ifs' of changes to humanity that soon turned into fantasy and science fiction novels. She writes about writing and her quirks of mind on her blog at:
www.rhobincourtright.com

Other Novels by

Rhobin Lee Courtright

New Novels

Stone House Farm – a Michigan romance – Amanda's old stone farmhouse might need repairs, but it has been in the family for generations, and hopefully neither her ex nor land developer-architect Wade Preston can grab it for their own profits.

Aegis Series:

Magic Aegis – Centuries ago, the witch Chloe cast the Aegis spell, binding four men and their descendants to protect Kaereya. Now, when needed most, magic is lost.

Change – Her mother demanded two things of Tyna...that she never expose her true nature and that she never enter Cygna, the land of witches. Now, her mother is dead, and her sister has abandoned her.

Acceptance – Responsibility and duty drove mercenary Kissre to find her estranged sister in Cygna, the land of witches.

Legend's Cipher – What Bertok had not related when the bishop gave him this mission was his most buried secret—he possessed an unnatural ability.

Black Angel Series:

Rogue's Rules – Traitor, mutineer, deserter—slanderous words fixed to Ensign Jezlynn Chambers' name.

Loser's Game – Jezlynn has plied the pirates' trade but won't let anyone use the signature of the Black Angel to hide their crimes.

Devil's Due – Command ordered Jezlynn into the Space Service Corp, yet it is one thing to think you can accomplish a goal, another to achieve it.

Angels Tread – Just when Jezlynn believes she has overcome her past it returns to haunt her

Home World Series:

Home World Aginfeld – On technically advanced but feudal Aginfeld, Alix Risseu is held for theft...the sentence is death. Only Alix is innocent.

Nanite Warrior – Hearing herself claimed as wife, Xandra gave a weak laugh. "Bad luck just won't end, but this time, I'm sure yours is worse than mine, husband."

Dragoons' Journey – Brigit has moved constantly for years, now a message offers her freedom on Aginfeld, a place her enemy, the Colonial Pact, desperately wants.

Home World Reax – Maera escaped the future planned for her on Reax, so what could make her return? Learning of her home planet's devastation.

The Carolingians:

Constantine's Legacy – Leonard must learn to be the Frankish warrior his father Radulf, the Dux Provinciae, demands. His difficult training is nothing compared to the dangerous deceptions he discovers.

Letter to Our Readers

Enjoy this book?

You can make a difference

As an independent publisher, Wings ePress, Inc. does not have the financial clout of the large New York Publishers. We can't afford large magazine spreads or subway posters to tell people about our quality books.

But, we do have something much more effective and powerful than ads. We have a large base of loyal readers.

Honest Reviews help bring the attention of new readers to our books.

If you enjoyed this book, we would appreciate it if you would spend a few minutes posting a review on the site where you purchased this book or on the Wings ePress, Inc. webpages at:

https://wingsepress.com/

Thank You

Visit Our Website

For The Full Inventory
Of Quality Books:

Wings ePress.Inc
https://wingsepress.com/

Quality trade paperbacks and downloads
in multiple formats,
in genres ranging from light romantic comedy
to general fiction and horror.
Wings has something for every reader's taste.
Visit the website, then bookmark it.
We add new titles each month!

Wings ePress Inc.

3000 N. Rock Road

Newton, KS 67114

www.ingramcontent.com/pod-product-compliance
Lightning Source LLC
Chambersburg PA
CBHW060621100726
47907CB00006B/1721